WHEN THE BOMBS BEGIN TO FALL

Eric Brady

The Jackson story
Part 1

COPYRIGHT

When the bombs begin to fall

This book is a work of fiction. People, places, events and situations are the product of the author's imagination, other than those events in the public domain. Any resemblance to actual persons, living or dead, is purely coincidental.

ISBN: 978-1-326-05279-9

Table of Contents

Many of the events in this first book of The Jackson story happened to Eric Brady and members of his family.

The Evacuation of some children from London to Folkestone (1939) and then their being moved onto South Wales in 1940 are true as were the experiences of some children of the way foster-parents chose the children they would foster. The different experiences of Kitty and Tim are also based on reality. When the foster-parents and children became close, as happened with Kitty, conflict could and did arise between them and their natural parents.

Children returned from Evacuation to London (and other major towns and cities) for reasons as varied as those of Kitty and Tim, with at times, problematic relationships developing as soon as the initial novelty of their return wore off.

Children had had to grow up fast when Evacuated and many parents too changed during the years of separation, by reason of their own sometimes traumatic experiences of bombing and war. In those days little was understood and Counsellors were non-existent for those situations.

The raid on Thompson Road school did happen as described but to Sandhurst Road School, SE London that Eric Brady and his sister Kitty were attending, Kitty being in the Senior part, Eric in the Junior. Tim's experience and injuries are those that Eric Brady had himself.

From that point on, the story is entirely fiction, for in reality Kitty did not survive the attack nor did their parents separate.

Chapter 1
Bombing threat

"Seen the latest May?" Jennie asked urgently, deliberately blocking her way as she was just coming out of her front door.

May glanced at the newspaper Jennie was holding out for her to see the Headline, then stared.

"The bombers will always get through", she read aloud with a sick feeling of dread.

"You'd better come in Jennie," she added quietly, pushing the sleeping Frank's pram back into the cramped passageway of the small, terraced Council house and then into the front room to get it out of the way.

Jennie, her neighbour and friend, followed her into the kitchen where May put a kettle on the gas, her dread now becoming mixed with a measure of triumph that her prediction of last year had proved to be exactly right.

Now Ron would have to admit that he – and that fool Neville Chamberlain – had been wrong when the Prime Minister had come back from that meeting with Adolf Hitler in Munich, waving that silly bit of paper, shouting that it meant 'Peace in our time'.

May swiftly read the full report that on an Exercise last night to test London's defences some RAF bombers had 'attacked' the city – and the defences hadn't even found the raiders in the dark let alone shot any down. And the bombers had all claimed to have 'hit' their targets.

"How soon d'you reckon Ron will be Called Up?" Jennie asked abruptly as May put the paper on the table.. That was already happening in the mid-summer of 1939.

May turned away to make the pot of tea.

"He won't be," she said, her back still turned. "Or rather he's counted as being Called Up already. As a Driver for NAAFI, delivering stuff to the Camps being set up all over the place he's classed as being in a Reserved Occupation."

She knew that Sam, Jennie's husband, wasn't. He was a Bus Driver, fit and in his mid-20s, so he was certain to go.

"But Ron has said he's going to join the ARP, so that when

the bombing starts he'll be in the thick of it. Because he 'wants to do his bit'," she added, the sneer obvious in her tone.

Theirs was not a particularly happy marriage now but the thought of Divorce had never really been considered. In their background it just didn't happen. There might be rows, there might be affairs, there might sometimes be violence but not Divorce. Not normally. Sometimes people walked out but mostly couples just muddled along especially if there were kids, and there usually were. She and Ron did anyway. Without real rows either and he'd never hit her, or even threatened to. And she didn't think he was running any affairs even though he was a lorry driver and away overnight at times, sometimes twice a week now that he was driving a bigger lorry and trailer and more Camps were being set up all the time.

But because she didn't really trust him, she'd taken measures to make sure she would find out if he did as soon as he'd started his 'overnights' with a Loader.

"Are you going to evacuate the children?" Jennie asked next.

The other big topic filling the newspapers. May handed her a mug of tea as they sat down at the table.

"Yes." May hesitated wondering whether to tell Jennie about her Premonition of what would happen to Kitty and Tim if they stayed in London. And then decided not to. Jennie was so practical and down-to-earth she would probably laugh at her.

"Ron tried to insist that I should go away with them. To look after them he said. And because I'm in one of the Priority Groups because of Frank." She smiled at Jennie sardonically. "And me leave him all on his ownsome here in London? For months on end? To play around as he liked? Not on your life!

"I didn't tell him that bit of course! What I said to him was that my place was here with him. Anyway, with the schools being in charge of the Evacuation I'm sure enough that Kitty and Tim will be properly looked after. Obviously Frank will stay here with me. What about you and Tommy?"

"Sam thinks Tommy should go. And as you're sending Kitty and Tim, I suppose it would make sense. Tommy and Tim will be company for each other and I can trust Kitty to keep an eye on them."

Jennie had a high opinion of Kitty, though she was only ten. Tommy and Tim were five.

It was just a few weeks later when May was peeling potatoes at the kitchen sink that the music programme she was listening to on the wireless was suddenly cut off. A pause, and then an announcement of a special news item. Moments later it came. It was that Parliament was to be recalled from Summer Recess because of the crisis over the Danzig Corridor and all Teachers were to report to their schools. The Evacuation Scheme was going to go into operation. More details would be given shortly.

She stopped the moment the music cut off, staring unseeingly through the window into the back garden. When the announcement finished, she gave a convulsive shudder, then dried her hands and went into the garden to find that Jennie was just coming out of her back door. They'd got a communicating gate in the joint fence.

"Did you hear ...?" they began together.

"So it's really happening then. The stupid fools with all the bombing that's going to happen as soon as the war starts," May snapped bitterly.

Now that the moment had come she was having qualms. Whether to keep Kitty and Tim here after all – and even more whether she and Frank should go with them.

But she had gone through this a hundred times before in her mind. And the horror of her Premonition that 'something terrible would happen to Kitty and Tim if they stayed here in London' still dominated her mind and feelings. They had to go, and she and Frank had to stay, she decided yet again. The Premonition had been more to to do with Kitty and Tim than she and Frank. And so she would still ignore Ron's arguments that she was certain he'd go through yet again tonight and remind him of the twice before her 'Premonitions' had proved to be right. The one about the war was the third – so this one about the 'something terrible happening' would be the fourth.

The night before Evacuation Day when May had put Frank and Tim to bed at their usual times, and Kitty had just gone up - Ron was still not at home. Not at all unusual with the hours he was now having to work but, she thought resentfully, he might have made the effort to be home early tonight of all nights.

She sat staring into the empty fireplace. She had nothing to do - except wait for time to pass, alone until Ron arrived home.

His dinner was in the oven, keeping warm, as usual. The children were in bed. Their cases had been packed. The letters she had written about them to whoever their foster-mothers would be had been put in their cases too. She had the small bags of sweets ready to give them as a special 'goodbye treat' tomorrow. The labels with their name, class, school and home address were done and ready to tie on their coats, as they'd been told to do.

Restlessly she stood up, sat down and stood up again to go into the corridor leaving the subdued hall light on to gave a glimmer of light into each of the bedrooms as she crept upstairs to look in at the children, asleep in bed. To give herself a last memory.

She checked Frank, then looked in on Tim. He was sound asleep, curled up in bed with his head on the pillow so she could see his face clearly even in the dim light.

She stood looking at him for a long time, wondering where he would be this time tomorrow night. Who would he be with? Would his foster-parents be kind and understanding? Would his room be nice? His bed as comfortable as this?

She glided into Kitty's room. She was lying on her back, hands behind her head. Her eyes flickered to the doorway as May came in.

"Hello Mum," she whispered.

"Hello. Can't you sleep dear?"

"No. Not really."

"Do you want to come downstairs for a bit?"

"Yes please!" Thankfulness echoed in Kitty's voice as she quickly slid out of bed. Downstairs, May sat in her chair and held out her arms. Kitty snuggled down in her lap, drawing comfort from her mother's close cuddling, big girl though she felt she now was.

"What were you thinking about when I came in?"

"Where me and Tim would be tomorrow night."

"I've been wondering that too," May told her quietly. "I have written a letter to the lady who'll be looking after you and Tim and put one in your case and one in his. So she'll know about you both even if you're not in the same place. To start with I mean," she added hastily.

Startled, Kitty twisted round in May's arms to look up into her face.

"But I thought we would be. We both did. We thought they'd be bound to put us together so that I can look after him. As we're brother and sister."

"I expect they will," May said quickly. "But I've done that just in case."

Kitty settled back, not completely satisfied.

"You and Dad will be safe staying here, won't you? When the bombs come?" she said after a moment, a tremor in her voice. Her abiding worry.

"Of course we will. After all we've got that Shelter at the bottom of the garden now, haven't we? Knowing you two are safe in the country will mean that we can do our jobs here without worrying about you," she added quickly, not wanting to give Kitty a chance to argue again about she and Tim having to go because 'it would be too dangerous for them to stay', while at the same time trying to re-assure her that she and Frank and Dad would 'be perfectly safe' here. Because of the Shelter.

"But if ...," Kitty began the question again. The sound of Ron's key in the door interrupted her.

"I'll just go and see Dad for a minute while you stay here, Kitty."

She heard a low murmur of voices in the hall briefly and then Ron came into the room while May went to get his dinner.

"Hello Kitty. Couldn't sleep then?"

He kissed her on the forehead, then swung her up in his arms to carry her across to his own chair on the other side of the fireplace.

"No Dad." Kitty smiled up into his face. It had been a long time since he'd done that. "I kept wondering where me and Tim will be tomorrow night." She wasn't willing to try arguing with her father about going.

"We've been wondering the same but I do know some things for sure. To start with you'll be going to a nice place to stay with some nice people. You see Kitty, the Government had worked out plans just for this kind of Evacuation years and years ago. So when Hitler started making trouble, they got the plans out again, brought them up to date and now everything's ready just at the time it's needed."

Kitty listened intently, staring into his face, beginning to feel a new flow of confidence. Because it was her Dad telling her again what her Mum had already told her. And because now he was in the ARP he'd be bound to really know, wasn't he?

May came in with Ron's dinner and put it at his place at the table already laid.

Kitty looked at it. It was her favourite! One of Mum's meat puddings with peas, and carrots and potatoes (all the vegetables fresh from Dad's allotment) and loads of gravy! Suddenly she felt hungry!

"Why don't you help me with this big dinner Kitty? And you May?" Ron suggested, standing up. "I couldn't possibly manage it all by myself."

A few minutes later all three were sitting round the table.

"Ready to go to bed now Kitty?" May asked gently when they had finished.

"Suppose so." Kitty was still reluctant.

"Try and get some sleep, Kitty," Ron said quietly.

She stood up and looked from Ron to May and back again.

"Will you be gone to work before I get up Dad?"

"Most likely."

"When - when will I see you again Dad?" Kitty asked in a rush, tears in her eyes. This could be the last time she'd see her Dad for ever so long. And they had never been away from home before, not even for a single night.

"I expect pretty soon. As I drive to Army camps and they're building them all over the place now, there's bound to be some near where you are. And then if I get sent near there I'll be able to pop in and see you. And Mum and Frank will be able to come and see you too. So how's that?"

That sounded a bit better, Kitty thought, just a bit. And the important thing was that Dad wouldn't be joining the Army. So he'd be here to look after Mum and Frank as well.

May went up with her to tuck her into bed, then came back to face Ron, carefully closing the door.

"And do you really believe all that you said to Kitty? Do you really believe everything will be as perfect as you made out?"

Her voice throbbed with cynicism, but with an undertone that was begging for assurance for herself.

"I do believe most of it May, and the basic facts certainly are true," Ron told her quietly, but emphatically. "The point is, people in the Government, and I don't mean just the politicians, have been thinking about this for years. And they've had plenty of time to do all the checking that they've said they've done. The Government will be wanting to get this right because of the muck-up they made over handling Hitler earlier, if for no other reason." The certainty in his voice carried conviction

"Okay, there's bound to be the odd hiccup along the line somewhere," he went on, "But they'll only be small ones and will get sorted out quickly. I'm willing to bet on that." He smiled faintly. "And you know I don't bet on anything less than a 100% certainty."

May looked at him searchingly. Ron looked back at her steadily, willing her to see only confidence, not his worry that things would go wrong all over the place with this massive shifting of people. Not just from London but from major cities all over the country. And his fear the children would be in one.

"You didn't eat your dinner like you usually do Ron." Her tone was half-accusing.

"The fact I'm sure the Evacuation will go off okay doesn't mean I'm not worried about things generally - about the war I mean. And that means I don't eat so well. You know me."

"I know exactly what you mean Ron. And neither of us are sleeping well either, what with Frank and everything else." She glanced at the clock and stood up. "I suppose we'd better try. It's late and we've all got a big day tomorrow."

Her lips began to quiver. Ron quickly gathered her into his arms to hold her close. As she began to sob, she clung to him, drawing comfort and strength from him as he was from her. The closest they'd been for years.

Chapter 2
Evacuation

As they walked to school with their cases, Tim and Tommy were larking about but Kitty was more serious, feeling the responsibility of having promised to 'look after' them.

They would have a foster-mother of course, but what would she be like? Would she (Kitty) have to stand up for Tim and Tommy against her? Or would she be as nice and kind as Mum was? Or Auntie Jennie. Which would mean she would take on the real responsibility for Tim and Tommy.

She was still worrying, her dread mounting, as they joined the others in the playground. Some children were running about, excited. Others were standing with their parents, an unusually large number of them waiting there this morning.

Rumours, often contradictory, were flying around, both among the parents and the children.

The parents' rumours were all about the oncoming war – or would it be peace at the last minute? Had Chamberlain pulled the rabbit out of the hat yet again with Hitler?

The children's rumours were of where they would be staying. Some said the country, some on a farm, others went for their idea of heaven – the seaside somewhere or other. The more imaginative were hoping to live in a castle.

Unnoticed in the excitement, Mr. Cutliffe, the Master of the Top Form and now Acting Headmaster, appeared at the Main Entrance to the school building. He hesitated a moment then raised his whistle to his lips and blew a long blast.

It slashed into the chatter, cutting it off short, creating instant silence.

It meant the real start of the Evacuation. It meant they were to go to their classrooms for the Registers to be taken, and then to be off. Into the unknown.

A short blast on the whistle. The summons to go in.

May kissed Kitty and Tim hurriedly.

"Goodbye Kitty. Here's a little present to take with you." She pushed the bag of sweets into Kitty's coat pocket. "I love you dear, never forget that. I'll come and see you as soon as I can."

To Tim who flung his arms round her, "'Bye Tim. Now you be a good boy and do as Kitty tells you. Here's your present. I love you Tim and I'll see you soon. I'll write to you and Kitty can read it to you. And - and send me the postcard of where you are. And ...,"

Another blast of the whistle interrupted her.

"Come on Tim," Kitty said in a shaky voice. "And Tommy."

Together, hand in hand, carrying their cases, the three went towards the school Entrance.

Once the children were safely out of sight inside the school, some of the mothers began to weep. They were losing their children to strangers. No one knew for how long. Almost no one really believed the rumour that it would be over and they would all be back 'in a few weeks'.

Mr. Cutliffe sat down at his desk and took out his fountain pen. As he opened the Register he looked round the subdued children. Just as all the other teachers were doing in their classrooms throughout the school.

"I am about to call the Register. Please answer to your names."

Which was exactly what he said each morning and afternoon. Deliberately acting as though this were a normal school day. And the familiar routine did bring its own comfort to the children.

Over half-a-dozen of them were missing but Mr. Cutliffe made no comment. He had rather expected it for most of them.

When he finished he put his pen away in his top pocket and stood up. Exactly as usual again. But instead of giving it to Kitty to take to the School Secretary, he put it into his suitcase. He glanced at his watch.

"In a few minutes the Assembly bell will ring. But we will not be going to Assembly this morning. The bell is the signal for us to go to the buses to take us to the railway station. Our class will lead." He paused as he looked round them. "As you are the Top Class in the school I expect you to set a good example to the younger children when we go."

Just as he finished, the Assembly bell rang.

Completely calmly, as though this was the most normal event in the world, Mr. Cutliffe picked up his own suitcase and gas mask from beside his desk.

"Make sure you have everything children. Remember, if as you go to the bus you see your parents by all means call goodbye. But do NOT, I repeat, DO NOT run to them for a last hug and kiss. Otherwise everyone will do it and we'll never catch our train. Kitty and Maralyn, lead on please."

Kitty picked up her case and gas mask and followed by Maralyn and then the rest, led the class out.

They had been best friends ever since they found themselves sitting together on their first day at school. Shorter than Kitty, inclined to tubbiness and wearing glasses, Maralyn admired Kitty who was more athletic. Kitty admired Maralyn for her cleverness and also her boldness in tackling teachers when she wanted to.

As Mr. Cutliffe watched them file out, quieter and more orderly than usual, he set his lips.

The Headmaster was not going with them. He had learned to sail and navigate as a hobby years before and had volunteered for the Navy. He was reporting for duty tomorrow so Mr. Cutliffe had been given responsibility for the whole school while they were evacuated.

Too old for Call-up this time, he saw his duty during this war as caring for the children in his charge so they would not experience the horrors endured by the French children he had seen nearly 25 years ago. Of small children, separated from their parents, frightened, lost and without food and shelter. He was determined that he would take care of these children, if necessary until they were old enough to fend for themselves, whoever was in control of Britain – British or German.

As he followed the last child out and closed the door firmly behind him, a wry smile twisted his lips. Of all the places to be Evacuated to! The very place where he and Elizabeth had just spent their summer holiday. They were going to Folkestone.

As Kitty and Maralyn followed by the long line of children as other classes tailed theirs reached the Main Entrance, the Marshal, wearing his distinguishing white coat, came out of the Head's office with him.

"Hello. Kitty and Maralyn isn't it?" he smiled at them as he jacked open both doors.

The parents by the Gate drew back to let the children onto the buses waiting for them.

Kitty saw May almost as soon as they came through the doors and kept her eyes on her all the way. When she was opposite her she called out, "'Bye Mum." She couldn't keep a quiver entirely out of her voice.

"'Bye Kitty. Send the postcards won't you, dear? And I'll come to see you as soon as I can."

"Okay Mum." And then Kitty was past her.

The Marshal stood by the front bus.

"In here Kitty and Maralyn. And the rest of you."

Kitty and Maralyn sat in the front seats nursing their cases, the rest following into the seats behind them. When that bus was full, the Marshall directed children onto the next bus, Mr. Cutliffe making sure there were no seats left empty.

As the last bus disappeared round the corner, the last shouted 'goodbyes' and waves stopped, silence descended on the parents. Slowly they dispersed.

Jennie linked her arm in May's. She'd come to see Tommy off of course, but it was just as much to support May. May was inclined to get upset and depressed too easily, Jennie felt. And these times were enough to get anyone depressed. And May was grateful.

Later, after Jennie had gone off to get Sam's dinner ready for when he came off shift at 2 o'clock, May sat on in the kitchen wondering what was happening to the children at this moment, how they were feeling, and what their foster-parents would be like.

Some of the papers had said they had been carefully selected and Ron had said the same. She had to believe them, just had to, or – or she'd go out of her mind.

But against that was the real feeling of relief. Relief that Kitty and Tim were now safe. Safe from the bombs that would be devastating London as soon as the war started. Everyone knew that was going to happen.

She stood up suddenly. She had stayed here to be with Ron. It wasn't only that she didn't trust him to behave himself if she wasn't here, not really. Not completely, she told herself. It wasn't just that. Though she had thought he had been getting just that bit too friendly with Josie, next door but one in the flats where they'd lived before they'd moved here three years ago.

She was staying to support him as well. Of course she was. So the first thing to do was to get the papers he'd been bringing home from the ARP training and see what that was all about.

As the bus turned the corner and the school, and Mum disappeared from view, Kitty turned to look through the big front window. They were finally off. Evacuated.

And suddenly her sadness fell away. This was going to be a great adventure!

And she wasn't alone facing the unknown either. She was with Maralyn, her best friend and the teachers were going to be there with them. And Mr. Cutliffe. And she was sure he'd back her if there was any trouble with a foster-mother.

It would be wonderful if she and Maralyn were able to stay in the same place. With Tim and Tommy as well, of course.

At the station, the Marshal disappeared inside but was soon back.

"They're all ready. Go to Platform 1, right to the end. There's plenty of signs."

At the end of the Platform was a WVS lady.

"Hello girls," she greeted them with a smile. "The train should be here soon, so just wait patiently. And keep away from the edge of the platform. We don't want anyone falling over it as the train comes in, do we?"

She looked over their heads towards the ramp. Kitty did so as well, just in time to see Tim and Tommy coming down. She felt vast relief now that she knew he had arrived safely because she had promised Mum, and them, that she'd look after them.

A train whistle blasted outside the station.

"The train's coming. Get back from the edge of the platform children. Move back. Move back." As they shouted the WVS ladies and the teachers got between the children and the edge of the platform, shepherding them away.

Slowly the long train pulled into the station, the engine coming to a halt just beyond the children with another big gust of steam.

Mr. Cutliffe blew a blast on his whistle and the children who had been excitedly grabbing for door handles, paused.

Teachers and WVS ladies opened the doors and took up their positions. He blew another short blast and despite entreaties and orders there was a mad scramble for places right along the length of the train. For some it was the first time they had ever been on a train, for others it was still a rare and exciting experience. Kitty and Maralyn found that others were closer to the doors than they were so they got the last seats in the middle of the compartment.

Once they were all aboard they expected to set off quickly, but time passed and still they were stuck there. Boredom began to creep in and the excited chatter faded away..

Sid, one of the older boys, stuck his head out of the door window and looked up and down the platform telling the others what was happening – or rather not happening.

"They're coming down checking all the doors are shut," he reported at last. And hurriedly pulled back as a porter whipped open the door, pulled the strap to close the window and slammed the door shut again.

The engine blew a long blast of its whistle and they moved. It stopped, jerked forward again, and then glided on steadily, picking up speed.

All along the train, children and teachers cheered. Everyone felt happier now they were actually moving.

They passed by small, crowded houses, more houses, bigger houses and then they were out in the country. Several times the train slowed, and once almost stopped before picking up speed again.

They were passing through a station when Dick Fanshawe suddenly announced, "I can work out where we're going." And jumped up to get his suitcase from the rack.

Everyone's interest was grabbed.

"How can you do that?" Maralyn asked for everyone.

"By this." Dick pulled a map from his case. ""When we go through the next station, look out for the name and I'll be able to tell where we are. And then maybe where we're going."

As he opened a book of road maps to one of South East England, they crowded round.

"When I was going to be Evacuated my Dad showed me how

to map-read." And impressed them by explaining the symbols.

Sid lowered the door window and stuck his head out.

"Mind Sid!" screamed Jane, seeing it. "My Mum said you'll get you're head knocked off if you do that!"

Sid hurriedly pulled it in then cautiously looked out again.

"Station coming up," he said, almost immediately.

They crowded to the windows.

"Harrietsham," shouted six of them.

A pause as they looked along the black line of the railway on the map.

"We started there ...," Dick said touching the map, " ... there's Harrietsham, so we're on this line. He traced the line to its end, and looked up. "We could be going to Folkestone then. The seaside."

There were choruses of delight.

"Unless it's one of the country stations before then," Maralyn said, drawing her finger down the line, pausing momentarily at each station.

"Don't be such a wet blanket, Maralyn!" laughed Kitty. "Let's just hope it is the seaside!"

They passed through a big town.

"Ashford."

And they didn't even slow.

More villages, each carefully checked.

"Mersham." Again without stopping.

"That means we must be going to Folkestone. There's no more stations before that one," Dick said quietly.

The atmosphere changed as the children looked at each other. The game of successful map-reading was over. The 'fun' railway journey was no longer such fun now they were so close to their destination. Because there they would be split up, going to strangers, to foster-parents they didn't know.

Houses appeared, then more houses, and the train began to slow. A platform appeared to one side as they slowed still more. And halted.

A loudspeaker blared into life. "This is Folkestone. This is Folkestone. Children of Cheslett School, all please alight here.

Make sure you bring your cases, bags and gas masks."

No one wanted to take that first step into the unknown. Then Kitty jumped onto her seat to grab her case and gas mask from the rack.

"Come on. We're the Top Class and we've got to set an example, Mr. Cutliffe always says."

There was a scramble for belongings but Kitty and Maralyn managed to be the first of them out.

She looked along the platform and caught a glimpse of Tim being handed down from the train by Miss Drew and then Tommy then child after child.

Mr. Cutliffe appeared to ask the question that all the teachers were asking.

"Have you all got everything? Are you sure you've left nothing behind?" And then checking round the carriages themselves - usually finding something.

The loudspeaker blared again. "Children of Cheslett School get into line, ready to move off to Bonar Lane school."

As it kept on repeating its message, children were ushered, pulled or pushed into line, Kitty and Maralyn automatically going to the lead positions of their class.

Mr. Cutliffe came up to them with a WVS lady and stood on a bench to be able to see right along the platform, checking that everyone was ready.

He blew a long blast on his whistle. Teachers checked their classes again, and waved to him to show they were ready. Satisfied, he stepped down.

"We're all ready Mrs. Simpson. Now children, step lively because we're much later than expected."

Chapter 3
Foster-mothers

A young man with a clipboard was waiting for them in the school vestibule. By him was a large blackboard on an easel with a plan of the school marked on it. Quick introductions followed.

"Would the teachers gather round please?" he called.

Word was passed down the line while the children waited standing in a long line across the playground.

"Ladies and gentlemen ...," he began, " ... my name is Paul Jenkins. On the blackboard is a plan of the school. Classrooms are numbered in red on the plan and on their doors. Your class numbers are marked in blue both on the plan and on the classroom doors. Foster-parents who expressed a preference for particular ages are in those rooms, otherwise I have spread them out where they are needed."

Mr. Cutliffe smiled, relieved and impressed by his efficiency.

"And what has happened when there are brothers and sisters of different age groups in different classes?"

Mr. Jenkins smile faded.

"I'm sorry Mr. Cutliffe. But that produced so many administrative complications at the planning stage that the Reception Committee decided that that could not be managed at this initial reception. We felt that that could be sorted out between foster-mothers later."

Mr. Cutliffe's smile had gone too.

"Do you really mean to tell me Mr. Jenkins, that just because of a few 'administrative difficulties', you are proposing to split up brothers and sisters at this very difficult time for them?"

His voice was quiet but his tone freezing.

"Mr. Cutliffe ...," Mr. Jenkins was suddenly equally cold, " ... if you wish to make an issue of this, you will need to take it up with Miss Carruthers herself. But I have no doubt that she will say that to alter the arrangements now will make an already complicated task infinitely worse. It is already late, the children must be tired and hungry and we do have foster-mothers here who have waited long past the expected time. And I have no doubt the foster-mothers themselves can sort out the moves between themselves, in the next day or two."

Mr. Cutliffe knew that he couldn't argue with what Mr. Jenkins had just said. It had had to be left with the local Reception Committees and Lodgings Officers to sort out their own arrangements so he had to accept this.

"Of course, Mr. Jenkins."

Kitty and the other children of the Top Class standing nearby were listening, Kitty with worry. That was sounding as though Tim would not be with her tonight after all.

"Teachers ...," Mr. Jenkins said loudly, " ... in the classrooms will be two copies of a list of foster-parents and the children allocated to them. Before each of them leaves with a child or children they will need to sign the two copies. The teacher will keep one copy, the other will be retained by the Reception Committee member there."

"Thank you Mr. Jenkins," Mr. Cutliffe said. "We'll take our classes to the rooms now, if that is all. But can we teachers all meet tomorrow morning at, say ten?"

"That is what I was to suggest, Mr. Cutliffe."

When Kitty's class arrived at Room 1, they found a group of women waiting at the front, facing the rows of ordinary school desks. As they went to the desks the two groups looked at each other curiously, apprehensively in some cases.

At the teacher's desk was a slim, serious-looking lady, wearing thin-rimmed glasses. She was neatly dressed in a quiet-patterned dress with a light jacket. Kitty thought she was maybe her mother's age, maybe a bit younger. Mr. Cutliffe went over to her.

"I hope she's not a foster-mother," Kitty whispered to Maralyn. "She looks really strict and as though she'd be cross about something or other all the time."

"Good afternoon. Mr. Cutliffe I presume?" she said in a cultured and pleasant voice, holding out her hand. "I am Miss Carruthers. You must have had a difficult journey."

"Difficult enough." He turned to face the foster-mothers. "On behalf of the children, their parents, and the school, may I thank you for taking our children in at this time. Now I'm sure you'll be wanting to get home and the children will too.

“Just one thing. A number of our children have brothers or sisters in different classes. I understand that at this point of time they are not necessarily going to be together." He was making the point as tactfully as he could. "Perhaps it might be possible for arrangements to be made for them to move in together in the next few days." He turned to Miss Carruthers. "Perhaps we could liaise over that speedily? At our meeting tomorrow morning perhaps?"

Miss Carruthers did not look at all pleased.

"Told you," Kitty muttered.

"We are holding a Review Meeting of the Reception Committee here are 7.30 tonight. If it is convenient for you to attend, it could be raised then," she said coolly.

"Thank you. I much appreciate that." He faced the children. The time had come for them to split up. Understandably they could be nervous, so he had to act as though everything was perfect. "Children, you will go with these kind ladies who will be your foster-mothers while you are in Folkestone. It has already been settled who you will be staying with.

"Kitty, Betty and Fred. Your brothers will be going with other ladies tonight, but they will be well looked after I can promise you.

"Remember, you must all behave yourselves with your foster-mothers and their families. I shall be round to see you in the next few days and we shall be starting school as soon as possible. Are there any questions you want to ask me?"

There was complete silence from the children

Mr. Cutliffe sat down in the empty chair by Miss Carruthers who passed him a typewritten list.

"Mrs. Banks," called Miss Carruthers

"Anita Atkinson," added Mr. Cutliffe.

Both stood up, looked at each other and smiled. Mrs. Banks trying to be re-assuring, Anita with mixed relief and still some anxiety. Mrs. Banks looked nice, but still ....

"Sign here please Mrs. Banks. And there. Thank you. Off you go Anita," Miss Carruthers spoke briskly. "Mrs. Bentham."

"I'll see you tomorrow, Anita," promised Mr. Cutliffe, trying to sound as confident and re-assuring as he could. "Jeremy Thompson."

The lists went on, children going off in ones and twos.

Finally Kitty and Maralyn were the only ones left. And there were no more foster-mothers.

Under the desk their hands stole together for comfort. What was going to happen to them? Miss Carruthers had said that all the foster-mothers were there, hadn't she? And now they were all gone. So had there been some mistake? Or - oh no! Were they really going to be staying with that awful Miss Carruthers after all? The lady who, to them and the other children from an 'overspill' part of London, 'talked posh', and was not like them at all.

Mr. Cutliffe smiled tiredly.

"Miss Carruthers, these two girls are Kathleen Jackson and Maralyn O'Conner. If I may say so without making them blush too much, they are the best girls in my class."

The girls glanced at each other. So they were going to be staying with her! With sinking hearts they picked up their cases and gas masks and went forward.

Miss Carruthers stood up and held out her hand.

"Good afternoon girls. Who is Kathleen and who is Maralyn?"

"I'm Kathleen."

"I'm Maralyn."

"I am pleased to meet you though I'm sure we all wish it had been under happier circumstances. Mr. Cutliffe, I understand you have made your own arrangements for accommodation?"

"Yes. My wife and I were here on our summer holiday a few weeks ago. We contacted the landlady and I'll be staying with her for the time being while we decide what to do for the longer term." He smiled briefly. "I'll just check in the other classrooms to see any children and teachers who may still be here."

"Of course. We shall be meeting later in the Headmaster's study by the entrance. Until later then. Come girls."

She left the room quickly. Kitty and Maralyn rushed after her with a quick goodbye in passing to Mr. Cutliffe.

"Miss Carruthers, can we stop a minute to see Tim please? He's my little brother and he will ...,"

"I am very pushed for time Kathleen but ...,"

"Oh please Miss Carruthers!" Kitty was so sure she was going to say 'No' that she interrupted. "He's only five and he's in a new place with new people, all by himself and he was expecting to be with me tonight. Please let me have just a minute to - to comfort him and tell him it will be alright. Please."

Miss Carruthers looked down at Kitty, almost quivering with anxiety, striving to convince this stern, unsmiling lady how important, how absolutely vital, this was. Her tension was in every note of her voice, every line of her body, in the strain on her face.

And Miss Carruthers suddenly wondered how her nieces, six year old twins, would cope in Tim's situation. Being separated from their parents to go to strangers, without even the comfort of each other, let alone a big sister.

"I was about to say when you interrupted, Kathleen, that we would take the time. But - five minutes?"

"Yes Miss Carruthers, five minutes," agreed Kitty, feeling weak with relief but trying to sound grown up.

"Maralyn, do you have a younger brother or sister you need to see?"

"No Miss Carruthers. I've only got Kitty."

Miss Carruthers looked at her a moment, taken aback by her answer, then she nodded.

"Very well then. Which class is Tim in, Kathleen?"

"Class 5, Miss Carruthers."

"Then let us go and find him."

In the entrance hall, she studied the blackboard for a moment.

"There we are. This way."

But there was only Mr. Jenkins and Miss Drew in the classroom. No children.

"I presume Tim Jackson has left, Mr. Jenkins," she said. A statement rather than a question.

"Yes Miss Carruthers. With a Mrs. Abbott. Is there some problem?"

Kitty's heart plummeted. "Was he - did he seem happy, Miss Drew?" she asked.

"His immediate question before he went off was whether you'd be alright without him. When I said you would be, he seemed happy with that. And with the toy car Mrs. Abbott had brought as a "Welcome to Folkestone' present."

"He would be. He loves toy cars." Kitty smiled slightly, then looked up at Miss Carruthers, summoning up the courage to ask if they could go to see him on the way home. To check for herself.

"Let me have Mrs. Abbott's address, Mr. Jenkins. And is she on the telephone?"

"She gave us no 'phone number on the form, Miss Carruthers," he replied as he scribbled the address on a piece of paper.

"Tommy Francis and Jack Saunders were with him Kitty," Miss Drew added quickly.

Miss Carruthers glanced at the address, at her watch and looked at Kitty, who was feeling a little relieved. At least Tim and Tommy were together.

"I am very sorry Kathleen. Mrs. Abbott lives on the other side of town from me and I simply do not have the time to take you there now. But if Mrs. Abbott is on the telephone you may speak to him tonight. And in any case I promise you we shall go to see him tomorrow morning."

Kitty knew there was nothing more she could do. And there was the promise of the 'phone call tonight and the visit tomorrow morning.

"Thank you Miss Carruthers."

"Then let us go home. Thank you Mr. Jenkins, Miss Drew."

She left the room quickly, Kitty and Maralyn hurrying after her, wondering if they had far to walk, or if they'd be catching a bus. They felt exhausted after their roller-coaster day.

And Miss Carruthers was thinking how mature this ten year old seemed to be. Caring so much for her younger brother, but being willing to accept what she had said without any real argument or making any unseemly fuss. She led them to a car and unfastened the boot.

"Put your cases and gas masks in there girls," she said as she went to open the car doors.

They were delighted. They didn't even have to walk to a bus stop and riding in a car was a novelty to both of them.

"Who wants to ride in the front?" Miss Carruthers asked as she got into the driving seat. Sarah and Janice always argued about that.

"You go Maralyn," Kitty said at once.

With a wide grin Maralyn dived into the seat, even if it did mean she'd be sitting by the awe-inspiring Miss Carruthers.

As Kitty got into the back, Miss Carruthers began to wonder whether taking on these two girls, that she had felt duty-bound to do, wouldn't be quite as bad as she'd feared.

Ten minutes of the journey passed in silence, when Maralyn twisted round.

"Look Kitty! There's the sea!" she burst out, pointing.

Kitty leaned forward to see for herself, just before it vanished from view behind a line of buildings.

"I had understood your name was 'Kathleen', but Maralyn has twice called you 'Kitty'," Miss Carruthers said a moment later.

"Well it is 'Kathleen' really, but everyone calls me 'Kitty'. So do my Mum and Dad."

"I see. Well I think I shall refer to you as 'Kathleen' while you are here. If you have no objection of course."

Kitty knew perfectly well that when a grown-up, especially one as much like a strict teacher as Miss Carruthers was, said to you 'If you have no objection', she really meant she was going to do it whether you had any objection or not. And when she was going to be your foster-mother for you-don't-know-how-long, you just went along with it if you were sensible. Not that it was worth making a fuss about anyway. So while she was here, she'd be 'Kathleen'

"Yes, Miss Carruthers," she agreed.

As they pulled into the drive of a detached house fifteen minutes later, Kitty's eyes rounded. This house confirmed what she'd already thought. Miss Carruthers was rich! Anyone who had a telephone at home, a car and a house as big as this, just had to be!

"Bring your cases in, leave them in the hall and then go into the lounge - that's the first door on the right. I shall ask Dorothy to bring us some tea there," Miss Carruthers directed as they got out of the car. She disappeared indoors leaving them to sort themselves out.

As they went into the hall they looked around.

It was so much BIGGER that the halls at home. There were

wide, dark oak stairs on one side giving off a faint smell of lavender polish, pictures on the walls and a dark oak coatstand on one side of the wide entrance door. A big grandfather clock with a loud tick was standing by the wall.

"That must be the lounge in there," whispered Maralyn.

They pushed open the door and went in.

This room was much bigger too, than theirs at home. Deep, comfortable-looking armchairs and a big settee were arranged facing a fireplace that had a big seascape above it. A writing bureau with a straight-backed chair by it was in a big bay window looking out onto the large front garden with its flower beds and tall silver birch trees. On the bureau by a telephone and typewriter was a photograph of a young soldier in uniform. Close to the bureau was a small table with two matching chairs. A nest of coffee tables were by a wall underneath another large seascape of a sailing ship approaching harbour.

They went to the settee to be able to sit together.

As they sank into the deep cushions Kitty whispered, "This is much better than the one we've got at home, Maralyn." And then wondered if she was being disloyal to her parents for even thinking that.

"Know what you mean Kitty – Kathleen," Maralyn whispered back.

Miss Carruthers came in briskly.

"Good. I'm glad you're sitting down," she said as she went to an armchair. "Please look on this lounge as being as much yours as it is mine. Except for the writing bureau of course. That is to be private to me. Dorothy will be coming in, in a moment with some tea and cakes for us. She is my Daily but as I have to be out tonight she has agreed to stay over to look after you till I return. To 'baby-sit' as she described it, though I feel you are rather old for that term to be used really. And she will give you your dinner tonight. Ah, here she is," she added as the door opened.

A stout, jolly-looking lady with greying hair came in, carrying a large tray. On it were an elegant teapot, matching cups, saucers and small plates, and a big plate of cakes.

"Dorothy, these two girls are Kathleen Jackson and Maralyn O'Conner. Kathleen and Maralyn, I'd like you to meet Mrs. Jones."

Both girls stood up quickly as though she was a teacher, the only patterns of authority they had met.

"Hello girls," Mrs. Jones said over her shoulder as she put the tray on the small table. "Nice to see you even if it is the war what's brought you here."

Miss Carruthers took the nest of tables and set the large one between the girls and put a smaller one by her own chair, gesturing for the girls to sit down again. Mrs. Jones poured out three cups of tea, put one by each of them, brought over the plate of cakes and hesitated.

"I'll have one Dorothy, then put the plate between the girls please. If they're anything like Sarah and Janice they'll finish the lot in seconds. Sarah and Janice are my nieces," she added to the girls. "They're just over six years of age. Twins."

She picked up her cup as Mrs. Jones left the room, and glanced at her watch.

"I have only a short time before I have to leave, so I want to explain some points now before I show you to your room."

Kitty paused in the act of taking another bite of the delicious angel cake and put it back on her plate to give Miss Carruthers her undivided attention. This was obviously going to be important.

"I have little experience of children - apart from contact with Sarah and Janice, so when I offered to accommodate evacuees myself I felt two girls old enough to be companions for each other and able to look after themselves to some degree would be best. Judging by the way you have behaved so far I feel we shall get on very well together."

Her smile lit up her face, transforming her severe look into a warm, attractive expression. That smile, to the girls, made her seem a much nicer, friendlier person.

"But I thought it would help us all if we had just a few rules. I'm sure you had them at home even if they were not called 'rules' as such, but they were ways in which your parents expected you to behave."

They nodded. Put like that they supposed there had been 'rules' at home.

"So I have made a list."

Miss Carruthers put her tea down, went to her writing bureau and brought back three sheets of paper, giving one to each of the girls and keeping the third for herself.

At first there seemed to be an awful lot of rules. But as they looked at them, they seemed to be only the things that Mum and Dad expected of them at home.

"As you see, they cover the things that we need to do to live together as long as this - this situation lasts." She picked up her cup and saucer, then put them down again, flushing slightly. "If - if you meet any - well, things that we might call 'personal matters', things you would normally talk over with your mothers I mean, I suggest you discuss them with Dorothy - or - or a female teacher you know at school - rather than me. Dorothy - Mrs. Jones - has had children of her own, though they are now adults and - well I'm sure she would be of greater assistance to you than I would be." She picked up her cup and saucer again.

The girls carefully didn't look at each other. What did Miss Carruthers mean about 'personal problems'? Girls growing up things? Or boys? Or what?

"The address of this house is on the paper as you see, so you can complete the postcards to send to your parents. You do have them to send I presume?"

"Yes, Miss Carruthers," replied the girls together.

"Is there anything you would like to ask me now?"

"Only about Tim. Timothy I mean," amended Kitty hurriedly. If Miss Carruthers was going to call her 'Kathleen' rather than 'Kitty', then she'd probably want to call Tim, 'Timothy'.

"Ah yes. Thank you for reminding me. I'll check the Directory." She went to the bureau, flicked through the pages, ran her finger down a short list of names and shook her head. "I'm sorry Kathleen. There is no 'Abbott' of the right address listed."

"Oh." Kitty's disappointment echoed in her voice. Her shoulders and the corners of her mouth drooped. She had been so hoping .... "Well thank you for trying, Miss Carruthers."

Miss Carruthers felt a surge of unexpected compassion for her. Having been an only child (even her 'nieces' were distant, being the daughters of a cousin) and her own parents having been pre-occupied with their business, they had never been a 'close' family. The only person she had ever developed a close emotional relationship with had been Gregory when she was seventeen. And he had died from wounds on the last day of fighting of the Great War.

And this little girl was only ten and she had been so suddenly wrenched from her home and parents and now her brother, by this new war.

"You miss him then?" she queried gently.

"Well - I suppose so. But the thing is, I promised Mum and Dad that I'd look after him. And I can't if he's somewhere else can I? And he's only five. Well, six nearly."

Miss Carruthers came to sit by her on the settee, just like Mum did when she wanted to be comforting, Kitty thought. Except Miss Carruthers didn't put her arms round her like Mum did.

"Kathleen, I can assure you with total confidence that Mrs. Abbott will be looking after Timothy very well indeed." She hesitated. "I could not accommodate him here I'm afraid, There simply isn't room for a boy because he'd need a separate bedroom of course. But perhaps Mrs. Abbott will have room for you to move in with him there. So when we go to see him tomorrow morning, as I have already promised we will, we can ask her. Does that sound satisfactory?"

Maralyn's eyes widened. She had been so relieved when she found she and Kitty would be together, that the thought of them being split up now came as a terrible shock. Would Miss Carruthers take another girl or would she be on her own here? Both had things about them that she didn't like.

"Yes please," Kitty said, perking up.

"Good. Then if you have finished your tea and cakes shall we go to see your room?"

She led them up the staircase to a wide corridor, the girls picking up their cases and gas masks on the way.

"There is the bathroom. There's the toilet - there's another downstairs. That is my room. That is the Study or Library. And here is your room. I hope you don't mind sharing."

She opened the door and led them in.

The girls looked round in delighted surprise. The large room had been freshly decorated and all the furniture looked new too.

There were two single beds with bright coverlets, a bedside table between them. A dressing table with a three-sided mirror, a chest of drawers and a wardrobe completed the furniture.

Colourful ornaments were on the dressing table and chest of drawers and seascapes were on the walls. The floor was newly carpeted. The large window overlooking the back garden had floral patterned curtains but blackout shutters were by them, ready to be fixed into position.

"I hope you like it." Miss Carruthers felt an unaccustomed diffidence. "I asked my cousin's advice - the mother of Sarah and Janice - what girls of your age would like."

"It's lovely!" Kitty's enthusiasm could not be doubted.

"It is!" Maralyn was equally emphatic.

"Excellent." Miss Carruthers found herself experiencing a degree of pleasure in their delight that she had never expected. "I will leave it to you to decide who will have which bed and decide on the drawers in the dressing table and chest of drawers. I am sure you can do that without squabbling."

But she spoke more in hope than expectation, judging them by her nieces.

"Oh yes," the girls promised together.

"May I see what clothes you have brought please?" Again she felt a measure of diffidence feeling it was an intrusion. But she did need to know what they had - and how clean it was. A Child Welfare Worker had told the Reception Committee that many of the evacuees would be from poor families so the foster-mothers shouldn't be surprised at anything they encountered.

Without demur both girls heaved their cases onto the beds and opened them.

Miss Carruthers flicked though the clothes and was taken aback. They were all new or clean - but there were so few!

"Are these all the clothes you had at home?" she asked gently.

"Oh no," both girls said together.

"I've got loads but we were told to only bring these or our cases would be too heavy to carry," explained Maralyn.

"Me too," confirmed Kitty. "Mum said she'd post on more when we sent our addresses. Oh, she gave me this letter to give to you. Well, whoever my foster-mother would be."

Miss Carruthers took it. "I must dash - after I've read the letter Kathleen. So unpack and then go down to the lounge or the kitchen where Dorothy - Mrs. Jones - is preparing your dinner. I shall not be back until late, after you will be in bed I expect, so I shall see you tomorrow morning." She went to the door and looked back. "So I'll say goodnight girls, even though it is fairly early. I do hope you will be happy here, in spite of the circumstances."

"Goodnight Miss Carruthers," they said together.

"And thank you for giving us such a lovely room," Kitty added.

Miss Carruthers stared at her, a sudden lump in her throat.

"My pleasure," she said softly. And left abruptly.

"Which bed do you want?" the girls asked together. Then laughed because they were so delighted with the room.

"You have the window bed if you'd like it," Maralyn said, feeling Kitty should have first choice as she had given her first choice of seat in the car.

"Thanks Maralyn," grinned Kitty. "Then you have first choice of drawers."

As they unpacked Kitty suddenly asked, "What d'you think a 'Daily' is, Maralyn? You know, what Mrs. Jones is."

"It's a servant. One that comes in every day instead of living in the same house. They had one in 'The House with the Red Roof', that I finished yesterday."

"Oh." Kitty was even more impressed with this evidence of Miss Carruthers' wealth.

When everything had been put away or hung up, they looked around the room with fresh delight.

"Lovely isn't it Maralyn?"

"It is!" She went to the window to look out of the window to see what was outside. "Kitty! Look! There's a squirrel! And there's another one."

Kitty joined her to look over the garden, to the big trees at the end of the lawn with its flower beds. Beyond the trees were fields of ripened wheat and barley with people at work harvesting. Three squirrels were darting from the trees, onto the lawn, pausing, moving in short rushes, then scampering back to the trees.

"It's beautiful," Kitty breathed. "Just like a picture. Except it's real." She looked round the room, then back out of the window.

"And this is where we'll be staying!" Maralyn exulted. The light abruptly died from her eyes. "Kitty ...," she faltered, " ... you will stay here with me, won't you?"

Kitty turned from the window, the light dying from her own eyes as she remembered about Tim, and her responsibility for him. Miss Carruthers said there was no room here for him, and she could see that herself. And that meant she'd have to go and stay with him, leaving this lovely room and garden and Maralyn. And where Tim was could not possibly be as nice.

"Well ...," And took refuge in the grown-ups form of words about unpleasant things that might be coming, " ... we'll see." Then seeing Maralyn's woeful face hurriedly added, "Let's go and find Mrs. Jones and see if we can go into the garden."

Not at all re-assured Maralyn went with her.

Kitty knocked on the door at the end of the hall and a voice from the other side called, "Come on in Kathleen and Maralyn."

Kitty pushed the door open. The big window looked out onto the garden and the back door was open as the early evening sun was still warm, adding to the heat from the stove.

"How did you know it was us?" Maralyn asked, puzzled.

"It had to be you. Miss Carruthers has gone out, there was only you two here besides me, it wasn't me what knocked on the door, so it had to be you. Pure deduction that was. Like a detective," she added complacently. "Would you like a drink while dinner's finishing? Orange? Lemonade? Or fizzy raspberry or a cup of tea. Take your pick."

"Lemonade for me please," decided Maralyn"

"Raspberry please," Kitty preferred.

"And I've already got my tea, so that's got us settled. Sit down at the table then." She put filled glasses in front of the girls, checked her cooking and sat down with them. "Do you like your room?"

"It's lovely," both girls agreed.

"Miss Carruthers had it done up special. It used to be a junk room - or 'Box room', as she used to call it."

"Miss Carruthers must be awfully rich," Maralyn said, after a pause. "I mean, with a telephone, a big car, a big house like this, doing up our room like that and - and everything."

Mrs. Jones frowned thoughtfully, staring into her cup as she considered it.

"I don't know about rich as RICH. But quite comfortably off I'd say. Nice ain't she?"

"When we first saw her at the school we thought she looked ever so strict. But she seems to be a lot kinder than she looks. I don't mean to sound rude," Maralyn hurriedly added.

"I know just what you mean, Maralyn. When I first came here I thought exactly the same. I thought, 'Hello, you're going to be a right awkward one you are'. She gave me a long list of Do's and Don'ts, all typed out like a lawyer would. But when you looked at them, they was only what a Boss would want of a Daily."

"We had a list like that. Well, not exactly the same I suppose." Kitty added, remembering the one about 'Do not play on the stairs'.

"She asked me what I thought should go down on yours seeing as how I'd had kids of my own. But she did put some of her own too.

"Anyway, a few days after I started here my Jack, he's my husband, took ill. He was real bad for a week to start with and Miss Carruthers told me to take off all the time I needed to look after him. After two days I came round to see her because Jack was still bad, thinking if I didn't I'd lose me job anyway. Because when a Boss says, 'Take off all the time you need', they usually mean just a couple of days but want to sound kind.

"But Miss Carruthers did mean it! She always means what she says, I've found. I asked if I could have the wages for the two days I'd worked before I went off, to get some of the special medicine the doctor said Jack needed. But do you know, she gave me the full week's pay, AND went off and got the medicine for us herself, and then went and had a talk with Jack's boss so that he kept the job open till Jack was fit enough to go back." She paused. "She's a real kind lady she is. You're real lucky to be here with her, I can tell you."

Chapter 4
Decisions

Kitty woke with a start. For a moment she stared round the strange room, not knowing where she was.

Then she remembered. She was Evacuated, and it was morning. And later this morning she would leave this lovely place, and Maralyn, and move into wherever it was that Tim was staying. Because he was bound to want her with him and she had promised to look after him.

At breakfast in the kitchen, while Maralyn chattered, Kitty was very quiet.

After glancing at her several times wondering if she was always like this, or if she was worried and homesick, Miss Carruthers asked her.

Kitty looked up from her plate at her.

"I was wondering, when I do go to stay with Tim - Timothy - if that place could be anything like as nice as what's here."

Miss Carruthers stared at her in astonishment. That had not figured in any of possible answers that she had thought of.

"I'm sure it will be Kathleen. This place is nothing special."

"Oh it is, Miss Carruthers, it is," the girls chorused.

When Tim realised that Kitty was not going to be with him at his new foster-mother's after all, he stared at Miss Drew.

"But where will Kitty be, Miss Drew?"

She looked at Mr. Jenkins who shrugged.

"I haven't got all the lists here, Miss Drew. But you needn't worry Tim, she will be with a lady who is just as kind as Mrs. Abbott," he replied quickly.

"So you go off with Mrs. Abbott and Tommy and Jack. After all, you know each other, don't you?" she encouraged.

"By the way boys, I nearly forgot," Mrs. Abbott broke in. "A 'Welcome to Folkestone' present for you each." She reached into her shopping bag. "I hope you like toy cars."

She handed Tim a Rolls Royce! His eyes widened. He loved

toy cars and for it to be a Rolls Royce! That was the prize of any collection!

"Thanks Mrs. ...." He'd forgotten her name.

"Mrs. Abbott. But call me 'Auntie Flo'. And here's yours boys." She handed presents to Tommy and Jack. "Come on then, if we hurry we'll just be in time for the bus home."

As they left, Tim much more cheerful now, the boys compared their presents. Tommy had had an aeroplane and Jack a ship.

The house proved to be just round the corner from the bus stop and Tim's heart bounded when he saw it. It was so much taller than home. And it even had windows in the roof!

After a drink and a cake, while tea was cooking, Auntie Flo took them upstairs to see their room.

The three boys looked round the big attic room with growing excitement.

"Golly!" Tim gasped. "It's just like camping in a tent! A great big tent."

The sloping roof with two skylights in, reached down to low walls. Painted plywood nailed onto the sloping roof rafters looked so like matt green canvas that it helped to reinforce that feeling. The walls had big pictures of merchant ships and foreign places with pride of place given to a cross-Channel ferry, 'The Sea Queen'.

"Well? What do you think? Do you like it?" asked Auntie Flo.

"It's t'r'ific!" burst out Tim.

"It's just as though we'll be sleeping in a great big tent! 'Specially with the camp beds." Jack spoke in an awed voice.

"They'll only be here till you get the proper beds delivered in the next couple of weeks." she warned them. "Now put your cases on the beds and we'll unpack them later. Tea should be just about ready by now."

They were sitting down at the big kitchen table when a huge man with a big beard came in pushing an elderly, white-haired man in a wheelchair, followed by a younger version of Wilf, almost as tall and broad as his father, but without a beard.

"My husband Wilf, you can call him Uncle Wilf, and Uncle Toby, and George, my lad. As he's older than you, you can call him 'Uncle George'. And this is Tommy, Tim and Jack who will be with us for the Duration, " introduced Auntie Flo.

The boys looked at the man in the wheelchair with interest.

So this was the man who was the wounded naval hero from the last war who'd won a medal for his bravery that Auntie Flo had told them about on the bus.

"Auntie Flo said you'd won a medal for being brave, Uncle Toby. What did you do?" asked Tim with a child's directness.

"Oh did she?" Uncle Toby growled grumpily picking up his fork. "Well there's nothing much to tell."

"Come on Dad, you're secret's out now, so you'd better tell them. If you don't, I will." grinned Uncle Wilf.

"Oh alright then," Uncle Toby said, still grumpily. And then he held the boys spell-bound as he told them about his part in the Battle of Jutland.

And then they looked in silence at the medal that Uncle Wilf took from its box kept in a sideboard drawer, that Uncle Toby had been awarded for rescuing burned and wounded sailors from their blazing turret.

When they went up to bed Uncle George went with them to show them how to make sleeping bags out of two blankets as he'd learned in the Sea Cadets.

As Tim snuggled down in his sleeping bag and the excitement of the day began to fade, he wondered where Kitty was and what she was doing. Could she possibly be in a place as perfect as this? With people as nice as those here? And what were Mum and Dad doing? And to think it was only last night he had been at home with them, in his own bed, in his own room. And now they were all so far away.

An empty kind of feeling came into his chest and stomach and he felt tears coming. He'd never felt quite like this before and he didn't like it. He was homesick.

He struggled not to cry. He didn't want Tommy or Jack to hear him, because they'd think he was a baby. Because big boys don't cry. But that didn't change the way he was feeling. That he wanted to be back at home with Mum and Dad, Kitty and Frank, all of them close by.

At last he fell asleep.

A voice was shouting for him to get up. It was a lady's voice but it wasn't Mum's.

Then he remembered. He was Evacuated and Mum was a long way away. Homesickness surged again. All he wanted to do was to go back to sleep. Then he'd be away from all this.

There was no sound from the other two beds so maybe Tommy and Jack were feeling the same as he was. Insidiously sleep began to creep up on him again.

"Tommy! Jack! Tim! On Parade in fifteen minutes!" It was a man's voice this time, shouting up at them.

All three boys shot up in bed staring at each other.

A Parade? What Parade? Who'd said anything about a Parade this morning? Or any morning?

"It's Uncle Wilf! Or Uncle Toby! Or Uncle George! It's got to be!" burst out Jack. "Tim, you take the bathroom first while me and Tommy get dressed, then we'll swap over."

Tim dashed out of the door, homesickness forgotten in his excitement.

Dressed and more or less washed, they clattered downstairs and stopped. Where was the Parade?

"In the kitchen," came the voice again.

They ran in to see George looking at his watch and counting.

"Three, two, one. Line up."

He marched to the doorway and snapped to attention.

"Crew ready for Inspection, Skipper," he called.

Uncle Toby wheeled his chair in.

"Crew – attention," snapped George. "Salute the Skipper," he muttered to the boys, who copied him

Gravely Uncle Toby saluted them back, then looked them up and down.

"Hands," he snapped.

The boys held them out.

"Over."

They turned them over.

"Did you wash ears? Necks? Clean your teeth?"

"Yes Uncle Toby," they said together.

"On Parade he's 'Skipper', not 'Uncle Toby'," George muttered out of the corner of his mouth.

"Yes Skipper," they amended.

"Good. Did you make your beds?"

"No Skipper," they muttered shamefacedly.

"We didn't have time, Skipper," Jack, as the oldest by a few months, spoke up in their defence.

"If you had got up at first call you would have had time wouldn't you?"

"Yes Skipper," they had to agree.

Skipper nodded. "Very well. You've done quite well on your first morning shipmates. Remember - up at first call in future."

"Yes Skipper."

Skipper had called them 'Shipmates', they thought proudly.

"Parade – dismiss," George snapped, saluting. "Salute the Skipper," he muttered.

The boys copied his salute, which Skipper returned.

"I hope you like porridge," said Auntie Flo from the cooker where she was stirring a pan of it.

They did. As they sat down, Uncle Toby wheeled himself to the table.

"Did you have porridge in the navy Skipper, I mean Uncle Toby," Tim amended, now that they were no longer on Parade.

"We did. And we've always had it here. That's why George and Uncle Wilf are so big. So you'd better eat it all up."

The boys eyed George who grinned at them.

"I remember once on board ship in Scapa Flow - that's in Scotland ...," began Uncle Toby.

The boys listened fascinated, as they plied their porridge spoons.

When they were asked what they would like to do that afternoon, Tim's answer was immediate, "I'd like to see some ships."

"Great idea!" agreed Tommy and Jack together.

"You play around here this morning and I'll take you down to see The Sea Queen sail this afternoon," promised George.

Straight after breakfast, Maralyn went in the car with them when Miss Carruthers took Kitty to Mrs. Abbott's house, this time with Kitty sitting in the front. Her case, re-packed, was in the boot.

"You know Kathleen ...," Miss Carruthers said as she started the engine, and then waited for it engine to warm up, " ... it may happen that Mrs. Abbott will not have room for you to stay there, just as I do not have room for Timothy here. But even if she has, if he is happy there and you feel, as I do, that the place is suitable for him, then I don't think you should feel that you have to move there just to be with him."

"But I promised Mum and Dad - and Timothy – and Tommy and Aunt Jennie that I'd look after them," she said in a low voice, staring at the dashboard.

Miss Carruthers drove off, paused to check the road then turned into it.

"I think you are to be commended for that, Kathleen, but what exactly did you mean, and your parents – and Aunt Jennie - understand you to mean, by that? To be responsible for cooking his meals, mending his clothes, darning his socks, buying him new clothes when they wear out, giving him pocket money, sending him to school, nursing him if he is ill?"

She glanced sideways at her. Kitty caught her eye and she smiled herself despite the way she was feeling. Of course Mum and Dad and Aunt Jennie wouldn't have thought that!

"No, of course they wouldn't have thought that," Miss Carruthers echoed Kitty's own thoughts. "Nor would anyone else. We arranged for foster-mothers to do all those things. As I was the person in charge of that in Folkestone, I know it was done properly."

"Were you?" Kitty was impressed and relieved. If it was Miss Carruthers who had organised it, then Kitty was sure it would be alright.

"So, as I have said Kathleen, if you find Timothy and Tommy are happy and agree the place is suitable, then I am sure your parents would be just as pleased for you to come back with Maralyn and me and for you to see the boys regularly, even if Mrs. Abbott does have room for you. And we would be very happy for you to continue to stay with us wouldn't we Maralyn?"

"Oh yes. Kathleen - do stay with us!" Maralyn begged.

"That is exactly my feeling too. But the final decision will have to be yours Kathleen." She braked to a halt. "Here we are. Maralyn, I think you should wait in the car for now. We'll leave your case as well, Kathleen, until we see what is decided."

They walked up the path through a garden that was not so well kept as Miss Carruthers, Kitty thought. Miss Carruthers knocked on the door, Kitty standing just behind her.

The door was opened by a young man with a mop of thick hair.

"Is Mrs. Abbott in please?" Miss Carruthers asked.

"She is. Please come in and I'll get her." George showed them into a front room that was obviously the best parlour. "Please sit down while I get my mother."

Kitty looked round the room. It was nice, but not as nice as Miss Carruthers'. How she hoped that Tim and Tommy were happy here - and as important, that there was no room for her.

"George, my son, said you wanted to see me," a small lady said as she bustled into the room, moments later.

"Yes please Mrs. Abbott, just for a few minutes. I am Miss Carruthers, Chairman of the Evacuation Reception Committee. I believe you have Timothy Jackson staying with you?"

"That's right. With Tommy Francis and Jack Saunders. I said I could take up to three boys. Is anything the matter?"

She was wondering if this was an Inspection Visit - and if she had been singled out or if everyone was getting them. And who that young girl was with this Miss Carruthers.

"This is Kathleen Jackson, Timothy's sister. How is Timothy getting on?"

"Oh he's fine. He's settled in really well. A bit uncertain at first of course, as was only natural. But he knew Tommy and Jack from school. They're out playing football in the back garden. And you're Tim's sister? He was wondering about you. But I had to leave with him and the other two quick last night to get my husband's tea before he went on duty with the ferry. He's First Mate on The Sea Queen, you know. I was going down to the office this afternoon but now you've saved me the trouble. Do you want to see him? It's this way."

Mrs. Abbott sprang to her feet. She had the quick movements and rapid way of talking that reminded Kitty of the darting movements of the squirrels she'd seen in the garden.

She led them down a narrow dark hallway (how different from Miss Carruthers, Kitty thought) to the kitchen. Through the big window they could hear the excited shouts of the three boys chasing a football.

"There they are," said Mrs. Abbott unnecessarily, pointing through the window.

The game was fast but friendly with Jack in goal, which consisted of two wide chalk marks drawn on a blank wall.

"Goal!" yelled Tim, throwing his hands up in the air, jumping up and down in his excitement.

"Okay. Three, two in my favour. Bet I get the next one," shouted Tommy in response.

Jack kicked the ball well down the big lawn towards the kitchen, while Tommy and Tim dashed after it.

Sitting in a wheelchair on a paved area near the kitchen door was an elderly-looking one-armed man with a blanket over his knees, cheering both boys on. George was standing by him, grinning broadly.

Mrs. Abbott smiled fondly.

"You know, those three lads have already done Toby a world of good. He's my father-in-law. In the wheelchair. He was proper mopey, what with his wounds from the last war troubling him all the time and now a new war starting. When Wilf, my husband, told him we were going to take in three lads he growled like a bear with a sore head and said he hoped they'd behave themselves, keep quiet and leave him alone. So on the bus I told them he'd been in the navy in the last war and got wounded and they were all over him. And look at him now!"

Another yell of triumph. mingled with shouts of protest rang out.

"It missed! It missed! It hit the post and bounced out," Tommy was shouting.

"It was inside! Inside!" Tim's shout was equally loud and just as definite.

"Let's ask Uncle Toby. He'd've seen," suggested Jack.

The three boys dashed over, Tommy and Tim shouting their versions. Uncle Toby held up his hand and they fell silent.

"The ball hit the wall just on the INSIDE of the chalk line, lads. With real goal posts it would have bounced off into the goal, so it counts as a goal. But from where Tommy was standing it would have looked as though it hit the post straight on. So

I reckon it's a goal Tommy, so it's three, three. And I reckon it's half-time."

The boys accepted his decision as final and flopped down on the ground near the wheelchair.

"If it's half-time I'd better go and get some drinks," said George, moving off.

"Why don't you go and join the boys, Kathleen?" suggested Miss Carruthers quietly.

Kitty looked from her to Mrs. Abbott and knew that meant there would be grown-ups talk about her. But it would give her a chance to find out what Tim really thought about being here.

"Hello Tim," she called as she approached them.

"Hello Kitty," Tim jumped to his feet, beaming all over his face, to hug her. He pulled her over to the others. "This is my big sister Kitty I was telling you about. This is Uncle Toby, but when we're on Parade we call him 'Skipper'. He won a medal in the last big war because he's a hero. And that's Jack. He comes from our school too. My Class. Where are you staying Kitty?"

"With a lady called Miss Carruthers, and Maralyn, in a big house, a bit like this one." Kitty sat down by them. "What's your bedroom like Tim?" She thought that would be a good lead-in.

"It's terrific!" his enthusiasm was obvious. "We've made it up like a camp because it looks like a great big tent and we've got real camp beds, not just ordinary ones. But Auntie Flo says we will be getting ordinary ones in a couple of weeks," he added disgustedly. "And it's got pictures all round the walls of 'planes and ships and things. And Uncle Toby has lent us some more pictures of submarines and battleships this morning and ...,"

"And some models," jumped in Jack.

"And some models. And Uncle Wilf is going to get us one of The Sea Queen ...,"

"That's the ferry my father works on," George explained, arriving back with a tray of drinks and handing them round, including one for Kitty.

She thanked him as she took it, then looked at Tim. She had to ask him, even if meant doing it in front of the others.

"So you really like staying here then Tim? Tommy?"

"It's t'r'ific!" they repeated emphatically.

"Everything is," Tim added. "Our camp. Auntie Flo and the Uncles. Tommy and Jack here. It's all t'r'ific." He really wanted to convince Kitty just how 't'r'ific' it was.

Kitty was convinced. There was only .... "Tim, suppose we couldn't stay at the same place? Would you mind?"

Tim hesitated. In the excitement of everything he hadn't given a thought to them being together, apart from when he was just going to sleep last night. They had thought they'd be staying together, and so had Mum and Dad. But he definitely didn't want to leave here, and he couldn't see how they could fit Kitty in, being a girl, so ...,

"Well if it's alright where you are, and I was staying here, I wouldn't mind. Because we can always go and see each other at each other's houses, couldn't we?"

"Of course we could. And anyway we'll see each other at school every day won't we?"

Kitty felt a vast relief. Tim was fine here, and he wasn't even thinking of her coming here to be with him. So was Tommy.

She looked towards the house in time to see Mrs. Abbott beckoning to her from the kitchen door.

As she stood up she made her decision. After all, Miss Carruthers had said it was her decision, so even if Mrs. Abbott said she could stay here, she would say, as politely as she could of course, that she'd prefer to stay with Miss Carruthers.

Mrs. Abbott put a motherly arm round her shoulders and guided her to a chair at the table where Miss Carruthers was already sitting, and pulled up hers to sit close by her.

"Now then Kathleen, Miss Carruthers has told me that you promised your Mum and Dad and Tim that you'd look after him while you're away. And Tommy. Obviously all that meant was that you'd be around to make sure he wasn't bullied and suchlike."

"Yes Mrs. Abbott," Kitty said quickly when she paused. "And ...,"

"And Miss Carruthers arranged for people like me to do all the other things. She says that you and Tim expected to be staying in the same place ...,"

"But that doesn't matter now Mrs. Abbott as Tim says ...,"

" ... but I've got no room for you to stay here with him," Mrs.

Abbott steam-rollered on. "I'm sorry Kitty - Kathleen ..."

"But I ...,"

" ... but you see, staying in this house there's already Wilf, he's my husband, and me, Wilf's dad that's Uncle Toby, one son who's in the navy and George my other lad you've just met. So while I was able to put three boys together in our top room 'cos it's so big, I can't put you, a girl, in with them, can I? But I've got a sister who I might be able to talk into taking you and Tim together ...,"

"Oh no, don't! Please don't do that Mrs. Abbott! Tim is so happy here, and I am happy with Miss Carruthers so can't we ...," She shot an appealing look at Miss Carruthers.

"It seems to me, Mrs. Abbott that things could not really have worked out any better, as Timothy is so happy staying here, and Kathleen is with me and her friend Maralyn. So I feel we should leave things just as they are. Kathleen, I really should go now as I have a meeting with your teachers, but if you would like to stay for a time I could ...,"

"I'll just say goodbye quickly to Tim and I'll come straight away, Miss Carruthers," Kitty said hurriedly, jumping to her feet.

She couldn't wait to tell Maralyn she'd be staying after all, and to get back to what she already felt was home.

That afternoon as they went down to the harbour, Tim trotting along holding Uncle George's hand, he felt on top of the world. He had seen Kitty this morning and she'd told him she was happy where she was. He was really happy with Auntie Flo and the others and wouldn't have to move away. He was staying at the seaside which was even better than the country. He was living with a naval hero and they might, if they were really lucky, be able to go on board The Sea Queen and even go on a trip on it and watch the big engines working.

It was all so very different and so much more exciting than all those rows of small, boring houses at home in London.

Chapter 5
It's war

At breakfast two days later, their first Sunday, Miss Carruthers refilled the toast rack and sat down again. She reached for a piece, methodically spread butter and marmalade on it and cut it into smaller pieces.

Kitty and Maralyn shot a look at each other. Something was in the air.

"Kathleen, Maralyn, instead of going to Church this morning as I usually do, I have decided to stay at home and listen to what Mr. Chamberlain, our Prime Minister, will be saying on the wireless at 11 o'clock. Naturally you are welcome to listen too, or play in the garden, if you wish, as the weather is fine."

"Do you think Mr. Chamberlain is going to say there's going to be a war?" Maralyn asked outright.

"If the news we have been hearing on the wireless in the last few days is to be believed then he may well do so. It is possible of course, that Herr Hitler has paid heed to what has been said and has given orders for his forces to withdraw from Poland, in which case there will be no need for us to go to war, and we can all go back to our normal lives." She paused. "I only hope and pray that is what will happen."

Just before 11 o'clock Kitty and Maralyn knocked on the lounge door. They were still wary about taking Miss Carruthers too much at her word when she had said they could treat the lounge as being as much theirs as hers, especially when she was at home.

"Come on in girls," she called out.

The wireless was already switched on as they went to sit down on the settee together, their usual places now, and waited.

Miss Carruthers was looking very serious.

"When we listen to what the Prime Minister says, girls, remember that he will be making a speech that will change the history of Europe, quite possibly the history of the world. He is about to begin so let us listen perfectly quietly."

"This morning the British Ambassador in Berlin handed the

German Government a Final Note stating that unless we heard from them by 11 o'clock this morning that they were prepared at once to withdraw their troops from Poland, a state of war would exist between us."

The quietly spoken and sombre tone of the Prime Minister was very clear.

"I have to tell you now that no such undertaking has been received and that consequently this country is now at war with Germany." He paused a moment.

"You can imagine what a bitter blow it is to me that all my long struggle to win peace has failed. Yet I cannot believe that there is anything more, or anything different, that I could have done and that would have been more successful.

"Up to the very last it would have been quite possible to have arranged a peaceful and an honourable settlement between Germany and Poland, but Hitler would not have it."

Kitty stole a look at Miss Carruthers as the Prime Minister was speaking. She was staring wide-eyed at the wireless, her face deadly pale, her hands folded on her lap were tight clenched.

"We and France are today, in fulfilment of our obligations, going to the aid of Poland, who is so bravely resisting this wicked and unprovoked attack on her people.

"We have a clear conscience. We have done all that any country could do to establish peace."

He continued talking but Kitty was no longer listening. She was terrified. Everyone knew that in a war London was going to be terribly bombed straight away. That was why she and Tim and all the others from the school were here in the country. To be safe from that. But Mum and Dad and Frank were still there.

After the Prime Minister finished speaking Miss Carruthers drew in a deep breath, stood up and switched off the wireless.

"Well - now we know. What would you like to do after lunch, girls?"

They looked at her, startled.

Do? After lunch? Just as though today was an ordinary day? Just as if the history of Europe if not the world had not just been changed? Because that was what Miss Carruthers herself had said just a few minutes ago!

"But - what is going to happen in this war, Miss Carruthers?" Maralyn asked shakily.

"And to London?" Kitty burst out. "I heard Dad tell Mum once that thousands and THOUSANDS would be killed in London. Straight off! And - and Mum and Dad are still there!"

Her eyes were wide with her fear.

Miss Carruthers sat down by them at the end of the settee, to be able to face them both, while being closer.

"I have seen many forecasts of what might happen in London, Kathleen. And only ONE of them spoke in such terms." Her calm voice cut through Kitty's terror. "All the other reports were much less pessimistic. They all said that the casualties - when and if the bombing did begin - would be very much less than that. As I recall the map, Catford where you come from, is a considerable distance from the centre of London."

"Yes Miss Carruthers, it is. I think Dad said once that it was about ten miles."

"And I would think that the German Air Force, if they do bomb London at all, would attack its centre rather than all round its outskirts."

Both girls nodded. They supposed that that was what Air Forces would do. If Miss Carruthers said so.

"And you have Shelters yourselves haven't you? And I've heard that they'll be building them in the streets too. So I do not think you need worry too much over the safety of your parents."

"Then why did we have to be Evacuated at all?" Maralyn asked a moment before Kitty.

"Because the Government, and your parents, quite rightly in my view, had the policy of 'better safe than sorry'." She paused. "Girls, because we can't see into the future we can't tell how this war will work out. So we must do what Mr. Chamberlain has just said - do our duty and carry on with our jobs. Your duty ...," she looked at both of them " ... is to work hard at school because people your age now will be the ones to re-make the world after the war is over. Whenever that will be. If it lasts as long as the Great War, the last war, which was four years, you will be coming to the age of starting work and could be very important in that."

Kitty and Maralyn stared at her and then looked at each other.

They had never looked on their futures and their lives like that. That they could be important. They had talked a few times of what they would like to do when they were grown up, but their ideas had been limited to things like working in a shop or maybe an office. But Miss Carruthers seemed to be thinking of things far beyond that.

And when they had talked about it, it had all been vague and far away. Almost unreal. But Miss Carruthers was making it sound as something to be working towards right now!

And that was exciting!

“But - it can't possibly last four years can it?" whispered Kitty.

"No one can know at this stage, Kathleen. We thought the Great War would be over by Christmas - in about three months then. With this one ...," she shrugged, " ... we'll just have to see.

“Now then ...," she went on briskly, " ... we can't sit here all day just looking at each other, and the sun is shining. So I shall get an early lunch and then we'll go for a walk along the sea front towards Sandgate where there are some nice tea-rooms where we shall have tea. Then we can come home up the Zig-zag path. Does that sound satisfactory to you?"

Still not fully re-assured, they agreed.

"Can we help you get lunch, Miss Carruthers?" asked Kitty.

For a moment she was about to refuse, then impulsively, "Why not? If you two can prepare the salad, I'll see to warming the pie and cooking the potatoes. Do you know how to do salads?"

Luckily, they did.

"There," Kitty said with satisfaction, hanging up the cloth to dry. "That's the washing up done too." They had listened to the 1 o'clock News on the wireless, dreading reports of waves of bombers sweeping in to destroy all of London as soon as the Prime Minister had finished speaking. But there had been no bombers at all.

The girls had suggested they do the washing up while Miss Carruthers went to the lounge with her cup of coffee. Now they had finished and were ready to explore some of Folkestone

"I'll get the gas masks from upstairs," volunteered Maralyn.

"And I'll tell Miss Carruthers we're ready."

Kitty knocked on the lounge door but there was no reply.

She opened it, and stopped abruptly.

Miss Carruthers was in there, sitting at her writing bureau, and holding the photograph of that soldier. And crying.

Kitty didn't know what to do. If Miss Carruthers had been a person like her Mum, it would have been easier. She'd have just gone straight up to her to hug her.

But Miss Carruthers was not like her Mum. Kitty didn't know how to put it into words, but Miss Carruthers seemed to be so much 'in control', as though she could do everything, that she was the sort of person who sorted things out for other people, as though nothing could ever upset her.

So for something to have happened to make HER cry must be truly terrible.

Maralyn arrived.

"I've got the gas ...,"

Kitty silenced her with a finger to her lips and a jerk of her head to Miss Carruthers.

"What'll we do?" Maralyn whispered.

Kitty decided. She knew that some grown-ups didn't like children to see them cry, but she couldn't just go away and pretend she hadn't seen this. Miss Carruthers had been so kind to them, and there was no one else there.

She crept over to Miss Carruthers and put her arms round her.

"I'm so sorry Miss Carruthers," she said softly.

"How many more fine young men like Gregory are going to be killed in this new war?" she sobbed.

Kitty knew that that was the kind of question grown-ups sometimes asked each other, not expecting an answer. How could anyone possibly know the answer to that one?

"Is that a picture of Gregory?" she asked instead.

Miss Carruthers nodded just once. "It was taken before he went off to France in 1915. He went through all the war and then was killed on the very last day of the fighting."

"Was he your brother?"

"No. He was my sweetheart. We were going to be married when he came home from the war." Her tears flowed faster.

Kitty didn't know what she could say. How could she say, 'It'll come alright', her Mum's usual words of comfort? Because a sweetheart being killed could never 'come alright', could it? So she hugged Miss Carruthers tighter and said nothing more.

Miss Carruthers suddenly sat upright as she realised she was being hugged by someone - and that someone was a ten year old child. A child she was fostering and who was the one who needed comforting! Fancy crying in front of her! What must she be thinking of her?

"I'm sorry Kathleen," she said, quickly reaching for her handkerchief. "That was very silly of me crying like that."

"My mother said that to cry when someone dies isn't silly, Miss Carruthers." said Maralyn, coming into the room from the doorway. "She said it was only natural. She told me that when my Gran died last summer. And I think it's much sadder when a sweetheart dies like that."

"Yes. Yes. Perhaps it is." Miss Carruthers dabbed her eyes and put the photo back in its place. "Thank you for - for your kind sympathy girls. I'll - I'll be down in five minutes and then we'll go for our walk."

As they walked along the seafront, Kitty was quiet and thoughtful, though Miss Carruthers seemed to have regained her usual cheerfulness. Because, for Kitty, Miss Carruthers was the first person she'd met who had had someone they loved killed by a war and it made this war come very close. But she gradually cheered up as Miss Carruthers told them about other places to see around Folkestone, as though she too had put away her sadness.

A tall grey-haired man and a lady crossed the road to speak to them

"'Afternoon, Miss Carruthers," he boomed, raising his hat to them.

"Good afternoon Colonel, and Mrs. Burns," she responded with a smile. "Your forecast proved to be correct."

"Chamberlain couldn't very well do anything else after all he's said," he grunted. "Erm - d'you have five minutes to spare now or shall I ring you?" He looked meaningfully at the two girls. "There is something else."

"May I introduce two young friends who are staying with me for a time? Kathleen Jackson and Maralyn O'Conner. Girls, this is Colonel and Mrs. Burns."

"Pleased to meet you, girls," the Colonel tipped his hat, while his wife smiled at them

"Will you be going off to fight the Germans?" Maralyn asked him excitedly.

"'Fraid not me dear. I retired from my Regiment more than a few years ago and they've already told me I'm too old to be recalled." He looked at Miss Carruthers. "Five minutes?"

"Girls, I can see an ice cream bicycle further down the road. Can you see him? I'm sure you can manage an ice cream, can't you?" She gave Kitty a half-crown. "Off you go."

"Thank you Miss Carruthers." The girls dashed off delightedly to catch the ice cream man before he moved on.

"Now then Colonel ...,"

Twenty minutes later as the Colonel and his wife left her, Miss Carruthers turned to look across the sea towards France, just about visible twenty miles away. Which was closer to Folkestone than London was.

The Colonel had been so convincing - that after conquering Poland, Hitler would inevitably turn his armies westwards to invade France - and equally inevitably, England. In which case they'd be bound to land on the South Coast. Just around here.

She had a mental picture of invasion ships coming to land troops on this very strip of shore where they were standing. With more ships crowding into the harbour only a few hundred yards away. The thunder of the guns, the screams of the wounded. The dying all around. Not only on this waterfront but in bombed and shelled buildings collapsing on people further inland.

And not only fighting men, but also women and children. Children like Kathleen and Maralyn. And her nieces, Sarah and Janice.

She shuddered.

"Wonder what he could have told her that was so important?" muttered Kitty. "And it must have taken much longer than the five minutes he said."

"Don't suppose she's going to tell us though." As Miss Carruthers drew nearer to the bench where they'd sat down to stay well away from the three grown-ups, "But she does look unhappy again, doesn't she?"

They stood up from the bench to meet her.

"Here's the change from the ice creams, Miss Carruthers," Kitty held it out.

"Change?" she echoed distractedly. "Change? Oh yes, change. Thank you Kathleen." She put the money back in her purse, hesitated a moment, then seemed to remember what they had been doing. "Yes. Well let's see if we can find those tea-rooms in Sandgate shall we? Do you think you could still manage a cake or two after the ice creams?"

They assured her they could.

"Was it bad news, Miss Carruthers?" asked Maralyn boldly after they'd been walking for some minutes in silence. "From Colonel Burns I mean."

"Was it about the bombing of London?" followed up Kitty swiftly.

"No. No, it was nothing about that at all. It was something else altogether. Nothing for you to worry about."

Kitty and Maralyn exchanged a quick glance. When a grown up said that, it usually meant that there WAS something to worry about - but that they weren't going to tell.

"You see that ship over there?" Miss Carruthers changed the subject hurriedly in case there were more questions. "That is bringing cargo to England, probably to London."

"How do you know that Miss Carruthers?" the girls asked together.

She took a pair of binoculars out of her big shoulder bag, showed them how to adjust them for a clearer view, and explained. Which provoked a stream of questions about ships and shipping, cargoes and foreign countries, just as Miss Carruthers had intended.

"Have you got things from some of the countries you've been to?" Maralyn asked just as they reached the outside of the tea-rooms.

"Quite a lot. If you are interested you can see them when we get home."

"How do you know so much about ships and things?" was Kitty's question when they had ordered.

"It's been our family business for three generations, including me. My grandfather began a ships' chandlers business, that's a shop that sells things to do with ships and boats, first of all here in Folkestone. Then my father took it over when he retired, my grandfather that is, after we had travelled a lot arranging cargoes for ships, and he set up another shop in Dover. I've opened two more, one in Hythe and another in Deal, so now we have four. But we now sell a lot of other things besides boating goods I was planning to open two more, one in Hastings and another in Ramsgate, but with the war I've put them on 'Hold' as we call it. I hadn't signed any Contracts for those so that won't cause any difficulties."

"Oh good," said Kitty, not having the slightest idea what 'Contracts' were. But she nodded to herself. That explained why Miss Carruthers was so rich.

It was as they strolled back that, in the most natural way, the girls had moved to walk one on each side of her and she found herself holding their hands.

With Sarah and Janice it was more to stop them dashing away or arguing, but with Kathleen and Maralyn it was - different. Companionable. They had taken her hands. As though they did it because they liked her. But it was absurd to think that they should have grown so close to her in this short space of time - barely three days.

At that moment Kitty looked up at her and squeezed her hand. She squeezed gently back, and Kitty gave her a beaming smile.

"Can we call you something different from 'Miss Carruthers' please?" she asked. "Only 'Miss Carruthers' sounds like - like you're a teacher and not as you really are."

"My Christian name is 'Anne'. So you can call me 'Aunt Anne' if you would like to."

"That's a nice name," Kitty commented.

"I've got a book where the heroine is called 'Anne'," Maralyn told them. "And she travelled to a lot of foreign places just like you did. Aunt Anne."

And Anne felt absurdly pleased.

They reached the Zig-Zag path that climbed the cliff face.

Part way up they all had to stop to catch their breath and look out over the sea. The girls were enchanted.

But the Colonel's warning intruded into Anne's mind, wrecking the happiness the girls' friendliness had given her.

She saw the German ships coming in, guns blazing. British troops were sure to be exactly where they were standing now, behind the natural breastwork of the wall.

And these two lovely children had come here to be safe! So they would have to be re-evacuated.

But - once the German forces landed could any place in England be called 'safe'?

That evening after the girls had gone to bed, Anne took her big Atlas down to the sitting room. To study it in the light of what the Colonel had said.

"Ron! Chamberlain is going to talk on the wireless in a minute. Are you coming in to listen or not?" Mingled worry and irritation lent asperity to May's voice.

"Coming."

Ron finished hammering in the last nail securing another piece of roofing felt to the chicken run that he had moved from the bottom of the garden to make room for the underground Anderson shelter.

He washed his hands in the kitchen sink and went into the front room.

"Hello Jennie. Sam working?"

She was clutching a mug of tea, sitting on the edge of the settee, tensed up.

"Supposed to be. But I'll bet that him and his mates'll be in the Depot listening to the set they've got there."

The Prime Minister began speaking as Ron sat down in his chair with a mug of tea. His first words confirming their fears.

They listened in silence until he had finished, then May very deliberately switched off the wireless and swung round to face Ron.

"Well Ron?" she demanded, almost triumphantly. "Do you remember what I told you when that idiot came back from Munich waving that stupid bit of paper? My Prediction? But you wouldn't believe me would you? Oh no! You knew better didn't you. 'Peace in our time', you said.

"But Chamberlain's just declared war on Germany hasn't he? In spite of what he's been told about the bombing that'll come. And all the deaths from it. And it is just inside the year, isn't it?

Just like I said it would be."

"But millions of people thought it meant peace May. Not just Ron," protested Jennie.

Ron looked up from his mug to May. He wasn't going to argue with her. And she was right anyway. They had trusted Chamberlain. And Hitler. And they had all been wrong.

"I'm going to finish the chicken run," he said standing up.

"Is that all you can say?" May demanded, fear adding to her fury. "Is that all ...?"

A distant air raid siren blared, immediately taken up by nearer ones, cutting her short.

"Get to the Shelter. Both of you. Get Frank. And take your gas masks. It's starting!" Ron snapped, grabbing his Warden's helmet and pack.

"Ron ...," began May.

"Don't argue woman! Do what you're told for once."

He dashed out of the house, grabbed his bike parked by the front door and peddled furiously down the road to the temporary Wardens' Post.

May stared after him open-mouthed. Ron had never, ever, sworn at her before. Stifling a smile, Jennie stood up.

"Can I join you in your Shelter May? Ours isn't finished yet."

"What? Yes. Yes. Of course." Suddenly May was galvanised into action "I must get Frank from upstairs."

She dashed upstairs as Jennie grabbed gas masks. And the tea tray.

The sirens were dying away as Ron arrived at the Post, the others arriving in minutes.

They were waiting for the 'phone to ring to say that bombers were nearing London. Or perhaps the first warning would be the drone of approaching aero-engines. Or the crash of bombs exploding, coming steadily closer to them. But as the minutes passed and nothing happened, tensions began to ease.

"Ron, Tom, Brian. Get out on your bikes and check your Sectors. Report back here when you've been round."

Ralph Smith leaned back in his chair feeling satisfied. His first war-time order had sounded good. Crisp, clear and decisive.

Ron cycled off in the bright sunshine, splitting his attention between the road, the houses and the sky. Barrage balloons were floating high up. Not all that many so far, but more were coming they'd been told. And more anti-aircraft guns.

Though the balloons looked pretty they had a deadly purpose. Bomber crews knew that there were steel cables tethering them to the ground somewhere, unseen and unseeable. But they could easily slice a bomber's wing off so the only safe thing to do was fly above them. Which made for less accurate bombing and easier targets for the anti-aircraft guns.

A few people were out in their front gardens staring into the sky for their first glimpse of German bombers. Most didn't have their gas masks.

Ron pulled up by one group.

"How long do you reckon you'll live if a Jerry bomber comes zipping up this road and drops a gas bomb on the corner?" he asked conversationally.

"And what's the chances of that happening Ron?" asked Fred Bentley with a grin and a wink at the others. He worked the allotment next to Ron's and had made a constant joke of Ron and the ARP.

"Fair to middling they reckon. Seeing the way the Jerries have been operating in Poland, and now that we're in the war too. They ain't used gas in Poland yet, but they've got loads of gas bombs. I've got a picture of what gas does that you can see."

He reached into his jacket and pulled out a close-up picture of a young soldier's face. Ruined sightless eyes stared out of a scarred and agonised face.

Silenced, the picture was passed round.

"That was taken in the trenches in the last war," Ron went on quietly. "It's what mustard gas does to you. It burns something terrible see, and if it does that to your eyes and face, just think what it does to your lungs. That's why the gas masks were given out in the first place." He paused. "I wouldn't like to see you in that state Fred. Or your Missus. Or Maisie." Maisie was their pretty 15 year old daughter. "That's why I always have my gas mask with me ...," " he patted it, " ... and so does my Missus. And we've got one for Frank, the baby." Ron took the photo back. "See you later."

Fred looked quickly up at the sky as Ron rode off to another group down the road to go through the same routine.

"Don't know about you lot, but having seen that, wherever we go our gas masks go too. My God! If Sall or Maisie ...!" He hurried indoors.

Half-an-hour later the All Clear sounded, with no bombers having been seen or heard. It had been a false alarm.

Chapter 6

Checks

Auntie Flo opened her front door to see a tall man wearing driver's overalls, holding two large parcels standing on the doorstep.

"Yes?" she said warily. She hadn't been expecting a parcel.

"Mrs. Abbott?"

"Yes." Even more warily.

"Tim Jackson and Tommy Francis are staying here I believe. I'm Tim's father. As I had to be in the area I thought I'd call in to see them and bring some more of their clothes."

Mrs. Abbott's face lit up with a welcoming smile.

"So you're Tim's famous Dad! Come on in. He's gone down to the beach with the others. They've taken Toby for a walk - well, he's in his wheelchair - Toby is I mean. He's my father-in-law. Wilf, my husband is with them so they're alright. But they won't be back till teatime. Can you wait till then? You will have a cup of tea, won't you?"

By this time they were in the kitchen and Flo had put on the kettle without having drawn breath once so it seemed to Ron.

"Yes please," he said quickly. "But I've ...,"

"I'm so glad you've been able to come and it's a shame he's out and there's no one here I can send out to find them, and I've no idea where they are really anyway except they were going to the beach as I've said. But if you can wait till teatime when they'll be back, you'll be very welcome to have stay and have some with us. Because ...,"

"Hold on Mrs. Abbott," Ron laughed, holding up both hands. "I was only able to come because I was suddenly told to bring an urgent order to a Camp in Dover. So I took the chance to drop in some clothes for Tim and Tommy. I was half-expecting them to be at school anyway."

"They're starting back next Monday. We had a letter yesterday. Here's your tea, help yourself to sugar. Still, if you can't stop, you can't. But ...,"

"How's Tim settled in?" Ron decided the only way to stop the stream of words was to interrupt.

"Fine, no trouble at all," Mrs. Abbott was off again without a pause. "The other lad I've got is about the same age as Tim and Tommy, they're in the same Class at school, so they knew each other already and they're all great friends now. And they've made a world of difference to Toby - they call him 'Uncle Toby' just as they call Wilf 'Uncle Wilf'. Toby had got real mopey what with pain he still gets from his wounds in the last war, and because of this one, but he's full of beans again now thanks to the boys. Do you want to see their room?"

The question, put suddenly in the midst of the stream of words, caught him by surprise.

"Yes please," he said quickly, and drained his cup.

He looked round the big attic room and stared at the camp beds with their blanket sleeping bags unhappily.

"The camp beds were only till new, proper beds arrived. They're in the shop now, but the boys begged to keep the camp beds for a couple of weeks longer, even with the new beds arrived. They say the camp beds go with their idea of this being a big tent. The same with making the blankets into sleeping bags and not using the sheets at all." She pointed at the green-painted sloping roof. "So we told the store to hold the beds for just one more week, then the boys'll have the beds made up proper."

"Tim was always on about going camping. This is a better way than most," Ron grinned, feeling a big sense of relief.

Still chattering, Flo led him downstairs again and only stopped as he turned to walk away, having managed to get in that he was pleased that Tim and Tommy were staying in such a nice place with nice people.

Twenty minutes later he walked up another drive, carrying another two big parcels.

His ring was answered almost immediately by a grey-haired, cheerful looking lady, with polish and a cloth in one hand.

Ron was taken aback for a moment, then guessed that she must be Mrs. Jones, the Daily that Kitty had written about.

"Is Miss Carruthers in please?" he asked.

"I'm afraid not," Mrs. Jones answered cautiously. "Who is it who wants to see her?"

"I'm Kitty Jackson's father. As I was in the area ...,"

"Oh please do come in Mr Jackson," Mrs. Jones said warmly, beaming at him, opening the door wide. "Kathleen and Maralyn have gone out for the day with Miss Carruther's cousin and nieces and won't be back till late. If only we'd known you were coming!"

"I didn't know myself till 8 o'clock this morning when I was told to bring an urgent delivery to a Camp near Dover," Ron explained following her into the lounge. "We had a parcel of Kitty's clothes ready to post so I took the chance to bring them. Maralyn's parents live near us so I got one from them for her." He put the two parcels on the floor.

"I'm sure Miss Carruthers would want to see you, Mr. Jackson. She can get here in half-an-hour if you can wait."

"Of course I can."

Ron was wanting to see this Miss Carruthers for himself. Kitty had written such glowing letters about her, and of being here, that he and May had been wondering how much of it was really true.

"I'll ring her then. Please sit down." She picked up the telephone. Moments later, "Miss Carruthers, Kathleen's father has just arrived. Are you ...? Yes. Yes, of course I will. Right. I'll tell him. Goodbye."

She grinned at Ron. "She said she'll be here in fifteen minutes. Goodness knows what that means for the speed limits! Would you like to see Kathleen's room first or have a cup of tea?"

"See Kathleen's room first please," Ron decided that as Mrs. Jones was using that version of her name here, then he would do so too. "How are things going with the girls?"

"Very well indeed. As Miss Carruthers chairs the Evacuation Reception Committee she felt duty-bound to take two herself. Mind you, I think she was dreading it. But they have really taken to each other, though it is only a fortnight they've been here. This is her room." Mrs. Jones pushed the half open door wide. "Kathleen and Maralyn share it, as you see." She stood back so that Ron could go in. "It was a box-room but Miss Carruthers had it done up for them."

Ron looked round the beautiful, sweet-smelling room, the beds neatly made, everything in its place.

"Do the girls look after the room themselves?"

"Of course." Mrs. Jones seemed surprised he should ask.

"Only it's far tidier than I've ever seen Kitty's - Kathleen's - room back at home," he grinned. "It's very nice, I must say. And she's said in her letters how happy she is here."

"Oh good." Mrs Jones spoke as though that was news to her, Ron thought.

He looked round the lounge while he waited for the tea Mrs. Jones was getting for him.

He couldn't help feeling uneasy because this whole house reminded him all too strongly of May's father's house. Big, luxuriously furnished by Ron's standards, even the grandfather clock in the hall looked the same.

The first few times he had called for May his reception had been friendly enough but later that had changed. He had no idea why. And when he had gone to tell her father he wanted to marry May the reception had become glacial.

The tea arrived, and Mrs. Jones excused herself to go back to the kitchen.

He poured himself a cup and to distract himself he strolled over to look at the big seascape over the fireplace. He had his back to the door when moments later Anne walked in through the half-open door.

She stopped abruptly in the doorway grabbing the door handle, suddenly dizzy.

It was impossible! It had to be. It couldn't possibly be Gregory standing there looking at the picture he'd always liked so much.

She had seen him for herself, lying in that hospital bed, his face waxen in the pallor of death, nearly 20 years ago.

A second of absolute horror as the man turned round to face her and then an overwhelming relief. For the man was a stranger. Not Gregory's ghost.

A stranger who had Gregory's build, his height and even his way of carrying himself. A very similar colour and style of hair. Even the same stance with one hand behind his back.

But the face was nothing like Gregory's.

"Miss Carruthers?"

His voice was nothing like Gregory's either.

"Yes," she managed to say.

"I'm Ron Jackson. Kitty's father."

He came towards her, hand outstretched in the usual greeting.

And his hand was nothing like Gregory's. This man's hand was strong, square, callused to some degree, a working man's hand. Gregory's hands had been slim with long fingers, a musician's hands, which he was. Had been.

"I'm pleased to meet you, Mr. Jackson. Please do sit down."

He sat down in the chair by the coffee table as Anne sat down opposite, now herself again, crossing her slim legs.

There was a moment's awkward silence.

From Ron because this pretty, sophisticated business-woman had a cool poise that epitomised everything that made him feel inferior. Her slight makeup was perfect, her light-brown hair was immaculately styled. Her house, her clothes, herself, all spoke of perfect taste, and the money to buy it.

Anne was silent too. Ron, though so like Gregory in many ways, was also the type of man she also respected. Hardworking, with a well-brought up daughter who had shown repeatedly in the way she had spoken of him how much she loved and respected him herself.

"Did Mrs. Jones tell you that Kathleen has gone out for the day? As school does not start till next week, Mr. Cutliffe set them a project on Harbours. After they had studied what books I have in the Library I asked Sonia, my cousin, if she would be able to take them to see those of Dover, Sandwich and, if possible, Ramsgate. I'm afraid they won't be back until perhaps 8 o'clock. Will you be able to wait?"

Ron shook his head. "I have to get back reasonably soon to the Depot in London." He hesitated. "Has she told you I drive a lorry for NAAFI?"

"She has. And that you have volunteered to act as an ARP Warden too. She is very proud of your doing two wartime jobs," Anne said quietly. She paused. "Kathleen seems to have settled down very well, though it is perhaps early days yet."

Her voice too was as Ron would have expected. Well-spoken, clear, an educated accent - contrasting with his own rougher London accent.

"The two letters we've had have been glowing with praise

about everything here. Did you see them before they were posted?"

He hoped in this way to check, tactfully, whether she may have influenced, or even suggested, that she write in this way. Or if Kitty had written this way because she'd expected Miss Carruthers would read them.

"No Mr. Jackson. I take the view that all letters are private, especially those between a child and her parents. So Kathleen writes and posts her own letters though I do give her the wherewithal to do so. Similarly with Maralyn. But I would hope that if she did write to you about any problems she was experiencing down here, that you would inform me so that they could be resolved at the earliest possible moment. But I would also hope that she would have sufficient confidence in either Mrs. Jones or myself, to approach us about them."

Ron began to feel a lot happier.

"You've made their room very nice," he said, just as Mrs. Jones came in with a cup of coffee for Anne and a fresh pot of tea for him. She smiled at him and left, closing the door.

"The girls do seem to like it. There was one thing that worried Kathleen initially, which was her promise to you that she would 'look after Tim and Tommy' as she put it. But having seen them at Mrs. Abbott's and receiving their assurance that they are very happy there, she now feels happy to stay here with Maralyn and me. Had she mentioned that to you?"

"She did." Ron grinned suddenly. "Tim likes sleeping in a camp bed in what he and the others think of as a big tent, she said. May and I were very relieved when we got Kathleen's letter saying how happy they both are."

"So May must be Kathleen's mother. And Ron's wife," Anne thought. Aloud she said, "Could you tell me about Kathleen? What she likes to read, her attitude to school, what her hobbies are? Things like that?"

As they talked Ron began to relax. Miss Carruthers, despite his first reaction, was really friendly, pleasant and very caring for Kitty.

And Anne found that Ron had a wry sense of humour, not unlike Gregory's and her own, but with elements all his own

They moved to first name terms as they talked of their families and, inevitably, the war. She saw him glance at Gregory's photograph.

"That is - was - Gregory my fiance." she said, picking it up and handing it to him for a closer look. "We were to be married after that war but he never came home. He was severely wounded by one of the very last shells fired by the Germans in the last hours of the fighting. He died three weeks later."

"The timing of that must have made it worse for you, Anne. Made it seem more - pointless. Right at the end like that."

"Yes." Anne nodded thoughtfully as she took the photograph back and looked at it. "Yes. That's exactly right Ron. You have put into words exactly how I felt but said it in a way that no one else has. More - pointless. Like much of war."

There was silence between them for some moments, but it was a companionable silence, almost an intimate silence between close, understanding friends.

"You know Ron, young as she is, Kathleen has the same kind of sympathetic understanding."

And she found herself telling him of how Kathleen had comforted her on the Sunday morning, something she had never intended to tell anyone, but that she now felt she could share with him. She felt the reserve she had always had about talking about personal matters, her deepest feelings, melt away in the warmth of the rapport she felt with this man.

The sudden, shrill ring of the telephone slashed into their intimate mood.

A moment's shocked silence, as they stared at each other, then Anne snatched up the telephone.

A brief conversation, then irritably, "Oh very well Mr. Blenkinsop, just keep him talking for another twenty minutes and I'll be there. Offer him a drink, a late lunch, anything but keep him there. Don't let him leave and do keep him happy. Start the negotiations yourself if necessary, you know my line on everything."

She put the receiver down and turned to face Ron, finding he was already on his feet.

"Ron. I'm most awfully sorry, but I do have to go. I'm terribly late for a meeting with someone from the Admiralty. It's so important I simply can't tell him to go away and come back another day."

"I'm sorry to have been the reason for you being late Anne, I mean Miss Carruthers. Goodbye. And thank you for giving such a good home to Kathleen. And to Maralyn."

His tone was of cool but friendly formality again, the warmth and intimacy of just a few moments ago gone. He held out his hand.

"It's still 'Anne', please Ron, not 'Miss Carruthers'." She took, and held, his hand. "After all, Kathleen calls me 'Aunt Anne'." The briefest pause. "When will you be back in Folkestone again? Or Dover? For us to be able to meet again?"

She was looking at him intently, standing close to him, still holding his hand.

She knew she was 'pushing herself' on him, which no 'respectable' lady would do, but she didn't care. This time of being with a man with whom she had felt so in tune, had been so abruptly interrupted that she was desperately wanting to make sure it could be resumed.

Just as Kathleen had so unexpectedly filled an unrealised gap in her life, so Ron now seemed to have started filling the gap that Gregory's death all those years ago had created.

Ron was very conscious of her closeness, of her being a beautiful woman who had been sharing personal matters with him. And with whom he had felt so at ease in a way he had not experienced for - well, ever before. A woman that was showing him a warmth of friendship that was in such contrast to the coolness (or coldness) he was getting at home. Had been getting for years it seemed. And he had a sudden, insane, desire to take her in his arms and kiss her.

"When ...?" he began, almost bemused at her totally unexpected question.

"When will you be back here again? For us to meet. To talk about Kathleen of course."

She smiled, making it plain that was just the excuse. A legitimising excuse.

"But Anne - this was just a special, urgent, one-off trip. Because other drivers cover this area. I cover ...,"

"Well can you change areas Ron? At least sometimes if you can't change permanently?"

She suddenly thought she was going too far, too fast, perhaps for both of them. So she crossed to her bureau. "Look Ron, here's my business card. That's the business number, This ...," she scribbled on the card " ... is my home number here. So give me a ring when – when you get the chance of another trip here. Or - or just give me a ring anyway. For a chat. Or - or to ask about Kathleen. And Ron, is there a number where I can get you? If there was an Emergency?"

Ron gave her the numbers of the NAAFI Depot and the Wardens' Post.

"But Anne, those can only be used in a real Emergency, not - not just for a chat."

"Of course," Anne replied instantly. "But my numbers are not just for an Emergency Ron. Any time you want to ring me, please do."

Ron looked from the card to Anne.

"Thanks Anne. I will."

They looked at each other for a long moment, neither wanting to make the move to end this meeting. Then both moved to the door together.

Ron arrived back at the big lorry and trailer parked in a wide road two streets away, at a run and climbed into the driver's seat, panting.

"Trouble?" asked Tony, rousing from a doze.

"No," Ron answered briefly, starting the engine.

He glanced in the mirrors and pulled away without giving the engine its usual warm-up time. They were well over two hours late leaving for their return run and the excuse of dropping off parcels of clothes for the children would cover only so much of that.

"So this foster-mother was a bit of alright then?" Tony asked with a sideways look.

"She's - both of them are good foster-mothers for the kids," Ron snapped.

"Oh sure!" grinned Tony. "But I noticed you spent a hell of a lot longer with this second one than the first one, didn't you?"

"That's because the second one was out and I had to wait for her. And then she asked a hell of a lot of questions about Kitty that the other one didn't ask about Tim."

"Oh sure," Tony said again. But he kept on probing. He was

determined to find out if there was anything he could gossip about. He wasn't malicious in his gossiping, looking on it as entertainment to while away the long hours of sitting beside drivers, doing nothing. He had caused real trouble twice before but that still hadn't stopped him.

Finally Ron lost his temper.

"For crying out loud, Tony! Can't you shut up about the ruddy woman? Can't you go to sleep or something and give me a bit of peace?"

Tony just grinned and closed his eyes.

Which gave Ron a chance to think about Anne. To wonder what her reaction would have been if he had kissed her. She had given him enough 'come ons' at the end hadn't she? Like holding his hand for ages. Giving him her 'phone numbers. Urging him to 'phone her 'for a chat'. To talk about Kitty - Kathleen - had just been the way of providing him with an excuse - the way she had looked at him when she said it, made that perfectly clear. Even suggesting he change areas to be able to see her. All of which added up to ...,

Unless she was like that with every Tom, Dick and Harry! He felt a chill and an instant revulsion at the thought. Surely she wasn't like that?

But how could he know? How could anyone really know another person? It wasn't as though he'd carried on with a lot of women to really be able to tell. In fact he'd never 'carried on' with anyone else at all He glanced at Tony. He'd be able to tell, if his stories about his 'other women' had any truth in them at all. But he certainly couldn't ask him - if he did the story would be round the whole Depot in less than five minutes of them getting back!

He had another thought that brought with it a great surge of relief. Anne couldn't be like that because if she was she'd never have taken two ten year old girls in to live with her for the Duration of the war, would she? Girls who were old enough to work things out if there were a stream of men visitors but still young enough to be indiscreet, to talk to other girls, or even a teacher. And with Anne having the kind of positions she had in town according to Kitty, she couldn't dare risk that kind of scandal. Even if she was that way inclined. Which she wasn't. Ron now thought he could be certain about that.

So he began thinking of asking for a change of area. After all he had the perfect reason for that with Kitty and Tim down there. Then he would have the perfect excuse to see Anne again. She had suggested that herself hadn't she?

And then his deep seated lack of self-confidence swept back over him. What the hell was he thinking of? She was a go-getting business-woman having negotiations with the Admiralty for God's sake! Owning four shops and had been planning more, Kitty had written! And what was he? Nothing but a lorry driver for NAAFI.

He'd obviously got it all wrong! All it was, was that she was being kind and considerate. Nothing more. And he'd started thinking ...! Thank God he hadn't ...!

"What you could do Ron, is see if you could swap areas permanent like with Joe or one of the others. You could say it was so you could see your kids. But then you'd be able to see that gorgeous Miss Carruthers regular wouldn't you?" Tony sat up grinning at him. "I wouldn't tell a soul the real reason why, Ron. Honest."

"Don't talk daft. Can you see Joe or anyone else want to change Kent for East Anglia, even if I wanted to? Which I don't."

Ron knew that that idea was now dead. Because whatever he said, if he did try to change area, Tony would tell everyone he had done it so he could see Anne. And as Tony was his regular Loader, presumably he'd change area with him. If fact Tony would make sure he did. And that would mean he would know every time he stopped off to see Anne. And then gossip back at the Depot.

So what was the use? Anyway, as he'd just been thinking, what the hell would a woman like Anne possibly see in him? A lorry driver! He sneered at himself. A pretty woman smiles at him and he goes all ga-ga! All that Anne had done was to show what a nice person she was. Just being as Kitty had described her, in fact. But when he thought about the way she had been .... So maybe, just maybe .... What he could do was ring her, say he was ringing to see how Kitty was - and see how she reacted. If he was going to do that though he'd really need to ring her at the shop ....

As soon as he walked indoors May put the kettle on and checked the state of his dinner in the oven.

"Ready in five minutes Ron," she called softly, not to disturb Frank. As he joined her in the kitchen "How were they? Do they really like it where they are?"

"I wasn't able to see either of the children - they were both out for the day till late - but I saw the foster-mothers. Tim's room is as Kitty described it. They were going to have proper beds last week but because the boys clamoured she's let them keep the camp beds for one more week. They're getting the proper beds delivered next week."

They went into the front room with Ron's dinner.

"And what's Mrs. Abbott like?" May asked as they sat down at the table.

"Very nice. Talks non-stop just about, but it's obvious she really cares for Tim and Tommy and the other lad. She's small, motherly and says that Tim's settled in fine. Just as Kitty said. He's starting school next week. So is Kitty but they'll be going to different schools as they're living in different parts of the town."

"Well that sounds pretty good. What about this Anne Carruthers? It seems funny to me that a young, single woman wants to look after two young girls."

"She's not young really. Probably around forty or so. (He deliberately over-stated his estimate of her age) She was out at one of her shops so Mrs. Jones, who's a motherly old dear, 'phoned her and she came straight away. I had a look at Kitty's room while I was waiting and it is as nice as she described it."

"So what's this Anne Carruthers like?"

"Pleasant. Spoke warmly of Kitty and Maralyn. She wanted to know what Kitty likes to read, attitude to school, things like that. She decided she ought to foster a couple of girls because she Chairs the Evacuation Reception Committee and I suppose she felt she ought to set an example as she's got a pretty big house."

"Then why didn't she take Tim as well?" May cut in. "Why did she decide to separate them?"

"She didn't. Not like that. She just wanted two, ten or eleven year old girls who could be reasonably independent and at the same time, companions for each other. And they'd have to share a room because there's only two bedrooms. What could have been the third bedroom is a Library. She couldn't put Tim in with Kitty because they're both growing up all the time and we've got no idea how long they're going to be there. In any case, while it's fine for Kitty, being a girl, it would be much too prim and proper for a boy like Tim. I'm sure he's far better where he is."

Ron felt on delicate ground here. When he had walked in, still with the memory of Anne's house in his mind, his own had seemed shabby, cluttered, untidy.

"One thing ...," he went on, " ... Anne Carruthers seemed quite shocked when I asked if she saw Kitty's letters before they're posted. She said that she regards them as private between her and us."

"Is she pretty?" May asked abruptly.

He had been thinking, at that very moment, just how pretty Anne had looked, sitting across from him as they had talked. So much more attractive in every way than .....

"Well - I suppose so. If you like those kind of looks."

"What kind?"

"Well - she's thin, nearly skinny you could say. Nice hair I suppose. Mousey coloured. Well dressed - but then she's got the money. Talks as if she expects to always get her way in everything. Bossy." He shrugged. "That's about it."

He felt contemptuous of himself for being so disparaging of a woman who was so nice, so attractive, so - so gorgeous.

But he was all too aware of how suspicious May could be, even though there was nothing for May to be suspicious about. Was there?

May knew she was liable to be unreasonably suspicious of Ron, but Peter Simpson had left an indelible scar when, even though they were Engaged, she found out he had been having a full-blown affair with his secretary all the time. And then she had married Ron 'on the rebound'.

And there had been that Josie in the flats four years ago now, before they moved here, that she had thought he had seemed to be getting a bit too friendly with. So she had made it very clear to him exactly what she would do if anything did 'happen'. And in spite of Ron's 'overnights' away, she was pretty confident nothing had.

Because at a NAAFI Christmas Social a couple of years ago she had made a point of talking to Tony's wife. As he was Ron's Loader he was always with him on those trips. Tony, his wife had said, always told her the gossip about the drivers, but Ron's name had never come up with gossip of 'another woman'. If it did, she had promised she would let May know.

But had there been - a certain something in Ron's voice when he'd talked about that Carruthers woman?

"When will you be able to go to Folkestone again?"

"Shouldn't think I will be. Today was a one-off. A sudden, urgent delivery and no other drivers that could be switched. You know I do East Anglia."

"Couldn't you ask for a transfer to the South East? Then you'd be able to see the children regularly."

The excuse was being given to him again, this time by May herself. The ready-made excuse to see more of Anne.

The trouble was, Tony had already suggested it. And if he did try to swap, even saying it was May's idea, Tony would be sure his idea about him and Anne was right after all, and spread the story. Whatever did or did not happen with Anne.

Ron pretended to think about it and then shook his head.

"It's just not on, May. With the number of kids Evacuated down there, there'll be any number of drivers wanting to do the same. And the drivers already doing it wouldn't want to swap for exactly the same reason. And even if someone was willing to swap, Malcolm will play safe and not pick anyone, because that would look as though he was playing favourites and that would only cause trouble among the rest. Anyway, now that it looks as though the Government's going to give cheap tickets for parents to go, you'll be able to go soon to see them yourself."

Relieved May took a sip of her tea. Her suspicions had to be groundless otherwise he'd have jumped at her suggestion of changing area instead of turning it down flat.

Ron thought about Anne's card. He wouldn't tell May about it. And he'd decide later whether to use it.

After the girls had gone to bed, Anne tried to work out her feelings about Ron, while listening to a Beethoven concert on the wireless. When he rang her, if he did, what should she say to him? What did she really want?

He was really nice. While his similarity to Gregory had been a shock at first, it was also an attraction. But though similar in some ways, he was also very different. He was intelligent, even if not particularly well educated by her standards. In some ways he seemed a very determined person but at the same time there was a lack of self-confidence that held him back. She was certain he had been about to kiss her, but at the last minute, almost the last second, had pulled back.

And she wondered how she would have responded if he had.

He was so different from Anton, her first boyfriend after Gregory. Rich, mad as a hatter (which his friends and hangers-on called 'delightfully eccentric') he had vowed his 'undying love' for her within ten minutes of their first meeting! The 'undying love' had lasted for only three months, but for her, it had been a time of frenetic fun.

And then Jonathan, who had been different again, being quiet and unassuming. But he had gone to South Africa to try and make better success than he was in England during the first Depression years. He had eventually stopped writing and her last letter had been returned marked, 'Gone away. Address unknown'.

And now, out of the blue - here was Ron.

She pulled a face, half-amused at herself. She had talked with him for less than an hour and a half and she was comparing him with Anton and Jonathan, and even with Gregory! Especially Gregory. More to the point, he was a married man and the father of one of the girls she was fostering.

But - she had found an instant rapport with him that she had previously only found with Gregory.

But the days and weeks passed. Early December arrived, and still he did not 'phone.

Chapter 7
Christmas at war

The postman arrived just as the girls were setting off for school and Anne for work, warmly wrapped up now that November was here.

"So who wants the letters this morning?" he asked holding them out, first to Kitty, then Maralyn, while Anne was locking up the house.

"It's my turn," claimed Maralyn, grabbing for them.

She sorted through the thin wad swiftly, giving one to Kitty, keeping one for herself and going back to give the rest to Anne. She put them in her bag to read them later and went to the garage to get the car.

While waiting the girls eagerly ripped open their envelopes. It was always nice to get letters from home and sometimes they contained Postal Orders.

"Aunt Anne! Aunt Anne!" Kitty shouted dashing over to her. "There's a letter in mine for you."

Anne immediately opened it, and swiftly read the letter. This had never happened before and it could be something bad had happened in London. What if Ron ...?

Kitty hovered by her, unsure whether to leave or stay. But what if it was about something terrible?

"There's nothing to worry about Kathleen," Anne said quickly. "It just says that your mother feels you should stay down here for the Christmas holiday and that she hopes to come down to see you for a few days after Christmas Day. She is asking for me to find somewhere for her and your baby brother to stay."

They had already begun talking at school whether they would be going home for Christmas or staying in Folkestone. Some who had already been told they would be going home for Christmas were wondering whether they would be coming back. Three had already gone home because with hardly any bombing there, was it worth staying away? So now Kitty knew what was going to happen to her and Tim. And she found she had mixed feelings about it.

"I haven't given Christmas a thought, Kathleen!" Anne said.

She called Maralyn over. "The letter was from Kathleen's mother saying Kathleen should stay here for Christmas. I think that you should write to your mother tonight to see what is intended for you. Now we must hurry or we'll all be late."

In her office Anne went quickly through her business mail, then sat back to re-read May's letter.

'Dear Miss Carruthers,

My husband and I think that it would be inadvisable for Kitty and Tim to come home for Christmas this year. Though there has been little bombing so far, it is expected at any time as you know. We hope that Kitty staying with you over Christmas will not cause you any problems. We shall, of course, be sending her and Tim Christmas parcels.

I would like to come down to see the children for a few days after Christmas, say from the 27th December. There will be just me and my five month old baby.

Could you find me somewhere to stay for that time please? I thought you would be the best person to ask as you were in charge of the housing for the Evacuees, Kitty tells me.

If you have a telephone number could you send it to me please? Then I could ring you from a call box to discuss the arrangements. If you tell me the best time to ring, I will do so as close to that time as possible.

Very many thanks for providing Kitty with such a lovely home.

Yours faithfully,

May Jackson (Mrs.)

PS I have also written to Mrs. Abbott to say I hope to be staying near by.'

So Ron would not be coming. And he had obviously not given May the card she had given him. So either he had thrown it away, lost it - or kept it private, personal to himself. In which case why hadn't he rung her?

Where to find lodgings for May and Frank would be no problem. Fewer children had come than had been expected and prepared for, and some Evacuees had since returned home, so she had plenty of spare addresses to call on.

That afternoon she and Mr. Blenkinsop were going through the monthly Accounts when the 'phone rang. Automatically she picked it up,

"Carruthers Chandlers."

"Is Miss Carruthers there please? It's Ron Jackson here. She gave ...,"

"Ron!" Anne nearly screamed excitedly. "It's me. Hold on for one second, just one second. Don't ring off whatever you do." She shot a look at Mr. Blenkinsop but he was already moving towards the door.

"There is some stock-taking I need to do ...," he murmured as he left the room.

"Ron. I'm alone now. It's been so long! I've wondered if you'd lost my card, or thrown it away or - or ..., But never mind that now. You're through and talking to me at last. How are you? What have you been doing? When will you be coming down here again?"

Anne knew she was chattering like an over-excited schoolgirl, but she didn't care. She simply didn't care! Ron was 'phoning her at long last!

At the other end of the line Ron caught his breath. Then Anne really did ...!

"Anne ...," he said almost unbelievingly, " ... were you really hoping that much that I'd ring?"

Anne laughed, happy now.

"Of course I was Ron! I've been hoping and longing, every day and all day! And I daren't ring you because you'd said that those numbers you gave me were for Emergencies only. And Kathleen hasn't even caught a cold or scratched a knee for me to pretend it was an Emergency. So I just had to wait for you."

"Anne, I really did want to ring you but - well I just didn't think you'd really want to speak to me that much. I thought you were just being the kind, lovely person you are, saying that I could ring about Kathleen if anything came up. But she and May are writing every week with all the news so nothing ever did.

"I nearly rang several times, pretending it was about Kathleen, but - well I suppose I wanted to still be able to hope ...," He stopped, not knowing how to put into words that would sound reasonably sensible, what he had wanted so much.

"You do know now, don't you Ron, that it was really and truly you I was wanting to talk to?" Anne said softly "I've – I've wanted it ever since we met."

She knew she would never have been as open as this if they had been face to face. But on the telephone ....

"Yes Anne, I do now. And I'm glad, more glad than I can say. How are you Anne? Are you really okay?"

"I'm fine now. How soon can you come down to Folkestone again? Or are you 'phoning to say you're on your way?"

"I wish I was. I don't know when I'll be able to come Anne. It depends on my boss sending me on a special run to Folkestone or somewhere near with a load. And those almost never happen because other drivers cover the area, not me.

"Why I rang now, and I'm really glad I did Anne, is that May is writing to you to ask about coming to see the children over the Christmas holiday. And she's going to ask for your 'phone number. I hadn't told her you'd given it to me months ago because - well I hadn't."

"I've already had the letter Ron. It came this morning in one to Kathleen. I guessed you hadn't told her so I was just going to give it to her, without mentioning the card I'd given you. But she talks of only her and Frank coming. Aren't you able to come?"

"No dammit. I've been organising a big Exercise for the ARP Wardens at my Post now for over a month. And we fixed the dates for just after Christmas because that's the easiest time for us spare-time people to get time off. At the time I started this May hadn't said anything about going to Folkestone, but it does make sense to visit during the school holidays."

"Could I make some excuse to say those dates are not convenient and fix some when you could come? At least we'd see each other then."

He hesitated, tempted.

"I don't think that would be fair to Kathleen and Tim, Anne. Because May must have already told them the dates in their letters."

"I suppose you're right, Ron," she agreed reluctantly. "Ron - what did you tell May about - here?"

"I said how nice Kathleen's room is ...." He paused.

"Did she ask about me?"

"She did."

"And?"

"I nearly told her not only how kind and sympathetic you are but that you are gorgeous. That your hair is a lovely light-brown colour that's beautifully styled, that your eyes are a deep blue like an ocean, that your skin is flawless, that you have a most beautiful smile that lights up your face, that your figure is - but we'd better not go into that on the 'phone."

"Oh do. Do let's go into that on the 'phone," she murmured.

"Anyway, I didn't think it would be sensible to tell her exactly what I was thinking - that I think - that I KNOW - that you are the most gorgeous woman I have ever met."

Anne smothered a delighted laugh.

"I should hope not Ron! If you had, she'd have been down here like a shot to tear my hair out! Her husband talking to her about another woman like that!"

"But why? If she, or you, said you'd met the most gorgeous man, it wouldn't bother me." He paused. "Well, not really". He paused again, wondering if he would be as indifferent as that if it was Anne that said it to him. "Well – maybe I don't know now," he admitted.

"Is there any chance we could meet Ron? If not here then somewhere else?"

"I wish we could Anne. The trouble is, I'm never alone. With the size of wagon I drive, I always have a Loader with me. He's called 'Tony' and he's the world's worst gossip. If we did meet up for a meal somewhere, by the time he'd finished telling it around the Depot, we'd have been away for a lost weekend together."

"If only!" she murmured, but loud enough for Ron to hear.

"But I'll tell Malcolm, he's the Depot Foreman, my boss, that if any more jobs come up in Kent, then I'm a permanent volunteer for them. And then hope that the load'll be small enough for me not to need a Loader."

"Please do that Ron. But – you will 'phone me before then, won't you?"

"Every week?" suggested Ron, hoping.

"Oh yes. I'm always at this number on Mondays and Wednesdays, and some other times too, but always Mondays. And we can talk more privately here than at home in the evening because ...," She stopped.

"How is Kathleen?" he asked, understanding.

"She's fine. Doing well at school. She's ...,"

"Caller, your time is almost up. If you wish to continue you must put more money in the slot," interrupted the telephonist.

"I'll ring next Monday Anne. About 11 o'clock if that's alright?"

"That's perfect Ron. So goodbye till then."

"'Bye Anne. Take care."

Anne slowly replaced the receiver, feeling a bewildering sense of delight and frustration. Delight that Ron had 'phoned her at last, and frustration over all the things she had wished now she had said, but hadn't had time for. And because it looked as though they would not be actually able to meet for a long time.

But at least Ron was going to 'phone her next Monday.

When Anne arrived home nearly a week later she found the girls had the tea-tray ready for her and her slippers warming by the fire as usual. They had begun doing this when she had arrived home exhausted one evening a month ago and had sat down for a rest before cooking dinner. They had gone into the kitchen to re-appear ten minutes later with the pot of tea for her. It became their regular custom, the tea appearing within a couple of minutes of her coming through the front door. She then realised that they must listen for the sound of her car's tyres crunching up the drive. As the nights had drawn in and the weather got colder they had grown to revel in the cosiness which had drawn them still closer together as they would tell each other about their day.

"Aunt Anne, in my letter that came this morning, my Mum said that if the bombing hadn't started before Christmas then I'd be going home for the whole holiday."

Maralyn's tone was not of complete happiness. They had been talking during the day of what Kathleen and Aunt Anne might be doing during Christmas.

"In that case what I think we could do would be for your mother to stay here with us Kathleen, and use Maralyn's bed.

And I'll borrow a cot that I'm sure we could squeeze in. If that's alright with you, Maralyn."

Maralyn knew that this was one of those things that grown-ups sometimes ask, all the time expecting you to agree without argument. Even Aunt Anne did that sometimes - as now. Not that she did mind of course, because she thought it was the sensible thing to do anyway.

As soon as May received Anne's letter, she telephoned to accept the offer. It would be the best possible way to check out Anne Carruthers. And she could check out the Abbotts by visiting them and seeing how Tim was with them.

On the last Friday evening just before the ending of term, the girls had barely sat down in the lounge than Anne picked up her briefcase that was resting, unusually, against her chair.

"Girls, we have something serious to discuss."

They looked at her quickly because her tone was as serious as her words. But then they saw she had a quirk of a smile at the corners of her mouth, so they knew that whatever else it was, it was not trouble.

"You have been here three months now. You have always kept your room tidy, though I would have expected that. But, in addition on your very first day here you volunteered to help in the kitchen, and you still do so. You always do the washing up and make a very good job of it too. You meet me every evening with a nice cup of tea and my slippers warmed now that it has got colder. So now I think it is time for Payday."

"Payday?" the girls echoed.

"Payday," Anne repeated with a smile. "Here you are."

And from her briefcase she took out two real wages envelopes and gave one to each.

"Thank you, Aunt Anne," they exclaimed together, opening them.

They each took out four brand new ten shilling notes

A boy at school had told them that foster-mothers were given ten shillings and sixpence for each evacuee each week for everything. And they had just been given a whole £2 each!

And that was on top of the half-crown Aunt Anne gave them every week as pocket money.

"Thank you Aunt Anne," Kitty said quietly, but with strong feeling.

As they had decided that she would spend Christmas Day with Aunt Anne at Aunt Sonia's that meant, she felt, she needed to get four extra presents. For Aunt Sonia, Uncle Arthur and Sarah and Janice. This solved the money problem for doing that.

"Now then girls. Where would you like to do your Christmas shopping tomorrow? If you want to do any that is. We could do it in Folkestone, or we could go to Dover, which has more shops."

They knew Folkestone but Dover was still largely unknown. So it would be more exciting to do their Christmas shopping there.

The evening before she was going home, Maralyn was both excited and sad. Travel arrangements were going to be easy because she would be travelling with a lot of other children going home for Christmas.

After dinner they gathered round the fire with a small lit up Christmas tree in the corner.

"Aunt Anne, as Maralyn won't be here Christmas Day, we'd like to give you your present from us now," announced Kitty

From behind her back Maralyn whipped a packet wrapped in Christmas paper.

"Happy Christmas, Aunt Anne," they chorused.

"Thank you very much girls, that is really nice of you. May I open it now?"

"Of course you can. That's why we gave it to you now," declared Maralyn.

Inside the wrapping was a blue presentation box. Anne carefully took off its lid, and found a delicately painted bone china lady wearing a sweeping ball gown.

"She's lovely girls!" Anne exclaimed, lifting her out.

"Do you like her? Really like her?" Maralyn burst out. "We chose her between us because she looked so beautiful and Kathleen said that if you dressed in a gown like that, you'd look just like her."

"Thank you for that compliment girls. And for this lovely present. Now - can you help me decide where to put her? I want her in a place where everyone who comes into the room will see her straight away."

They tried various places from the table to the mantelpiece and then settled for the writing bureau by Gregory's photograph.

The three of them stood for several moments looking at the ornament and the photograph, Kitty on one side of Anne, Maralyn on her other. Anne slipped an arm round each of them.

"She is going to be very special to me for two reasons. First of all because you gave her to me, and second because Gregory took me to a ball once when I was dressed in a gown very like that one. So it is exactly right to put her by him." She bent down to kiss them both on the forehead. "Would you like your presents as you have given me mine?"

"Yes please!" They had no doubt about that.

Anne took from the bureau two slim packages each with a name tag.

"This is yours Maralyn, and this is yours Kathleen."

Anne went to her seat by the fire and watched them open their packages as carefully as she had opened hers.

Inside the Christmas wrapping Maralyn had a green box, Kitty a pink. They opened the boxes.

"A watch!" they exclaimed together.

Slightly different from each other, they both glinted gold in the light. The faces were small and elegant, but the numerals were clear, and on their backs they saw their names and 'Christmas 1939' engraved.

Sitting between them, Anne showed them how to set the time and how their luminous dials worked.

"Thank you Aunt Anne. It's the most wonderful Christmas present I've ever had."

And spontaneously Kitty reached up and kissed Anne on the cheek. After all, Aunt Anne had kissed them for her present.

Maralyn did the same.

As the girls put on their watches and admired them, Anne looked at them with an affectionate smile on her lips. Yet again she marvelled at all the ways they had enriched her own life and how thankful she was that she had taken them in.

And it was through Kathleen that she had met Ron. Wherever that might lead. If anywhere.

"What would you like to do when we have seen Maralyn off tomorrow, Kathleen? You could come back here, Mrs. Jones will be here of course. Or I could take you to Aunt Sonia's. Or I could take you to spend the day with Timothy. Or you could come with me to Deal. I've got some things to do there for a few hours so you'll need to take something to amuse yourself there - unless Mr. Jordan the Manager can find you something to do in the shop."

Kitty decided at once that she would go with Aunt Anne and hope she could help in the shop.

Over the past few months she and Tim had been seeing less and less of each other as they had become more absorbed in their own foster-homes and lives. And as they were at different schools they didn't meet there either. So their previous close relationship had weakened swiftly.

Later that night, as they lay in bed, both girls were awake and thoughtful.

"Kathleen, are you awake?" Maralyn whispered softly.

"Yes."

"You know, I almost wish I wasn't going home for Christmas, but staying here with Aunt Anne and you. Do you wish you were going home?"

"Not really. Because ...," She stopped. To have said more, she felt, would be disloyal to Mum and Dad.

"I do hope Mum and Dad let me come back. Not because of the bombing but to be with Aunt Anne and you again." Maralyn's whispering became animated as she turned on her side to face Kitty. "We haven't got anything like the books at home that Aunt Anne has got here. All those books on science. And that Children's Encyclopaedia that she found for us! And the maps and atlases. And the way she explains things to us. Like the luminous bits on our watches f'r'instance. She's made me want to be a scientist when I grow up. To find out all sorts of new things."

"What about? What'll you be a scientist about?"

"Don't know yet. But something." Maralyn turned onto her back, her hands behind her head, staring up at the ceiling in the total darkness of the blacked out windows. "I began thinking about it after she talked to us about doing our part in helping to re-build the world after the war. You know, after that broadcast by the Prime Minister about the war. Have you thought about what you'll do?"

"I'm going to go into business like Aunt Anne," Kitty replied promptly. "I'm not so sure it'll be ship's shops though - but something in business. Maybe in fashion. Clothes. Not ordinary clothes but things like that ball gown that little statue had that we got Aunt Anne and that she wore at the ball with Gregory. Yes, I think that's what I'll do."

Silence fell, each dreaming their dreams until sleep crept up on them.

At this first Christmas of the war the shops were still full of toys and goodies. The blackout meant that the traditional bright lights were not there and the measure of worry of what 1940 would bring gave an edge of desperation to the gaiety of the shops and shoppers.

But Kitty and Tim still had a Christmas filled with fun and laughter, and adding to it was the knowledge that two days afterwards they would be seeing Mum again.

Anne, Kitty and Tim were waiting at the railway station when May's train steamed in. The children hurled themselves at her, hugging and kissing her while she hugged them back.

Over their heads May caught Anne's eye - and saw that she was jealous of the spontaneous affection they were showing to her. She knew it had to be Kitty Anne was jealous over, not Tim. So her hug became one of possessiveness.

At the same moment Anne realised that she WAS jealous. Intensely jealous. Kathleen had never acted towards her like that. With such an outpouring of impulsive affection.

She swiftly reminded herself that she had no right to be jealous. It was May who was Kathleen's mother, not herself. And May was Ron's wife. And that thought produced a still stronger surge of jealousy.

She went forward, holding out her hand, a welcoming smile stitched on her face.

"Hello May. It's lovely to see you at last. Kathleen has ...,"

"Her name is Kitty," May interrupted.

"Kitty," agreed Anne. "But only as long as YOU'RE here," she added mentally. "The car's outside," she said aloud.

"Kitty, Frank's pram is in the Guard's van. See up there, he's just putting it out. Run along and get it will you?"

When Kitty arrived back with it, Anne picked up May's suitcase, May carried Frank while Kitty wheeled the pram and Tim clung to May's other hand.

Anne looked in consternation from the pram to the car boot.

"I'll never get that in there! Never mind, you sit in the car while I ask the Station Master to send it up in the Station van."

She let them into the car then wheeled the pram back into the Station.

"How do you get on with her, Kitty?" May asked swiftly, as soon as Anne was out of earshot.

"She's been lovely to us, Mum. Just like I've said in my letters."

"I wasn't sure how far you had to write like that because of her reading them before they were posted."

"But she never has read any of my letters to you," Kitty protested. "Or yours to me. When we first got here she gave Maralyn and me a writing pad with envelopes and stamps for us to write to you - well me to you and Dad and Maralyn to her Mum and Dad. We can write whenever we want to but she always reminds us every Friday night, just in case we've forgotten."

Kitty was feeling uncomfortable. It was seeming to her that for some reason she couldn't understand, that Mum didn't seem to like Aunt Anne very much. And she really wanted the two most important grown-up women in her life to like each other because she loved them both.

"So you're happy enough to be here then?" May persisted.

"Yes," Kitty said simply.

May was not sure she liked the quiet emphasis in Kitty's tone. Nor the way Kitty was picking up Anne's way of speaking either.

But she had to be glad, she thought guiltily. On the whole.

"Has she asked much about me? Or Dad?" she asked, after a pause.

"A bit. 'Specially at the beginning. What we liked doing as a family, you looking after Frank, Dad being a driver for NAAFI, and an ARP Warden. She asked Maralyn the same things too. Except her Dad isn't a Warden and he works on the railways."

"Auntie Flo and Uncle Wilf asked me those things like that," put in Tim. "They're t'r'ific they are Mum. They're really looking forward to meeting you, they said. And they've got a Christmas present for you too. I know what it is but I mustn't tell you or it'll spoil the surprise."

"Did Anne give you anything for Christmas Kitty?" May asked.

"This watch." Kitty moved up her sleeve to show her.

"She gave you that valuable watch at your age?" irritation rasped May's voice. To her the gift of a watch was a significant 'growing up' thing.

"Yes." Kitty looked at her quickly wondering why Mum seemed so cross about it. "She gave one almost exactly the same to Maralyn too." She glanced out of the window. With almost a feeling of relief, "She coming back now. And she hasn't got the pram."

Anne whipped open her door.

"That's all settled. They'll be bringing it up in a couple of hours. Let's get home and into the warm, shall we?"

A few minutes later, "That's a very nice watch you gave Kitty for Christmas, Anne."

Anne shrugged, noticing the barely concealed disapproval in May's voice. "I felt that Kath ..., Kitty, was old enough and sensible enough to be trusted with one. And that she deserved it. I felt the same about Maralyn too." She paused. "I hope you don't disapprove. I didn't think to check with you."

"I think you were - very generous."

Anne said nothing, but she was furious. And it was now, seeing Kathleen (as she thought of her still) with her mother, that she realised just how much she had come to love her. When the Child Welfare Worker had talked at one of the meetings Anne had arranged for the foster-mothers, about the emotional ties they could form with the children and that they had to guard against them otherwise all kinds of problems could arise with their natural parents, Anne had been inclined to dismiss it as over-stating things.

But that was exactly what had happened to her with Kathleen.

And there was Ron. One visit, a couple of 'phone calls and she was feeling about him in much the same way as in her early days with Gregory. And though she told herself - repeatedly - that she was being silly (after all she was no longer a seventeen year old girl) it made no difference to the way she was feeling about him.

And May? So far she wasn't too different from the mental picture she had built up from what Kathleen had said from time to time over the months. But she would reserve judgement herself until after the three days that May was planning to stay.

As Kathleen was showing very clearly how much she loved May, she would have to be very careful not to say or imply anything against her after she had gone. Not least because that could turn Kathleen against her, not her mother. Not that she wanted to do that anyway, she told herself quickly.

And underlying everything in her thoughts was the chilling knowledge that May could take Kathleen away from her in an instant, and there was not a thing she would be able to do about it.

"You've got some more presents children," May was saying brightly. "They're in the case. And Dad sends his love."

Before Anne could take the opening to ask, very casually of course, how Ron was, Tim cut in, "And Kitty and me have got some presents for you and Dad under the Christmas tree at Auntie Anne's. And she gave me a model 'plane. It's a Hurricane and it really flies!"

Once in the warm house and taking off their coats Anne asked Kitty to take them into the lounge while she made some tea.

May looked round the hall and then the lounge before sinking into the big, comfortable settee with a sigh of relief. She unwrapped Frank and sat him up in her arms.

"This is lovely," she said appreciatively. "I used to live in a house like this before I married your father, children."

Kitty said nothing. She knew they weren't rich like Aunt Anne even though Dad worked so hard.

"Were you able to get Anne a Christmas present, Kitty?"

"Yes. Maralyn and I clubbed together to get her this." She went to get the figurine to show to May. "Aunt Anne decided she wanted it by that picture of the soldier. He's Gregory. They were going to get married but he was killed in the last war. He took her to a ball in a gown like that one so she really likes it."

She took it back quickly from May as Tim came over to look.

"Don't you touch it Tim. It'd be awful if you broke it." She let him see it, then took it back to the bureau.

"That must have cost you a lot of money, Kitty. Or did Maralyn put in most?"

"Well - no. We put in the same. But Aunt Anne had given us some money and ...,"

"So you felt you had to spend it all on her," interrupted May in a flat tone.

"No Mum." Kitty was feeling uncomfortable again. "You see ..., Oh here she is with the tea."

Relieved, she jumped up to put out the coffee tables as Anne brought in the tray.

"There's some cakes in the kitchen, Kitty. Would you get them please?" asked Anne as she put the tray on the table.

When she came back with the cake stand, May and Anne were talking about Frank and his attainments.

She handed round small plates from the tray and then the cake stand, Tim being delighted at having cakes like this rather than an occasional one at teatime for a special treat.

By the time they had finished Frank was getting restless.

"I'd better change him," said May. "Kitty, could you show us our room?"

Tim trotted upstairs with them not wanting to be away from May a moment longer than necessary.

May looked round the bedroom as she lay Frank down on a bed.

"This really is a lovely room," she said, impressed.

"Aunt Anne had it 'specially decorated like this for Maralyn and me, Mrs. Jones said. Well - not for us exactly but for whoever she was going to have to stay. My bed is the one by the window. And she borrowed the cot for Frank."

As they were going down the corridor Kitty showed them the toilet and bathroom, then opened another door.

"This is what we call 'The Study' or 'The Library', and we do our homework here. We have a fire on when we're using it but it's cold now because of the holiday. See all the books, Tim? And the pictures of other countries? Aunt Anne has been to all sorts of places across the seas, and when we do our homework, we can use any of the books we want to look up things. That's why we've been getting good marks at school Mum. Maralyn wants to be a scientist now when she grows up."

Tim was mightily impressed by 'The Study' or 'The Library' never having seen anything like this in someone's house before though he had been to the Public Library at home. And this had made Maralyn want to be a scientist, had it? He wasn't exactly sure what a scientist was, but it sounded very important.

"Have you any ideas about what you want to do Kitty? Be another scientist perhaps?" May was more amused than serious.

"No Mum," Kitty was serious. "I don't think I've got the sort of brains like Maralyn to be a scientist, so I don't think I'd be much good as one. I want to be in business like Aunt Anne. Not in ships shops though. But a business of some kind." She decided she wouldn't say anything about wanting to be a fashion designer just yet, not even to Mum. "But I am going to collect books like this. And when I have a house of my own I'll have a Study just like this."

May set her lips, irritated. Kitty was bright, her school reports showed that. But to be in business for herself? Anne was filling Kitty's head with unachievable nonsense - with ideas right out of her range. Anne would have to realise that and stop building up Kitty's ambitions so much to avoid massive disappointment in the future. Kitty being a business-woman indeed!

Later after Tim had been taken back to the Abbott's, while Frank was being fed and put down to sleep, Kitty laid the table in the Dining Room. Normally they ate in the big kitchen but this was a special occasion. Anne had told her to put wine coasters by the table mats.

"Is wine a nice drink, Aunt Anne?" she asked, eyeing the bottle standing in an ice bucket in the kitchen.

"This one is. But wine is not for small girls, even when they're becoming bigger girls. Unless your mother says you can try it."

"Is there anything I can do to help?" May asked coming into the kitchen, hearing voices.

"Not really. I should be able to dish up in a few minutes. Would you like a sherry while we're waiting?"

May hesitated barely a second. This house, Anne's style, took her back through the years to her own background.

"Yes please."

"Can I try some sherry too?" Kitty had no idea what sherry was or what it was like.

Anne smiled at May. "Kitty was already hinting about trying wine with dinner as I am putting it out for us. I've never given the girls any alcoholic drink, nor drunk it in front of them but as you are here you should make the decision I feel."

"You can try just a little wine at dinner, but raspberry for now."

Kitty sighed but not too loudly. It had been worth trying and wine would be a new thing anyway. Anne poured the drinks, solemnly putting Kitty's raspberry into a sherry glass.

"How is - erm - Ron, isn't it?" Anne felt she could ask after this length of time out of ordinary politeness.

"Fine. He's being kept busy with this ARP Warden's Exercise he's running."

"What exactly does he do as a Warden? All ours seem to ever do is scream at us if we show as much as a glimmer of light after the blackout."

May laughed. "There is a lot more to it than that. Or there will be once the bombing starts."

Anne looked at her sharply. Conscious of Kitty's presence, and to change the subject, "Is the sherry satisfactory?"

"It's lovely. It's years since I've had sherry. We used to have it regularly, and wine with dinner. When I was at home with my parents I mean, before I was married. But Ron doesn't approve."

"Oh?" Anne was surprised at someone not approving, but she was still glad to get back to talking about Ron even by this route.

"He joined the Band of Hope - the children's Temperance Movement thing - years ago when he was a boy. And he's still stuck to his promise not to drink alcohol at all."

"Why did he do that Mum?" asked Kitty, so curious about this about her father as to butt in.

"Well ...," May hesitated, " ... look Kitty, you are not to tell anyone about this, not even Tim. But as you've asked I'll tell you. Your grandfather, that's your father's father, not my father, used to get drunk a lot. And when he was drunk he used to make trouble. So your father decided never, ever, to drink alcohol himself. And then one of your father's older brothers, Uncle Samuel, started to do the same. Which made him more determined than ever."

"What sort of trouble did they make?" Kitty asked wide-eyed. "And was it always?"

"They'd argue a lot. And sometimes get into fights with other people and do other silly things. That's why we don't go to see them. My family never did those things because we always drank sensibly."

"But we don't go to see them either, Mum," said Kitty, puzzled.

"That's for other reasons," snapped May. "This is a really nice sherry Anne." she added to forcibly change the subject.

"I'm glad you like it, because it is my favourite." Anne checked the saucepans. "Dinner's just about ready."

After Kitty had climbed into bed, weary but happy, May sat on the bed beside her.

"Did you mind us not having you home for Christmas?" May asked her quietly, not to disturb Frank asleep in the cot on the other side.

Kitty hesitated.

"Some went home from school like Maralyn. She doesn't know whether she'll be coming back."

"But did you mind? And Tim?" May pressed, after a pause.

Kitty felt in a quandary. If she said she did mind, would Mum then be upset for keeping her away? But if she said she didn't mind because Christmas with Aunt Anne and the others had been such fun, then probably she wouldn't like that either.

"We were sorry we couldn't be home for Christmas, but with what you said to Aunt Anne about the bombing starting at any time, I know you were right not to. Even though the bombing didn't start."

May smiled and Kitty breathed a silent sigh of relief. She must have said the right thing.

"Did the children who have gone home for good, say why they

were going home?"

"Most've said that because there had been no bombing their Mums and Dads said they might as well go home. Some just wanted to because they were unhappy where they were. Tim and I think we've been very lucky where we are."

"So you're happy enough to stay here? For a time anyway?"

"Yes Mum," Kitty replied promptly. There was so much more here than at home she thought. But she did not say that aloud.

"Good." May stood up to go, then, as if as an afterthought, "Does Anne ask about us much?"

"A bit at the beginning. And she asked Maralyn about her Mum and Dad," Kitty yawned sleepily. "Then when you were coming we talked more. Especially since Maralyn went home and there was just Aunt Anne and me here."

Kitty yawned again. She'd told Mum that already, in the car when she'd asked.

"Has she asked much about Dad? What he likes? And the things he likes to do?" May tried to sound casual.

"Not really."

"Does - does he 'phone her at all?"

"No. 'Cos if he did he'd speak to me too, wouldn't he?"

Not if he 'phoned her at work, thought May. But he did say he hadn't got her 'phone number when I asked him. Maybe she was getting things out of proportion, but why had he described Anne so disparagingly that time he came down here with the parcels - when all the time she looks like a woman out of a fashion magazine? Was that to put her (May) off the scent?

But, just in case he did get transferred to the Kent area or made some more trips down here, and he had got some ideas, she had already worked out how she would kill it. As far as Anne Carruthers was concerned anyway.

Anne was in the lounge, the wireless on softly where the News was just ending.

"Both asleep?"

"Yes. Sound. Anything much on the News?"

"Nothing really. Everyone still seems to be waiting for the other side to do something." Anne shook her head. "It's an odd way to fight a war. Especially as we're supposed to be in it to help Poland and the delay in doing anything has meant that Poland has already been over-run."

"It won't last much longer. It can't," affirmed May. "Then when the bombs begin to fall we'll wish for this time back again. Do you mind having Kitty here?" she asked without a pause.

"I did at first, I'll be honest about that. Not because it was specifically Kitty and Maralyn ...," she added quickly, " ... but simply the necessity of taking in Evacuees at all. But I felt that if I was asking others to do so, then I should do the same. But Kitty's lovely. So is Maralyn. Now I wouldn't have missed having them for the worlds. Shall we finish off the wine?" she added, holding up the still half-full bottle.

"Why not? It's a very pleasant wine isn't it?"

"It is. When the war began looming I bought several cases of it, because it seemed to me that one way or another it would be bound to affect supplies."

She poured out two glasses on the coffee table between them.

"Kitty tells me you've talked to her quite a lot about Ron and me," May said trying to be casual as she picked up her glass.

"Yes, that's right," Anne replied at once. "A Child Welfare Worker we had to talk to the Reception Committee and then groups of foster-mothers, said that we must make sure that the children do not forget their parents. Especially the smaller children, say of Tim's age. So we should talk to the children about their parents and encourage them to write to them. She said children tend to live so much 'in the moment' as she put it, that they could tend to forget them. Not forget them completely of course, but that they should sink into the background." She laughed. "But being a mother yourself, I'm sure you know more about children than I do."

She leaned forward to re-fill May's half-empty glass and poured just a few drops into her own still nearly full one.

"Is there anything you feel you want to know about me? Or Ron?"

Anne sat back in her chair, nursing her drink. There were hundreds of things she wanted to know about Ron. But few of them that she could ask his wife.

"I only had that brief conversation with your husband when he brought the parcels of clothes for Kitty and Maralyn soon after they came here. So all I know is what they have told me over the time. It's a very difficult balance to strike - keeping parents in their minds without making them homesick."

"Yes. Yes. I suppose it can be." May paused. "Did you know I suggested to Ron that he change his area from East Anglia to Kent?"

Anne struggled to keep from staring at her. That was just what she had suggested to him! And coming from May it would have given him the perfect – and legitimate - excuse.

"What did he say to that?" she managed to say.

May laughed, an indulgent note strong in it.

"Anne, you must understand. Ron is a dear man with a number of good qualities, but being bright isn't one of them. Do you know, I had to actually explain to him that he would then be able to stop off for an hour or two to see the children if he did. But he still put up all kinds of difficulties." She laughed again. "It almost made me wonder if he's got a girl friend over in East Anglia somewhere. He has to stay away overnight a couple of times a week you know."

Anne managed to keep up an appearance of still being relaxed. She knew Ron was intelligent - that had come across very clearly. Which meant he must have some reason not to change area - if it was as easy as May appeared to be saying. But - a girl friend in East Anglia?

"Do you think he has?" she asked.

"Not really. You see, he's not only not very bright but he's not at all enterprising either. For example ...," May took another sip of her emptying wine glass, knowing that she was now really going to hit the target of belittling Ron to this go-getting businesswoman. " ... when the Depression hit soon after we were married, he was told they were closing the Department where he was Foreman, which meant he'd be out of a job. But they did have a vacancy for a Driver that he could have if he wanted it, but it would mean quite a drop in wages. He took it and he's stayed only a Driver ever since. I'm certain he could have found another job, a better one, if he'd tried and been ready to take a chance, but he wouldn't. He said that being a married man with a wife to support he daren't take the risk. Even when things began picking up he still said he'd stay where he was. With a million still unemployed he said at least he was in a job that was secure. And my father was a bank manager," she added, apparently inconsequentially, but with a depth of bitterness in her voice.

"But he did show enterprise in courting and marrying you, didn't he May?" Anne asked with a smile as she poured more wine into May's glass, and again added just a few drops to her own. She felt that the unaccustomed wine was probably making May more talkative that she would have been otherwise.

"Thanks Anne. The thing was, he caught me on the rebound as they say. I had just given my fiance his marching orders. I'd found out that while we were Engaged and planning our wedding, he was having a full blown affair with his secretary. He was well-off, on his way up in a big City firm, wildly exciting and I loved him passionately. I then met Ron at a dance and he was everything that Peter was not - quiet, dependable, hard working and persistent. I'll certainly give him full marks for persistence! He stuck to me like glue for months, without me giving him the slightest encouragement!"

"But you began courting," Anne prompted after a pause.

May shrugged.

"He was persistent, he was male, he was available. Good looking when properly dressed." She sighed. "All my friends had boy friends, and were getting Engaged. I kept hoping that Peter would come to see me when he heard I'd found someone else, but he never did. So I stayed with Ron and eventually married him." She paused. "He's still quiet, hardworking, dependable and ...," bitingly, " ... deadly dull and boring! At least Peter would have been exciting. And I'd have been living in a house as good as this one instead of a pokey little Council dump."

Anne looked into the fire, now understanding a lot more about Ron, and May. And their marriage.

"Suppose - just suppose, you found he did have a girl friend in East Anglia?" she said finally.

"I'd Divorce him," May snapped immediately. "With the greatest possible amount of publicity in the local papers where she lived. Wherever she lived," she added looking directly at Anne. "And I'd make sure he never saw any of the children again."

"A clear warn-off," Anne thought. "I wonder if she suspects, or if it's only a just-in-case." Aloud she said, "I think you're absolutely right May. I'd do exactly the same in your position."

May looked surprised at Anne's immediate support for her strong line. For a moment she wondered whether to tell her about her arrangement with Tony's wife, but then decided not to.

"Have you any idea whether Maralyn is coming back here after Christmas, May?" Anne asked, deliberately closing off Ron as a topic of conversation.

"As far as I know she is."

"Good. Because Kitty and she are really close friends and she would miss her if she didn't. And so would I if it comes to that."

Chapter 8
Exercises

In London Ron shut his front door feeling unutterably weary and depressed. The Exercise was showing up all manner of weaknesses in their responses to an air raid incident.

On paper their organisation looked pretty good. But in practice some of their people were simply not up to the demands of even the fairly minor incident of the Exercise - two bombs dropped, one at each end of a street.

The Warden's job was to be first on the scene, start rescue themselves then direct the survivors to helpers and helpers to the survivors. In a small incident they might have to handle everything themselves, especially if there were other incidents nearby taking the Heavy Rescue Units away to deal with them. So they had to be fit enough to run to a scene, dig into rubble and keep cool under the pressure of demands coming from all directions at once. While bombs were still falling around them.

He flopped down in his chair in the cold front room, too tired and depressed even to make a cup of tea.

There was a knock at the front door. Ron ignored it. Whoever it was could go away.

But it was repeated. More persistently.

Ron pulled himself to his feet muttering. It could be someone with an urgent message from the Warden's Post. But most likely it would be nothing.

"Hello Ron," a soft, feminine voice spoke in the nearly total darkness as he opened the door.

"Jennie?" he queried doubtfully.

"Yes, it's me."

"What's the trouble?"

"No trouble Ron. The thing is, I've made twice the amount of dinner I really need. I saw you come home, so as May is away and Sam's away in the Army now, and you not having had any time to get anything to eat yet, I thought you might be able to help me eat it."

Even to her, her carefully rehearsed speech sounded totally

phoney. To have 'accidentally prepared' twice the amount of needed food - nowadays? With rationing? To have seen Ron coming home in the complete darkness of the blacked-out street with no moon shining? With May, and Sam away ...?

To Ron, who suddenly realised just how hungry he really was, a hot meal in a warm house with Jennie. It sounded wonderful!

"Can you give me just ten minutes to have a quick wash? Because ...."

"Sure. And a drink will be waiting."

He rang her doorbell fifteen minutes later, washed, shaved and changed.

"Come on in Ron. Drink?"

"Tea'd be great, Jennie."

Not the drink she'd had in mind, but tonight what Ron said was what went.

He sat down in one of the comfortable fireside chairs and looked round the cheerful, warm room appreciatively. It struck him how light and spacious it seemed in contrast to his own. Then he realised what made the difference. The walls were papered with a light pattern, the paintwork was white instead of his darker brown, the furniture was smaller and lighter (fireside chairs in contrast to his bulkier armchairs and settee) and the table was a fold-up type, though it was now half-opened and laid for two.

"Tea," Jennie announced coming in. "And dinner will be on the table in five minutes."

He watched her sway out of the door, the picture of her close-fitting blouse that complimented her full breasts, and her full, shortish skirt swinging to show a length of leg, still lingering in his mind.

She came back in with two steaming plates that she put on the table, switched off the main light so that there was only the softer, more intimate light of a lampstand on a sideboard. There was a music programme on the wireless, playing softly.

"Ready?"

"This looks terrific, Jennie!"

"Then I hope it tastes as good as it looks."

Seconds later, "It does, Jennie."

Later, "How is the Exercise going, Ron?"

As he ate he told her. And of his worries of how they would cope when the bombing really began.

Jennie asked intelligent questions and made some comments that gave Ron fresh angles to think about.

They finished their dinner as they finished the subject.

"Ron ...," she said, when they were sipping creamed coffee by the fire, " ... from what you've said, the main trouble seems to be the fitness of the men you've got."

"That's right Jennie, but it's not so much that they're unfit and need some exercise to put 'em right, it's just that almost all of them are so old! Alright, some of us are younger, like me, in Reserved Occupations, but George White is 67, and Martin Goddard has got to be in his 70s. So what can you expect?"

"Then why not take on younger, women Wardens? I'd join given half a chance."

"You?" Disbelief echoed in Ron's voice.

"Yes, Ron Jackson – me," she grinned at him. "What's wrong with me?"

Ron openly let his eyes roam over her and grinned back. "Not a thing from where I'm sitting. But it would be dangerous out there with the bombs falling."

"So?"

"Well - women should be in the Shelters. Rescue is men's work."

"Who said?"

"Well ...," Suddenly his male prejudices seemed harder to justify.

"You listen to me, Ron Jackson. The last war showed that women can do things as well as men can, didn't it?"

"Well yes, but ...,"

"And I'm doing war work right now - well not this very minute but you know what I mean - work at the Arsenal that only six months ago they'd have said was men's work."

"Well yes, but ...,"

"And women nurses have been in War Zones, in the thick of danger, for ages, haven't they?"

"Well yes, but ...,"

"And there are women in the Services now aren't there? On Air Force Stations that are likely to get bombed aren't there?"

"Well yes, but ...,"

"And there are Women Wardens already. There's a picture of one in the papers. Look." She pulled a newspaper from under her chair, open at a picture, producing it as her clinching argument.

"Well yes, but ...," Ron checked the picture.

And there she was. A woman dressed in Warden's gear outside a Warden's Post, smiling into the camera. And the caption underneath rammed the point home. "But ...," Ron stopped, not knowing what to say. Jennie grinned at him triumphantly, her point made.

"And I bet there are things that I can do that you can't."

"Oh yes? What are they then?" Ron's mind was still on bombs and rescue, feeling he was on safer ground with that.

"Having babies for one," she shot back at him.

He looked up from the paper, speechless for a moment at the complete switch. Then he laughed, dropping the paper to the floor.

"Okay, I'll admit that one. But I can do things you can't."

"Such as? I bet there aren't."

"What about putting you in that way?"

Jennie grinned back at him.

"Alright. So that's one each. But I bet I'm fitter than you are."

Ron joined in her game willingly enough. "And I bet you're not."

"I bet I can lift you, but you can't lift me."

Ron looked at her slim figure. She looked fit enough, but stronger than him? When he was obviously taller and heavier? Equally obviously she was leading this somewhere.

"I bet I can and you can't."

"I'll have you know that I'm stronger than I might look, Ron Jackson." She stood up. "So we'll have to put this to the test. Come on."

He felt a tingle of anticipation as he put down his coffee cup and stood up in front of her.

"You challenged first, so you have first go," he said, still wary of taking the initiative.

She put her arms round his waist, rested her head on his shoulder and heaved up.

He barely rocked. But her could feel her body pressed hard against him, and his own body responding.

"I'll have another go," Jennie panted, not altogether from exertion.

She heaved up again. To encourage he stood up on his toes.

"I did it a bit!" thinking just for a moment she really had. "Now it's your turn to see if you can do any better with lifting me."

She raised her arms, deliberately accentuating her breasts and smiled at him as he hesitated.

"Come on. You can't back out of the challenge now, Ron Jackson," she said softly, stepping close to him and taking his hands to put them round her waist. She rested her hands on his shoulders. "Now show me just how strong you really are, big boy."

He held her tight to him, feeling his body responding still more to the pressure of hers, and knowing she knew it. With little effort he lifted her 18 inches and held her there.

"Do I win my bet?" he asked, wondering what she had planned for next, and how much he could claim as his 'winnings'.

"That one. But I bet you can't turn round to face the way I am now, still holding me up like this."

"Bet I can."

He pivoted and faced the full length mirror, fully aware that she was wanting him to see what he was seeing - how far her skirt had ridden up to reveal her knickers.

"Bet you can't lower me, very gently, still holding me tight," she whispered.

Wordlessly her let her slide slowly down, both knowing how high her skirt was now riding up. Faces level she kissed him gently then more passionately. She leaned back slightly to look at him. He kissed the side of her neck, still holding her tightly. She drew in a shuddering breath, then her lips sought his again.

After long moments, "I bet you can see an awful lot of my frilly knickers."

"Only the smallest bit," he lied, and kissed her again.

"I bet you want to see more."

"How did you guess that?"

Jennie reached behind her and undid the two buttons of the waistband of her skirt.

"I bet that if you let me go, my skirt will be round my ankles in two seconds."

Ron made no reply. He just stood back and Jennie's skirt dropped to the floor.

"It took three seconds, but I won't lodge an objection on that point. But I still can't see all of them. Your frilly knickers I mean, because your blouse is hiding some. So I must lodge an objection with the Jockey Club."

Smiling slightly, she undid buttons and tossed the blouse onto a chair. She stood with her hands resting on her hips, one knee slightly bent, head well up and back, well pleased with the effect on Ron she was having.

"And I bet my bed upstairs has frills on like my undies."

"I shall need to inspect that before I pay up on any of the bets, ma'am."

"I would expect nothing else, sir. So If you would kindly come this way ...,"

Afterwards, when Jennie began caressing him again, Ron's eyes flew open.

"Jennie! I didn't ...,"

"I did, so don't worry. I won't get pregnant."

He relaxed. A smile came to his lips as he turned to face her in the soft bedroom light.

"You planned all this, didn't you Jennie?" But it was more a statement than a question.

"Of course I did! From start to finish. And boy, what a finish!"

"Jennie, you are what is called a 'scarlet woman'," he murmured, caressing her breasts.

"Scarlet? They were pale blue ones if you remember. They are over there somewhere, where you flung them after tearing them from my quivering helpless body. But I have got some scarlet ones. Red ones anyway."

They lay in each others arms in contented silence for a long time, then Ron roused himself.

"I suppose I'd better go Jennie, or we'll go to sleep and then it'll be daylight. I could be seen and your reputation will be ruined."

"You are an unfeeling brute you are, Ron Jackson," she responded drowsily. "You have your wicked way with a sweet, innocent young maiden and then you cast her aside." She kissed his cheek, then moved to lie across him to kiss him more intensely.

"You? An innocent maiden?" Ron echoed incredulously, long moments later. "You taught me how to do things tonight that I'd never even thought of before!"

"Then all I can say is, you're a mighty quick learner." She slid out of bed and pulled on a dressing gown. "Back in a sec."

Downstairs again, they stood in each others arms and kissed gently.

"Ron ...," Jennie hesitated, " ... Ron, tonight had no strings attached. Either way. We both - well we've both got other commitments haven't we?" She hesitated again. "But we will both be alone again tomorrow night - tonight now - so ...," She stopped.

"I've got some fish that needs eating up, Jennie."

"I know a wicked way of cooking fish, Ron. So if you brought it round ...,"

"I should be home from work about seven ...,"

" ... then while it's cooking you can tell me about joining the Wardens."

He looked at her gravely. "You may have to go out on patrol with a man. Could even be me. Could be dangerous."

Jennie sighed theatrically. "The risks I am prepared to run for our King, country and the War Effort!" she murmured.

While Ron waited in the cold railway station for the train bringing May back from Folkestone he tried to work out his feelings about the women that were now in his life. Three of them if he counted Anne, even though he had only met her once and spoken to her twice on the 'phone.

They were such different women. And his feelings for them

were so different too.

May? Well she had gone against her family to marry him and had then just about cut herself off from them. Whether that was for his sake because she loved him or because she was now ashamed of him or simply a determination to defy them still and not to let them know that she now felt she had made a mistake in marrying him at all, he was not really sure. He thought it was one or both of the last two but, occasionally, she could seem quite affectionate. She was the mother of his children and she did all the things a wife was supposed to do. So maybe he should just settle for that - as he always had done. Up to the past few nights anyway.

And Jennie? The last two nights had been a revelation! Jennie was someone he could laugh and joke with. She was very sexy, someone who really enjoyed it herself, not someone who just lay back and 'permitted it' because they believed it was their marital duty to do so. Like May did.

He felt a twinge of guilt, not so much over May as over Sam, Jennie's husband. As he was away in the Army was that being fair to him? Then he shrugged. From the way Sam had talked before he went off he certainly wasn't going to let himself go short. So if he was doing it, why shouldn't Jennie? And if so, why not with him?

But the last two nights wouldn't be able to happen again, not with May back. Not unless .... An idea occurred to him.

And Anne? She was vastly different from both the others. He liked her, liked her a lot. And she seemed to like him. At least she'd been glad he'd 'phoned her and made it obvious she wanted him to keep on doing so. And she wanted them to meet again.

But would he ever be able to meet her like that again? There was no sign of any more trips down to Folkestone.

Was she looking on him as a kind of substitute, a stand-in for her dead boy friend Gregory? Come to think of it, things with Anne were a bit like things had been when he'd first met May. Someone he thought as being 'above' him, that he could look up to and admire, someone he could dream of 'bedding', but never in this world set out to do it. Though he had with May - once they were married.

But Anne had responded to him much more positively than

May had at the beginning of their relationship. So did he have some kind of real chance with Anne? If he got any more trips to Folkestone?

And here was May's train pulling in. And once more he had to be the dutiful husband.

As they walked home, May pushing Frank in the pram, Ron carrying her case, May talked. About the children, about the Abbotts, the children's Christmas party she had gone to with them, even the weather there and here. Without mentioning Anne once.

When she ran down, "How did you find Mrs. Jones and Miss Carruthers?" He was careful to put Mrs. Jones first.

"Mrs. Jones is nice. But I don't trust that Anne Carruthers."

"Oh? You mean she's got a bad attitude to Kitty? That Kitty's unhappy there in spite of what she's written?"

"Oh no. Kitty's definite she wants to stay there, and their living conditions are good, and she's looking after the girls well. I can't deny that. But she's filling Kitty's head with nonsense. Kitty's now saying she wants to be a business woman like her, believe it or not!"

Relieved, Ron put a puzzled note in his voice.

"But May, we've often said we want the children to do better than me, haven't we? And if it turned out that Anne Carruthers can help Kitty do what she wants in some way ...,"

"I know, but ...," May stopped short. How often they had said that they hoped the children would do better. But their ideas had been limited to Kitty being a secretary or something in the City. But for her to be a business woman like Anne Carruthers? Even with her help in some way or other?

"Kitty's too young to be getting ideas like that yet," she snapped. "Anyway, what have you been doing over the last couple of days? How did the Exercise go?"

"Good and bad. Good that it showed up the weaknesses, bad that we've got them."

"What were they?" May was genuinely concerned, because she realised how important the Wardens would be when the bombing really started.

"Basically a lot of the people we've got are not really up to it. Some of us are young enough, like me, but George White and

Martin Goddard are in their late 60s and 70s and could be having to shift rubble after a 200 yard dash to get there. Some of them can hardly manage the 200 yard dash, let alone shifting rubble straight after."

The following night when she gave Ron his mug of tea on arriving home, May said, "Guess what Jennie told me today?"

Inwardly Ron jumped. Had Jennie let something slip? But May was smiling with amusement. So he smiled back.

"How can I possibly guess what women will talk about?"

May ignored that,

"She told me that she, Mary Dyson and Jill Payton are going to volunteer to be Wardens."

"And does Jennie, and the others, realise that will mean digging smashed and dead bodies out of rubble?" he asked, sounding sceptical. "Still, they could stay in the Post and do Admin. jobs I suppose, though there isn't all that much of that."

May laughed aloud.

"I told Jennie you'd think like that. But don't you believe it. Jennie at least, is dead set on doing everything you men do. And when she sets her mind on something she's as unstoppable as a steamroller."

"Then it'll be interesting when she sees Ralph about it. I should think some sparks will fly then, because I'm sure he'll think like me."

But by the middle of February Jennie, Mary and Jill had been fully accepted by everyone in the Post. Now, their training complete, Ralph was having to decide where to put them next week.

Ron spun out the tidying up after the training session till he and Ralph were alone.

"Decided which of the women you'll be allocating to who, Ralph?" he asked as casually as he could as he picked up his gas mask to leave.

"I'm wanting to give one of them to you Ron. Any preference?"

"Well, Jennie does live next door to me, so ...,"

"So you don't want her then?"

"What I was meaning was that as she does live next door then it would be handy for passing messages to us if we're covering the same Sector."

"Good. I was thinking that way too. I'll put her with you then."

Ron walked out grinning. He'd tell May as soon as he got home of course, saying that it was at Ralph's insistence.

To his relief May said she was glad it was Jennie, Ralph had decided he should be with, not one of the other two. Especially Jill. Stories were already circulating about Jill. But she knew she could trust Jennie. If Ron did try anything on with her then Jennie would slap him down mighty quickly.

Two nights later as Ron and Jennie began their first patrol together, the darkness was intense. The small moon was hidden behind thick clouds, so not even a glimmer of stars was in the sky. The streets were silent and deserted even though it was barely 9.30. They both carried torches with masked lenses so that only a sliver of light was seen when they briefly switched them on.

"Creepy, isn't it?" whispered Jennie after a time, glad she had not been sent out alone.

"You get used to it," he muttered back.

Their hands brushed, then held. She squeezed his tightly.

"It's been so long, Ron," she whispered.

"It has. Down here."

He guided her down a narrow grassy path, their shoes hardly making a sound. He stopped. The briefest flick of his torch, and he unlocked a door and guided her through. She stood in pitch darkness, shivers running up and down her spine as she heard him close and bolt the door. Another brief flash of his torch and then another.

"Good. No one's been in," he whispered and flicked on a low powered light.

She looked around as her eyes adjusted.

"Ron! What on earth ...! How on earth ...?"

"Keep your voice down!" he hissed.

"What is this? Where is it?" she breathed.

"Back of Mrs. Murgatroyd's. She went off to stay with her son for Christmas and then the Duration and she asked me to keep an eye on her house. I asked if I could set up this out-house as a sub-Post and she was only too willing. She let me have the stuff and – here it is."

"And who else knows of this - this sub-Post? I haven't heard anyone else mention it."

Ron struck his forehead. "I knew there was something I kept meaning to tell Ralph!"

Jennie looked round the large outhouse with a black-out blind fixed firmly over the small window high up in the wall. Ron had made it into a neat, clean room with a small fold-up table, two wooden fold-up chairs, and a small heater. A mattress lay across the table with two blankets folded on top of that. Even though it had been closed up it still smelt fresh.

"All mod. cons. I see," Jennie said smiling, touching the mattress. "But isn't it a bit risky to use it on top of the table?"

"That item of Warden's equipment goes up there when the Post is not operational, Ma'am. When it is, as now, it goes there," Ron pointed to the lino on the floor. "It - erm - hasn't been tested yet. The mattress I mean."

"Tut-tut, Warden Ron," Jennie murmured, putting her arms round his neck. "And I've been instructed that ALL equipment must be tested BEFORE an Emergency arises."

Ron put his hands on her hips.

"There has been no earlier opportunity Ma'am. But if you should agree that we can spare the time from active Patrolling ...,"

"As you are in Command of this Patrol sir, I am ready to take any orders you may give. And I am all prepared."

"So am I this time," Ron grinned.

They quickly laid down the mattress and blankets, then reached for each other.

Chapter 9

Uprooted again – Kitty's story

It was a warm late afternoon in early May 1940 as Kitty and Maralyn trudged up the drive. Kitty rang the bell and Mrs. Jones opened the door almost immediately as this was the usual time they arrived home from school.

"Hello girls," she greeted them cheerfully.

"Hello Mrs. Jones," they replied.

She took one look at their faces and saw that something was badly wrong.

"Come into the kitchen and tell me," she said quietly. "Now what's the trouble?" she asked as soon as they had sat down at the table while she bustled around getting drinks.

"This." Kitty passed a note to her. "Maralyn's got one too. We're being Evacuated again."

"Evacuated again? Why? When? What for?" Mrs. Jones was shocked.

"The Government thinks there's going to be an invasion and that the Germans will be coming to Folkestone and other places near here," explained Kitty.

"And because our soldiers will be coming here to stop them, when the Germans come there'll be huge battles. So we've got to go away again. And the other children who live here will be going away too."

"And what's worrying us, is what's going to happen to you and Aunt Anne. Because if you're still here, you'll be in the middle of the battles, won't you? So can't you come with us too?" burst out Kitty.

"Now just you wait a minute before you get all upset girls. It's not 'when' the Germans come, it's 'if'." Mrs. Jones was trying to be re-assuring. "Who says they'll get anywhere near Folkestone in the first place? We've got our soldiers over in France haven't we? And the Germans have got to get through them first before they can even THINK about coming on here.

"And there's all the French soldiers too. We've got our Navy in the Channel, and our Air Force in the air to attack them. And then we've got big guns that fire huge shells for miles and miles. So they'll sink the German invasion ships before they get anywhere near here."

"They invaded Denmark and Norway didn't they?" Maralyn said. "It was on the News."

"And we're still being Evacuated again. So can't you be Evacuated with us?" persisted Kitty. To her, this was the important thing.

To the girls the idea of an invasion, German soldiers actually landing on the beaches they knew so well, just a mile or so away from where they were sitting this very minute, was much more dangerous than the idea of bombs falling from an aeroplane high up in the sky that could hit anywhere. This was someone coming right up to you to hurt you badly - even kill you. And what could a not very big girl do to stop a big man who'd got a gun doing just that? Or Aunt Anne or Mrs. Jones?

"The best thing for us to do is to show these letters to your Aunt Anne. But the thing is, we both have our jobs to do here, so how could we go? What would we do when we get to where you're going and the Germans don't come after all? Because then all we've done for years would be wasted wouldn't it?"

The girls had no idea what to say about that. All they knew was they were frightened for Aunt Anne. And Mrs. Jones of course.

"So we'll show these to your Aunt Anne and see what she says. Now you get changed and do your homework while I finish these veggies for your dinners."

When Anne walked in she found the girls were preparing her tea tray as usual but instead she went up to them, holding out her arms, as soon as she came in.

She had been contacted that morning as, having Chaired the Evacuation Reception Committee, it was thought she would be the best person to organise their re-Evacuation. They were surprised to find that she already had plans drawn up. She had listened to the warning of Colonel Burns months before.

They ran to her to be hugged and held tightly.

"My dears," she said, a break in her voice.

"Aunt Anne, please say you'll come with us. I couldn't bear it if you got hurt in the battles," Kitty sobbed.

Anne squeezed her tightly. No one, it seemed to her, had ever cared, really cared, for her as much as Kathleen did. The thought flashed through her mind, she had no reason to be jealous of May any more. Kathleen loved her!

After a time they released each other and dried their eyes.

"When do we go? Mr. Cutliffe said he didn't know," Maralyn asked.

"Or he wasn't going to tell."

Anne took them into the lounge, then Kitty darted out for the customary tea tray. Anne poured their teas out, then sat back in her chair with hers.

"Sunday week," she said quietly.

"What!" gasped Kitty appalled. "But that's less than two weeks away!"

"That's right. You see girls, the Government thinks that all this could happen very quickly. So a lot of our soldiers are coming down here very soon to get all the defences ready. And so you are being sent to another, very beautiful part of the country."

"Where's that, Aunt Anne?" Maralyn asked the practical question while Kitty was still silenced by the suddenness of the re-Evacuation as well as its happening at all.

Anne sipped her tea, thinking quickly.

"You must not tell anyone just yet of what I am going to tell you now. Come to the Study and I'll show you exactly where it will be."

They stood in front of a map of the British Isles on the wall.

"Where is Wales?" she asked.

Both girls reached out to touch the map.

"That's right. And obviously South Wales is ...,"

"Oh no! Not there, Aunt Anne!" burst out Kitty.

"You said it was a beautiful place! But it's all coal mines and slag heaps there. We did it in geography three weeks ago!" exclaimed Maralyn, equally horrified.

"While there are a lot of coal mines and attendant slag heaps in places, there are also very many beautiful places." Anne touched a place on the map. "Those are called the Brecon Beacons. As you see it is a range of mountains and moorland. It's a lovely area with wild ponies, foxes and all kinds of other animals and flowers. You will be in a town right on its edge."

"But Aunt Anne, you will come with us won't you?" Kathleen pleaded desperately.

"No Kathleen. I have my work here." Anne's tone was quiet but final.

"But ...,"

"No 'buts' Kathleen. But I will tell you another secret that you must not tell anyone until the war is over. And then, if it still matters to you, you can. The day your father Kathleen, came with clothes for both of you, I had a meeting with a very important man from the Royal Navy."

"Golly!" whispered Maralyn, impressed.

"And the agreement we made meant that I would keep our Navy, well a small part of it I should say, supplied from my shops and warehouses. As well as keeping many other people supplied with all the other things I sell. So I have to stay here to keep on doing that."

Later, while they were making a pretence of eating dinner, Kitty looked up suddenly as a wonderful idea occurred to her.

"Aunt Anne, when we were Evacuated here, a lot of children didn't come at all. And a lot more have gone home since. So we can choose whether we go or not, can't we?"

Anne hesitated. "Well ...,"

"And they wouldn't put us, or you, in prison if we stayed, even though it is the Government that says we've got to go, because they didn't before so they won't now!" supported Maralyn, seeing what Kathleen was getting at. "So we ...,"

"Girls, you are going." Anne's quiet tone was final.

There was a silence.

"Girls, you know that I love you both tremendously. Too much to keep you here when it would be so dangerous if there IS an invasion. If I did keep you here and you were injured, or even more if you were killed, I would never forgive myself. And your parents who sent you here to be safe from the bombing of London, would never forgive me either. So I must send you away, so that you will be safe. If the invasion happens of course," she added quickly. "And I'm sure your mothers and fathers will agree with me."

There was another silence, the girls staring at their plates.

"You do believe I love you, don't you?" Anne asked quietly.

"Oh yes, Aunt Anne."

Kitty ran from her place to fling herself into Anne's arms. Anne immediately held out an arm for Maralyn to come to her as well.

Later that evening Kitty looked up from the book she was pretending to read. "Will we be going together, the same way we came here?"

"Yes. We're keeping to the same kind of arrangements because they worked last time."

But Anne knew that the shortage of time they had this time meant that things were not working out like that at all.

"So Kathleen and I will still be together then?" Maralyn asked swiftly.

"I'll let you into another secret. Tonight is a night for secrets isn't it? As soon as I heard this morning what was going to happen, I wrote to the person who'll be doing the job in Wales that I did here, the Lodgings Officer as they call him, asking for you both to be placed together."

"What about Tim?"

Though Kitty did not feel the pressure to 'look after him' in the way she had last time, and though they had grown further apart, she still wanted to know.

"Tim will be going on the same train as you, to the same town. In my letter about you and Maralyn I also mentioned that Tim is your brother. Now whether they will be able to put all three of you together is another matter. More likely they will put him with Tommy and Jack as they are of an age and they have been together here."

To Kitty that really did seem as though that would be the best arrangement.

The night before they went Anne gave them presents. A pretty nightdress with a matching dressing gown for each, and a book. Kitty had 'Fashion through the ages', and Maralyn had 'Scientific Marvels'. They had confided to Aunt Anne their ambitions. And she had treated them seriously.

They had scoured the shops of Folkestone, where they were allowed to go by themselves, and had found a figurine of a gentleman in evening dress to match the lady in the evening gown they had given to Anne for Christmas.

They gave Mrs. Jones a brooch.

The four of them arrived at Bonar School in Anne's car but they knew she would have to leave them to make sure that everything was working as it should. Though they had said their goodbyes at home, Anne hugged and kissed them again before hurrying off. So they would not see her tears rather than because she was rushed. Then Kitty and Mrs. Jones stood by the cases while Maralyn dashed off to the toilets.

"Kathleen, I want to tell you something," Mrs. Jones said quickly, as soon as Maralyn was out of earshot. "Aunt Anne was always very careful never to play favourites between you and Maralyn, but she - well she really loves you, you know Kathleen. Not that she don't love Maralyn but she loves you special. She told me so last night when she actually cried over you going away. And I've never, ever, known her cry in all the years I've known her. I'm telling you that so as to make sure you write to her regular. Every week like you do your Mum and Dad. So you will write, won't you Kathleen?"

"Oh I will, Mrs. Jones, honest I will! Aunt Anne and you have been so kind to us, I'll never ...,"

A long whistle blast blown by Mr. Cutliffe cut through the babble in the playground.

"That's it Kathleen." Mrs. Jones hugged and kissed Kitty. "God bless you dear Kathleen. Be good and write to us. And you'll come back and see us when all this is over, won't you?"

"Of course I will. I ...,"

Maralyn dashed up and hugged and kissed Mrs. Jones quickly, then grabbed her case and haversack.

"Come on Kathleen! Off we go again!"

Now that the moment had come she was bouncy and excited.

But Kitty wasn't. She felt even more upset about leaving Aunt Anne than she remembered being about leaving home in London. She wondered why.

After the children had all gone and the last of the volunteers who had helped them had been thanked, Anne drove slowly home. She felt too drained and anxious to go to the office to do any work and in any case she had kept the whole day clear for the Evacuation. She dreaded going home, but there seemed nothing else to do.

Before the girls had come last September the house had always had the quiet of peaceful comfort. But now they had gone she expected it to feel like the quiet of the grave.

The essential thing, she told herself severely, was that the girls would be safe from the invasion battles. And with the way the German Luftwaffe had reportedly destroyed the centre of Rotterdam with huge casualties, just four days ago, as they had destroyed Elverum in Norway earlier, it had been the right thing to do. Just as it had been right for the girls' parents to have Evacuated them last September.

But - the thought came as well - how soon after landing here, would the Germans be attacking Wales? Her only hope was that that attack, and those battles, would be less intensive than the invasion landings here were bound to be.

She stood in the sitting room where only a few weeks ago she had been so happy with the girls. Especially Kathleen. The forecasts of Colonel Burns had long ago been pushed to the back of her mind. But then the German invasions of Denmark and Norway had happened in April and that had made her look again at her plans for the re-Evacuation.

She went upstairs, hesitated, then went into the girls' bedroom. As she'd expected, it was as tidy as always.

And there was an envelope on the bedside table.

With an exclamation she hurried over to it. What on earth could the girls have forgotten!

Then she saw it was addressed to her, to 'Aunt Anne'. In Kathleen's round handwriting that she would know anywhere.

She sat on Kitty's bed and turned the envelope over. It was stuck down on the very tip of the seal. She eased it open.

Dear Aunt Anne,

I am going to leave this letter on the bedside table for you to find after Maralyn and I have gone.

There is so much I would like to say to you but I don't know how to. Except that I love you to bits Aunt Anne and when I grow up I want to be just like you.

You were so kind to take us in, even though you did not

know what we would be like. And you gave us such a lovely room here and let us use your Study with with all your beautiful books. And you have been so kind to us all the time.

Please say 'Thank you', to Mrs. Jones for us for all her love and kindness too.

I shall write to you often. If you have time could you write to me too please?

When this war is finished I'd love to be able to come and see you. And I am sure that Maralyn would want to do that too.

I shall never ever forget you, dear Aunt Anne. Or Mrs. Jones.

All my love,
Kathleen Jackson

Anne re-read the letter with a smile, but tears too.

"Are you alright, Miss Carruthers?" It was Mrs. Jones from the doorway. "I thought I'd heard you come in."

"Yes thank you Dorothy. I came up to - well, look at the girls' room. And I found that Kathleen had left this letter. She mentions you in it too."

She held it out for Dorothy to read.

"She's a lovely girl," Dorothy said a minute later as she handed it back. "So's Maralyn."

"They are. I'll never forget them." Anne paused. "I wonder if Kathleen will write. It's so easy for children to make promises like that, with every intention of keeping them of course, but then forget in their new activities and interests."

"Kathleen won't forget, I'm sure of that, Miss Carruthers," Dorothy spoke confidently. "I was just going to make a pot of tea if you feel like some. I was wondering, if you're not too busy, if we could look at those snaps again you took of the girls at Christmas."

"That's an excellent idea, Dorothy." Anne carefully re-folded the letter and re-placed it in its envelope. "And this goes into my Treasure Box."

As soon as the train left Folkestone, Dick got out his maps and the compass he'd been given for Christmas.

"We'll now be able to work out where we're going even better than when we came to Folkestone," he announced.

"Anyone know where we're actually going to in Wales?" asked Samantha.

Kitty looked at Maralyn. Surely, now that they were actually on their way, they could say?

"Get the map of South Wales and I can show you exactly where," Kitty said quietly. "Aunt Anne - I mean Miss Carruthers - where we were staying and who was in charge of all this, told us."

Dick turned to the map as the others in the compartment crowded round.

"There. On the edge of the Brecon Beacons." Kitty put her finger on the spot. "And then Maralyn and I looked the place up in some of Aunt Anne's books she's got in her Study."

For the next half-hour Kitty and Maralyn told the rest all that they had found out.

When Dick told them they were in Wales, they all looked out for the 'beautiful scenery'. Finally the train slowed, slowed more as they drew into a station, and stopped.

"We must be there. Here," said Kitty, unnecessarily.

But they weren't. They needed to change trains, and then they were off again. Through a valley with mountains on each side. And then the mines and slag heaps. Many more of both. And the villages close by them seemed cramped and crowded together. And it began to drizzle out of a grey sky.

They stopped again and were told to get out. They really had arrived.

Again they stood in a long line on the platform, the Top Class at the front, Kitty and Maralyn at the head of that. A lady who said she was from 'The Council' was waiting with others. They had a quick talk with Mr. Cutliffe and the other teachers.

The teachers and one of the ladies with each of them went off to their classes and talked to them, while Mr. Cutliffe turned to face the Top Class.

"Listen to me children," he called. When there was silence, "We shall be going off in separate classes to where the new foster-mothers will be waiting. The ladies with the teachers know where those places are, so will be showing them the way.

Though the school will be split up, I shall be keeping in touch with everyone. We will now go to where we are due." More quietly, "Lead on Kitty."

They set off but Kitty was wondering about Tim and Tommy. Then she decided she'd just have to trust Miss Drew to look after them. Because she wouldn't be able to, if she was going somewhere else altogether.

They walked through narrow streets of crowded houses, even more crowded than the houses at home in London, she thought. Mr. Cutliffe exchanged a few words now and again with their guide.

Finally she pointed to a church building they were approaching.

"The Reverend Jones, the Minister of the Bethel Chapel has kindly given permission for you to use the Hall for this class. The children will have to use trestle tables as desks, and they, and the chairs will have to be stacked at the back on the evenings that it is going to be used for Chapel activities. And on Fridays for the weekends of course."

"Of course," agreed Mr. Cutliffe.

"And you will be responsible for any damage or breakages."

"Of course," he said again.

Kitty and Maralyn followed them in through the open door, a quick glance taking in the rows of chairs, the lady sitting at a trestle table at the front and the group of foster-mothers waiting for them. They went to the chairs in the front row furthest from the door and sat down. The rest of the children followed, filling up the front row then the others behind.

Kitty looked over the foster-mothers - and the one foster-father.

She saw him whisper to the lady on the seat beside him who gave a slight smile. He whispered to her again. She shot him a startled glance and then looked directly at Kitty.

Politely Kitty smiled back at her.

The lady looked back at the man, whispered to him, then both looked at a card he was holding, and then back at her.

Kitty flushed. What were they staring at her like that for?

"Maralyn ...," she whispered, " ... that man and that lady keep looking at me."

Maralyn glanced at them, back to Kitty and back at them.

"Maybe they know you've been matched with them," she suggested.

"But how could they know it's me? I haven't got a sign round my neck with my name on it, have I?"

Mr. Cutliffe had gone over to the lady at the table.

"Good afternoon. I'm Mr. Cutliffe, the teacher of this class and Headmaster of the school."

"I'm pleased to meet you," she said briskly. "I'm Mrs. Judson, responsible for this Reception Centre. As the children are all seated, shall we begin?"

"By all means. May I have my copy of the lists of the foster-mothers and the children they are matched with?"

"Matched with, Mr. Cutliffe?" she echoed incredulously. "Mr. Hughes our Lodgings Officer has had no time for 'Matching' anyone. We're lucky to have got the number of volunteer foster-mothers we have." She looked over to the group waiting. "Who has Card Number 1?"

A lady sitting close to her stepped forward and handed over a Card.

"What do you want? A boy or a girl?"

"I'll take a boy. That one." She pointed at Dick.

"Come forward boy. What's your name?" directed Mrs. Judson.

"Richard Fanshawe Ma'am." He picked up his case, eased past two children to get to the end of his row and approached the table, outwardly as self-possessed and confident as always, but inwardly as anxious as any.

"You're to go with ...," she glanced at the Card, " ... Mrs. Griffiths."

"Yes Ma'am." He smiled at his new foster-mother. "Good afternoon, Mrs. Griffiths."

"And could you make sure he is back here for - shall we say 10 o'clock tomorrow morning, Mr. Cutliffe?"

"Yes, 10 o'clock will do very well, but ...,"

"Sign here please Mrs. Griffiths. Thank you." With barely a pause, "Card number 2"

"That's me. I want a girl. I'll take that one." She pointed to

Samantha.

"Come forward child. What's your name?"

Mr. Cutliffe opened his mouth to protest, then closed it again. He thought this way of foster-mothers choosing the children as though they were puppies in a pet shop, was bad, but Mrs. Judson was right - there had been very little time. So he - and the children - would have to be grateful for what had been done. Any glaring mistakes would have to be sorted out later.

Kitty had been covertly watching the man and lady. When Card Number 2 had been called and she said she wanted a girl, she had stiffened but relaxed again when she had chosen Samantha.

"I reckon they want you," Maralyn whispered who had been watching them too.

"If I go first I'll ask her if you can come too," Kitty whispered back.

"And I'll do the same for you."

When Card Number 6 was called, the man and lady stepped forward quickly and said something to Mrs. Judson.

"You," she called, pointing at Kitty. "Come forward please. What's your name?"

"Kathleen Jackson, Ma'am." They had all followed Dick's example of calling her that.

Closer up the lady looked older than Aunt Anne, and whereas Aunt Anne had been tall and slim, this lady was shorter and plumper. She was wearing a nice dress with a light coat and hat. She looked pleasant but anxious about something.

The man with her, who Kitty thought must be her husband, was only slightly taller than the lady and had greying hair. He seemed to have an air of quiet authority about him - a bit like Mr. Cutliffe, Kitty thought.

The lady bent down slightly to talk to her.

"Would you like to come and stay with us, Kathleen?"

"She has the same scent Aunt Anne uses," flashed through Kitty's mind. "And she ASKED me to go!"

"Yes please. I'd like that," she replied politely. "But can you take Maralyn O'Conner as well please? She's the girl sitting next to me and she's my best friend. We were able to be together in Folkestone and we would really like to be together again."

"Oh dear," the lady said in consternation. "I'm terribly sorry but we only have a small bungalow with only one spare room and that's only big enough for one person. So I don't really see ...," Her voice trailed off as she looked up to her husband to solve this dilemma.

"That's that then. Maralyn O'Conner will have to go somewhere else. Sign ...,"

"Just a moment if you please, Mrs. Judson." The man spoke quietly but with authority. "My dear ...," he said to his wife, " ... didn't Gaynor say something to you about taking an Evacuee?"

"Yes. Yes she did Hywell," she said with sudden hope. "Can we contact ...?"

He turned back to Mrs. Judson. "I suggest that both girls wait with my wife to one side while you continue with the other Cards and I make a quick telephone call. I hope then to be able to take both girls."

"But Mr. Davies ...," she began with asperity.

"I am sure Mr. Hughes would agree with my suggestion." Without waiting for a response he looked at Maralyn. "Will you sit with my wife and Kathleen please? I shall only be a matter of moments." He smiled benignly at Mrs. Judson. "Please don't let me hold you up any longer."

She set her lips angrily. But she knew that Mr. Hughes would not have gone against the wishes of Town Councillor Hywell Davies, the influential General Manager of the Four Valleys Omnibus Company.

"Very well, Mr. Davies," she snapped ungraciously. "But please be as quick as you can. Card Number 7."

Mrs. Davies pulled chairs over for Kitty and Maralyn and moved over to one side herself while the other foster-mothers continued to pick the children they liked the look of.

"We've got a lovely room that I'm sure you will like, but it really is only big enough for one girl. But our next door neighbour, Gaynor Williams, Mrs. Williams that is, has a bungalow just like ours with a spare room and she did talk the other day about taking an Evacuee when I told her we were. If she agrees now, you'll only be next door which is almost as good as staying with us, isn't it? And she's very nice Mrs. Williams is. And so is Mr. Williams."

She seemed desperately anxious to convince both girls. She turned back to Kitty.

"Do we call you 'Kathleen' or something else for short? Like 'Katy' or 'Kitty' or 'Cathy'?"

"My Mum and Dad call me 'Kitty', but Aunt Anne, the lady we stayed with in Folkestone, called me 'Kathleen'. So I don't mind really."

"You liked your Aunt Anne then?"

"Oh yes." Kitty's simple and definite answer spoke volumes.

"She's lovely," supported Maralyn.

"Then Gaynor and I will have a lot to live up to," Mrs. Davies smiled.

She looked round as the door swung open and her husband hurried in, smiling. He gave them a quick nod and went to the table.

"It looks as though we've got good news," exclaimed Mrs. Davies, losing her anxious expression.

Mrs. Judson finished the Card she was dealing with, then looked sourly at Mr. Davies.

"Mrs. Williams has said she will take Maralyn O'Conner. I will sign as the person having responsibility to take Maralyn to her. Mr. and Mrs. Williams live next door to us, at number 42."

"Very well Mr. Davies. Will you complete a Card giving their details on her behalf and please ensure both girls are here tomorrow morning at 10 o'clock? Card Number 20."

Mr. Davies swiftly completed the Cards for himself and the Williams, put them on the table and smiled at his wife and the girls.

"Shall we go home then?"

"The car's just a little way down the road," said Mrs. Davies to the girls as they left the Chapel. "No trouble with Gaynor or James then?" she added to her husband.

"None at all when I told them the situation. But I was very fortunate - I caught them just as they were about to go out. They offered to cancel but I told them we would look after Maralyn till they got back."

Both the girls were glad. It meant they would be together that bit longer.

They drove just a short distance out of the small town before coming to another village. They pulled into the drive of a small, neat bungalow, one of a street of similar small, neat bungalows. There were no trees in the front or the small back gardens they discovered the next morning, so no squirrels to watch from the bedroom window. But there were lots of mountains around.

"I'll check the casserole and put on the kettle while you show Kitty her room, my dear. You go as well Maralyn if you wish."

As Kitty looked round her room, she could see that Mrs. Davies had been right - there was only room for one. And though it was nice, it was not as nice as their room at Aunt Anne's. That had had a touch of elegance that somehow was lacking here.

"It's lovely Mrs. Davies," Kitty said politely. "Are those of mountains near here?" She indicated the paintings on the walls.

"Would you like to call me 'Aunt Edith', not Mrs. Davies, Kitty?"

"Of course, Aunt Edith."

So she was going to be 'Kitty' here then. Well that helped to keep the way she was with Aunt Anne something different and special. Which, she decided, she preferred.

"Those mountains are the Brecon Beacons. Out there." Aunt Edith waved a hand vaguely towards the back of the bungalow. "Uncle Hywell and I often used to drive over to them, but the petrol rationing has rather put a stop to that."

Maralyn looked closer at one of the paintings, a shallow lake set in the middle of mountains.

"Aunt Edith, this one's got 'E.D.' on it in the corner. Does that mean you painted it?"

"She painted all of them, Maralyn. Good artist isn't she?" Uncle Hywell said proudly from the doorway. "The casserole's fine Edith and the tea is ready. So if you want to come down, we can get to know each other."

When the girls sat down together on the small settee, as they used to do at Aunt Anne's, Kitty saw that behind Uncle Hywell's armchair was a telephone on a small table.

A telephone! If Uncle Hywell let her she could actually speak to Aunt Anne tonight! She knew 'phone calls were expensive but she was positive she had enough to pay for it. But how to ask and say that?

At that moment he came in with a tea tray.

"Kitty, Maralyn, I've had a thought. Are your parents or Aunt Anne on the telephone? If they are, you could ring them to say where you are, if you like."

"Aunt Anne is. Mum and Dad aren't," the girls said together "I've got Aunt Anne's number here," Kitty added, whipping a small notebook out of a pocket and opening it. Though she knew both Anne's home and business numbers by heart.

"I'll get her then." Uncle Hywell took the notebook, went to the 'phone, and dialled the operator. He replaced the 'phone. "The lines are busy at the moment but the operator will connect us as soon as she can. Now tell us about yourselves. What you like doing, your favourite books and your hobbies."

It wasn't until an hour later that the 'phone suddenly rang, just as Kitty was wondering if the operator had forgotten them.

Uncle Hywell went to the 'phone, listened a moment, then said, "Is that Aunt Anne?"

Kitty nearly laughed. Partly with relief, partly because it sounded funny to her that a grown man like Uncle Hywell should call her 'Aunt".

"My name is Hywell Davies. My wife and I are Kitty's new foster-parents in Wales. I have Kitty and Maralyn to speak to you."

He held out the 'phone to Kitty.

"Aunt Anne! Aunt Anne! It's me, Kathleen. Are you alright?"

Anne had been so restless she had wondered about going to Sonia's to get away from the awful quietness of the house. But she had stayed because she felt she'd be such bad company for them that it would not be fair to go.

Now she was thanking heaven she hadn't!

"All the better for hearing you, my dear. How are you? What kind of journey did you have?"

Five minutes later, Kitty, reluctantly, handed over the 'phone to Maralyn, who later handed it to Uncle Hywell, who talked to Aunt Anne for another five minutes.

"Thank you so much for letting us use the 'phone Uncle Hywell," Kitty reached into her pocket for her purse. "How much ...?"

"Put that away my dear," he said at once, seeing what she was doing. "A 'phone call is the least we can do to welcome you to Wales."

As she lay down to sleep that night Kitty was fairly content though not completely happy. She wondered where Tim was. And Tommy. Had they been as lucky again as she and Maralyn had been, both in their new foster-parents and where they were staying? She would have to ask Mr. Cutliffe where he had gone and go to see him.

And sometime in the near future, Aunt Edith had promised them, they would catch a bus from somewhere called Merthyr Tydfil to Brecon which went right through the middle of the mountains. The Brecon Beacons, as Aunt Anne and Aunt Edith had called them.

Funny names they had in Wales, she thought sleepily, as well as a funny way of talking. But come to think of it, maybe the London way of talking sounded funny to them.

Uncle Hywell had shown them a book of photographs. In it had been an old one of a 10 year old girl and he asked if they recognised her. Maralyn had said straight away how like Kitty the photograph was. And it had been a picture of Aunt Edith when she was ten!

They had said they had 'never been able to have any children though they had always wanted some'. Then added 'till now', smiled at each other and then at her.

Kitty couldn't understand that. They must know how it happened surely! She decided to ask Maralyn what she thought about that tomorrow.

There was plenty to write to Mum and Dad about tomorrow when she gave them her new address. And how lucky to have been able to actually TALK to Aunt Anne tonight! But most of the time she'd write letters to her.

Chapter 10

Uprooted again - Tim's story

When Tim first heard they were going to Wales he thought it was to another seaside place where there would be a lot of the huge fish that Uncle Toby had told them about. When he was told the truth he was disgusted.

"Then why do they call it 'Wales' if there aren't any?" he demanded with all the indignation of a six year old who feels he has been cheated. "So if there are no whales there what is there to look at?"

"Coal mines," put in Uncle Wilf, who had been listening. "Lots of coal mines. Going even deeper underground than the one at Betteshanger. That's near Deal, a bit up the coast."

"I went down Betteshanger coal mine in my last year at school when I did a Project on it. I've got some pictures in a book if you'd like to see them," offered Uncle George.

All the boys did.

The more he thought about it, the more sorry Tim was to leave Auntie Flo and the Uncles. But at the same time he was looking forward to seeing the coal mines. Maybe he could even go down one like Uncle George did!

And maybe the next place they'd be at would be as nice as here, and if he was really lucky perhaps he could share with Tommy and Jack again.

At Bonar School, where they all met to go on the same train, he and Kitty saw each other briefly as they were going to their classes, and waved to each other.

The train journey was as boring as the one to Folkestone and even longer. But at last their train pulled into their final destination in the late afternoon. Ladies from the Council were there to meet them, but this time the classes separated at the Railway Station.

As Tim and the rest of his class walked through the narrow streets in a long crocodile, Tim and Tommy looked around eagerly for the coal mines expecting to see them at every corner. Passersby stared at them, a few with hostility, but more with simple curiosity. Until they came opposite a group, mostly of boys around 13 years of age, and their jeers quickly becoming shouts.

"Here's them London 'Vaccies". "Send 'em back to the London Gov'mint, they can 'ave 'em, we don't want 'em," began to be chanted.

As the cat-calls kept on and became louder, some of the children began to look frightened. They were tired and hungry, and already worried about meeting new foster-parents. And this was awful!

Miss Drew glanced along the line of children, then marched over to the group. The yells died away as she approached.

"Be quiet you horrible children!" she snapped. "These youngsters ...,"

A big 14 year old pushed his way to the front of the group and glared back at her defiantly.

"Look missus ...," he interrupted, " ... we don't want you London 'Vaccies down 'ere. None of us does. Because when we needed the London Gov'mint to back us against the mine owners, did they? 'Course they didn't! What they did do was to send the soldiers in against us, that's what Churchill did. You ask my Dad. And now Churchill's in charge of the London Gov'mint ain't he? So why should we back his war? That war's got nothing to do with us down here. We ain't said we wanted to be in it."

There were murmurs of agreement from some of the crowd gathering round, but there were also murmurs against.

"That's it. You tell 'er Ted," wheezed a middle-aged, ill-looking man. "I lost me lungs in the mines missus and the London Government ain't been bothered none about me, so why should I be bothered about them?"

"But those children were nothing to do with the Miners' Strikes! They weren't even born then! They are victims of this war, just as much ...,"

"This war is between two lots of Capitalist Imperialists and nothing to do with the working class. We don't want nothing to do with it," interrupted Ted.

"Who do you think the German bombs and guns killed and are killing and injuring at this very moment in Poland, Denmark, Norway, Holland, Belgium and France?" snapped Miss Drew. "Only the rich? Only the Capitalists? Of course not. It's ordinary people. People like you and me and these children and you people here." She pointed around the listening group. "And does your father work in the mines?" she demanded turning back to Ted.

"Yep. And me brother. And I will be. Because there's nothing else to do round here. And if me Dad wasn't doing overtime right now, he'd be telling you exactly what I am."

"So your father and brother are producing coal right now, to produce electricity to run the factories to make weapons and ammunition to fight the war aren't they? And the Royal Welch Fusiliers is one of the bravest Regiments in the British Army aren't they? And they're over on the Continent fighting the Germans at this very minute.

"So the coal your father and brother are producing right now helps the factories to make the very weapons and ammunition that YOUR VERY OWN REGIMENT NEEDS SO URGENTLY! So that means that your father and brother ARE already working to fight this war aren't they?

"And the places where these children have come from, London and Folkestone, are all from working class areas and soon they will be enduring the same bombing that towns on the Continent are at this minute. And those places will be the front line of any invasion too.

"And don't you forget Ted and the rest of you ...," she said looking round, " ... if the Germans aren't stopped on the Kent beaches, they'll be coming down this street right here before too long afterwards! They certainly won't be stopping at the English-Welsh border just because you say you don't want to be in the war."

There was no response from Ted or the crowd and Miss Drew went back to the children, feeling she had won that argument.

"Shall we go on to where we're going?" she asked the Council lady quietly.

They walked on leaving the still silent crowd behind them, impressed by Miss Drew.

But she was badly worried. If that Ted was typical, then this town was not going to be a happy place to be evacuated to.

Would there even be enough foster-mothers for them? While that was the responsibility of the Lodgings Officer here, of course, she felt responsibility for the children too.

"Sorry about that, Miss Drew," said Mrs. Hughes quietly once they were well out of earshot. "Not everyone thinks like Ted Jones and his father do. They're Communists they are."

"What worries me is that if a lot of people do think as they do, will there be enough foster-mothers for the children?" Miss Drew spoke equally quietly so that the children would not hear.

"There will be," Mrs, Hughes said confidently. "Once the Town Council said that the money for the 'Vaccies will be there, we got plenty of names." She paused. "Don't think we're a lot of money-grabbers, Miss Drew, but we are a poor town compared with a lot of other places and people here simply couldn't afford to suddenly take on a growing child just like that, for who knows how long. And while we're sorry, very sorry for the children themselves, we simply don't trust the London Government and what they promise. Not with the way they've treated us in the past. With our own Town Council it's different. We'll trust them to provide the money first off and then for them to get it back from the London Government. And once people knew that, then we could do what we really wanted to do - provide the children with good homes." She indicated a building. "We go in here."

They went up a flight of stairs into a large hall, filled at one end with desks and chairs. In the middle part of the room were lines of hard wooden chairs, while near the door as they came in was a group of women talking to one man who had a harassed expression.

It cleared as he heard the noise of them coming up the stairs the inner door open and saw Mrs. Hughes walking in followed by Miss Drew and the children.

"Sit down in the chairs, children," instructed Miss Drew.

"Good afternoon Mrs. Hughes," he said as she came into the room behind the last children. "Miss Drew I presume? I am Elwyn Hughes, the Lodgings Officer, no relation."

"I am very pleased to meet you, Mr. Hughes." Miss Drew looked at the group of ladies appraising the children, who were looking back at them apprehensively. "Are those our foster-mothers?"

"Yes they are. Now if you will come with me ...,"

But Miss Drew was already moving towards them.

"Good afternoon ladies. I am Miss Drew the teacher of this

class of children. I want to thank you very much for being willing to take them in at such short notice at the present time. We really ...,"

"Yes, yes, Miss Drew ...," butted in Mr. Hughes, " ... I echo that, indeed I do. But it is most important that I get you to your lodgings straight away. Miss Gordon was most particular that I get you there by 6 o'clock and we shall only be there in time if we leave now. I can assure you that everything has been arranged for the children by these VERY capable ladies."

"Yes Mr. Hughes. But ...,"

"There is nothing for you to do here tonight, nothing at all," he said emphatically. "This room will be your classroom and Mrs. Hughes will be here at 9 o'clock tomorrow morning to hand you the keys, give you a list of which children are with which foster-mother and answer any questions you might have. Now please come this way."

In the face of such insistence Miss Drew felt she could protest no longer. It was obvious that to stay would only cause resentment, and she had already seen plenty of that.

"Very well, I'll see you tomorrow morning Mrs. Hughes. I'll just have a quick word with the children." She faced them and said one word, "Children."

And there was immediate silence.

"Children, you already know from before what happens now. These two ladies have arranged for these other kind ladies to look after you, just as you were in Folkestone. I have to go now but you can be sure that everything has been arranged, so there is no need for you to worry about anything at all. We shall all meet here tomorrow morning at 10 o'clock, though I shall be here at 9 o'clock." She looked at the foster-mothers "Will 10 o'clock be convenient for you to have them here for then?"

There were murmurs of agreement.

"Then I'll see you all tomorrow morning. Now children, be good all of you."

She picked up her case and followed the impatient Mr. Hughes while Mrs. Hughes joined Mrs. Jones at the table.

"Who has Ticket Number 1 please?" Mrs. Hughes asked the foster-mothers.

When Mr. Hughes had been given the job of finding foster-mothers, he had put advertisements wherever he could, giving a list of places where children of different ages would be sent to when they came. Peoplc willing to take evacuees collected numbered cards from the Town Hall for the various Reception Centres, and then told when they would be coming. As they arrived at the Reception Centres they were given another number starting at '1'.

"That's me." A cheerful looking lady went to the table. "I'm Mrs. McDonald. I can take one girl."

"Thank you." Mrs. Hughes took the card and passed it to Mrs. Jones who noted her name in one column on a sheet of paper "Which girl do you want?"

Mrs. McDonald looked round the children, staring at her.

"I'll take that one." She pointed at a neatly dressed, pretty child.

"Come here. What's your name?" Mrs. Hughes beckoned.

"Debbie Edison," she replied, slowly moving forward, reluctant to be the first to leave her familiar friends to go off with a stranger to a strange place.

Mrs. Jones handed a postcard to Mrs. McDonald. "Send that off to her parents in the next couple of days will you? To let them know where she is." To Debbie. "You do know your home address don't you?"

"Do you mean where I've just come from or London?" she asked. Both were 'home' to her now.

"Where your parents live."

"Yes. But I know the other one too."

"Good. Sign here please, Mrs. McDonald."

Mrs. Hughes looked at her as she signed. "Any difficulties you'll be able to sort out with her teacher tomorrow. Ticket Number 2," she added, before they had moved away from the table.

The process went on. Children went in ones, sometimes twos. Tommy was chosen fairly early on. His foster-mother wouldn't take Tim or Jack. Then Jack went.

"Ticket Number 17," Mrs Hughes looked at the last lady, smiling, relieved the job was over.

"I can only take one child," the lady said.

Mrs. Hughes smile vanished. There were two children left.

"Why not take them both?" she asked.

Mrs. Williams looked from Belinda to Tim, sitting in the same row but apart from each other.

Belinda put on her nicest smile. Tim copied. Not that he wanted to be stuck with that awful Belinda for the rest of the war. What he really wanted was to be with Tommy, but that was impossible. He'd already gone. And as this was the only foster-mother that was left ...,

"I can only take one, I haven't got room for two," Mrs. Willams said, studying them. "I'll take the girl. Just her."

Belinda snatched up her bags and hurried forward in case the lady changed her mind and took Tim instead of her.

As the door closed behind them Tim suddenly realised he had nowhere to go. No foster-mother. Unless one of those two ladies took him.

"Well I've got no room to take him," Mrs. Hughes said quickly to Mrs. Jones.

"Nor have I," Mrs. Jones said immediately afterwards, dashing Tim's hopes.. After a pause, "So what are we going to do with him?"

"Take him to Elwyn Hughes of course. He's the Lodgings Officer, so it's up to him to sort it out, not us. Our job was to put the 'Vaccies and the foster-mothers he gave us together, not to hunt out new ones ourselves at this late stage."

The two ladies at the table were talking quietly, carefully not looking at him, but Tim could still hear every word in the now silent room. And he felt relieved. So that Elwyn Hughes, whoever he was, would find him a home even if there were no more foster-mothers here.

"But suppose he can't? He lives by himself doesn't he, so he can't look after a small boy, can he? What would people say?" Mrs. Jones asked worriedly.

"It would be even worse if we were stuck with a girl wouldn't it?" declared Mrs. Hughes. "Anyway, it'll be up to him to sort it out. But we can wait a bit longer, just in case someone turns up late. We've got these forms to sort out and we might as well do it here as anywhere else."

Tim was frightened again. If he couldn't stay with that Elwyn

Hughes, and he couldn't find him a foster-mother what would happen to him?

He remembered a picture he had seen in one of Uncle Toby's really old books they had looked at one wet Saturday afternoon. It was of a boy in Victorian times sitting on the steps of a railway station trying to shelter from the pouring rain. Underneath it was the title 'The Waif'. He'd asked Uncle Toby what a 'waif' was. Now he felt just like that boy must have felt.

It was a long worrying time later, when the forms were almost finished, that there came a clatter of feet running up the wooden stairs and all three looked towards the door with sudden hope.

"Are there any of them 'Vaccies left?" a lady asked quickly as soon as she opened the door. "I only heard about the Council paying for them an hour ago and I had to go to the Town Hall to Register, and they told me to come here."

"We've only got one left. Him." Mrs. Hughes pointed to Tim.

The lady swung round to look at him.

Tim tried to copy Belinda's nicest smile. If this lady was the only foster-mother around, then it was better to go with her than be a waif sitting on steps of a railway station in the rain.

"I wanted a girl, not him," she said finally, not softly. "Are there any other places with 'Vaccies left?"

"They'd have all gone by now. Like they have here apart from him. And there's no more 'Vaccies coming to this town, so if you don't take him, you'd have gone to all that trouble and ended up with no one."

"Oh."

"And that would be a real shame, Mrs. ...?" put in Mrs. Jones.

"Morgan."

Tim looked at the only possible foster-mother unhappily. She didn't want him, didn't seem to even like him. She wasn't a bit like Auntie Flo.

Mrs. Morgan studied him then made her decision.

"Oh alright then I'll take him. As there's no one else."

The Council ladies heaved a sigh of relief. Their problem was over. The last of the 'Vaccies was off their hands.

"If I can have your address Mrs. Morgan. And just another

couple of details. They won't take more than a minute," Mrs. Jones added hurriedly, not wanting to say anything that might make Mrs. Morgan change her mind. "And if you could send this postcard off to his parents at some time. Just to let them know where he is. It's already stamped."

"Come on lad," Mrs. Hughes said cheerfully to Tim who was already moving slowly along the line of chairs. "You'll be going with Mrs. Morgan. What's your name?"

"Tim Jackson, Miss."

"Right. Off you go then. Oh, Mrs. Morgan, he's supposed to be back here at 10 o'clock tomorrow morning. His teacher and the rest of the class will be here then because this is going to be their classroom."

"I'll see he's here. Come on then Tim, shall I carry your case?"

Wordlessly Tim handed it over, feeling near to tears. The kindly tone in Mrs. Morgan's voice now was so different from the way she had been talking about him to those other ladies only a couple of minutes ago.

They walked the few yards to the main road in silence and then past the closed shops. He heard a clock strike seven.

To think this time last night he was still at Auntie Flo's. And now he was in this strange place where everyone talked funny and he was going to have to live here for ages and ages. With a lady who didn't want him, she'd wanted a girl, and who didn't even seem to like him much.

"Is there anyone else where we're going, Mrs. Morgan?" he asked in a small voice.

"There's Mr. Morgan, my husband, and our boy, Gareth who'll be your foster-brother of course. He's thirteen. You'll be a bit of a shock to him - he's expecting me to come home with a girl. Up here."

They turned off the main road and began climbing a long hill that seemed to go straight on to the distant mountains as far as he could see

His legs began to ache. He longed for a 'carry' when Uncle Wilf would swing him up on his back and carry him for miles as though he weighed no more than a feather.

"Is it far now?" he asked.

"At the top of the hill."

Tim's heart sank. The road went straight on to those mountains - and she called it a hill! And they had to go to the top of it!

That far out in the country meant it had to be a farm of course, but if he had to walk all that distance every day to school and back! But maybe the farmer would bring him in a lorry. Or a tractor. Fancy going to school on a tractor!

"Not far now Tim."

And to his immense relief they turned down a level side road of small terraced houses, just before the tarred road became a wide stony track going on up into the mountains.

"Here we are." Mrs. Morgan took a doorkey from her bag. "I'm home," she called as she went inside, Tim following. "Shut the door after you," she added, over her shoulder.

A boy came quickly from the kitchen/living room as they went past the closed door of a front room. His smile of welcome vanished as soon as he saw Tim.

"You said you was getting us a girl 'Vaccie, Mam. And he ain't no girl."

"Clever aren't you Gareth, to notice that. This is Tim Jackson, Tim this is Gareth. Come on through and meet your foster-dad."

She went into the kitchen, Tim following, trailed by Gareth, still scowling.

A small, wiry man, was sitting in a wooden tall-backed chair with just a thin cushion by a black kitchen range. A table that was already laid for four places was set against the window that looked into a back yard.

The man looked up from the newspaper he had been reading and grinned at Tim.

"Hello there, boyo. Welcome to Wales."

Tim smiled back. The first really friendly voice he'd met since he'd arrived here.

"Hello," he replied.

In the background he heard Gareth say quietly, "You said you wanted a girl too, Mam. Can't you send him back? Or swap him for a girl with someone?"

"Now you be quiet," his mother replied, also quietly but just as audibly. "He was the only 'Vaccie left or I would have picked a girl. You make sure you're kind to him because he's come a long way to get away from the German bombs and, don't forget, they could be coming any time now." More loudly, "Tim, Gareth will show you where your room is. But be down in ten minutes because tea will be on the table then."

"Alright Mam. Come on you," grunted Gareth, and walked out, hands jammed sulkily in his pockets.

At the top of the stairs he pushed open a door with his foot.

"In there."

Tim went in and looked round the barely furnished room. A small bed was jammed against one wall, a small battered chest of drawers was against another wall at the foot of the bed facing it, with just enough room between them for the drawers to open. A wooden fold-up chair was by the bed and a mat was on the bare floorboards. But the bed had been made with new looking bedclothes.

All the same, it was nothing like the big room like a tent he had shared with Tommy and Jack at Auntie Flo's. There were no pictures on the wall, no models around. But maybe they'd let him put up some of the pictures he'd brought with him.

Gareth leaned against the door jamb, hands in his pockets watching Tim put clothes from his suitcase in the chest of drawers as he'd seen Auntie Flo do.

"What part of London do you come from?"

"Catford."

"Is that near the London Docks?"

"Do you know that part of London then?" Tim asked, looking at him with sudden interest.

"Never heard of Catford. But is it near the London Docks?"

Tim didn't really know, but he'd heard his father talking of sometimes going there.

"It's not far. Why?"

"Because them Docks are going to get blown to bits by the bombs so if you come from near there your Mam and Dad'll get blown to bits too won't they?"

Tim looked at him uncertainly, not sure how far to believe him.

"How do you know they will?" he asked finally.

"Dad said so when him and Mam were talking about having a 'Vaccie here to stay. We wanted a girl really but we're stuck with you. So you can think yourself bloomin' lucky to be here away from all that bombing. And don't you forget it."

He turned and went downstairs leaving Tim terrified. If Mum and Dad were blown to bits that'd be awful! Not just because of that, though that was awful enough, but because he'd then have to stay here for years and years and years. Right until that impossibly long time in the future when he'd be grown up himself.

"Tim! Your tea's on the table. Leave your unpacking for now and come down," Mrs. Morgan called.

Tim shut the door after him and slowly went downstairs.

A nice tea was there, with cake he saw, but he could hardly eat. He was terribly tired, homesick for Auntie Flo - and Mum and Dad were going to get blown to bits and he would have to stay here with that rotten Gareth for years and years and years. It was all too much.

"What's up then boyo?"

Tim looked up at Mr. Morgan.

"My Mum and Dad are going to get blown to bits and I'll have to stay here for years and years and years," he gulped, tears very near the surface.

"What makes you think that Tim?" asked Mrs. Morgan in a very gentle voice.

"Gareth said that he said ...," Tim nodded to Mr. Morgan, " ... that the London Docks will get blown to bits and because we live somewhere near them, then my Mum and Dad will get blown to bits too."

"Gareth's talking stupid about your Mam and Dad, Tim," snapped Mr. Morgan angrily. "And if you talk to Tim again like that Gareth, I'll take my belt to you." He turned back to Tim, his tone as gentle as Mrs. Morgan's had been. "Tim, if the Germans do drop bombs on London, your Mum and Dad will go to the Shelters, won't they? And they'll be safe in them. All the newspapers say that."

"And a lot of people have got Shelters of their own now. Have you got one?" asked Mrs. Morgan.

"Yes, we have. Some men came and dug a big hole at the bottom of our garden, poured in some stuff, I think they called it concrete, to make some walls and a floor and then put some metal stuff like half a ring on top of the walls. Then we put a load of dirt on top of that. It looked ever so strong and safe." The memory began to re-assure him. "They did that before I was Evacuated to Folkestone, so I watched them do it."

"There you are then. And the papers have said they're even building Shelters in the streets too, and they're bound to have them in all the Docks. So if your Dad was near them when the bombers came, he'd dive in them, and he'd be safe wouldn't he?" Mr. Morgan was being as convincing as he could.

"Yes, he would, wouldn't he?" Relief rang in Tim's voice, and he reached to get a sandwich from the big plate in the middle of the table.

"Does your Dad work in the Docks or will he be Called up?" Mr. Morgan asked.

"He won't be Called-up, Mum said. He drives a great big lorry for NAAFI and he takes stuff to Army Camps all over the place. And Navy and Air Force places. And my Mum said once that he takes special, secret stuff to secret camps. He's not allowed to tell even Mum what he takes then," he added, remembering how that had impressed Jack when he'd told him about that once at Folkestone. Despite himself Gareth was impressed too. His Dad didn't do anything like that.

"Are you going to be Called-up, Mr. Morgan?"

"Call me Uncle Maynard. And she's Auntie Blodwyn. No, I won't be Called-up because I'm a miner."

Tim stared at him wide-eyed.

"A miner! Uncle George, where I was before, told me about them! You must be ever so brave to go right under the ground like that to dig it out!"

Uncle Maynard looked startled, and saw that Tim's admiration was genuine. No one had ever admired him or called him brave before for being a miner.

"How thick is your coal seam? Uncle George said they can be big but sometimes they are ever so narrow."

"The one I'm working now is about three foot high. That's so high." He measured it with his hands. "Did your Uncle George show you a miner's pick?"

"No. He wasn't a miner, but he went down the one at - at ...," Tim tried to remember but couldn't. "It's near some place not far from Folkestone. But he said you went much deeper under the ground in the Wales ones."

"Then he wouldn't have shown you this."

Uncle Maynard went to the outhouse in the yard and came back carrying a short, sharp pickaxe.

"This is the kind of pick I use to dig out the coal with."

Tim examined it.

"It's smaller than the one they used to dig the hole for the Shelter at home."

"That's because we haven't got so much room to swing the pick underground. Sometimes I have to lie on my side to dig the coal out in this seam."

"Crumbs!" Tim was even more impressed.

When Tim went to bed he was much happier than when he had first arrived. Mum and Dad were going to be safe Uncle Maynard had said, so that had just been Gareth being rotten. And he thought that Auntie Blodwyn and Uncle Maynard liked him now. And fancy Uncle Maynard being a real, live miner!

Chapter 11

School life

"Gareth! Tim! Time to get up. Or you'll be late for school!"

Tim jerked awake, bewildered. Gareth? Who was Gareth? And where was he? This wasn't the room he slept in with Tommy and Jack.

Then he remembered. He had been Evacuated again. And that wasn't Auntie Flo calling him, it was Auntie ... who? He couldn't remember but it was a funny name. A Wales name.

"Now then Tim ...," his foster-mother said over breakfast, " ... I'll show you the way to your school this morning, and meet you tonight. Then when we go tomorrow, you show me the way there, and coming home, then if you get it right both ways you'll be able to go by yourself, won't you?"

"Yes Auntie ...." Tim still couldn't remember her name so he said, "Yes Auntie" again.

They had just gone a few yards down the road when Tim saw a familiar figure come out of another house with a lady that must be his foster-mother.

"Tommy! Tommy!" he yelled, dashing forward. The boy turned round.

"Tim!" he yelled, equally delighted, and dashed back to meet him.

They set off together, both exultant that they were going to be living so close together, while their foster-mothers walked together behind them.

"So how's your 'Vaccie doing, Blodwyn?" asked Tommy's while they were still close enough to hear.

"That's it!" Tim thought triumphantly. "She's Auntie Blodwyn."

Aloud, when they were far enough ahead for her not to hear, "What do you call your foster-mother, Tommy? Mine's got a funny name. She's called 'Blodwyn'."

"Mine's ordinary. She's called 'Mary'. But she thought my Mum's name was funny. But 'Jennie' isn't funny is it?"

"I don't think it is. But I'm not a Wales person."

"They're called 'Welsh' the Wales people are," Tommy told

him, a trifle smugly.

The room that was now to be their schoolroom looked different from yesterday. Mrs. Hughes and Miss Drew had moved the desks that had been piled at one end into rows, and arranged the chairs into semi-circles at the front. Mrs. Hughes and Miss Drew were chatting with some children and their foster-mothers who had already arrived. More were coming up the stairs behind them.

"Children, go to the desks now. Sit where you want to. Ladies, would you take seats please, now we're nearly all here."

Within minutes they all were.

Looking at the children, Miss Drew clapped her hands. "Quiet children. Quiet as mice please."

The familiar words had its own comfort and brought silence. Miss Drew turned to the foster-mothers.

"Thank you for bringing the children this morning, and even more for taking them into your homes. Now are there any matters you would like to raise with Mrs. Hughes or myself? We may not have all the answers, but those we don't we'll find out as soon as possible." She smiled in her friendliest way.

There were some questions about starting and finishing times, school holidays, mid-day meals, but both Miss Drew and Mrs. Hughes felt there were other things on people's minds.

"I think perhaps I should take the children out into the garden for some fresh air, and leave you to talk," Mrs. Hughes announced, standing up. "Come on children, outside and see who can find the first and best buttercup and dandelion. But you must stay inside of the gate."

There was a stampede for the door.

As the clatter on the stairs died away, Miss Drew said, "I'm sure we can all talk more freely now. So perhaps I could just make a few general comments.

"First of all these children are only six or seven years of age. They were taken from their parents and familiar homes when they were even younger, about seven months ago, and put with complete strangers. Then, even more suddenly, when they had just about got used to them, they've been suddenly whipped away and placed with more strangers in a strange place, only having had a very short time to get used to the idea of moving again.

"Secondly, they don't know how soon their parents are going to be killed." She paused to look round the foster-mothers. "It could be next week, next month, even tomorrow, whenever it is that the German bombers start raiding London, where of course, their parents still are. Unless their fathers are in the fighting Services where they are in even more danger."

She again looked round the silent foster-mothers for a moment.

"I don't want to over-dramatise the situation but that is the reality that those small children are living with. Just as you are living with that same fear if you have loved ones in the Services.

"They won't understand the details of course, but you know as well as I do that now the German forces have started their invasions, sooner or later London, and other towns, are going to be bombed as badly as Rotterdam and those towns in Denmark and Norway. And if the German troops do succeed in landing on our beaches they will be coming here at some time."

She paused and looked round them again knowing she had made the impact she'd wanted. "Now - your questions please."

Questions and comments flooded. Some were favourable to the evacuees, some were not. She found she was able to answer virtually all the questions and promised to find answers to those she needed to.

When those had been dealt with, she said, "Now I would like to ask for your help with something. Now that we are here I'm wanting the children to learn about coal mines. I can tell them a lot of things of course, but that is simply things that I have read about because I've never been down a mine myself, let alone dug out coal.

"It would be far more interesting to the children, and to me as well, if one of your husbands or sons who is a miner would come and tell the children just what it is like down there. In fact, if we could have people who do different things in a mine to talk to them, that would be even better. So if you could give me names and what they do, I could get together with them to work out some lessons for the children.

"One final matter, I have to go to a meeting this afternoon with the rest of the teachers to sort out with the education officials at the Town Hall how we are going to educate our children while they are here. So just for today could you collect the children at 2 o'clock? Then school will start at what will be the usual time of 9 o'clock tomorrow until 3.30. Thank you very much."

As the foster-mothers stood up to leave, there was a buzz of interest and now support.

A short time later Miss Drew had the children all sitting at their desks. It was just gone 11 o'clock but already she was feeling exhausted with a splitting headache.

And underlying everything was her nagging worry over Arnold, her fiance. She hadn't heard from him for three weeks and the fighting on the Continent had been very heavy.

She perched herself on the side of the desk near the children. However she felt, she had to be cheerful for their sakes.

"Now then children, we are all together again. In this nice room and with a garden for a playground. Aren't we lucky to have a garden!

"The town here, and the people might seem a bit strange at first, but so did Folkestone didn't it? But as we got to know it, we got to like it didn't we? The seaside, the ships and the countryside, which were all so different from London. It was nice wasn't it?"

There was a murmur of agreement.

"Wish I was back there now," said Clarissa loudly,

"Of course we do. But here there's all sorts of NEW things to see and find out about aren't there? And to start with I'm arranging for a real miner, who goes right under the ground to dig out our coal, to come and talk to us about it. Yes Tim?"

He had put up his hand.

"My foster-dad's a miner. And last night he showed me the pick he uses under the ground. It's smaller than the one they used to dig the hole for our Shelter at home."

"If he's the one who comes to talk to us perhaps he'll bring it along so we can all see it. Can anyone else tell us something they have found out about Wales?"

Hands went up and she knew she had their interest, and some were already beginning to look happier.

Four days later Tim, Tommy and Sam, who they found lived near them too, were making their way home through some back streets. They had found that this way though more complicated was shorter than going through the town and up the hill. Partway along Sam pointed to a tabby cat sunning itself on a window ledge.

"That cat's just like the one we've got at home!" he burst out excitedly. "Kitty, kitty, kitty," he added enticingly, rubbing his fingers together as he moved slowly towards it.

Pleased with the friendly attention, the cat began purring loudly. Sam tickled it under the chin while Tim and Tommy looked on admiring his touch with animals.

Four boys, all a few years older, stopped on the other side of the road.

"They're London 'Vaccies they are," said Evan contemptuously. "You can tell that from the stupid way they talk."

"Shall we chase 'em off then?" suggested Daffyd.

"Yeah, let's do that," Evan agreed at once.

The four crossed the road.

"Hey you. Leave that cat alone," Evan ordered.

"'S'alright," Sam replied amicably, looking over his shoulder. "We was only looking at it, not hurting it. See? It's purring. It likes us."

"It's a Welsh cat. It don't like London 'Vaccies."

"It likes us alright. Look," asserted Sam, tickling it behind the ears this time, producing more purring.

"Leave it I said," Evan snapped, giving Sam a shove, hard enough to send him sprawling on the ground.

"Leave him alone," Tim shouted, giving Evan a push in his turn.

It was Daffyd who swung the first punch, hitting Tim on the side of the face. Tim whirled to meet this attack and the fight became general, the cat vanishing with a terrified yowl.

Minutes later the boys felt hands grabbing their shoulders and arms, pulling them away from each other as adults appeared from the houses round about to put a stop to the obviously unfair fight.

"Now what's all this about?" demanded the man holding Evan and Tim apart.

There were shouted accusations, counter-accusations and denials.

"Shut it, the lot of you," shouted the man over them all. "Now you ...," he shook Evan by the arm he was holding, " ... you say what happened."

"That 'Vaccie was torturing a cat that was ...."

"He's a liar, Mister!" yelled Sam furiously. "I wouldn't torture no cat! And that one was just like our one back home."

"Liar yourself, 'Vaccie," snarled Evan.

"Anyone see how this started?" the man appealed to the small crowd, feeling he was getting nowhere.

"I did." They all swung round to stare up at a 'teenage girl half-leaning out of an upstairs window. "I was looking out and I saw them three 'Vaccies go up to Mrs. Jones's tabby. That one ....," she pointed to Sam, " ... started stroking it real gentle and them four stopped right under my window. That one ...," she pointed at Evan " ... said them three were 'Vaccies and that one ...," she pointed at Daffyd, " ... said 'Let's chase 'em off' and then they went over and started it."

"There y'are Mister!" the London boys shouted together, triumphantly.

"So why did you four pick on the three of them when you lot are all bigger?" demanded the man.

"'Cos they're yellow 'Vaccies they are!" yelled Daffyd. "Coming down here, where we don't want 'em, and they say it's to get away from bombs - when there ain't been none there."

"You're a young fool you are," snapped the man. "Haven't you seen the pictures in the papers of what the Jerries did to Rotterdam? That place in Holland? And London's going to cop it any time. The Jerries are already starting to drop bombs all around ain't they? You just wait till they get really started, and you'll be damn glad you're down here not up there. Now clear off and leave them 'Vaccies alone in future. Go on. Clear off."

He pushed Evan away and the others followed sullenly as the man stood and watched them.

"Alright lads ...," he said, turning to the three Londoners, " ... which way are you going? Up there? Okay, off you go then."

"Thanks Mister," Tim called after him, as the man went back indoors.

He just waved a hand in response, without turning round.

"And thanks Miss," Sam called out to the 'teenage girl.

Malcolm, the Depot Manager, poked his head round the Canteen door and saw the man he wanted was just about to sit down with a mug of tea in his hands.

"Ron ...," he called. " ... I've got a job for you. In my office."

Ron sighed. He had just got back from an overnight trip to half-a-dozen Camps around East Anglia and was due out on Warden Patrol tonight. Though that would be with Jennie, the longer summer daylight and so more people out working their gardens growing vegetables, meant that their use of the 'sub-Post' had become severely curtailed.

He followed Malcolm, carrying his mug of tea.

"It'll only take a minute, Ron, because I know you'll want to be off. But I need you to do a rush job down Folkestone way tomorrow."

Ron nearly spilled his tea. That could mean a chance to see Anne.

"What about my run to Colchester?"

"Trevor, the new lad, will do it."

"Fair enough. So where do I go?"

"It's a new airfield. Here." Malcolm twisted the map on his desk round for Ron to see him trace the route. "Your best way is down the A20, and then go this way."

Ron nodded and made a quick sketch of the route from the main road.

"Will it be the lorry and trailer?"

That would mean he'd be taking Tony. So he'd have to work out some kind of excuse to dump him somewhere if he was to spend any time with Anne. And that wouldn't be easy.

"The lorry only. So Tony will be able to go with Trevor and show him the drops on the route. And there'll be plenty of Erks at the airfield to help unload anyway. You'll be coming back empty."

"Fair enough," said Ron again, somehow keeping his voice

deadpan.

"Your kids were with those that were re-evacuated last month, weren't they?"

"Yeah."

"Pity. If they had still been there you could have dropped in to see them, like that other time."

Ron shrugged. "They'll be safer in Wales. Especially if there's an invasion."

He stopped at the first telephone box on the way home, praying that he'd be able to get through easily. And that Anne would be at home. She was.

"Anne? It's Ron here."

"Ron! It's so lovely to hear you so soon! I wasn't expecting .... Nothing's wrong is there? Nothing's happened to Kathleen?" She was suddenly terrified.

"No. Everything's fine. Anne, I've just been told I've got a trip down to near Folkestone tomorrow. I was wondering if there was any chance we could meet somewhere? I'll be alone on this trip so ....,"

"Tomorrow! Oh yes Ron! That'll be wonderful. Tell you what, why don't we meet at home? Here? Then I can get you something to eat. What time can you be here?"

"Early afternoon I should think. That alright?"

"It's perfect. Oh, there is one thing though ...,"

"What's that?" Ron asked, disappointment replacing the elation.

"I had thought of giving Dorothy (you remember, Mrs. Jones?) the afternoon off tomorrow. Which will mean there'll only be the two of us in the house."

A delighted grin spread over Ron's face.

"I expect we'll manage to struggle along somehow," he said.

"I'm sure we will Ron," she murmured softly.

He parked outside Anne's house as the lorry was too large to pull onto the drive. He was careful to remove the rotor arm from the distributor - not to immobilise your vehicle was now a criminal offence, and he particularly didn't want that to happen outside Anne's house. He walked up the drive trying to look casual and rang the bell.

Anne opened it immediately. She had seen him from the sitting room window where she had been waiting for the past hour.

She was wearing a light, summery dress and had bullied her hairdresser into seeing her first thing this morning, ahead of her other customers and she had been quietly confident of looking her best.

Until Ron rang the bell - when her confidence vanished. Would Ron, on seeing her, still see her in the way he had spoken to her on the 'phone so often? Or would he see her as someone not at all as he had remembered her?

And Ron was suddenly painfully conscious, facing the glamorous lady that had just opened the door to him, of being dressed in driver's overalls, that though clean this morning were not new. And he was sure he must smell of the stores he had carried today even though he had not needed to touch them himself.

"Anne, you look gorgeous!" he blurted. Not at all the sophisticated greeting he'd worked out - and now completely forgotten.

But for Anne it was the perfect thing for him to say. Her face lit up, her self-confidence restored. "Oh Ron, it's so lovely to see you at long last! Do come in."

Her spontaneous warmth restored his self-confidence too.

She shut the door after him and Ron gently took her into his arms and kissed her full on the lips.

For a split second, taken by surprise, Anne hesitated, then her arms went round his neck and she responded equally.

She held onto him feeling the strength of his hold upon her. He moved his lips to the join of her neck and shoulder, and Anne quivered as thrilling shivers swept through her.

He moved to gently touch her breasts with one hand while still having his other round her waist.

For a second she froze. That reminded her too strongly of the way Anton had acted on their first date. And then the memory vanished like a wisp.

This was Ron kissing and caressing her. Reliable, dependable Ron, who had maintained the telephone contact week after week, month after month, with no apparent chance of them ever being able to meet again.

Ron, still caressing her, looked her in the eyes.

"You really are lovely, Anne. Even more beautiful than I had remembered you," he said softly.

She smiled, her hands resting on his muscular arms, the sensations in her body still sweeping her.

"Do - do you want some tea, Ron? Or something to eat? Or - or ...," She turned her head to look very obviously at the stairs, then back to him. "Dorothy isn't here."

Anne marvelled at herself. A few months ago she would never have given such a blatant invitation to anyone. Even to Ron. But things were different now. Folkestone was having a lot of bombing, which had carefully avoided the harbour area, raids when she could be killed or crippled at any time.

And there was not just the raids either. There was the expected invasion. She was under no illusions - an inevitable part of such things was rape. And, unless she was killed first, which she half-expected anyway, she was almost assuming that would happen to her.

And she wanted to have a happy memory of genuine love-making before that.

The last war had robbed her of Gregory. She was desperate not to let this war snatch away her second chance.

And there was Ron. How long would he survive the bombing that was bound to hit London any time now? Or the invasion?

So like everyone else, she was going to grab whatever happiness there was to hand, before it was gone for ever.

He drew her towards the stairs.

To Ron her bedroom was a delight of feminine elegance, that he felt perfectly mirrored the type of person Anne was.

Kissing and caressing her gently, he undressed her as though it was the most natural thing in the world for them to do. He gently lay her on the bed. She watched him, a serious expression on her face, with thrills of anticipation sweeping through her as he stripped quickly

Afterwards, she was never sure whether at her climax she whispered, 'Oh Gregory, my love', or whether that was only an echo in her mind.

Ron never referred to it, if she had said it, and his manner to her never wavered.

As they lay together afterwards Anne was filled with wonder at the experience Ron had given her. Alright, it was her first time, but how on earth could May have described Ron as being unenterprising and deadly dull? With her, he had taken control of their love-making, taken her to heights of ecstasy she had never imagined possible and murmured words of love to her that filled her with a wonderful sense of being treasured by the man she loved.

Ron, as he lay with one hand stroking Anne, shot a heartfelt message of thanks to Jennie. For it was she who had taught him how to 'pleasure' a woman, as she had called it. And that Anne had been 'pleasured', she had made plain.

And he knew his feelings for Anne had changed. He knew they had become deeper over the months. But meeting her again, and after this shared love-making, he ....

Slashing into their peaceful, cocooned world, a close-by air raid siren screamed. Ron's Warden training sent him leaping from the bed to his clothes before his conscious mind registered what he was doing.

"Ron!" Anne's plaintive cry as she sat up, wrenched him back to this reality.

He stopped hauling his shirt over his head to look at her.

She blushed, lifted the bedclothes to cover herself, then flung them aside.

"It's a bit late to try to be modest in front of you now, Ron," she laughed as she dived towards her own clothes. "Do you want to go to the place under the stairs or do you want to eat what I've got ready? And do you have time for either?"

Ron listened a moment. There was no sound of aero-engines, bombs or gunfire.

"Huddling close to you under the stairs sounds good. But can I eat with you instead if it stays peaceful?"

"Of course." Clothed now she went to his arms. "I'm so glad you can spend a little more time with me Ron," she said softly.

"I'm going to be held up really badly by traffic and Alerts going back to London," he grinned.

"Then if ...?"

"Don't worry Anne. I said last time that's the standard excuse for a lorry driver." He looked into her eyes and said seriously, "Anne, you are the most desirable, loving person I've ever met." He kissed her long and gently.

Anne clung to him. She wasn't going to let herself be unhappy yet. That would come later, after he had gone. But that was only because he had gone, and because they did not know when he could come back again.

Not for what they had done together.

Chapter 12
The bombers come

Ron and Tony had almost finished loading their lorry and trailer at the dockside when they heard the wail of a distant siren.

"Jerry again Tony."

"Yeah," Tony responded sourly, ramming the last few cases aboard the lorry. "Wonder who'll cop it this time? One thing, the raids ain't been too heavy, just a few ...,"

Closer sirens sounded.

"Get a move on. It could be us this time," Ron was suddenly urgent.

Tony rammed the last case in as Ron dashed for the driver's cab. Tony slammed the big doors of the trailer shut.

The siren just outside the Gate wailed into deafening life, as the drone of aero-engines suddenly became louder.

"Bugger me! Look at that!" whispered a docker standing by Ron's cab with a clipboard ready for Ron to sign. "They must be coming for us this time. And look at 'em all!"

Tony glanced into the sky as he dashed for the cab. The sky was filling with apparently hundreds of bombers and fighters heading straight up the Thames, harried by fighters as they had been from the coast but tracking steadily through the bursts of anti-aircraft shells exploding near or among them.

Ron revved the engine and rammed into gear as Tony slammed his door and the docker began a run for the Shelter. Ron leaned on the horn as the heavy lorry and trailer began lumbering towards the Gate.

The policeman on duty swung both gates wide as Ron approached so he would not have to stop.

Ron slowed briefly as he came to the main road then swung to the right, away from the whistling of the bombs already on their way down and the crump of the first explosions.

The main road ran parallel with the Docks with narrow side streets leading off on the side away from the river, too narrow for this lorry and trailer. But 100 yards on was a wider road that he could get down.

Tony was leaning far out of his window, staring back the way they had come.

"Ron! You can't outrun them bombers! They're catching up!" he yelled.

"How far are they spread out this side of the river?"

"'Undreds of yards! And if you don't get off this road bloody quick they'll be laying their eggs right on top of us!"

"Corner coming up. Hold tight!"

Ron swung the wheel and the lorry swirled round the corner.

The trailer mounted the pavement, missed the corner of a shop by less than twelve inches and then they were roaring up the side street, horn blaring, Ron's foot hard down on the accelerator.

They crossed one intersection, then another, and another and then they were away from the track of the main bomber stream that were concentrating on the ribbon of Docks on the river.

Ron slowed and stopped.

"How far back did they start dropping the bombs Tony?"

"Not far from the Arsenal. Or on it."

"That's what I thought," said Ron quietly. He was feeling a mixture of relief and guilt at feeling that relief.

Jennie was not on this shift at the Arsenal. She had been on earlies this week so would be safe at home by now. But others would be dead or injured, because it had been their shift.

He watched as the last of the bomber stream finished their run and turned for home.

He started driving forward.

"The Depot's that way Ron. We got our full load just in time." Tony jerked his thumb over his shoulder.

"That's right. And the bomb damage is this way."

He swung the wheel to head back towards the river.

Tony stared at him, then shrugged.

Moments later Ron braked. Yards ahead the side road heading back down to the Docks was blocked with rubble from a destroyed row of houses.

"Come on," Ron switched off the engine and got out of the

cab.

"No thanks. I saw more than enough dead and injured in the last war, so I'll stay right here and look after the lorry."

Ron glared at him through the open door.

"We're not going gawping. We're going to pull people out of that stuff. So come on."

He went round to raise the bonnet, took out the rotor arm, dropped the bonnet with a crash and set off at a run.

"Oh bugger it!" Tony growled. But set off after him.

Ron stopped by the nearest pile of wreckage. He listened. Was that a child's whimper?

"Anybody under there?" Ron yelled. "Shout or scream but just answer."

"Thank Gawd! Yes, mate. Under 'ere."

Ron began throwing aside timbers and bricks.

"How many of you?"

"Me, me missus and two kids."

"Tony, get shifting that stuff from there," ordered Ron, pointing. "Any injuries down there?" he called out.

"Me leg's broke I think. Otherwise okay. We got under the table just in time."

"Good for you. Now keep talking so we can keep track of you. How old are your kids?"

Ron kept them talking as he and Tony dug through the wreckage. Then Ron knelt to peer through a gap.

"I can see a table. Hello kids. We'll soon have you out of there. Tony, give us a hand with this rafter. The other end is on top of the table. With a bit of luck I can lever it up for them to crawl through."

His idea worked. Ron rested the end of the rafter on his shoulder, holding it with both hands, supporting more wreckage with it.

"Right Tony. I'll hold this up while you get through to pull the kids out. You're smaller than me to get through that gap. You come out backwards pulling them. Got it?"

"You reckon I'm a bleedin' 'ero, don't you Ron Jackson?" Tony grumbled, already crawling into the tunnel. "And I ain't. I'm a ruddy coward I am. Now kids, which of you's coming out first?"

A grimy hand and a small, scared face appeared. as Tony pushed aside a lump of masonry, helped by a man's hand.

"Come on ducks. What's your name?"

"Melissa," the three year old answered, the fear beginning to fade from her face.

"Both hands Melissa and I'll pull you out. That's it." Tony grasped her wrists. "Give her a shove behind."

Then he was crawling backwards, pulling the little girl.

Once in the open, "Go and stand over by that big man there, Melissa while I get your sister out."

"It's me bruvver."

"Your brother then." Tony was already back into the gap.

After the boy he got the woman out, shaking and fighting to control her tears. The man had already begun crawling out after her, dragging his broken leg, when Tony started to go back the fourth time. He helped him out the last few yards

"Everyone out?" gasped Ron, still straining to hold up the wreckage with the rafter.

"That's everyone," confirmed the man, staring at the wreckage of his home. "Blimmee! That little lot's going to cost me landlord a bob or two to fix!"

As Ron tipped the rafter off his shoulder, to crash down, the man stared down the wreckage-strewn road towards the Docks where flames were now leaping up with a roar.

"You okay Tony?" Ron asked.

"Yeah. What about the next house?"

Ron slapped his shoulder. "Good for you Tony." He turned to the man. "You got somewhere to go mate?"

"Sarah's got a sister up the road. Looks as though her place was missed by the bombs."

"Right. A First Aid Post will be set up round here soon, so you can see about getting your leg fixed there. The rest of you can go to your relatives." He swung back to Tony, that problem being sorted. Other people would have to be the ones to give them further help. "Come on Tony."

An hour later Ron turned from helping load a body into an ambulance and found Tony beside him supporting an elderly man waiting for a place in the ambulance too. He looked around. Firemen, Wardens and volunteers were there now.

"I reckon we can go Tony," he said quietly. "They've got plenty of people here now. I'll just let the Chief Warden know."

Tony looked round while he waited for Ron to come back. And decided he had never felt so good. He'd hauled more people out of wreckage, been thanked by terrified but now re-assured people who believed he had saved their lives, and been told by Wardens and Firemen that he had done a great job.

Ron came back, filthy, dust-covered, a wide smear of blood across one sleeve of his overalls from a badly injured 'teenager. Tony's overalls were scarcely better.

"Let's go Tony."

As they made the half-hour trip back to the Depot, both men were silent until they were nearing the Gate.

"Is what we did back there what you do in the Wardens, Ron?"

"Part of it. What we did back there was what we call 'Initial Rescue'. But we also do First Aid, Casualty Evacuation, Salvage Collecting, and Recording."

"Oh." Tony hesitated. "Are there still any vacancies?"

"Should think so. Your best bet would be to ask at the Wardens' Post nearest to where you live. And after what you did today, I'll give you a first-class reference if you want one."

"Where the ruddy hell ...?" Rod, the Deputy Foreman began as he came out to meet them. He stopped as they climbed down from the cab and he saw the state they were in. "You'd better come and have some tea. The kettle's just boiled."

When they were sitting down, "The lorry's in one piece so I guess you got out of the Docks before they were hit. So how did you get in that state?"

"It was Ron's fault," said Tony promptly. "I was scared stiff and wanted to run but he insisted."

"You scared?" Ron scoffed. "Rod, what that clown went and did was ...,"

Rod listened as they talked, each of what the other had done as they unwound from the shock of their first close experience of bombing.

By the time Ron was still not home two hours later than the time he'd expected, May was certain he had been killed in the Dock's bombing. She knew he was to load up there sometime today, and distant though they were from the Docks she had heard the rumble of the explosions of hundreds of bombs and the crash of the anti-aircraft guns.

She felt cold with fear despite the warmth of the day. Fear of what must have happened to him, the agonies he might have been in before dying. Or had he been killed instantly? How would she tell the children he was dead when she had assured them repeatedly that he would be safe even though they had stayed in London?

How would she manage for money? She had some as Ron had given her the housekeeping last night. But they had no savings to fall back on so she'd have to get a job of some kind. But who would look after Frank while she was working?

As Ron peddled the last couple of hundred yards home, the calm of this street seemed a million miles away from the carnage he had just come from. Thankfully he opened the front door into his familiar home that was still in one piece, not a pile of rubble. And there was May coming to meet him in the hall. Safe and sound. And Frank running after her.

"May ...," he began, about to tell her how thankful he was that she was safe and well, not among the dead and injured he had just come from.

"You might have taken the trouble to spend just a few coppers and a couple of minutes to 'phone the Wardens' Post to let me know that you were not dead in the Docks but sitting in the Depot guzzling tea and gossiping," she snapped freezingly.

Ron stared at her unbelievingly, his words dying on his lips.

"And next time you're going to be this late, you'd better make sure you do just that because next time I won't be sitting here like a stuffed dummy meekly wait you to roll up just when you happen to feel like it."

"May ....," Ron said in a low very controlled voice, " ... I was lucky enough to get out of the Docks seconds before the first bombs hit. Then me and Tony went back to wrecked houses. And we've been digging out dead bodies, smashed bodies of men, women and children since then. Ten year olds like Kitty. Six year olds like Tim. Babies like Frank. Some had been blown to bits, but some were still alive. Some were injured, some not. Some we got out of wreckage just seconds before more walls fell on them which would have killed them. Or the fires that would have burned them alive. Would you really have wanted us to just drive away and not do anything to help? What if it had been this house that had been hit and those kids had been Kitty, or Tim or Frank?

"Sure. I could have 'phoned the Post. But you know damn well because I've told you enough times, that that 'phone is for War Emergencies only, not a Message Centre for your personal convenience. Especially with a raid on." He snatched his helmet and haversack from its peg. "I'm going to the Post. I'm on Duty."

"Ron! I didn't ...,"

But Ron's slamming the front door cut her off just as the siren at the end of the road began its wail.

As sirens were to do continually as German bombers came back constantly that night, and succeeding days and then nights, to bomb the heart out of London. A bombing that made the bombing of Rotterdam seem almost small in comparison, and was the presager of what was to follow on Coventry, Liverpool and many other cities.

When Ron walked into the Post, Ralph was sticking pins into the big wall map of London along the Thames going up-river from Woolwich Arsenal.

"The bombs hit a bit further out from the Thames on the south side than that Ralph. Out to about there I should think." Ron touched the map over Ralph's shoulder.

Ralph turned round and saw the state of his overalls.

"What the hell's happened to you Ron?"

Because this was the first time anyone in the Post had had first-hand experience of the real thing, Ron went into detail. As he was talking Wardens dashed in to report and go to their Sectors, but stayed to listen. Jennie came in, heard a few words and made and silently handed him a mug of hot, sweet tea. When he had finished Ralph looked round the silent group.

"So that's how it's done. Thank God our training seems to be pretty spot on. Okay. Get off to your Sectors, and remember Ron's experience if it happens like that round here." After the others except Jennie had gone, "You okay Ron or do you want to go off now rather than later?"

"I'm alright. And I'd sooner be out." He had no wish at all to go home.

Ralph nodded, guessing there were undercurrents around somewhere.

"Fair enough Ron. But let me know if you do decide you want to go off early."

Ron and Jennie left to patrol their Sector.

"What's the matter Ron? Has what you saw got to you?" Jennie asked after they had walked some way in silence. "Or is there something else wrong?"

They walked on, the thunder of bombs falling again on the area around the river and the anti-aircraft guns a rumble in the distance.

"When I got to the end of our road after digging those people out of all that wreckage, kids as well, and everything round here was so - normal, I felt ... well how tremendously lucky I was. That the house was still there - and that May and you were alright. And that Kitty and Tim were safe in Wales."

Jennie said nothing at the bracketing of May and her together, not sure how she felt about that. What had started with Ron had been a simple and uncomplicated sex thing, but over the months her feelings for Ron had deepened quickly. Now she was ....

"Then I walked indoors ...," Ron interrupted her thoughts, " ... happy, relieved and really pleased to see May coming into the hall to meet me, safe and well after all I had just seen. Out of the blue she slung at me that I hadn't rung the Post to get a message sent to her that I was alright. She knew I was going to be loading at the Docks some time today, but that could just as easily have been this morning as this afternoon. In fact it would have been, but we got held up at the Depot. And she knows damn well that the Post 'phone is only for Emergencies and that's even more so when a raid's on."

"I can understand why May reacted like that," Jennie said quietly, a few yards later.

"You what?" Ron demanded incredulously.

"I can understand why May reacted the way she did," Jennie repeated. "If I had known that you were going to be anywhere near the Docks and could have been in the middle of that lot ...," she waved a hand at the sky glowing red from the still burning fires, " ... then I'd have been frantic too."

"You would?" And remembered. "But your parents live over there don't they?"

"Not now, thank God. A farm in Kent where they used to go hop-picking every year was short-staffed and the farmer asked Dad to go there permanently. So they moved there a couple of months ago.

"But to get back to you and May. You mustn't blame her Ron. Haven't you ever told off one of your kids when you'd been terrified for them and then found they were safe after all? I did that with Tommy once when I lost him in Lewisham. And that was for only ten minutes. But I gave him such a telling off! And May would have been thinking a lot worse had happened to you. She must have thought you were dead. Or crippled. So no wonder she was frantic."

They walked on again.

"Jennie. You said that you'd have been 'frantic' too."

After a pause. "Yes."

"'Bothered', I can understand. But 'frantic'? Like May?"

"Yes. 'Frantic'. Because – because I love you, you big baboon!"

They faced each other in the pitch darkness of the blackout.

"You ...? Oh Jennie."

He took her in his arms, and they kissed gently, then more urgently as the memory of what could have happened to him, engulfed them both.

"Ron Jackson, if you ever let yourself get killed, I'll - I'll ...," she stammered in a muffled voice, her face buried in his shoulder.

"Kill me?" he suggested, a smile in his voice.

"Yes. At least that." She hugged him again, then stood back to straighten her hair by feel. "Thank God for the blackout or the whole neighbourhood would have seen us."

They walked on again, arms round each other, each busy with their thoughts, knowing that what Jennie had said signalled a change in their relationship.

And Jennie was now wishing she hadn't said it at all. Before, 'without strings' had suited them both, because both were living for the moment like so many others were, leaving the future to take care of itself. Because in wartime anything can happen at any time. As could have happened in the Docks today to Ron. Or if it had been her shift at the Arsenal.

But now it had been said.

"Jennie ...," began Ron hesitantly.

"No Ron. Don't say anything. I shouldn't have said what I did. You're a married man with three kids, I'm a married woman with one kid. And we live next door to each other." She faced him. "We said 'without strings' at the start and that's still got to apply. It will as far as I'm concerned, and it's got to apply to you. Or - or I'll go away and not tell you where I'm going. The complications of anything else are too – simply too horrendous to even think about."

"Okay Jennie, okay. But can we still carry on as we have been? Still 'without strings'?"

"If you want to."

"Thank God for that!" Ron took her in his arms and held her close. "I do want to."

"Me too."

Ron hurled her bodily over the low garden fence, landing on top of her, almost winding her.

The massive explosion as the bomb, that Ron had heard whistling down bare seconds before it hit the house opposite, shredded the fence they were lying by. Debris cascaded down onto and around them.

Ron leaped to his feet.

"You alright Jennie?"

"Yes," she replied shakily and breathlessly. "Was that a bomb or you being enthusiastic?"

"A bomb. Get to the 'phone at the Brown's if it's still working, and report to the Post. Then get back here."

As Jennie ran off Ron dashed across the road.

Flames were leaping up from a shattered gas cooker, threatening to start more fires, adding to those already burning.

The house that had taken the direct hit was wrecked totally, others nearby on both sides of the street were badly damaged.

"Get stirrup pumps and water," he yelled to the few neighbours now emerging, as he climbed over the wreckage to the blazing cooker. "Does anyone know where the gas stopcock is?"

"I know." A sixteen year old boy was clambering towards him. "It'll be just round here. I live three doors down, same kind of house."

They began throwing wreckage aside to get at a smashed cupboard. Other neighbours joined in.

"Anyone know if people were in the house?" shouted Ron, still working.

"John, the lad that lives here, told me this afternoon they were going to start sleeping in the Shelter tonight because of the bombing in the Docks," volunteered Trevor.

"I'll check that out. You others get to the gas and turn it off. And get those stirrup pumps going."

In the light of the fires Ron climbed over the rubble to the garden path and ran up to the half-buried Shelter. Behind the blast wall, the door of the Shelter was open. He flashed his torch inside. It was empty.

"Damn!" he muttered.

As he ran back to the houses the cooker fire snuffed out. And stirrup pumps were being used on the others.

"Quiet everyone!" Ron shouted. "They're not in the Shelter so it looks as though they are under this lot. I want to check."

Silence fell. The raid had gone further into London and the drone of aero-engines kept up just a background noise.

"Anyone under the wreckage there?" yelled Ron. "Shout or scream, but let us know you're there."

No answer.

"Everyone listen carefully. I'll try again," Ron shouted again.

"I think I heard a groan over here, Warden."

Ron got across using his shielded torch.

"Here?"

"Yep. Thought it was anyway."

Ron peered down, trying to probe through the tangle of bricks timber and furniture. He needed more light if he was to stand any chance of seeing anything. He pulled the shielding off his torch. Shining it down he thought he caught a glimpse of something white. He flashed the torch around the closest walls of neighbouring houses to check how stable they were.

"Put that light out!" shouted an on-looker, trying for a laugh.

The perpetual cry of the Wardens.

"Do something useful for once in your life, you bloody idiot! Get over here and shift some wreckage," Ron rapped, irritated.

Jennie arrived back panting.

"Got through to the Post, Ron. Reinforcements coming, ambulances too. Said you had the fires under control so didn't need firemen. There aren't any to spare anyway. They're all at the Docks."

"Right. Check the houses next door, both sides. Check if the neighbours know whether they were occupied tonight. You know the drill."

"Got it." Jennie moved off.

Ron shone his torch into the wreckage again.

"There is someone down there. Woman I think. Anyone know their name?"

"Gladys Evans," It was the sixteen year old again.

"Mrs. Evans. Gladys," shouted Ron "Can you hear me?"

There was no response or movement that he could see.

"Shift that, that and that," Ron snapped, pointing. "Then I might be able to get to her."

They were shifted. Ron hung head downwards into the gap, He got a hand down and touched her face. It was icy cold. He touched the side of her neck, and thought he detected a faint fluttering pulse.

"She's alive. Help me get this stuff moved. We'll start here, but don't let anything fall onto her. Check carefully first, every time."

"Warden. I think there could be someone here," a voice shouted a few yards away.

Steven had been copying Ron, shining a torch down through the wreckage moving from spot to spot. "

"Keep going to reach Mrs. Evans. I'll check this one out." He moved across. "What have you found?"

"I think it could be a leg. See? Down there."

"You're right mate." Ron raised his voice. "I need more volunteers over here."

They heard an ambulance arrive.

"Stretcher needed here. Casualty." Jennie's voice shouted from where Gladys Evans had been found.

"And here," Steven shouted, close to Ron's ear.

"Give us a hand with this," Ron ordered taking hold of a length of broken floorboarding.

Together they heaved it up and thrust it clear. Ron shone his torch down.

"Oh my God!" Steven choked and turned away to vomit.

Ron stared down at the shattered head, crushed under the rafter, nausea rising in his own throat.

"Stretcher here. Where's the casualty, Warden?" a voice said beside him.

"No hurry with this one, mate. He's dead." Ron shone his torch down again for the ambulance man to see.

"Mum! Dad! What's happened? Where's my Mum and Dad?" a boy's voice rose to a half-scream.

"That'll be John, their son. He must have been out somewhere." muttered Steven.

Ron went across to meet him. Another of a Warden's jobs. Neighbours were grouped around the 15 year old boy who was crying and shaking with shock, a lady having an arm round his shoulders.

"What's your name son?" Ron asked with a calming authority, even though Steven had just told him.

"John - John Evans." The boy got an edge of control in his voice. "Mister, what's happened to my Mum and Dad? Are they alright?"

"I'm sorry John. Your house took a direct hit. Your Dad didn't make it, but your Mum was alive when I got to her." He looked round and saw a stretcher being loaded into the ambulance. "That'll be her. Being put into the ambulance."

The ambulance doors slammed, and next second, bell ringing, it was off.

"Mum!" John screamed, starting to run after it

"Hold it son." Ron grabbed his arm. "They've got to get her to the hospital as quick as they can so they can't stop to wait for you, can they? Anyone know where it's gone to?" he added to the crowd.

"I heard 'em say Lewisham," contributed a volunteer.

"Right. Now listen to me John. You can go to the hospital to see your Mum tomorrow. So is there somewhere you can go to for tonight?"

"I - I could try my girl friend's, I suppose. But her Dad don't like me."

"You can stay with us till things get sorted, John," said Steven coming up.

Ron turned away. There was still more work to be done here, maybe more people to be pulled out from the damaged houses. Others were taking care of John.

Hours later Jennie and Ron walked home together silently, the final tidying up of the wreckage would be done tomorrow in daylight.

"It was a lot less than what they've got to cope with over there," Ron nodded in the direction of the Docks area where the sky was still lit by raging fires.

"It must be awful. We only had one bomb to deal with. They must have had hundreds."

They turned into their road.

"May will be glad for the message you sent her from the Brown's saying ...," Jennie began off-handedly.

"Message?" interrupted Ron, puzzled. "I didn't send any message. Oh Lord, I suppose I should have done. Oh hell. Now I'll get another dose of belly-aching from her."

"As far as May is concerned you did send a message, Ron. I told the Brown's to tell her that you told me to tell them that you were fine but you and I would be busy dealing with the bomb and there was no need for her to worry."

"But ...,"

"Listen Ron, I'm sure you'd have told me to do it if rescuing those people hadn't been so much at the front of your mind, so we'll take the will for the deed and then I don't get May calling me a liar tomorrow."

"Thanks Jennie. You're a great girl."

"You just keep on thinking like that, Ron Jackson."

They stopped at her gate, both conscious that May might be watching out for Ron from a darkened room.

"Goodnight Jennie."

"Goodnight Ron."

As soon as Ron had shut the front door, May ran to him and threw her arms round his neck.

"Ron, I'm so sorry for the way I spoke to you earlier. And thanks for letting me know you were safe after that bomb fell. I'd have been sure it had got you if you hadn't."

As Ron put his arms round her, he thanked heaven for Jennie thinking of it. And thinking to tell him. Otherwise he'd have really put his foot in it!

"I've moved all the bedding into the Shelter. With the bombing of the Docks, and this, it looks as though it's really starting."

Chapter 13
Close call

A week later May had just laid Frank down on the settee for his afternoon nap, when there came a soft knock at the front door. With an irritated sigh May hurried to answer it in case whoever it was made a louder banging and woke him up.

"Hello Linda. Anything wrong?"

May knew Linda slightly as she worked in the local newsagents and lived in one of the blocks of flats behind May's house. The quiet, shy mother of a twenty year old son, now Called-up, there was no husband around and depending on which gossip was believed she was a widow, a deserted wife or an unmarried mother with her 'Mrs' being by courtesy rather than by matrimony.

"I can't stop now May, I'm just going back to work but - look, would you mind terribly if I came into your Shelter for tonight? Just for tonight? Please. I - I don't like to ask but ...." She stopped, tongue-tied, partly with embarrassment, but, now more transparently, sheer terror.

"Well - yes. Of course. Ron's away tonight driving, so that will be easy enough."

"Oh thank you May," Linda's relief was tangible. "Can I come at say, 7 o'clock?" Suddenly she seemed anxious to get away.

"Fine. See you later then."

May was puzzled because the blocks of flats had Shelters of their own, big ones to take all the flats' tenants. But, it suddenly occurred to her, maybe Linda had had a bad experience in hers. While it was no problem tonight, which was all she'd asked for, if she was thinking of it as a permanency, when Ron was at home there would be. Because there was no privacy, and no room, in their small family shelter. So after tonight she'd suggest she could ask Jennie as she was alone in hers. Maybe she'd even be glad of the company.

Exactly on time, Linda knocked on the door, carrying a large cake tin and a shopping bag, with another large bag over her shoulder.

"I've brought a chocolate cake I've made, and some tea, milk and sugar," she said in a rush as soon as May opened the door to her.

"You didn't have to do that Linda!" May exclaimed, but delighted all the same. "Come into the kitchen, I've got the kettle on." Once in the kitchen, "Where on earth did you get the things for a chocolate cake nowadays? Or shouldn't I ask?"

"I've - well the truth is May, I've got a little store of things. You see, I always look on the dark side of things so I expected that there would soon be war, after Chamberlain came back from seeing Hitler that time, waving that silly bit of paper and ...."

"Did you? So did I!"

"Really? Well I began gradually buying in things then, things that would keep. And - and I've got a friend who lives in the country and he lets me have things from time to time. Eggs for example."

"Lucky you," May said enviously. Then quickly in case Linda thought she was going to ask about the 'friend who lives in the country' (which she wanted to) or cadge something (which she wasn't) she asked casually, "Is something wrong with the flats' Shelters Linda? Has something happened in them?"

Linda hesitated. "No. Not yet. But I know it will tonight."

"How do you know that Linda?" May asked quietly as she poured boiling water into the tea pot. She emphasised the 'know' as well.

Linda hesitated again, then decided May's question was genuine.

"Do you believe in Premonitions, May?"

"Yes."

Linda was relieved at May's unequivocal reply.

"Then you'll know what I mean by 'know'."

May handed her the tea.

"Are you sure it is a Premonition Linda and not just the worry we've all got?"

"It's a Premonition," Linda said flatly, with such certainty that May felt a chill run up her spine.

"Well, we have to take notice of Premonitions Linda. I always do."

They heard distant air raid warning sirens. Linda's head

snapped up as almost immediately, the siren at the end of the road started.

"Time to go," May said abruptly. She whipped the tea things onto a tray. "You take these, I'll take Frank."

As they hurried down the path, nearby anti-aircraft guns opened up as the drone of bombers came closer.

"I'll go in first with Frank," May said as they reached the two-brick thick 'blast wall' in front of the low Shelter door.

She sat on the edge of the entrance, kicked off her shoes and slid in. She put Frank on his bunk, took the tray from Linda who was huddling petrified behind the blast wall. She dived into the Shelter as May quickly lit a candle before shutting the thick wooden door and sliding the bolt across.

"There. We're safe and sound now Linda. So will you cut the cake while I settle Frank?"

Linda relaxed visibly.

"I can't say how much I appreciate you letting me into your Shelter May. I must have sounded really silly coming to you like that. But I know something awful is going to happen tonight."

"Don't worry about it Linda," interrupted May. "You have to listen to Premonitions. As I said, I always do."

The rumble of exploding bombs penetrated into the Shelter, going on for nearly half-an-hour before the drone of aero-engines faded away and the guns fell silent.

"Closer, but not on us. I'm going out for a look."

May opened the door and climbed out. She looked all around. Fires were blazing, lighting up the sky, not only in the direction of the Docks but up-river too. And more were over in the Croydon direction. The All-Clear siren sounded and May knelt to look into the Shelter.

"Do you want to come out for a breath of fresh air, Linda? Because we'll have to get back in sooner or later, I'll be bound."

Linda joined her outside, but minutes later the warning sirens began again. A pattern that lasted for hours as bomber streams came back repeatedly. Each time they sat back in their positions on the bedding, hugging their knees and listening.

"Bombs again. Coming closer than before," whispered Linda

tense and wide-eyed with fear.

May nodded in the dim candle light. "They've started a long way out from the Docks this time."

More explosions, closer still, and Frank began to cry as he was woken. May picked him up to comfort him.

"This is their 'terror bombing', isn't it May? There's nothing military around here," jerked Linda.

More explosions. Close by. Closer still.

Then came a massive double explosion, sounding almost as one, that shook the underground Shelter itself. Both Frank and Linda screamed as May shot out a hand to grab the candle holder before it fell from the ledge onto the bedding.

The Shelter shuddered repeatedly as huge pieces of debris crashed down onto the three feet of earth covering the corrugated steel roofing.

Screaming hysterically, Linda slumped sideways, curling into a foetal position, frightening Frank still more.

May leaned across and slapped her face.

"Linda! Shut up! You're frightening Frank, and you're perfectly safe," she yelled.

More explosions still, but they began fading into the distance as the bomber stream went on its way.

May herself was shaking. Nothing had ever been that close before, or that big as to actually shake the Shelter.

The two women began to relax and Frank quietened.

Fire engine and ambulance bells could be heard, some close by.

"It sounds as though the worst is over for now. Take Frank while I go out for a look."

May opened the door, and paused, listening. There was an odd flickering red glow outside and a strong smell of burning all around her. And a lot of shouting going on nearby.

She levered herself out and looked around in the darkness.

"Oh my God!" she exclaimed.

"What's the matter? What's happened? What can you see?" demanded Linda, still crouching inside the Shelter, clutching Frank.

"Put Frank in his bunk and come out for a look. He'll be

alright."

Linda clambered up beside May

"Oh my God!" she whispered. "Just look at that! The flats! And the Shelter. Where I would have been!"

The three-story block of flats where Linda lived was a gutted blazing inferno. The Shelter for those flats had a huge gaping hole in it.

"It must have been one of those massive sea mines they've taken to dropping to do that to that Shelter," Linda went on. "May. If you hadn't taken me in ...."

"It was your Premonition, Linda. Oh Lord!" she added in sudden consternation.

Linda turned to follow May's look at her house and the others in the long row of terraced houses, lit by the flames from the burning flats. All the windows had gone, and a lot of the tiles in May's house and more of the nearer neighbours.

"May! That's awful! Your house has gone!"

May grinned in spite of the shock.

"Yours has even more gone, Linda. Keep an eye on Frank while I check the state of the building."

She reached into the Shelter for the big torch they kept by the door but which they used only very sparingly. Batteries were hard to come by.

"May? It's Des. From the Post. Are you alright?" shouted a voice from where their fence had been.

"Yes. I was just going to check the house."

"Hang on a sec. I'll come with you."

As he clambered over the debris of the flats, the All-clear sounded again.

"This is Linda. We decided she'd spend the night here. If we hadn't she'd have been in that lot." May waved a hand at the wrecked flats and Shelter.

"Then the Good Lord was really with you tonight Linda. Just about everyone in both were killed."

May and he checked over the house as well as they could with their torches as other neighbours were checking theirs.

"Stupid though it sounds May, I think you've been pretty lucky, all things considering. The blast seems to have gone straight through the house. Okay, it took the windows and some tiles, but at first look the structure itself still seems solid enough. We'll get a tarpaulin over the roof till proper repairs can be made and plug the windows."

May felt a degree of comfort. Des was an architect so he knew about such things.

Inside, some of the furniture had been damaged but Ron and she would be able to fix it. More or less. Some glasses and pictures were cracked and the kitchen cabinet had had a door ripped off.

"Look at that May! That'll make a good bomb story for the local paper," Des pointed.

Inside the cabinet, a jar of marmalade had been smashed to splinters. But right beside its remains on the shelf was an egg. Not even cracked.

Chapter 14
Evacuation relations

For Tim, Tommy and Sam, the summer holidays came as a welcome respite. Not simply escape from the rigours of school, but from the daily problem of choosing their way home, either to go through the town or the back streets, to avoid meeting Evan, Daffyd and the others. Whenever they met there was always name-calling that the Londoners were 'yellow' to come to Wales when no bombs had hit London, which led inevitably to fights unless there was speedy intervention by adults.

The holidays meant that their paths from school to home, which were on the opposite sides of the town for both, no longer crossed.

The long summer holiday also meant that Tim and Gareth saw more of each other even though Tim spent as much time out with Tommy and Sam as possible. But on wet days, when both perforce stayed in, their bickering was almost continuous.

A fight nearly erupted when Auntie Blodwyn was out one day and Gareth snatched a comic out of Tim's hands on his way past him. But this time Tim went after him and snatched it back as Gareth sat down in his father's chair. He leaped up to get it again.

"Come on then Gareth. You just try to get it back," Tim snarled, tossing the comic behind him and putting up his fists.

He was fed up with Gareth, and Uncle Toby had told him you had to stand up to bullies and when you did they often backed down. And Mum had said the same kind of thing, years ago.

The many fights with Evan over the months had toughened Tim, and Gareth suddenly realised that if he was to get the comic back he would have to fight Tim for it, and much younger though Tim was, Gareth was not at all sure that he would win. And even if he did, it would not be easy.

"Didn't want to read the silly thing anyway. It's only for stupid kids," he sneered to save face as he sat down again.

Tim sat down at the table to read the comic, elated. After this Gareth certainly wouldn't be so keen to bully him again! And he laughed out loud frequently, twisting round to look at Gareth to show just how good the comic really was.

But the holiday ended and the Blitz on London began.

"The paper said yesterday that our 'planes always shoot some of the Jerries down, so they can't keep the raids going much longer. Not with their planes getting shot down all the time," declared Sam confidently as they talked yet again on their way to school on the first day of the new term.

"But they must be making more 'planes all the time too," Tim said gloomily. "And they're shooting ours down as well, ain't they?"

"The thing is, who's going to run out of 'planes first?" Tommy had asked the vital question.

"I hope Auntie Flo's alright," muttered Tim. "Uncle Maynard's paper said Folkestone's been bombed again. And Mum and Dad in London."

Suddenly, round the corner came Evan, Daffyd and the others, effectively trapping them.

"Hello Vaccies," came Evan's hated voice. But instead of the usual name-calling that presaged a fight, Evan shuffled his feet as he hesitated. Then, "We went to the pictures last night."

"Ain't you the lucky one then," Tommy replied, both sourly and apprehensively. Tim and the others had almost forgotten about the Welsh lads in their worry about home.

Evan ignored the interruption, and stubbed the pavement with a foot.

"And they had on that Newsreel thing. You know, when they show things that are happening about the war, before the main picture. Well, they showed some of the places what have been bombed. You know, in London and places."

"Did they show Folkestone?" asked Tim quickly.

"Don't know. They didn't say what the towns were, just that they was on the south coast. And 'specially London." He kicked the stone again. "I didn't know that bombing'd be like what they showed. None of us did. You know, houses being blown apart. People getting killed and going off to the hospitals and such.

"And me Dad said that if he'd been your Dads, he'd've done just the same as yours did. Sent me and me sister away to a safer place before it ever began, I mean. Before it was too late, he said. And me Mum said you all must be dead worried about your people still being in London. I know I would be if I was you. Seein' what it's like now." He hesitated and looked at the others. "So we reckon we ain't been fair to you 'Vaccies, calling you 'yeller' like. And so there won't be no more bother from us. That's right ain't it?"

There was agreement from the others.

"Good. We're glad about that, ain't we?" Tim looked at Tommy and Sam.

"Not 'alf!" they agreed fervently.

Kitty and Maralyn read the newspapers too, and listened to the News Programmes on the wireless every evening with dread.

The Battle of Britain, far away from Wales, raged through the summer and the autumn, then came huge relief when the likelihood of invasion seemed to recede, so Kitty's worst fears of a big German soldier rushing up to Aunt Anne with his gun aimed to kill her, subsided.

But the Blitz on London together with the bombing onslaught on coastal towns caused other fears.

"Your Mum's written to you Tim." Auntie Blodwyn passed over the letter, opened as usual, when he arrived home from school, cold from the winter chill outside.

He was used to that now, but he still resented it. Auntie Flo had always given him the letter to open himself even though she'd then had to read it to him until he had learned to spell them out for himself.

"And she's written to me to say she'd like to come and see you and your sister sometime in November between your birthdays. She wants me to find somewhere for her to stay for one night and then she'll go on to spend another night where your sister is."

"Mum did that last Christmas at Folkestone," Tim said excitedly. "Except then she stayed with Auntie Anne where Kitty was."

The five weeks before she came seemed to last for ever to Tim, but at last the great day came.

Uncle Maynard took him to meet the local train from Newport. As it steamed in, he swung Tim up onto his shoulders so that he could see over the heads of the passengers streaming off the train.

"Tell me when you see her Tim."

"There she is! There she is!" screamed Tim moments later, pointing, then waving both arms frantically.

May had spotted him at the same moment, and waved back, excited herself. She picked up her suitcase again, and pushing Frank in his pushchair hurried towards them as quickly as she could, while Maynard pushed his way towards her, Tim still waving and shouting.

Gratefully Maynard let Tim slide down from his shoulders to hurl himself into May's arms. She dropped her case to hug him tightly, then held him out at arms length as the last of the crowd surged past them, unheeding and unheeded.

"My! You have grown Tim! And here's Frank who was a baby when you last saw him. Hasn't he grown?"

Tim looked at the eighteen month old boy in the pushchair who surveyed him solemnly, sucking a thumb.

Of course he'd grown, thought Tim prosaically, that's what boys do. Though Mum still looked exactly the same as he'd remembered her.

"Hello Mrs. Jackson. I am Maynard Morgan, Tim's foster-father."

They shook hands, quickly assessing each other.

"I shall take your case, shall I? And you'll be alright with the youngster will you?"

They were the last to go through the ticket barrier, Tim walking beside May, clutching her hand, face wreathed in smiles.

"Blodwyn is getting the tea ready for us," Maynard went on once they were in the street and able to talk more comfortably. "Ieuan Smith and his wife, where you and the youngster will be sleeping tonight, are just next door to us, so that is convenient as you will be taking all your meals with us." They walked on a few more paces. "When we told some friends that you were coming from London to see Tim they asked if they could meet you so that you can tell them what it is really like in the Blitz. We get the papers and see the Newsreels of course, but there is nothing like actually meeting someone going through it is there?"

"I'll be pleased to. And as Tim's father is a Warden, I know more than most of what it is really like," May answered promptly.

When the friends crowded into their best parlour that evening, Tim nearly bursting with pride, May talked of the bombing, the dangers, the rescues, the heroics that were being done day after day, night after night, with no medals being given to most. Extraordinary things being done by otherwise ordinary people.

It was only after the youngsters had gone that she talked of the horrors of the injuries and deaths that the rescuers encountered too. Producing silence among her listeners.

"I suppose that now you've come you'll be taking Tim back with you, won't you?" Gareth said almost casually while they were having breakfast next morning.

Tim looked from him to Mum, an enormous flare of hope surging through him. Had Mum really come to take him home?

"No, certainly not. We don't want him at home now with the bombing as it is." May looked from Gareth to his parents. "What's the difficulty? Is Tim causing you trouble?"

"No. Tim's no trouble at all. He can stay with us as long as he needs to." Maynard's answer was prompt, not knowing about most of the arguments between the boys and remembering all that May had described last night.

"Oh good." May's relief was obvious.

Tim was stunned, heart-sickened. His hopes had been dashed just as suddenly as they had been raised. Only now it was worse.

To him the important words in May's answer had been, 'Certainly not. We don't want him home now'. And then, she had even asked if HE was the one causing the trouble! When it wasn't him at all. It was that rotten Gareth!

For May, her important words had been ' --- not with the bombing as it is.' And to her, her question was natural. Though she looked at Tim, she saw nothing of his inner turmoil.

The day was mild and May did not have to catch the bus to go to Kitty till early afternoon, so she suggested to Tim they go for a walk. She wanted to get to the bottom of why Gareth had asked that question. When asked he had just shrugged and said that he'd thought she'd want to.

"How do you get on with the Morgans, Tim?" she asked as soon as they had turned the corner to go down the hill to the town.

"Alright." Tim was being guarded now after what his mother had said.

May looked at him sharply, sensing that something was wrong.

"How do you get on with Gareth?"

"Rotten. But he's not been so bad since I stood up to him."

"What do you mean by that?"

Tim became animated as he described what had happened. And because he had done what Mum had always said you should do with bullies, face up to them, he was sure she would approve of what he had done. It hadn't even come to a real fight because he had.

"What did Blodwyn say? Or Maynard? You did tell them I hope."

"'Course not. That'd be sneaking. And no one likes a sneak." Surely Mum wasn't ...?

"In future Tim, whenever there's trouble between you and Gareth you always tell Blodwyn or Maynard. Or one of these days there's be a real fight between you and Gareth and they'll want to get rid of you. And then what'll happen?" May stopped walking to emphasis what she was saying, staring hard at him. "Do you understand?"

"Yes Mum," Tim muttered, miserable again.

Far from being proud of him, even though he'd only done what she had always said you should do to bullies, stand up to them and they'll often back down just as Gareth had done, Mum was talking again as though he was the trouble.

It had all gone wrong. He'd been so excited about Mum coming all the way from London to see him and he'd been telling everyone how t'r'ific it was going to be. But this morning she'd said she didn't want him home any more, and now she'd said he'd got to sneak on Gareth.

Well, Auntie Blodwyn wouldn't like that one little bit if he did, would she? If Mum blamed him straight off for the trouble, then

Auntie Blodwyn was bound to do the same only ten times worse because Gareth was her kid wasn't he? And he was only a London 'Vaccie.

When the time came for May to catch the bus to go to Kitty, May forced herself to be as outwardly calm and as matter-of-fact about it as she had appeared at the first Evacuation. The way she had always acted with the children no matter how she was feeling herself. She didn't want to upset Tim by showing how upset she was at leaving him, knowing he wasn't really happy with the Morgans. But the thought of bringing him back to the Blitz was simply too terrible to contemplate. Especially after the flats. Especially because of that ghastly Premonition she'd had just before the War started.

As they waited for the driver and conductor to come out of the Canteen May wondered whether to tell Blodwyn what Tim had told her about Gareth's bullying. Then she decided not to. They only had a couple of minutes and she had already told Tim what to do. And it would be better for Blodwyn to have an actual incident to deal with, rather than make a general accusation now.

The bus crew came out and it was too late to say anything anyway.

She kissed Tim quickly, and hugged him tightly.

"Now you be a good boy Tim and do what your Auntie Blodwyn tells you. And remember what I've told you to do."

She climbed on the bus with Frank, her case and the folded pushchair were handed in, and the bus pulled out as May waved to Tim through the window.

Tim did not wave back.

Not when Mum had told him only this morning that she didn't want him back home again. And hadn't said to him how t'r'ific he'd been to stand up to a bully like she'd told him to do before. And because she'd blamed him when Gareth asked that question. And then she'd said how he'd got to sneak on Gareth, which'd only cause a load more trouble if he did.

So he wouldn't do what she'd said.

Blodwyn glanced down at his sad face and felt a surge of sympathy. He was only a little lad and his mother had just gone off back to the dangers of the bombing. And after May's talk last night she now had a better idea of what that was really like.

She took his small, cold hand. "Let's go to the shops and get some cakes for tea shall we Tim?"

"Yes please, Auntie Blodwyn."

His sad voice made her feel still more sorry for him.

May found that the Davies's too had arranged the same kind of 'meeting with a few friends', as the Morgans had. And she was quite happy to explain to another friendly audience what life in the London Blitz was really like.

Much later, after they had gone and Kitty had gone to bed, Edith asked a question that had been worrying her.

"May, what happens to the children who survive an incident but whose parents are killed or have to go into hospital for a long time? Or even for a short time?"

"I suppose the first place would be with relatives or neighbours. If they can't look after them then I suppose - I suppose they'd have to go into a Children's Home." May was uncertain, never having thought about it.

Edith glanced at her husband.

"It must have been very hard for you to decide to send Kitty away," commented Hywell. "Didn't you have any relatives or friends that the children knew, to which they could have gone? So that it would have been less of a wrench for them?"

"No," May shook her head decisively. "I've got one sister who lives with our mother but they're in London too, and while Ron has family further out they wouldn't have been at all suitable for Kitty to go to. Or Tim."

Though wondering what could have possibly happened to make them 'not at all suitable for Kitty to go to', but at the same time for May being willing to trust complete strangers to be 'suitable', they changed the subject.

"Kitty speaks very highly of her Aunt Anne in Folkestone," Edith remarked.

"She was good to her, but it was rather unfortunate. She's filled Kitty's head with a lot of nonsense about becoming a rich businesswoman. Anne Carruthers herself had been very lucky in inheriting a very prosperous business and it's been a simple job to keep it ticking over. And she's had the help of an excellent Manager, of course." May's tone was dismissive.

"Yes, I see," Hywell nodded. But 'keeping it ticking over with the help of an excellent Manager' didn't match at all with what Kitty had told them about Aunt Anne.

The next morning May went with Kitty to see their local waterfall as an excuse to have a private talk.

"How do you like the Davies's?" May asked as soon as they were a short distance down the road.

"They're lovely," Kitty tone was completely convincing.

A little later, "Do you see much of Tim?"

"No. I went to see him once but he didn't seem much bothered about seeing me. It was like that in Folkestone. Aunt Anne took me to see him the day after we got there but he was more interested in being with Tommy and Jack and the Uncles there. And - well ...," Kitty didn't know how to put it into words. "I mean it wasn't like it was at home before we were Evacuated. But Mrs. Jones at Aunt Anne's said it was only natural really, him being a boy and me being a girl and us both growing up and not living together as well."

"I suppose you mean you and Tim have drifted apart. With being away from each other as well." May had put into the words what Kitty had felt.

"Do you hear anything from Folkestone? From Miss Carruthers?" May asked casually after a pause to admire the waterfall.

Kitty had been wondering if Mum would ask that, going on how she had seemed not to like Aunt Anne when she had come to Folkestone last Christmas for those few days. So she had prepared an answer.

"A bit. We write to each other sometimes." It was easier to say that, than to tell her that they wrote to each other every week without fail and that Aunt Anne still sent her regular Postal Orders too. And Aunt Anne always telephoned her the first day of every month and she always telephoned her on the middle Monday, both Kitty and Uncle Hywell paying half its cost after Kitty had tried to insist on paying it all.

"I see. Well now that you're here in Wales, Anne Carruthers is in the past isn't she? And you can't keep in touch with everyone from the past can you? So I'm sure she'd understand if you concentrated on your life here now and dropped off your writing to her altogether."

May felt that the Davies's were more level-headed than Anne Carruthers. They would never have encouraged Kitty in this ridiculous notion of becoming a rich businesswoman.

Kitty made no reply, but thought angrily that she would never stop writing to Aunt Anne who had done so much for her, and was encouraging her in her fashion design ambitions too. "So Mum and I have drifted apart too," she thought. "Just as Tim and I have."

May stared at the letter she was holding

"The cheek of them!" she muttered furiously and went storming in to see Jennie.

"Read this Jennie and tell me what you think of it," she snapped, pushing it into her hands as soon as she was inside the door.

Jennie unfolded it apprehensively. Had someone written to May about her and Ron?

Dear Mr. and Mrs. Jackson,

We are writing this very difficult letter because we honestly and truly have the best interests of Kitty at heart.

When you were with us two weeks ago you described in such graphic detail the effects of the bombing in London which gave us a much better understanding of your situation and the plight of children left orphaned and homeless after their parents had been killed or injured and were lying in hospital.

This has made us wonder what your wishes might be for Kitty and Tim if any of those awful things should happen, which of course, we pray won't happen.

We gathered that you felt strongly that there would be difficulties about your relatives having care of them.

We would like to assure you that should the necessity arise we would be only too pleased to continue to look after Kitty as though she were our own. We understood from you that Tim is happy where he is.

One of our friends who was present when you spoke to us is a solicitor.

When we met by chance a few days later we asked, in general terms only, about the wider family's responsibilities in these situations. He said as the law stands those families are held to be liable to take on the responsibility if at all possible. Which, of course, means they would have first claim on them and foster-parents would have none.

Consequently any of those relatives of whom you disapprove so strongly and feel unsuitable to have care of Kitty, could simply whisk her away from here without a moment's notice if they so chose.

The only way to prevent this, we understand from him, would be for you and Mr. Jackson both to sign Consent Documents for us to Adopt Kitty should any disaster happen. Quite obviously if no such events occur they simply do not apply, and naturally we hope and pray that they will not happen. We are simply wanting to provide for a more secure future for Kitty in any eventuality.

Should you feel that this is the best way to provide for Kitty's safe and secure future if disaster should happen, then arrangements for the Consent Documents can be done through the post.

Naturally we have not mentioned any of this to Kitty and will not do so unless you feel it should be.

Yours sincerely,

Hywell and Edith Davies

"Don't you think that's an appalling letter Jennie? I've a good mind to take Kitty away from them right away!" snapped May when Jennie looked up from reading it.

"You said when you came back from seeing them that you liked them, that you preferred them to Anne Carruthers and that they were giving Kitty a good home," Jennie reminded her quietly.

"That was before I knew they were plotting to get her away from me!"

May felt furious – and hurt and betrayed. Betrayed by a couple she had felt she could trust completely to look after Kitty, that they could be trusted more than she had felt she could trust that Anne Carruthers.

And all the time they had been plotting to steal Kitty from her! Even during the time they had seemed so friendly during her visit such a short time ago. She had never met anyone as two-faced as the Davies's!

Jennie looked at her soberly.

"May, ever since the bombs got both of Sam's parents and my Dad's accident on the farm and the way my mother's going, I've wondered what would happen to Tommy if I copped it. So I'd be glad if I got a letter like that from Tommy's foster-parents and I tell you this May, I'd sign straight away. At least I'd know he wouldn't get shoved into some orphanage."

May snatched back the letter.

"Well I'M not going to let anyone take MY kids away from ME."

"No. But what if the bombs take you and Ron away from THEM?"

"Well, then ....," May paused. What would happen to Kitty? Because maybe Tom and Marie would try to get her. Given her age. "Nothing's going to happen to me," she snapped.

That evening when May put Ron's dinner in front of him she sat down opposite.

"We had a letter from the Davies's today."

"Oh? Well that's not altogether unusual is it? Kitty alright?"

"It wasn't about her. Well, it was in a way, but not in the way you think. That's it."

She pushed it to him across the table. He took it out of the envelope and read it twice while he was eating.

"We've been talking about this kind of thing down at the Post."

"You mean a lot of foster-parents are suggesting adopting?" May demanded.

"No. I mean about orphaned children. Leslie Thompson's brother has had several down in Stepney. Welfare takes them away and they do their damndest to persuade relatives, any relatives, to take them. If they won't or can't, they try friends. If that doesn't work the kids have to go into orphanages. And brothers and sisters don't always go together either."

"And what happens to Evacuated children?"

"I'd have to ask. I should think the same thing applies, because while they're being fostered the Government pays, when they're with relatives they aren't. That way ...," he pointed to the letter with his knife, " ... we'd be making sure that Tom couldn't take her. Nor Marie. And at the age Kitty is coming up to, I can see them trying. And then push her out to work at the first chance. Or worse could happen to her," he added ominously. "You said you liked the Davies's, and Kitty does seem happy there going by her letters. And by what you said she said to you."

"So you're saying you're perfectly happy to sign away the future lives of our children to complete strangers?" gritted May, pushing away her own worry about Tom and Marie.

"No," Ron replied patiently. "What I'm saying is that we could sign those Consent Documents for the Davies's to adopt Kitty, with the Clause written in that they apply ONLY if we are killed or incapacitated and only then. Which is what the Davies's have already said, but we would have it actually written in.

"They want to take on that responsibility. And they are not 'complete strangers', are they May? Kitty's already with them, she likes them, and you've met them and liked them. The thing is May, without that, the best we could hope for Kitty is that she would stay where she is with no interference from anyone. But the worst is that Tom would get his hands on her. Or Marie."

Ron spoke in a very calm voice. May would have to come round to see the sense of what he was saying.

"I might have known you'd side with Jennie," May snatched the letter back.

"What's Jennie got to do with it?" wondering if May had heard something and was leading into it.

"I showed her the letter, and you've taken the same line as her. Well - it amounts to the same line."

"So we happen to agree on that," Ron shrugged. "But she's a mother isn't she? So if, as a mother, she thinks it's the best thing to do, then surely that shows it does make sense? What's she going to do about Tommy? Did she say?"

"She said something about she'd snap up the offer if his foster-parents made it about him," May admitted reluctantly. “For the same reasons you said.” she added suspicions back.

There was silence for several minutes. May poured them both some tea and they went to sit in their chairs on either side of the fire.

Abruptly, "Ron, I don't trust the Davies's now. And I can't really see Tom or Marie being interested in Kitty. Why should they be? We haven't had any contact with them for years, not since Tom went to prison. And Marie didn't go, did she? Alright, I know she was involved just as much ...," she added hastily before Ron could interject, "... but why should they be interested now?"

"Because Kitty's almost of working age. And because she's a girl! As I said just a minute ago," Ron snapped back.

"Well I don't think they would be." Defiantly. "The Davies's said that both our signatures would be needed and they certainly won't get mine!"

Ron said nothing. But he was going to ask around about it because to him the Davies's suggestion did make a lot of sense. And Wales was a hell of a lot safer than Folkestone for Anne to adopt Kitty. Though the likelihood of invasion there had receded, the town was often being bombed and shelled.

"And I want to bring Kitty home right now."

Before Ron could snap a refusal the Air Raid Warning wailed into life, followed immediately by the crash of the anti-aircraft guns at the end of the road.

"Bring her back to this? Don't talk so bloody daft May!" Ron shouted as he jumped for his Warden's equipment.

May did not reply to the Davies's letter and with a surge again in the bombing of London she didn't mention bringing Kitty home again either. But she was determined to do so.

The Davies's debated worriedly whether they should write again in case their first letter had been lost in the Post - enough were in the bombing. Or perhaps the Jackson's reply had been lost coming back to them. Or perhaps they had not known what to say so were not replying at all and to write again could provoke a response they did not want. So they finally decided to do nothing further. And if anything did happen to Ron and May they would use every weapon they could find, to keep the girl they had come to love as their own.

Chapter 15
Back to London

"What's the matter Ron?"

Jennie's worried voice seemed to Ron to be coming from a vast distance through the maze of cottonwool that was stuffing his head. His chest felt clogged, his legs heavy and uncoordinated, feelings that had been getting steadily worse over the past few days.

"I'm alright Jennie. Just a bit tired I suppose," he mumbled.

No one complained about mere tiredness. It seemed that almost everyone you met was tired to exhaustion. Working all day, and then Warden Duty, Home Guard Duty or some other Duty most nights. Or simply being kept awake by the night-time bombing now that daylight raids were less common.

And this had been going on for two years. Now that America had come into the war after the Japanese attacked Pearl Harbour last December and they had declared war on Japan (in retaliation) and Germany and Italy (because they had declared war on America in support of Japan), most people felt they now had a chance.

But only in the long run. A very long run because in March 1942 the enemy still seemed to be carrying everything before them.

"There's more to it than just that Ron. You're coming back to the Post with me right now to see the Doc." Jennie's tone was determined.

"But we're nearly at our sub-Post. I'll have a rest there."

Jennie stopped to stare into his face in the faint starlight.

"Ron, a rest - or even what I can give you - isn't what you need." She paused and in the near total silence could hear his rasping breath.

And was shot through with fear. When she had last heard that kind of breathing it was her father, who had nearly died of pneumonia.

She took Ron's arm and pulled him, gently but insistently.

"Come on. Back to the Post. There's no Alert on so we're not neglecting anything."

Feeling relieved, because with Jennie being so worried and insistent he could not be accused of malingering, he allowed himself to be towed while being supported by her. Because his knees were now feeling even more rubbery. And he was feeling light-headed too in a dreamy kind of way that was not altogether unpleasant.

And suddenly he found himself inside the warm Post.

"Doc! Thank God you're here! Check Ron over will you, 'specially his chest. I think he's ill, seriously ill."

'Doc' was not really a doctor, but he had been in the St. John Ambulance for years. He was too old to be used officially, so he'd taken on this unpaid, unofficial job as Post First Aid Instructor and Consultant.

"Pull your shirt up Ron, so I can get to your chest," he ordered crisply.

Ron did as he was told while Doc got his stethoscope. He gave him a thorough check over, then told him to get dressed.

"I reckon he's got pneumonia Ralph. Bad," 'Doc' muttered to the Chief Warden. "Can I use the 'phone to get Doctor Sullivan?"

"Sure." Ralph pushed it to him. "Ron, you're off sick as of now and you only come back when Sullivan gives you the all-clear."

"But ...,"

"No 'buts' Ron. Jennie, will you take him home and then report back here. Thank God it's a quiet night so far here." To 'Doc' as he put down the 'phone. "What's his verdict?"

"Agrees with me. He'll call out to Ron's in about half-an-hour unless he gets held up. In the meantime he's to go to bed."

"Off you go then," Ralph ordered.

As they went Ron felt a vast relief. Now he was under doctor's orders he could admit to himself that he was ill.

"Put your arm round me Ron," commanded Jennie as she put hers round him.

He wanted to make some ribald comment but his head seemed so full he couldn't think of one. In any case his lungs felt as though they were filled with lead so it was easier not to talk. Which meant he could use all his concentration on staying upright and putting one foot in front of the other.

There came a change of direction that made him stumble as they went through his front gate, followed by thunderous crashes as Jennie knocked his front door quietly, hoping desperately that May hadn't yet gone to the Shelter with Frank. If she had, she'd have to sit Ron down on the wet ground while she dashed through her own house to get to the back gardens. But seconds later May half-opened the door, the hall in darkness.

"Who ...?" she began.

"It's Jennie, May. Ron's ill and 'Doc's' sent him home. Dr. Sullivan ...,"

May had the door open wide and was helping Ron stumble in over the threshold.

"What's the matter with him?"

"It's pneumonia, 'Doc' says. And Sullivan agrees. He's on his way to see him."

May had begun leading Ron upstairs, not daring to risk the damp Shelter if it was pneumonia, Jennie pushing him from behind as he concentrated on the immense labour of lifting each ton-weight leg onto the next stair.

Then they were in the bedroom and Ron collapsed onto the bed. He stared up at them dazedly.

"Ain't I lucky one?" he wheezed. "Two beautiful women to be my devoted nurses."

And was racked by a fit of coughing.

"Get a bowl or something quick, May. He's going to be sick," Jennie snapped, pulling Ron into a sitting position and supporting him.

May got back just in time as he vomited up rust-coloured sputum. His coughing eased.

"Get a warm, damp face-cloth so we can wipe him down. And a towel of course," ordered Jennie, laying Ron back against heaped up pillows.

When May came back, Jennie had taken off Ron's coat, jacket and boots and was looking at him uncertainly, not willing to presume to undress him further in May's house.

She took the face-cloth and wiped his face and neck then gently dried him while May watched jealously. Jennie seemed to know what to do whereas she didn't.

"My father had pneumonia badly once, so I've got some idea what to do," Jennie explained, half-apologetically. "He needs to be put to bed the doctor said - shall I leave that to you if you can manage him?"

"I can manage," May said shortly.

A marked coolness to Jennie had developed since she had not supported her ideas about the Davies's letter, four months ago now. And she had begun wondering about her and Ron being paired on their Warden Sector. How exactly had that come about? Had they arranged it somehow? And was she right to have been as trusting of Jennie as she had been?

She begun unbuttoning Ron's shirt.

"Can you see yourself out Jennie? I must get Ron comfortable." It was an obvious dismissal.

"Of course I can May. Just let me know if there's anything I can do for you or Ron. Or Frank."

"Thanks," May's reply was brief as she unbuckled Ron's belt.

Jennie closed the front door behind her quietly and stood on the doorstep for a moment. She wanted to talk to the doctor after he'd been, but she thought that May would see it as going behind her back and she might then begin to suspect. If she didn't already going by her coldness over the past months.

And as Ralph would be expecting her back at the Post, she'd better get back.

In the early hours of the morning after a bomber-less night, Jennie walked home. She had already decided it was too early, or too late, to knock on May's door to ask about Ron and what the doctor had said. And Ron might be asleep.

A few hours later, at 8 o'clock, she knocked softly on May's door. Even though it was now broad daylight, all the blackout screens were still in place at the windows. May opened the door, bleary-eyed with fatigue.

"Is there anything I can do to help, May?" Jennie asked, changing what she had been about to ask.

"Oh you angel!" Relief throbbed in May's voice. "Could you give Frank his breakfast and wash and dress him?"

"Of course I can." Jennie stepped into the hall and shushed Frank who had come dashing up to his Auntie Jennie. "How's

Ron doing?"

"Poorly. The doctor said he'd come in again this morning." She passed a hand worriedly across her face. "I think he's a bit delirious. When you've finished Frank could you come up and see what you think."

Half-an-hour later Jennie was listening to Ron's laboured breathing and occasional incoherent mutterings. His half-closed eyes were unfocussed as he twisted and turned restlessly on the bed, his forehead burning with fever.

"Kitty," he said suddenly, very clearly, and went off again into a jumble of words, sometimes only half-formed.

"Has he said 'Kitty' like that before May?"

"Quite a lot in the past hour. D'you think he might be wanting her here? They always were close."

"Has he mentioned Tim or Frank?"

"No. Only Kitty. And you."

"Me?" Jennie put blank amazement into her voice. "What on earth did he have to say about me?"

"Couldn't make it out, apart from your name. And that was as clear as Kitty's name just then." She looked at Jennie, her suspicions rising.

"Kitty. Kitty." The name trailed off again into muttering.

"I think you're right May. He is wanting Kitty," Jennie said decidedly, not least to distract May.

"You really think so?" May's voice was eager. "Do you think I should send for her? The bombing has eased off again."

It was obvious that May was wanting confirmation for what she had already more than half-decided to do.

"Yes, I do," replied Jennie positively. Both because she did believe it and also knowing it would restore her to May's favour.

"I'll send the Davies's a telegram," said May with sudden determination.

"Why not 'phone them? If they're not on the 'phone themselves at home, he must be at work as he's a Manager. Another thing, why not use the Post 'phone? I'm sure Ralph would agree in the circumstances - after all it is an Emergency isn't it? And it could take forever and cost a fortune in a 'phone box. I'll go and sort it out if you like."

"No. Thanks all the same. It'll have to be me to talk to the Davies's. Can you look after Ron and Frank for me?" her suspicions seemed to be forgotten for the moment. "Goodness knows how long I'll be."

"Of course I will May. My shift at the Arsenal doesn't begin until two, and this takes priority over that if it takes you longer. So you take as long as you need."

"I'll be as quick as I can Jennie." May looked anxiously at Ron, still restless, and hurried out of the room.

Jennie heard her tell Frank to be good and to do what Auntie Jennie told him, and then the front door close. She checked to make sure that Frank was playing happily with his bricks in the next room and sat on the bed by Ron.

She took both his hands in hers and talked in a low clear voice while gently massaging their backs with her thumbs. Her father had told her several times that it was her mother doing just this that had penetrated through the fever of his illness and brought him back.

"Come on Ron, my darling. It's your Jennie here now. Come on, fight that fever. Come on Ron. Come back to me. To me, your Jennie. You're very strong and you can beat it. And I do need you, my love, my darling. This is your Jennie speaking to you."

Her low, quiet voice kept on and on, talking through Ron's mutterings.

Finally, "Jennie?" he queried, eyelids fluttering.

"That's right Ron, it's Jennie here. Come on big boy, battle that illness. You're going to make it just fine. I know you are."

"Kitty?"

"Sure. Kitty's coming. She'll be here soon. So you rest. Lie still. Relax and listen to me just chattering on. Don't forget that I love you. Do you remember that time when we were out on Patrol under that huge, bright moon a few months ago when we ...."

Ron had relaxed for a few moments when he erupted into a paroxysm of coughing.

Jennie whipped him up to a half-sitting position, grabbed a bowl and held it in position while he brought up more sputum.

When he'd finished she lay him down again and mopped his

face and chest.

He went off again into incoherent muttering while Jennie went on with her low-voiced, one-sided conversation till he fell asleep.

When Jennie heard May's key in the door nearly two hours later, he was still asleep, restless, but Jennie thought less so than before.

"How is he?" May whispered, creeping into the room.

"A bit better I think. At least his breathing seems a shade easier. What do you think?"

May listened a few moments.

"I think you're right Jennie. It is."

"Were you able to get through to the Davies's?"

"In the end. Then I had to wait for him to ring back with the time of the train. He's going to put Kitty on the 8 o'clock from Newport to Paddington, which is supposed to arrive about three. But you know what trains are like nowadays." She hesitated a moment. "Jennie. Could ...?"

"Of course I'll stay and look after Ron and Frank. Or would you rather do that and I meet Kitty?"

"I'd sooner meet her. But - what about your job, because that time goes right into your shift?"

"That's no trouble. I'll tell the Foreman I can't go in tomorrow. He's used to what he calls 'Domestic Emergencies' happening among us women." She paused. "Mr. Davies understood then?"

"Oh yes. He said he'd get her a Month's Return so that when Ron's better she's already got her ticket to go back."

"Ah." Jennie had noticed an odd note in May's voice, a kind of suppressed triumph.

"But we'll have to see about that, Jennie," May said, giving her a sly half-smile. "The important thing right now is that she is coming home. Later on? Well, we'll see."

Mr. Cutliffe glanced at his watch. Just on time for the lunch break.

"Put your books into your boxes and close them quietly."

The children carried out the first part of his instruction, but were less successful with the second.

"You may go - but don't be late back."

He smiled, as always, at the stampede for the door. Kitty and Maralyn, as usual waited in their seats for the bottleneck to clear before leaving themselves. They had just got to their feet when Mr. Davies came in. He smiled and nodded at them, but went straight over to Mr. Cutliffe.

Both girls sat down again, feeling a clutch of fear. This was the first time he had come to their classroom in the nearly two years they had been in Wales, so it must mean that there was something wrong and that could only be that something had happened to their parents in the bombing. So were they hurt? Or - dead?

After saying only a couple of sentences to Mr. Cutliffe, both men came across to them.

"What's happened?" demanded both girls together.

"Nothing too worrying," said Mr. Davies. "But Kitty, your mother has just telephoned me at my office to say that your father has been taken ill, and is asking to see you. As the bombing is now so much less, she wants you to go home for just a short period till he is better. So ...,"

"What's wrong with him Uncle Hywell? Is he going to die?"

"No. He is not going to die." His re-assurance was quiet but definite. Even though May had told him that Ron was very unlikely to survive, according to the doctor. "He has pneumonia but not to a degree that is dangerous." He hoped he was lying convincingly, to keep her from knowing what May had really said, till the last possible moment. He saw no reason to cause distress to Kitty any earlier than was absolutely necessary. "But your mother feels that if you were with him at this time then he will recover more quickly."

"Did Mrs. Jackson say how long Kitty will be away?" Mr. Cutliffe asked.

"When I said I'd get Kitty a Month's Return, she said that would be fine. So it should be no longer than that, more likely just a couple of weeks. It will depend on Mr. Jackson's recovery of course."

Early the next morning both Uncle Hywell and Aunt Edith went with Kitty to get the early local train to Newport to put her on the London train. Looking around the other passengers they saw a lady with two sons who were going to London too. She promised to look after Kitty till she was met by her mother. They left Kitty's case and haversack in her care while she re-joined the Davies's on the platform for those last few minutes.

Kitty was excited at travelling all the way to London by herself - well, almost by herself, to going home and seeing Mum and Dad and Frank for a couple of weeks. But this was overlaid by the worry of how ill her father really was.

Aunt Edith fussed over her, with tears not far away. She checked Kitty's coat was buttoned up tight against the March morning, cool at this time, patting it, straightening the collar.

"Now you will take care, won't you Kitty? About crossing the road. Who you talk to. And - and the bombs. You will take care about the bombs, won't you Kitty? And make sure you always ...,"

"Edith, Edith!" cut in Uncle Hywell's calming voice. "Do stop fussing so. I am sure that Kitty knows perfectly well what to do and how to behave. And London is safe enough now. Do you really think that May would dream of taking her back if there was any kind of danger?"

The Guard gave a warning blast on his whistle. Aunt Edith gave Kitty a last kiss and hug, then gave her a gentle push towards the train, not trusting herself to speak.

"Sit with Mrs. Harris till you get to London, and then wait by the Platform Gate till your mother gets there, though she should be there waiting for you," Uncle Hywell spoke in a shaky voice, very unlike his usual, "Goodbye my child. For a short time."

Kitty flung her arms round both for a quick hug, then jumped into the train.

"See you in a couple of weeks," she called out as the train began to move.

The three waved to each other until the train vanished round the curve.

"Come Edith," said Hywell at last, taking her arm. "She will be back soon. We'll find a cup of tea and then see about getting the train back home."

"She will be alright won't she Hywell?" Edith was begging for re-assurance.

"Of course she will Edith. And she'll be back again with us so soon it will be as though she'd never been away."

As the train ran through the outskirts of London, Kitty and the two boys stared out of the window at the increasing signs of bomb damage as they came closer to the centre.

May was waiting at the Platform gate and they saw each other at the same moment to their great relief.

"It's so lovely to see you again," May exclaimed, hugging Kitty tightly to her.

"How's Dad?" were Kitty's first words.

"He's beginning to improve but there's still a long way to go yet," May replied, relieving Kitty's immediate fears.

Goodbyes and thanks were said to Mrs. Harris and her boys, and minutes later they were on their way.

As they left Paddington Station, Kitty stopped still with shock. Seeing bomb damage in Newport, pictures in newspapers and coming through on the train had still not fully prepared her for the sight of the devastation around her.

More damage was to be seen as they travelled on the bus from Paddington to Charing Cross and then on the local train home.

May talked on about Ron, Frank and how Auntie Jennie had helped such a lot, but Kitty barely heard a word.

"Mum. Is all of London like this?" she cut in, pointing out of the window.

"Not all of it. We've been pretty lucky where we are really. It's worse round the Docks though because the Germans really went for them. It did look a lot worse, but it's been tidied up."

She spoke with the casualness of adult familiarity, not realising how shocking it was to the 13 year old Kitty, seeing it for the first time.

When they were walking home from their local Station, Kitty's depression lifted a little. Mum was right, there wasn't all that much bomb damage around here. She stared at the two big anti-aircraft guns in what she remembered as being a small open area at the corner of their road.

But the road seemed - odd, somehow. Narrower than she had remembered it. The terraced houses smaller, more cramped, crowded closer together, the gardens smaller. And everything seemed a lot dirtier and shabbier. Even the air seemed smellier.

In Folkestone the last few hundred yards to Aunt Anne's house had had tall trees in the gardens, and there were the fields behind Aunt Anne's house. The gardens and the houses were bigger and further apart. In Wales the bungalows had been separated by neatly kept, if small, gardens. And there were mountains not far away that could be seen from the gardens and the street.

Here, there were just buildings, buildings, and more buildings.

"Here we are. Home at last. It's been a long day's travelling for you hasn't it dear?" commented May as she opened the door and they went into the hall.

How small and DARK it seemed! thought Kitty.

A small boy came clattering down the thinly carpeted stairs.

"Mum! Dad says he's feeling better and ...,"

Frank stopped and stared at this big, strange girl standing behind Mum.

"Frank, this is your big sister, Kitty. Do you remember her?"

"Hello Frank," said Kitty briefly. "I'm going up to Dad, Mum."

And without even stopping to take the haversack from her back, Kitty ran up the stairs.

She stared at the man lying in her parents' bed. The father she remembered from nearly three years ago, the last time she had seen him, had been a tall, strong-looking man. Now he was much thinner and ill-looking.

"Dad!"

"Kitty!"

She dashed over to him.

Later she was sitting on the edge of the bed, Ron and Jennie smiling, listening to her chattering enthusiastically about her life in Wales when May came in carrying a tea-tray, followed by Frank.

"I've got some things just right for tea!" exclaimed Kitty, reaching for her haversack.

One after the other she handed out to her mother pieces of different types of slab cake, jam tarts, mince pies, custard powder and dried eggs and dried milk.

"How on earth could the Davies's have sent all that!" gasped May. "Don't they have rationing in Wales or has he got his own private Black Market?"

"Yes. No. I mean yes, they do have rationing in Wales and no, Uncle Hywell wouldn't use any Black Market. But last night Aunt Edith told some of the neighbours that you talked to when you came to see Tim and me, that Dad was ill and I was coming home to see him, and they made the cake and got the other things from their own private stores and brought them round last night. And they sent these for Frank."

She handed him a large bag of sweets which May promptly whipped away, and gave him three which stopped his yowl of protest.

"You can have a few at a time," she declared. "Now for some cake."

Later after Jennie had gone. "I've put your case in your room Kitty. Do you want to unpack or shall I? Because I think Dad should rest for a bit now."

"I can do it Mum. See you later Dad."

She kissed him, and snatched up her coat and haversack as Ron lay back and closed his eyes.

It was lovely to have Kitty home for a few days. As long as those bloody bombers kept away. His chest still hurt when he breathed but he was feeling a lot better though he also felt as weak as a kitten.

Kitty turned right out of her parents' room and stopped abruptly on the threshold of her room.

Or what had been her room. Now very obviously a boy's room. Frank's room.

"Your room's the other one," May's voice said quietly behind her.

Kitty turned into the smallest bedroom, May following her.

"Kitty, if we had all been here, you'd have still had to move into this room so that Tim and Frank could share what had been your room, when Frank was old enough to move his cot out of our bedroom."

"Of course they would," Kitty agreed. And it was sensible for him to start off in that room, she realised. And in any case she would only be here for a couple of weeks.

As she pushed back the lid of her case to get out her clothes, she caught a glimpse out of the window.

"What happened to the flats Mum?" she asked, crossing to the window to see better. "And wasn't that where one of the flats' Shelters was? Where that big hole is?"

"What we call a landmine - which is a big sea mine dropped on a parachute from a bomber - hit the Shelter. And then another one, or a big bomb, hit the flats. It blew some of our roof tiles off and smashed the windows but that was all. We were in the Shelter so we weren't even scratched. It was a long time ago and we didn't tell you in case you got worried."

Kitty stared at the places for a long time.

"They must have all been killed straight off," she whispered. "And all of you could have been killed. Just a few yards this way and you ...," She stopped.

"But we weren't, and not everyone was killed or even injured. Because blast does funny things." All those things were true, May told herself. She, Ron and Frank weren't killed, Linda wasn't (even if that was only because she had been in their Shelter, not the flats), and blast does do funny things. "So you finish putting your things away and play with Frank while I get tea, and then we'll be able to spend the evening with Dad."

That night Kitty lay awake in the darkness for a long time. Thinking about all the people who had been killed just a few yards away from where she was lying at that minute.

And it could have so easily been Mum and Dad and Frank. If the bombs had been just a few yards this way ....

And then what would have happened to her and Tim? Someone at school had said that sometimes your relatives came and took you away. There was Uncle Samuel and Dad's dad that Mum had told Aunt Anne about that Christmas, and they sounded awful. And someone had once said something about an Uncle Tom and Aunt Marie but she'd never even met them. And then there was Auntie Joan, Mum's sister and her mum, that they hadn't seen each other for ever so long either.

But - if something did happen to Mum and Dad why couldn't they stay where they were? Her with Uncle Hywell and Aunt Edith and Tim where he was?

When she got back to Wales she'd ask Uncle Hywell if they could do something so she would stay with them if - if .... And she'd ask Aunt Anne too. If anyone could fix it, she could.

Three days later May had taken Frank out leaving Kitty to get anything Ron might need, he made his way gingerly downstairs. Hearing his movements Kitty jumped up from the table and ran to see what he was doing. He grinned at her and came into the front room. On the table was big sheet of paper, pencils, a rubber and a large book.

Leaning on the table, breathing heavily, Ron looked at what Kitty had been doing.

"That looks good Kitty - though I know almost nothing about ladies' frocks. Are you drawing it for school?"

"I'm not just drawing a frock Dad. I'm designing one." Kitty spoke defensively.

Ron pulled up a chair beside hers to look at it more closely.

"It'd take a terrific number of clothing coupons wouldn't it?"

Kitty realised he was treating her and the designing seriously.

"It's for after the war, Dad, not now. The war may be over by the time I leave school and I - well, I want to go into clothes designing. So Aunt Anne said I should start now and build up experience and a portfolio." She looked at her father sideways to see how he was taking the news.

Anne had told him a long time ago of Kitty's interest in this during one of his weekly telephone calls. But he had to pretend it was news to him, of course. He glanced at the large book on the table, 'Fashion through the Ages'.

"Did Anne give you that?" he asked.

"Yes. When I was re-Evacuated to Wales." She passed it over to Ron to see.

He looked at Anne's message to her, written in the front. 'To Kathleen with my fondest love and best wishes, your Aunt Anne' and then looked through some of the designs.

"Have you got any more drawings I can see?"

"Yes. I'll get them."

Kitty ran upstairs and returned a minute later with a long cardboard tube that had just fitted across her case.

"I'm keeping them in this tube that Uncle Hywell got me to keep them neat and clean. Then when I get an idea I can work on them." She drew out half-a-dozen sheets. "I'm designing a complete range. Daytime (that's the one I'm on now) evening, ballroom gowns and formal and informal dresses. Aunt Anne suggested that. The ballgowns are really hard."

"I can imagine! And I suppose every designer's work has got to be different."

"That's right Dad. Everyone wants an exclusive design and will pay big money for it, Aunt Anne said. But at the same time, each season at least, they've got to have something that shows it's a Kathleen Jackson design," she added with a touch of self-consciousness. Then she grinned at him. "That's what the fashion design books that I've had as presents and from the Library say anyway."

"So you really are planning your own business? In fashion design?" Ron looked at her seriously.

"Yes." Kitty spoke the single word with determination. "I know it will be really hard work and I'll have a lot of disappointments but Aunt Anne says she thinks I've got the - the imaginative flair for design, she called it." She looked at him soberly but proudly. "Aunt Anne really does believe in me, you know Dad."

"I believe in you too Kitty," Ron said quietly. "But as Anne would know far more about those things than I do, her opinion is worth that much more."

Kitty squeezed his arm. "She might know more about dresses, but I want you to believe in me too, Dad."

There was a moment's silence.

"Dad ...," Kitty asked hesitantly, " ... you do like Aunt Anne don't you?" It was more an appeal than a question.

"Yes, I do," his reply was quiet but emphatic. "Mind you ...," he lied hastily, " ... I've only seen her that once when I took your clothes to Folkestone that time, but she struck me as a very kind person. And she gave you a very good home. And Maralyn of course."

"Then why doesn't Mum like her in the way we do?"

"How do you know she doesn't?"

"Well - it was the funny kind of way she kept on asking about her that Christmas when she came to see us. And then when she came to Wales that time, she wanted me to stop writing to her." She thought that might not sound very convincing to anyone else but she was sure she was right. "Has Mum said anything to you about her?"

"She said that Christmas she was very pleased with the way Anne was looking after you. Did you know that Mum worked in fashion before she married me?" he asked without pause to change the subject. To keep on talking about Anne might raise some tricky questions.

"That was only millinery, not fashion," Kitty's tone was disparaging.

"From what she said once, sometimes the one can be as important as the other. Take that dress you've marked 'Ascot', for example. Your Mum told me once that someone once came into the place where she worked, desperate for a special hat to go with a special dress for the race meeting, that would get her noticed. So why not talk to her about your ideas? Maybe you could work on something together."

Kitty looked at him doubtfully. If she was right about Mum and Aunt Anne, would Mum look on her ambitions in the way Aunt Anne did?

Kitty opened her eyes, woken by the noise. Her bedroom was in pitch darkness because of the blackout screens across the windows. She listened to the rain on the windows and the noise of the distant thunder. And then she realised that the way the thunder was going on and on, it couldn't be thunder though the rain was real enough. In that case it had to be bombs and guns.

The transom window over the door lit up and her door opened quietly.

"Are you awake Kitty?" May whispered.

"Yes."

May came in and sat on the edge of her bed

"Did you realise that noise like thunder is really an air raid very many miles away?"

"I guessed it was."

"Do you want to go to the Shelter?"

"Is everyone else going?"

"Dad can't. Not with the way the weather is outside, the damp in the Shelter and him just getting over pneumonia."

"Then I'll stay."

"Would you like to come into our bed then till the All Clear goes?"

"No thanks," Kitty's reply was swift.

She was very conscious of the way her thirteen year old body was developing and though secretly proud of her swelling breasts she was shy of appearing in front of her father wearing only a nightie.

"Alright then. But we'll be staying awake till the All Clear so if you change your mind, come in."

But the noise stayed distant and eventually Kitty fell asleep before the All Clear sounded.

Kitty had been home nearly two weeks when Ron decided he was fit enough to walk down to the Wardens' Post, taking Kitty with him. They spent a pleasant hour there then walked home.

"It's a funny thing Kitty ...," he said when they were nearly there, " ... but it's only a few weeks ago that we were getting Alerts all the time, though we didn't get too many bombs actually falling round here. There are raids in other places of course, and Jerry could turn his attention back to us at any time. I am better now so ...,"

He let the sentence hang there, but Kitty guessed that he must be thinking she should go back to Wales now and was trying to break it gently.

But, Kitty thought, he has no idea how much I do want to go back! That Wales, with Uncle Hywell and Aunt Edith, is now far more 'home' to her than this place, even though London is where her parents are. And Folkestone was 'home' most of all!

"I've been thinking May ...," Ron said that evening after Kitty had gone to bed, " ... I'm fit enough now, and while it's been nice having Kitty home, I think she ought to go back to Wales now, don't you?"

"No."

"What?" Ron was startled.

May looked up from her knitting.

"I said ' No'. Kitty is not going back to the Davies's."

"You told me that when I was delirious I was asking for Kitty so you brought her home to be with me till I was better. I am better now so there is not that need for her to be in London any more, so she can go back to the safety of Wales."

"It's safe here. There's been no bombs dropped round here for months and months. So there's no need for her to go back to the Davies's."

"It's less than four weeks since the last bombs fell here. Remember Sycamore Grove? And in Kitty's first few days here there was that raid not far away. And there are raids on some part or other of London every night and they could switch back here any time. So I'll contact Hywell Davies and make arrangements," he finished in a tone of finality, picking up a newspaper.

"As soon as you do that I'll take her and Frank to my mother's and leave you for good. I shall Divorce you and make sure you don't see either of them again. Ever. Or Tim," she added as an afterthought.

Her voice was quiet, steady, and totally determined. She had made up her mind, as she was going to the Post to telephone the Davies's for Kitty to come home, how she was going to handle this when Ron raised it as she was sure he would as soon as he was better.

Ron stared at her dumbfounded. May had never spoken like this before. Of Divorce and getting the Judge to bar him ever seeing the children again.

"I mean it, Ron. If you try to force our daughter to go hundreds of miles away from me to those people in Wales for no good reason, then I'm finished with you. I certainly won't want anything more to do with you and I'm just as sure Kitty won't either when I explain to her what you were trying to do. She's been really happy being back home and you just want to ruin it."

"But ...,"

"There's no 'but'. It's simple, Ron. You try to make her go back and I'll take them both away immediately, Divorce you and convince the Judge that you should be barred from ever seeing any of them again."

"And what about the bombing?"

"There hasn't been any round here for - well alright, four weeks. You think they'll come back here again, I don't."

“And what about your Premonition that made you agree to send them away when the war started?” he challenged.

May blinked. She had forgotten that Premonition in her anger against the Davies's. For a moment she wondered whether ....

“The time of that danger in London has now passed,” she snapped. “And I know this just as certainly. If you send her back to Wales something terrible will happen to her there. And you know my Premonitions are never wrong. Just as Linda's wasn't that time."

Ron was silenced. He had an almost superstitious fear of May's Premonitions. They had been right before just as Linda's had been, and if he did go against this one, and it turned out to be right and 'something terrible' did happen to Kitty in Wales – then he'd never forgive himself.

But whether or not that was right, there was still May's threat of Divorce and getting the the Judge to ban his Access to the children.

Ron knew that had happened to another Driver at the Depot, though for different reasons, when the Judge had believed the wife's lies. And May had already said she would poison Kitty's mind against him as well.

But he'd need to check this out properly somehow. Would a Judge really go along with an argument like that from May? He wasn't bothered at all what any neighbours might think if May tried to poison their minds against him with any account she might give them, but he was bothered about Kitty.

Inspiration. Anne would know, or could find out about the legal angles.

But there was still May's Premonition. Unless it was not one of those at all and she was just saying it to bolster her argument.

He tried to salvage some pride.

"Alright May. We'll leave it as you want for now. But if we get the bombing back as it was before ...," He let the words hang in the air. The implication was there, but as long as he didn't actually put it into words he hoped she would not challenge it.

Knowing she had won, May said nothing.

Ron fidgeted with his paper, then flung it down and stood up.

"I'm going down to the Post. See what's happening," he

growled.

There was no response from May.

On his way he 'phoned Anne from the Call-box not far from the Post. Her delight at his 'phoning vanished as he told her.

The next night when he 'phoned again Anne told him her solicitor had said he was 80% sure May would win her case given the arguments she was using, especially the point that so many parents were already bringing their children home. If she cited her Premonition as an argument though, that would almost certainly be discounted. It was even possible that Access could be barred though that was less likely unless she claimed fears that Ron would kidnap Kathleen. If Kathleen did say she wanted to stay at home May's chances of success would rise to 90+%. If she said she wanted to return to Wales then May's chances would be lessened but she would still almost certainly win the case.

"I've been thinking Kitty," May said abruptly the next evening as they were washing up.

Kitty looked at her expectantly. Now that Dad was better, Mum must be about to tell her about going back to Wales, and trying to break it gently, just as Dad had. Not realising that that was exactly what she was wanting!

"The nearest school for your age that's open is the one in Thompson Road. It'll mean a bus ride but that'll be alright. We'll go to see them tomorrow for you to start there Monday."

Kitty stared at her, wide-eyed with shock.

"School? Here? But I thought I'd be going back to Wales now that Dad's better."

"Why? The bombing has stopped. There hasn't been any round here for – well, ages. So what's the point of you going back? And as you're staying you've got to go to school. It's as simple as that."

Kitty had never before experienced such a maelstrom of feelings.

Shock, grief, the abrupt dashing of her hopes. And not just her hopes but her expectations. Her mother had told Aunt Edith and Uncle Hywell that her return to London was just until Dad was better. So she would be going back to Wales when he was.

And it wasn't just them who had been lied to about that – she had been lied to as well. By her own mother. About such an important matter too.

Then anger surged, swamping all the other feelings.

"You planned to do this from the beginning, didn't you!" Kitty said quietly but with intense bitterness. "You meant all along to keep me here once you got me back. And yet you still let Uncle Hywell get a Return Ticket even though you knew you were going to stop me going home to him and Aunt Edith."

"Don't be ridiculous Kitty," snapped May. "This your home - here in London, not in Wales. And I am your mother, not your precious Edith Davies or Anne Carruthers. So your place is here."

"But Dad said ...,"

"Your father agrees with me," May butted in quickly.

Kitty was stunned. The way Dad had talked to her only the other night on the way back from the Wardens' Post had made her think that she was going back to Wales! In the next day or two. Yet he must have been in on this plan too! Lying to her as well. Pretending one thing while all the time knowing he was going to keep her here. He was as bad as Mum. Mother. Keeping her here, stuck in the middle of all these horrible shabby buildings, in a dark, horrible shabby house, in a dark horrible shabby room! Leaving Aunt Edith and Uncle Hywell thinking even now she'd be back with them very soon..

"So that's settled," May broke into her whirling thoughts. "You're staying here. And there's still the wiping up for you to finish."

Mechanically Kitty reached for another plate in the rack.

She knew she would have to stay. Because even if she managed to get some money from somewhere for her train fare to Wales and get there, Mum and Dad would only come and drag her back and, even worse, get Uncle Hywell and Aunt Edith into awful trouble if they tried to keep her there.

Last term Dick Fanshawe had suggested they have a Class Debate on 'The rights and responsibilities of foster-parents' in school and so they had learned all about it.

But she would keep on writing every week to them, and to Aunt Anne of course, (mother couldn't stop her doing that) and as soon as she was old enough to leave school, which would be next year, and get a job, she would go straight back to Wales. Or to Folkestone to Aunt Anne.

She wouldn't cry now! She wouldn't let mother see her do that. She'd show her she could act like a grown-up.

And she was glad she hadn't said anything to her about her fashion ambitions. Because that would be something special between her, Aunt Anne and Aunt Edith and Uncle Hywell.

Within days, May began to wish she had sent Kitty back to Wales as Ron had said, but she wouldn't change her decision. Before she had come home, May, Ron and Frank had formed a small, cosy family unit. Frank was an easily controlled three year old, but now they were having to cope with a permanently angry, permanently resentful 'teen-ager, who by accident, had soon found a weapon against her mother.

The day after she was told she was staying May pulled her up for the way she was ironing a blouse.

"This is how Aunt Anne showed me, and Aunt Edith said the same," Kitty flashed back.

And was amazed at the fury that had flushed May's face.

Thereafter whenever possible, which was frequently, she would say, "Of course, Aunt Anne ...," or "But Aunt Edith ...," to gleefully see the same reaction.

Ron refused to be drawn into the on-going conflict between May and Kitty. When May demanded one night that he support her in reprimanding Kitty, he simply shrugged. "You said she was happy here. She clearly isn't and wants to go back to Wales. So the obvious thing …," And looked straight at her.

"No," May snapped at his unspoken suggestion. "She can learn to like it here."

Chapter 16
A way out?

The morning after May's thunderbolt Kitty dropped three letters into the postbox at the end of her road. They were to Uncle Hywell and Aunt Edith, to Maralyn and to Aunt Anne. Her last letters had been cheerful and saying that 'Dad' was getting better quickly and that she hoped to be back 'in Wales and its lovely mountains' soon.

These were of the bitter news that she was being kept by her 'mother and father' in the 'prison' of London, even though her 'father' was now better. And in the letters to Uncle Hywell and Aunt Anne she said that she would be able to leave school in about a year and would they please be able to find her a job, 'if possible in a fashion-designers but if not any kind of job will do, in any kind of place, just so that she could leave here and live with them'.

At school she met another girl who had been brought back from being Evacuated to a farm in Somerset and found that she hated living back in London just as much. So, though Kitty felt Gladys could never replace Maralyn, at least she had a friend who could understand what she was feeling.

On the following Saturday morning there was the clatter of post being pushed through the letter box.

Kitty dived into the hall, closely pursued by Frank.

"Let me Kitty, let me," he squealed frantically. "Let me get the letters!"

"That wretched girl!" snapped May, starting to her feet.

"You can have that one," came Kitty's voice from the hall.

"I want that one too! I want that one."

"That one's mine. See? It's got my name on it." Knowing perfectly well that Frank couldn't read yet.

Frank dashed in carrying one envelope.

"Mum, Kitty won't give me that letter," he burst out, pointing.

"It's my letter, so you'd only be giving it to mother who'd give it straight to me, so what's the point?"

"Frank always gets the letters, so why couldn't you let him

have that one? Who's it from anyway?"

"Aunt Edith. And it's been sent to me," Kitty added, defiance in her voice, putting the letter behind her back.

"Let me see it," May ordered, holding out her hand.

Kitty flushed angrily.

"Aunt Anne and Aunt Edith NEVER tried to snoop into my letters. I'm not a kid any more mother, so stop treating me like one. I can leave school next year and get a job and then I can choose for myself where I want to live. And it certainly won't be here in this prison with YOU!"

She turned on her heel and stalked out of the room, slamming the door behind her. May heard her run up the stairs and then her bedroom door slam.

May was speechless with fury for a moment, then sat down slowly as what Kitty had said sank in.

Kitty had taken to calling her 'mother' and Ron 'father', no longer 'Mum and Dad' as though choosing that less affectionate way of addressing them to distance herself from them.

And she was right about being able to leave school in just over a year. While May was not 100% sure she would really have the legal right then to decide where she lived when that was against her parents' wishes, when she was earning the bulk of her own living it would be ridiculous to try and force her to stay here.

If she was being 'difficult' now, she would become totally impossible then if she even tried! She knew, just as well as Kitty did, that the Davies's would jump at having her. And if she was still in touch with Anne Carruthers, so would she.

And she would lose her daughter for good. The very last thing she wanted.

It was true, she realised, she had been treating Kitty as though she was still the ten year old who had gone away in September 1939. But now in April 1942 she was a thirteen year old 'teenager who had grown up fast. Even as a small child she had always had a mind of her own and being away for nearly three years at that vital stage of development, had made her even more independent.

May slowly made her way upstairs. She reached for the door handle to Kitty's room, then paused. Instead she knocked and waited.

Kitty opened the door and looked at her, saying nothing. She had obviously been crying. Whether that was because of the row they had just had or because of what the Davies's might have written in their letter, May couldn't guess.

"I think we need to talk Kitty." May hesitated the briefest second, "Can I come in?"

"It's your house, not mine," Kitty said coldly, retreating to the foot of her bed.

"I think we've both got things to apologise for and I'll start," May said, following her in and pushing the door to. "You were right. I have been treating you over the past couple of weeks as though you were the same ten year old girl that was Evacuated nearly three years ago. And of course, you're not. You've grown up a lot and I hadn't realised just how much. I'm sorry."

She waited but Kitty did not move or say anything. Nor did her cold expression soften.

"And I'm sorry you feel you are being 'kept here' in a 'prison'. Which of course it isn't."

"Then can I go back to Wales?" It was a demand, not a question.

"No."

"Why not?"

"Because - because ..., Well you can't. I'm sorry, but that's the way it is."

"Aunt Anne once said to me that saying sorry is only really meant, if - if the behaviour changes, she said. If it doesn't then just saying 'sorry' doesn't mean anything at all."

May suppressed her anger at Anne Carruthers being quoted as an example against her.

"I shall be treating you as a thirteen year old girl from now on, I promise you."

"And can I go back to Wales?" This time it was a challenge.

"No."

"Why not?" The question she daren't answer, was back.

How could she tell Kitty it was because the Davies's had suggested they sign Consent Documents for them to Adopt

Kitty if anything happened to them in the bombing? If they were killed. If Kitty knew that, she would agree wholeheartedly. And become against her even more.

"I - I can't explain now Kitty. But you'll understand better when you're older."

"I must be old enough to understand now. Now I'm not ten. And you said you'd treat me as a thirteen year old. Almost old enough to leave school, go to work and earn my own living."

"I mean when you're a mother yourself." May ignored the fact that Jennie was a mother and yet had agreed with the Davies's suggestion wholeheartedly. "Believe me when I say that it is better for you to stay here at home now, and that you will understand when you are older - when you're a mother yourself," she amended hastily.

Kitty did not believe her. At all. But there was nothing she could do about it right now. That Debate at school had made that perfectly clear. But in a year's time it would be different.

"Will I." she replied, but it was not as a question.

May went forward to hug her. It was several moments before Kitty responded, and then it was only for a couple of seconds and transparently half-hearted. At least it was not a total rejection, May thought.

"Let's have a cup of tea and then decide what we're going to do for the rest of the day, shall we?" May suggested briskly, ignoring Kitty's level of response.

"Alright. Mother," Kitty said, almost indifferently.

And May knew that Kitty had not forgiven her. That she was still going to keep the distance of the less affectionate 'mother'.

"Look Mum, this is all dirty. It wasn't me what did it," Frank added quickly to exonerate himself from all possible blame holding out the letter he'd just picked up from the mat.

Kitty was at school so there had been no argument over this one.

"It must have had some adventures getting here then, to arrive in that state," May responded, wiping her hands from the washing up.

The envelope had dirt smears across the front and back, though the typewritten address was clear enough as was the name and postmark. It was stuck down so securely it could not be steamed open without that being very obvious.

"Now then ...," thought May, " ... if that smear was a little further ovcr and up ...,"

She went out into the garden comparing soil colours and the marks on the envelope. She rubbed her thumb and fingers in a dry patch, went back into the kitchen and resting the envelope on the table, carefully rubbed across its front. All that now could be made out was the address and 'M Jackson. The 'Folkestone' postmark was completely obscured.

Satisfied, she ripped open the envelope and unfolded the long handwritten letter. A ten shilling Postal Order fluttered to the table. She skimmed through the letter then read it again more slowly and then for a third time. She looked at the Postal Order, made out to Kitty, replaced it inside the letter and put that back into the envelope thoughtfully. And with dread.

The letter was warm and loving. Not at all the kind of friendly but cool, letter written by an adult to a child that she had fostered for a brief period two years ago. It was far more the kind of letter that would be written by a mother to a well-loved daughter. And it was obviously just the latest of an on-going long term exchange of similar letters between them.

So her attempt to cut off Kitty's contact with Anne Carruthers while she was living in Wales had failed completely. Both Kitty and Anne Curruthers had clearly kept it very much alive.

She hoped that Kitty would believe her explanation that she had opened the letter by mistake: that with the full name and postmark obscured and it being a typewritten envelope she had thought it was an Official letter to her, never thinking that Anne Carruthers would be sending her (Kitty) a letter, especially in a typewritten envelope. And of course, as soon as she had realised it was for Kitty, she had not read the letter.

Whether Kitty believed her or not, at least she now knew how Anne Carruthers and Kitty were writing to each other. And she resented it intensely.

When Kitty came home from school she listened to May's explanation without comment but obviously total disbelief, said a neutral-sounding 'Thank you', and took it up to her room to read.

Ron looked even more sceptical when May repeated the same

version to him that night.

On the Friday Kitty was at school when the postman knocked with a Registered Letter and a joke about the amount of mail they were now getting. May signed for it, and examined the reinforced envelope as she went into the front room. It was addressed to 'Miss K. Jackson' and when she turned it over she saw the return address was the Davies's.

"Now what on earth could they be sending Kitty in a Registered Letter?" she wondered aloud.

She knew she wouldn't be able to repeat her 'smudge' trick again, especially with this kind of envelope.

"There's a letter come for you Kitty. A Registered one," May called as soon as Kitty entered the front door.

She came into the room to get it, checked to make sure this one had not been tampered with and struggled to open it, too excited to take it upstairs to her room first.

"Here's some scissors," May offered her a pair.

Kitty snipped, then peered into the envelope.

"Oh. It's my Savings book from Uncle Hywell," she said, taking it out and putting it on the table, while reaching into the envelope again to ease out a thick letter.

"A Savings book?" echoed May, trying to keep her tone to one of mild interest only. "Where did you get one of those?"

"Post Office," replied Kitty briefly, engrossed in her letter.

"I know where you get them," May snapped. "You didn't have one when you went away. And how much have you got in it?"

"Ten pounds." Kitty's tone was off-handed. "No! It's ...," She picked it up to check the last entries. "Golly! Uncle Hywell's put in another two pounds!"

"Kitty! Listen to me. Where did you get all that money?" May spoke loudly.

Kitty looked up from the letter.

"Aunt Anne. Uncle Hywell. And you."

"Me?" repeated May blankly.

"Yes. You sent me pocket money sometimes. Aunt Anne does. Did. And Uncle Hywell gave me money sometimes. And as I didn't spend it all, I've saved it. That was Aunt Anne's idea. She said money is only any use when it's working by buying things to use or by being invested. She said banks work by ...,"

"I know exactly how banks work," interrupted May impatiently. "What I want to know is, how is it that you've been given so much money that you not only had all you wanted to spend, but so much over that you can save all that!"

"I've already told you, mother!" Kitty snapped back, irritable herself now. "Aunt Anne used to give Maralyn and me pocket money when we were living there and then when we moved to Wales we found she was still sending it to us. Uncle Hywell was going to give me pocket money, but when Aunt Anne said she was still going to send it to me, I said I didn't need any more. But he still would give me some when I did things - like helping in the garden f'r'instance. I think he telephoned Aunt Anne about it once," she added, going back to reading her letter.

"Did he!" May exploded. Neither of them had mentioned it to her when they occasionally wrote about Kitty's progress.

"And then, Aunt Anne, and you, sent me Postal Orders for birthdays and Christmases and things, so over time it mounted up. As Aunt Anne said savings do," she added. "Aunt Anne said ...,"

"I don't care what Anne Carruthers said," shouted May furiously. "And I'll look after that Savings book," she added, reaching out for it.

She didn't want Kitty to have that amount of money so readily available. It was more than enough for her to get a train ticket to Wales and Kitty could be determined enough to run away and do that. Ron would back Kitty staying in Wales and she was not really sure she would win a Divorce Court battle with him over Kitty staying in London, knowing little about Divorce Courts. She had been bluffing from the beginning.

Without looking at her, Kitty snatched it up and walked out of the room, saying "I'd better go and get changed."

"Kitty!" rapped May.

When Kitty did not come back at once with the book May took one step after her – then stopped short. If Kitty wasn't going to hand the book over when she was told, May was not going to try to get it from her by force. She was wanting to improve whatever relationship there might be, not ruin it totally.

It was when Kitty had been home six months that May decided it wasn't fair to keep Tim away as she was still steadfast against Kitty going back. So though London was still being subjected to occasional raids, she asked a neighbour going to Wales for her own boys, to bring Tim back as well.

When at last Tim and May turned into their own street (May had gone to meet him at Paddington) Tim heaved a sigh of pure happiness. It was so t'r'ific to be home again and away from that rotten Gareth! And Mum HAD wanted him at home after all! As they went up to the front door he had a sudden thought.

"Mum, when is Kitty coming home?"

The front door opened and there she was. Bigger, older, different from the sister he'd last seen nearly three years ago. But still Kitty.

And Kitty stared at the bigger and tougher-looking boy than she remembered, standing on the doorstep.

"Hello," they said together, a shade uncertainly now that they actually met.

"Let's go in then. No sense in just standing on the doorstep," said May briskly.

Later that evening Tim happily looked round the room that he'd be sharing with Frank. He had put up on one wall the big picture of 'The Sea Queen' given to him by Uncle Wilf when he'd been sent to Wales, and set out his toy cars on a chest of drawers. Watched all the time by an admiring Frank who was happy to at last meet his 'big bruvver Tim' that Mum had told him about, and who was now here for him to play with.

So happy that he hadn't minded too much when this newcomer had grabbed toys and books claiming them as his own when Frank had grown up believing they were his. But over the next few months that produced innumerable quarrels and tears that drove May to exasperation.

Kitty poked her head round the door. "Frank, mother wants you downstairs."

Once he'd gone, Kitty came into the room that had once been hers but was now so different.

A wave of homesickness for her room at Aunt Edith's, and even more for her room at Aunt Anne's, swept through her.

"It's rotten being back here, isn't it Tim?" she said quietly.

"Rotten?" Tim stared at her, amazed that she should think such a thing. "Of course it's not rotten! It's t'r'ific!"

It was Kitty's turn to stare. "You mean - you're GLAD to be back?"

"'Course I am! Ain't you?"

"No I'm not! I hate it here! I want to be back with Aunt Edith and Uncle Hywel in Wales. And with Maralyn. And even more with Aunt Anne in Folkestone!"

For the next half-hour until Frank came up to bed they swapped stories of what had happened to them while they had been Evacuated, both surprised at how different their lives had been. And at how differently they felt about being back in London again.

In the gloom of a mid-November morning Ron set off for Folkestone with his usual sense of excitement at seeing Anne again. He was 'phoning her at least once a week between these 'Emergency' trips to one or other of the growing number of camps and airfields near the south coast, which were now happening almost every month.

Anne opened the door to his ring, demurely dressed in a respectable-looking housecoat. The last time she had worn that to greet him, what she had had on underneath had belied the outwardly respectable appearance.

"Good afternoon Miss Carruthers," he said formally, as he had done for very many months.

"Good afternoon Mr. Jackson. How is Kathleen?" Their standard greeting to give the reason for his visit, just in case anyone was listening.

But once the door was safely closed, they hugged and kissed each other hungrily.

"It's been such ages," Anne sighed, as they made their way upstairs.

"Seven weeks is far too long," Ron agreed

Later, dressed and downstairs again, as they were having the light meal that Anne always had ready for them to share before Ron returned to London, Anne looked up at him.

"Ron, I've been doing some checking about that suggestion

you made to me last time." At his quizzical look, "That business suggestion I mean. About transport."

"Oh." Ron pretended disappointment, which Anne openly, but smilingly, ignored.

"If you remember, you suggested I should start up a Transport subsidiary, basically to move my stuff, and use any spare capacity as a general carrier."

Ron looked at her sharply. "And?"

"I've checked it out. It really could work, Ron. Because of the war work I do I'd be able to get all the Permits I need, and still be able to use what spare capacity I'd have for other work."

She looked down at the coffee table they were sitting at, and then back to him. Now that the moment had come she was suddenly nervous. Because in moments she would know whether Ron saw her just as - 'a bit on the side' as some people called it - or whether he really did love her. Love her enough to come down here, leaving his wife and, she desperately hoped, bringing Kathleen.

"The point is Ron, I don't know anything about actually running a firm like that. I know about the chandlery business, I know how to organise an office, getting the capital and the Permits and so on - what I don't know is how to organise a Yard, the right kind of vehicles to get, the runs and the drivers. So I'd need someone to run it. If I went ahead with it."

She looked down at the coffee table again, fiddling with the teapot.

Ron's head spun for a moment. It was obvious Anne was thinking of him to run it. And he could run a Yard! He'd run the Depot at NAAFI for brief periods when Malcolm and Rod had both been away. And Anne would be there to do the office side.

"Would it be a Reserved Occupation?" he asked suddenly. "Because of the war work side?" Because to leave NAAFI to run this and then be Called-up would not bring he and Anne closer would it?

"Yes. I've checked," Anne smiled.

"Can I submit an Application for the job?" Ron asked grinning.

"Your Application is accepted, you've been interviewed – and the job's yours! Oh Ron!"

Anne flung herself into his arms, crying tears of gladness.

Everything had come out so right! To have Ron with her. And Kathleen as well. If she wanted to come of course – and she didn't have the slightest doubt she would. Then she would feel really complete and fulfilled.

"I'll get cracking on the Permits, organise the capital and line up possibles for a Yard and lorries - and then ...," She drew in a deep breath.

"Perhaps just one lorry and one van to start with, Anne. Because until we see the level of trade we get and so whether we can take on more drivers there'd not be any point in buying more. And let me know what kind of stuff we'll be delivering and then I can make suggestions about the size and type of lorry to get. Though we might have to put up with what we can get to start off with."

On the way home Ron was busy with making other plans. Say a couple of months for Anne to get things organised down at Folkestone. That would bring it to the New Year. And then when everything was tied up - he'd spring the news on Kitty. A hell of a bust-up with May - and the children could decide where they wanted to go. But he was pretty sure that only Kitty would opt to come. He'd have to organise Maintenance for May and for whoever of the children stayed with her - which reminded him. Wages hadn't been even mentioned! Fancy him taking a job without sorting that out! But with Anne it was no ordinary job of course when wages were the priority.

Kitty woke up with a start. An Air Raid Warning close by was winding up its screech, and then the one at the end of their road started. And Frank, woken up by them, began crying, adding to the noise.

She sat up, heart pounding and reached for the watch Aunt Anne had given her three Christmases ago. The luminous hands showed 1 o'clock in the morning. What a way to be woken up on Boxing Day morning! Didn't the bombers believe in Peace and Goodwill at Christmas!

She got up and slipped into her dressing gown and slippers, as May came into the room.

"Get dressed and come downstairs quickly. And bring your bedclothes," she added as she hurried into the boys' room.

They trooped downstairs Tim still half-asleep, where May re-lit the fire in the chilling room and then bundled them up in the bedclothes, huddled under the table she pushed against the inner wall of the house.

"Where's Dad?" asked Kitty, in her anxiety forgetting to refer to him as 'father'.

"On Warden Duty."

"What's that noise?" Tim broke in, suddenly wide-eyed.

"Bombers engines," snapped May. "Be ready to run for the Shelter if I tell you."

The anti-aircraft guns at the end of their road suddenly thundered into life with a whole series of mighty crashes.

"Wouldn't it be better to go to the Shelter now rather than wait for the bombs to actually hit us, mother?" Kitty demanded over the noise.

"It'll be cold as icicles down there. And damp. And there's no bedclothes down there because we've ...,"

There were a series of explosions, coming closer and closer.

May was terrified. Her Premonition flamed into her mind!

She knew only too well the talk of her 'Premonition' about 'something terrible would happen to Kitty if she went back to Wales' had been a sham. A lie. She'd never had that 'feeling' about Wales. Only London. But those Davies's ---!

If anything happened to the children now she'd never forgive herself! The 'real' Premonition would have come true.

Perhaps Ron had been right for Kitty to go back to Wales and for Tim to have stayed there.

More bombs were exploding, but now they were starting to go away from them towards the centre of London yet again. More bombs, still further away. Their guns fell silent though more distant ones were still firing furiously.

"They've gone! They've – gone." May tried to control her near hysterical reaction now that they were safe from this lot of bombs. As the bombers' engines faded into the distance, she thought perhaps her 'Premonition' had been wrong after all. It was now better to think that rather than think it was yet to happen.

"We'll – we'll stay down here for a while. Kitty, help me make up better beds against that inside wall. Then see if you can get some more sleep. I'll be staying awake so there's no need for you to worry."

They lay down, still fully clothed. May switched on the hall light and nearly closed the door to put them in a dim light.

The boys soon fell asleep, but Kitty stayed awake for a long time. Thinking of the people who that lot of bombs had hit. The injuries and deaths.

And if - or when - this part of London would get hit again. And what might happen to them.

Anne lifted the telephone as it rang. It was one of the days that Ron often rang.

"Carruthers' Chandlers" she said into it, hoping.

"Hello, you beautiful girl."

Anne settled back into her chair happily.

"Hello my handsome lover," she replied softly. "And how are you today?"

At the other end of the line Ron grinned. "Somehow managing to cope in this bitter cold so far away from your love which is the only thing that keeps me warm."

Anne laughed. "Ron! How on earth do you manage to dream up all those nice things you say to me! You have a real poet's soul underneath those overalls."

"It's you that inspires me, of course," Ron replied. "But to return to earth - any news about our plans?"

"Yes. The best. I've been promised the last Permit I need for next Wednesday, the 20th January. So then it'll be up to us when to start. I've got some Yards in mind for you to see, and a few lorries to see."

"So shall I ring you Thursday? Then if you've actually got the Permits, I'll talk to May and Kitty - Kathleen - and come down on say the Friday? I'll put in my week's notice here tomorrow."

"Oh Ron! That'll be so marvellous! With you, and Kathleen here with me - well, I feel as though I shall then be – complete."

Chapter 17
The Bombers

Tuesday, 19th January 1943. Luftwaffe Base, France

The final preparations were being made for the daylight Intruder raid on England. Under the cover of a sweep of fighters and fighter-bombers along the south coast, a group of specialised FW 190A-4U3 ground-attack fighter-bombers would swing inland to attack six high-priority targets in South East London.

Intelligence had long ago reported that since early in the war many schools emptied by Evacuation had been taken over by the Air Ministry and aircraft firms, with top level scientists working in them on Top Secret projects designing ever more new weapons and aircraft, which were now in production and helping to overwhelm the far-flung German forces. So still newer ones would be coming.

Somehow that had at last come to the Fuehrer's notice and he had ordered that action should be taken. It would also show the British and their Allies that the Luftwaffe could still strike hard at the very heart of London in daylight when they wanted to and not be confined just to coastal attacks, so it would be a Propaganda Victory both at home and abroad as well.

Wednesday, 20th January 1943. 8.00 am, London

"Come ON, Tim!" exploded Kitty. "Come on, or we'll miss the bus!"

"I'm coming. I'm coming." Tim hurtled down the stairs to where Kitty was standing. "'Bye Mum. 'Bye Frank." He dodged past Kitty to stand near the gate. "Come ON Kitty!"

At the school they separated, Kitty to go into the Senior section, Tim to the Junior.

Wednesday, 20th January 1943. 11.15 am. Luftwaffe Base, France.

Aircraft engines roared into life, not just at this Base where the Intruder Force was located, but others where more Squadrons would be providing the bigger attacking force that really was the diversion.

At 11.30 am they were in the air, converging into their attack formations

Wednesday, 20th January 1943. 11.30 am. Kent

"Sir. Build-up of enemy aircraft near Abbeville," reported a WAAF to the Air Controller as she began to move counters across the huge map of the French and English coasts that stretched inland to north of London.

More WAAFs moved more counters showing how the raiding force was building up as more reports came in from radar posts, showing it moving towards Folkestone.

"Standard Alerts," the Air Controller ordered quietly.

Klaxons at Bases sounded and fighters scrambled. Civilian Air Raid Warnings sounded in Folkestone.

A short-lived strafing there and those attackers turned west and roared along the coast attacking towns and villages indiscriminately. A typical 'Jabo' hit-and-run raid. If a lot bigger than normal.

Then another group came to attack towns in the Thames Estuary.

The Air Controller frowned. These raids were splitting the defence fighters. But they had to go where the attackers were actually operating.

Ahead of the attackers, sirens were wailing, fighters scrambling. But inland, no action was taken. None was needed. Obviously the raid was not coming to them this time. Not that these hit-and-run raids ever did. They only ever hit the coastal towns.

Wednesday, 20th January 1943. 12.10 pm. London

"Oh Kitty. Just a word please."

Kitty stopped hurrying across the Hall while Gladys carried on

When your Headmistress wants 'just a word' with you, you simply stop going to the Dining Area with your friend and listen. Even if you are starving hungry.

Tim and Trevor were already in the Dining Area on the Ground

Floor, eating their sandwiches and arguing over whose bit of shrapnel was the best, which they had begun at morning playtime.

Wednesday, 20th January 1943. 12.10 pm. Kent

Close to Eastbourne the Intruder Force section of the raiders banked sharply to the right and began their top-speed run into London while the others carried on their attacks along the south coast and the Thames Estuary.

The Intruder Force found the anti-aircraft balloons were all close-hauled right along their line of attack, so marvelling at the defenders' laxity they dived down to rooftop level. They roared low over Hailsham, by-passed Tunbridge Wells, flew directly over Biggin Hill Fighter Station, beating Air Raid Warnings that wailed only briefly behind them, when they sounded at all. Because the threat of their attack had often gone before anyone even had time to hit the button. And Warnings were only sounded in areas of direct threat. Had been like this for years because too wide Warnings had resulted in too much disruption. But the Biggin Hill fighters roared off to catch the Intruders on their way back.

Wednesday, 20th January 1943. 12.20 - 12.45 pm. London

The Headmistress broke off what she was saying, frowning.

"That sounded like an Air Raid Siren in the distance. Kitty. Go to the Dining Area and tell Mrs. Sullivan to get the children to the Shelters immediately."

As Kitty ran for the stairs, Miss Brown hurried to get to her office at the other end of the hall and down some stairs to sound the General Alarm. She knew the entire school could be in the Shelters within three minutes of that sounding.

Just as Kitty got to the Dining Area door, an FW of the Intruder Force swooped low over the school, the roar of its engine deafening.

It was too late to go to the Shelters.

"Get under the tables children! Get under the tables!" screamed Mrs. Sullivan above the noise of the engines as the aircraft began a return flight.

"Tim! Where are you?" Kitty shouted, staring around, over the clatter as children dived for whatever shelter the wooden trestle tables could give.

"Here Kitty!" yelled Tim, waving his arms frantically above his head a short distance from the doorway..

Kitty saw Tim and dashed towards him as he scrambled back under the table.

"Make room for my sister!" he shouted to the others.

He was feeling tremendous excitement. His first 'real' air raid! After this the Christmas one wouldn't count and now he'd be able to tell some real stories! Tommy and Sam would be mad jealous when he wrote to tell them!

Wednesday, 20th January 1943. 12.45 – 16.00pm. London

As Kitty rushed towards Tim through the obstructing tables, chairs, benches and screaming children, fear tore at her. Not just for herself but for all of them. She was old enough to understand about bombs, death and injury in a way that Tim didn't. She had to get to him to take care of him. She had got to the end of his row of tables as the bomb dropped by the FW hit the school roof.

"Come on Kitty!" Tim was yelling, leaning out from under the table.

"If only I'd been with Aunt Edith or ...," was flashing through Kitty's mind, as the five seconds delay fuze exploded the bomb and rubble of the collapsing school fell down onto them, smashing the tables onto the children and the teachers lying underneath them.

As Tim saw the ceiling begin to fall down to where he was, he flung himself back under the table. His excitement vanished. He was terrified.

"Kitty!" he screamed briefly.

And blackness swamped him giving almost no time for him to even feel the pain of the block of masonry smashing onto the floor and toppling to crush his left wrist and hand and slam into his head. Or the smaller piece that smashed his left ankle.

May grabbed Frank seconds after two Intruder 'planes flew directly over the house as she heard the bomb exploding, knowing with an appalling certainty that it was the school that had been hit.

Her Premonition! It had happened.

Somehow, anyhow, she bundled Frank into his overcoat and ran down the road, hoping desperately she would not have to wait for the bus to get her to the school.

She was lucky. As she turned the corner, the bus arrived at the stop.

"Thompson Road," she panted to the conductor. "And make the bus go as quick as it can. Please."

"What's up Missus? Late for the dentist?" grinned the elderly conductor.

"I've got to get to the school that's just been bombed. My children are in it," she jerked.

The conductor blinked once. "Hold on a sec. Missus."

He ran to have a quick word with the driver, came back and rang the bell. The bus started forward and went faster than May had ever known a bus travel. But for all that, to her it seemed to crawl.

She knew, logically, that the bomb could have missed the school altogether. It could have hit any of the houses crowded around it. Or way beyond it. Nowhere even near it. After all, why should the Germans aim for a school that was crowded with children? But she knew, knew with a terrible certainty that grew - that it had. That ghastly Premonition had been true all the time!

"Don't you worry Missus ...," jerked the conductor clinging to a seat, " ... we'll get you there as quick as we can. How old are your kids?"

"Thirteen and nine. A girl and a boy."

Without needing to stop for any passengers, the bus arrived at the stop nearest the school.

A cloud of smoke and dust was still rising from the shattered building. Ambulances were arriving, a fire engine was putting out a few small fires. Rescue vehicles with heavy lifting gear were arriving with their equipment and more men.

On legs that felt stiff, her whole body rigid yet trembling, May walked the hundred yards from the bus stop to the corner from where she would see the school.

In her arms three year old Frank stared round. He could have walked himself, but May was cluching him tightly as if trying to gain support for herself from him.

She turned the corner and stopped as if turned to stone, feeling numbed and dazed. The noise and shouts of the rescuers and even the screams and cries of frightened and injured children seemed to fade to a distant hum.

As soon as the bomb had exploded, rescuers had dashed from nearby houses to the shattered school and screaming children. Dozens of them who had been playing in the playground were uninjured but terrified.

They were bundled away from the sights while rescuers with bare hands, tore at rubble, floorboards and rafters, broken desks and school equipment, desperate to get to the children buried underneath.

A Warden arrived and co-ordinated the work so people did not get in each others way, setting them to clear lanes into the rubble from three directions towards the Dining Area where most of the children were. Right under where the 1,000 lb bomb had exploded.

Some of the older children got to work, whitefaced with shock themselves. Others comforted younger children.

Parents arrived, some nearly overcome with relief at finding their children safe after all and taking them off home. Others, nearly overcome with fear for their children, were waiting.

Like an automaton May moved forward.

A shout and stretcher bearers rushed forward.

A small, limp body was quickly lifted onto the stretcher and carried at a swift walk past May towards the nearby Church Hall that had already been made into the First Aid Station and temporary mortuary. Ambulances were too precious to take dead bodies to a mortuary when there were living, injured people needing them.

Numbly May followed the stretcher just in case it was Kitty or Tim.

As they paused to manoeuvre the stretcher through the doorway, May looked down at the child. And turned away from the sight of the injuries to the eight year old girl, shuddering and feeling sick with horror. It was not just her broken and twisted limbs. It was her torn and bleeding face.

But she was not Kitty.

May began to walk slowly over to join a small group of mothers, waiting like her.

As she passed behind two waiting ambulancemen unseen, she heard one say, "It's bloody stupid all them kids being here and under all that lot."

"What yer mean Tom?"

"What I say. What the hell are parents doing having their kids back from Evacuation yet? That school was empty and closed once, apart from some air force people. Now it's crowded with kids. The war's still on and you never know what devilment the Jerries'll be up to next. Like who'd have expected them to bomb kids in a school, fer God's sake! And they could start another all-out Blitz on London at any time couldn't they? I tell you Bert, it's the parents what's to blame for them kids being in there."

"Parents to blame." whispered May. And collapsed in a faint, pitching Frank to the ground.

The ambulancemen whirled round at his yell and immediately knelt down to check them over.

"Fainted," diagnosed Tom swiftly. "It's alright youngster. Your Mum'll be okay in a jiff." He turned back to May, gently tapping her face. "Come on Missus, come on. Wake up. You've got this little'un to take care of, you know."

"Give her a whiff of this Tom." Bert held out a bottle of smelling salts.

Tom waved it under May's nose. In seconds she began to cough and splutter.

"That's it Missus. Come on now, wake up."

May opened her eyes.

"The school. My children." she panicked.

"Yeah, I know, I know. But it's no use you hanging around here. You've got this one here to look after. You get off home and leave the rest to us. You can contact the hospital later for news."

"Ambulances!" came a shout.

"Get her into the First Aid Station Bert and leave her there while I move up the Ambulance. And get back here bloody quick," Tom ordered urgently.

May felt herself pulled bodily to her feet and moments later found herself in the warm Church Hall, sitting on a hard wooden chair, Frank standing by her knee. She felt faint, dazed, sick, barely aware of her surroundings.

Tom's words kept whirling in her mind. "It's the parents what's to blame for them kids being in there."

"Kitty. I shouldn't have kept you here. I'm so sorry. So very, very sorry," she whispered, tears flowing.

"May. May."

A familiar voice cut through her daze. She looked up. It was Jennie.

"What are you doing here, Jennie? It's not Tommy in the school. He's still safe in Wales isn't he? It's Tim and Kitty."

"Mrs. Lock told me she'd seen you running for the bus after the bomb dropped so I guessed you'd come here to see if it was the school. Any news yet?"

"No. They've not been brought out yet. Only a few have. I've - I've seen some of them Jennie. It's - it's ghastly what they look like."

Jennie, who had seen it before on Warden duty, nodded.

"It can be. But now I think you should come home." She over-ran May's protests. "When they do bring the children out they won't allow the parents to travel with them to the hospital. They'll need all the space they've got. And we do need to get Frank away from all this. Doc's in his car outside so he can take us all home. Come on. Let's go."

She put a hand under May's arm to lift her.

"But Jennie, Kitty ...."

"No 'Buts'," interrupted Jennie firmly, lifting her up. "Come on Frank, we're going home."

Then Doc was there, taking May's other arm, and they were leading her out into the cold afternoon air.

Back home Jennie made May lie down on the settee while she got her some hot, sweet tea and Frank something to eat and drink. She sat down by May on a hard chair with a cup of tea herself.

"Jennie. It's all my fault that the children are in there. In that school," May sobbed.

"How d'you work that out?" Jennie's tone was deliberately abrupt. May had to break through the shock gripping her.

"Kitty so wanted to go back to the Davies's after Ron was better, but I wouldn't let her. And then I insisted on Tim coming home too. Ron thought they would be safer in Wales but I - I threatened I'd take the children away, Divorce him and get the Judge to bar him ever seeing them again, if he tried to make them go back. Except Kitty wouldn't have had to be MADE to go. There was nothing she wanted more. If I hadn't done that, they'd have been safe and well now. So it is my fault. And I heard the ambulance people say so too."

May stared at her, and then broke into a torrent of crying hiding her face in her hands, rocking backwards and forwards in despair and grief.

"It's alright Frank," Jennie re-assured Frank, looking at his scared face. "Mum's just a bit upset at the moment but she'll soon be alright. I'm here to look after your Mum, so you get on and eat your tea."

Slightly re-assured Frank went back to eating his jam sandwich.

All the time Jennie had been patting May's shoulder

At last, through sheer emotional exhaustion May's crying eased, and finally she sank back against the settee's arm, covering her face still.

"That is absolute rubbish May," Jennie said firmly as though there had been no break in their conversation. "You are not to blame at all. Thousands of parents have done what you've done haven't they? Bringing their children home, I mean. And whatever Kitty may have said, I know that Tim was delighted to be home with you. It was the German pilot's fault and his alone. Not yours. There were dozens of children in the playground and so he must have known it was a school. Flying as low as he was he couldn't have mistaken it for anything else. And there's something else May." She stared into May's eye's almost hypnotically. "I've seen people pulled out alive and completely uninjured from wreckage every bit as bad as that school. Remember I'm a Warden, so I've seen plenty of bombed buildings. So there's no saying that Kitty and Tim are not perfectly safe and well, without even a scratch."

Hope flooded across May's face and she grabbed Jennie's

arm convulsively.

"You do mean that don't you Jennie? You're not just saying that, are you? There is a chance - some kind of chance - that they could be alright?"

"Yes I do mean exactly what I've said," Jennie said flatly. Because that was the kind of answer that May needed at this moment. "The odds are that they're perfectly alright, safe and secure under a table or in the school Shelter and just waiting around for the way to be cleared to get them out."

"If they are Jennie, then I swear that they'll go back to Wales right away. Or wherever they want to go that's safe. I won't object to Kitty going back to the Davies's any more. I'll - I'll even agree to sign the Consent to Adopt papers for them in case anything does happen to Ron and me. I'll agree to anything, to do anything, just as long as the children are safe."

"Sure you will," agreed Jennie, who had heard desperate people make all kinds of vows before. "Now have you any idea what time Ron is expected home?"

"What? Ron?" May was bewildered at the sudden change of subject. "Oh, about seven or eight. Unless he's held up by something. Oh my God!" Another dread swamped her. "What's he going to say to me about this!!"

But Jennie's thought was a heartfelt thanks that Ron wasn't away on one of his 'overnights'. Aloud she said, "I'll stay with you till he comes and then we'll settle whether he or I go to the school or the hospital. If the children haven't already come home themselves by then." she added hastily.

Dazed and bewildered, Tim stared upwards, not recognising where he was. He was lying on his back, on something very hard and uncomfortable.

Across his face, very close, was a plank of wood. With other planks and things lying criss-crossed on top of that. There was some light coming though but not much, so he couldn't see very well.

And there was a terrible weight on his left hand and head. He tried but he couldn't move that arm at all. It seemed fixed to the ground above his head somehow. He could turn his head just a bit one way, but when he tried it the other he banged it on something hard right on the spot where it was already hurting.

And his ankle was hurting too. Badly. He tried to move his leg away from whatever it was but he couldn't move that either. And trying to move it made it hurt worse. His right leg he could move just a bit.

So what could have happened?

His mind seemed to drift away into a kind of fog and then to drift back, this time with some memories. He could remember that someone had shouted something about getting under tables. Or something.

Noise began to impact on him. Then he realised it had been going on for some time.

The noise of children crying. Or screaming. Or shouting.

And then he remembered that Kitty had been running towards him. That had been after the teacher had shouted to them to get under the tables. The noise of aeroplane engines. A bang. Then a huge bang and the ceiling falling down on them. And Kitty ...!

"Kitty!" he screamed in sudden panic. "Kitty! Are you alright?"

But there was no answer from her.

"Tim? Is that you?" came a tearful voice from somewhere down near his legs.

"Yes. Who's that? Have you seen Kitty? You know, my sister?"

There was a bubbling cough and the noise of spitting.

"'S Trevor, Tim. I'm hurting real bad. Me chest and me back and ...." There was the noise of spitting again. "Tim, I keep bleeding into me mouth. Like when I had a tooth out once but it's a lot worse. Tim ...," more spitting sounds. Tearfully, "Tim ...,"

"I'll shout Trev. My Dad's a Warden and he rescues people like us. So hold on." He took a deep breath, coughed because of all the dust and shouted as loud as he could.

His shouting made his terrible headache worse but he kept on shouting as long as he could. For Trev's sake as well as his own. And Kitty's. But finally he had to stop, sobbing with the pain of his head, his arm and his leg.

"Trevor," he called.

There was no answer.

"Kitty," he called, louder.

No answer.

And he cried.

Until a kindly black tide rose up and swamped him.

When he regained consciousness the already dim light had almost gone and it was even colder.

Now his arm and leg had no feeling at all, they were just numb. And that big lump was still pressing against his head.

"Kitty," he called weakly.

No answer.

"Trevor."

No answer

And he thought that the noise of other children crying was less than it had been before.

Much later, darker and colder, he heard other noises. Diggers. People talking and calling.

"I'm here! I'm here! Help!" he shouted as loudly as he could, suddenly excited.

People were rescuing! Just like Dad did! Maybe Dad was even there with them, just by him! And he'd pull him and Kitty out and they'd go home, he'd get warm and everything would be alright again!

"Help! Dad!" he shouted as loud as he could, but it didn't sound very loud even to him. And then some others joined him in shouting.

But gradually silence fell among them again. They were too exhausted and in too much pain to keep it up for long.

And Tim lapsed into unconsciousness again.

Wednesday, 20th January 1943. 17.45. Folkestone

Anne Carruthers shut her front door, humming cheerfully.

Using her torch sparingly she groped her way into the kitchen, and switched on the light seeing from the intense darkness that Dorothy had already put up the blackout screens. She smiled as she saw the letters waiting for her on the kitchen table, put there by Dorothy. Once again the postman had come after she had gone to work. There was the weekly one from Kathleen and one of the more occasional ones from Maralyn.

They would make the perfect end to the perfect day. When Ron 'phoned tomorrow morning she'd be able to tell him that, as promised, the last of the necessary Permits had arrived today, so everything was set.

He and – she was sure - Kathleen would arrive at the weekend and her life and family would be complete with the two people she adored.

As she put on the kettle she flicked on the wireless. It was almost time for the Six o'clock News.

She made the tea as the News preliminaries finished and the Newsreader began the Headlines.

"A school in South-east London was attacked by enemy aircraft soon after mid-day today. There are many casualties." He went on with the other Headlines.

Anne's smile and cheerfulness vanished. "Those poor children. And their parents," she thought.

A surge of pure terror engulfed her.

"No!" she whispered, "Oh God, no! Don't let it be."

She held her breath, waiting for the Newsreader to get back to the main story.

He repeated the Headline, then, "Thompson Road County School was crowded with more children than usual this lunchtime because ...,"

The voice went on with Anne no longer hearing. She had the name of the school now and it was the one she knew Kathleen attended.

The next question was who could she contact to tell her whether Kathleen was safe or - or in hospital? And which hospital? Or - or whether .... Anne pushed that ghastly thought away.

She grabbed for the diary in her handbag as she went into the lounge.

Years ago Ron had given her the number of the Warden's Post 'For Emergency Use only'. This was the worst possible kind of Emergency and they would be bound to know something. With shaking fingers she dialled for 'Trunk calls'.

After what seemed an age she heard the 'phone ringing in the Post. It was answered on the second ring.

"This is Miss Carruthers. Ron Jackson gave me your number a long time ago. I have just heard on the News about Thompson Road school being bombed this lunchtime. I was Kathleen Jackson's foster-mother in Folkestone. Do you happen to know if Kathleen is safe or - or ...." She had managed to keep her voice steady as the words rushed out but now found she could not put her awful dread into words.

"I don't have any details here, Miss Carruthers because Thompson Road is out of my area," Ralph said quickly. "But I do know that the casualties are being taken to Lewisham Hospital at least to start with. So your best bet would be to contact them. Their number is ...," he checked the list pinned to the wall in front of him and read it over to her. "Tell them that you were her foster-mother and I'm sure they'll treat you as a member of the family for news."

"Thank you. And - and if Mr. or Mrs. Jackson should come into the Warden's Post could you ask them to contact me please? My number is ...." She gave it to him.

"I certainly will. Would you like me to send a message for them to ring you now?"

Anne hesitated just for a moment.

"Perhaps not at this time thank you. If - if anything has happened they'll be too - busy I'm sure."

"If you change your mind don't hesitate to call us again. And I'll ring you myself if I hear any news about the children."

"Thank you very much." That meant she'd have two contacts for news.

When the hospital told her that neither Kathleen's nor Timothy's names were on either the 'Killed' or 'Injured' lists she was relieved but not re-assured. Because all that that might mean was that they were still under the wreckage, or had not yet been identified. Or – she could hardly let herself dare to believe it - they were safe, unhurt. She would wait a few hours then ring the hospital again. In the meantime she would sit by the 'phone and wait. In case Ron or someone rang with some news.

When it rang less than five minutes later such a great surge of hope ran through her that she felt physically sick. Perhaps it was Ron 'phoning to say Kathleen was safe!

"Hello? Is that you Ron?" she asked, her voice trembling.

"No Anne. I'm sorry. This is Hywell Davies. Have you heard the dreadful news about Kitty's school?"

Anne sobbed, her hopes dashed.

"Yes. On the Six o'clock News." She pulled herself together. "I've been able to find out that they would have been taken to Lewisham Hospital. When I 'phoned them five minutes ago Kathleen's name was not on either the 'Killed' or 'Injured' lists."

"Thank God for that!" Relief thrummed in Hywell's voice.

Anne heard a woman's voice, it must be Edith's, in the background and Hywell repeated what Anne had just said.

"But Hywell ...," Anne forced herself to say, " ... that may only mean she - she hasn't been found or identified yet. It ...," Anne couldn't finish.

"I know Anne. But at the very least there are some grounds for hope! And one hears of people being brought out unharmed from the most appalling devastation."

Anne wondered if he was saying that to re-assure Edith, himself or her. Or if he really believed it. But nevertheless what he was saying was true! People were! Anne permitted herself the barest touch of hope.

"You are right Hywell, we do. So we must just hope that that happens with Kathleen. And Timothy of course."

"Or she may not have gone to school at all today!" he burst out. "One hears of such co-incidences. Premonitions. Almost miracles."

"One does," Anne agreed again. Not because she believed that herself but because Hywell so obviously wanted to. "I shall be ringing the hospital again later. When I get any news from them, or - or anyone else, I'll let you know of course. Or you could 'phone the hospital yourself. Do you want the number?"

"I'm sure the hospital will be very busy so rather than us both 'phoning them about the same person it might be better if we left that to you and for you to contact us with news. But I will have the number just in case I do find I need it."

Wednesday, 20th January 1943. 18.00. London

When Tim opened his eyes again, he nearly panicked. Had he gone blind as well as everything else? It was pitch dark, he couldn't see a thing. And it was colder than ever.

A flicker of light flashed across his face. Then another. And another.

"What's that?" he shouted.

"Hold on lad, we're coming for you. We're right up close to you now."

"Oh - t'r'ific!" Tim burst into tears of relief.

He could hear wreckage being moved. But it didn't sound all that close to him.

"What's your name lad?" the voice called. Wanting to keep him talking to reassure him and to keep him located.

"Tim Jackson. My Dad's a Warden."

"That's good. We'll check if he's here when we can. My name's Joe Saunders and there's another chap with me. He's called Kevin Daniels. Are there any more kids near you?"

"Yeah, loads. And my sister Kitty's somewhere near too. And Trevor. But they haven't talked to me for ages. Well, Kitty hasn't at all."

"Okay Tim." Then in a shout, "Floodlight over here. There's a lot of kids straight down here." He turned back. "Now then Tim, we're going to be shifting stuff to get to you as quick as we can, but you've got to be patient for just a bit longer, and so have Kitty and Trevor. Because we've got to do it careful, and now that it's dark it's not so easy."

A glare of light suddenly blazed across them as a floodlight was swung over.

As the rescuers got to work they talked continuously to the children. Comforted, the children waited, though some were sobbing with pain and the bitter cold.

A jolt of fear shot through Tim as the wail of the Air Raid Warnings sounded.

"Douse them lights!" roared the Chief Warden.

Blackness clamped down immediately.

"Are you going to the Shelters, mister?" shouted Tim, frightened of being left again.

"'Course not Tim. We ain't going to let a few Jerries scare us off like that. There's enough light for us to see to shift some bits and we'll use the torches as soon as we can. Come on Kevin, grab that timber."

Overhead the drone of the fleet of bombers grew louder. Searchlights and flashes of anti-aircraft gunfire lit up the sky.

The drone died away with no bombs being dropped just here and the nearby guns fell silent. This part of London was not the target for these bombers tonight.

Tim's eyes jerked open. Lights were flashing across his face as the rescuers' torches probed through the wreckage. This was to become the stuff of terrifying nightmares for Tim for years afterwards.

"I can see someone down here! That you Tim?" a voice called down from straight overhead.

"Yes. Yes. I'm here," Tim shouted.

Part of the broken trestle table was lifted away and Tim had to shut his eyes quickly against the glare of the powerful torch shining directly into his face.

"Hold on now Tim. We'll have you out of there in two ticks."

The torch flickered round, picking out other children, then focused back on Tim.

He felt dizzy with relief. And he felt kind of 'funny' as well, a kind of feeling he'd never had before. Nasty. But it didn't matter now. They'd have him out in 'two ticks' and then he'd be able to go home. And maybe Kitty hadn't talked to him because she'd been dug out already.

"Now then ...," Kevin lay down on his stomach to lean right into the gap they had made in the wreckage while he reported back to the more experienced Joe, as he shone his torch around. "There's a block of masonry leaning against Tim's head it looks, but it can't be too heavy against it or he'd've been a goner already." He shone his torch round to Tim's other side. "I can see quite a lot of kids down there with him, so I reckon if I can get Tim out of this hole then we can reach a whole load of others."

He backed out and threw aside more timbers.

"Take your time to check around Kev. Make sure the kids are clear and everything is stable before you try to move anyone," Joe urged him.

The trouble with Kevin was that he was young and just that bit too eager to get people out quickly. While that was okay of course, it did have its dangers.

Kevin slid back into the gap. The trouble with Joe, he thought, was he took his time just that bit too much. He'd already checked everything hadn't he?

He rested his torch on a brick and lifted the lump of masonry from Tim's ankle and handed it up to Joe.

"Ooooh!" gasped Tim.

"You okay Tim?" Joe called down.

"Yeah. It's a bit better now that's gone."

"Now Tim, I'm going to pull you down towards me to clear the lump of bricks by your head and then lift you straight up through the hole to Joe up there behind me."

Joe nodded approvingly. Always tell the casualty what you're going to do before you do it if you can. Then they can work with you.

"But mister ...,"

Kevin grabbed Tim's knees with both hands and pulled.

"Aaah!" groaned Tim. "Mister, my ...,"

"Don't you worry Tim, that block isn't going to fall on you," Kevin interrupted, and pulled sharply.

"Mister! It's me arm ...," Tim shouted in panic.

Kevin guessed that Tim's sleeve must be caught somewhere. Trust a kid to worry about a silly thing like that! And he'd bust his back to pull the coat clear if he had to! Because then he'd be able to get to the other kids that much quicker. So he yanked really hard.

Tim screamed in agony and fainted. He had barely moved.

"Something's wrong with the kid, Kev. Get out and let me see," snapped Joe.

But Kevin was already shining his torch around and pushing aside lathes and plaster, just as the floodlight clicked on.

"Oh my God!" he muttered.

"What's the matter?" demanded Joe.

"That block's pinning down his hand. I can see that now that I've shifted that plaster and stuff and the floodlight's back on. What I thought was Tim's hand down there is another kid's."

"Get out and let me look."

A shaken Kevin climbed out.

Gently Joe felt up the length of Tim's arm then carefully eased him back to take the strain off the arm. Squirming he managed to peer behind the block. There seemed to be a small gap that he could lean it in to. He checked above it. Nothing was now resting on it to fall when he moved it.

He braced himself and pushed steadily against its top.

It teetered then rocked backwards off Tim's hand. Joe eased the arm towards him so it would be out of the lie of the block when he let it come back.

Even deep in his faint, Tim groaned.

Gently Joe lifted him up from the floor and knelt up to pass the unconscious boy up to Kevin.

"Take him and for God's sake don't hold him by that left arm. Tell the stretcher-bearers the same and for them to tell the Medics that that arm is badly injured."

"Joe ...," began Kevin, as he took Tim's weight.

"Later. There's more kids down here to get out and you're needed."

The stretcher-bearers hurried with Tim to the Church Hall, his arms across his chest. They hefted him quickly but gently onto a trestle table by a waiting team.

"Rescuers say the kid's left arm's badly injured Doc," one said quickly.

The doctor felt round Tim's neck

"Ah. He's got an Identity Disc. That's something. Name's Timothy Jackson."

An Auxiliary Nurse standing by him printed the name onto a new Medical Card, and added his name to a growing list on a clipboard. Those without an Identity Disc had a brief description only - 'Boy, brown hair, about 8 yrs.'

"Bad head injury ...," dictated the doctor, " ... severe concussion certain, check for brain damage. Reported arm injury (left), shoulder out of position relative to head so probable spine injury, possible broken neck." He felt Tim's arm through his clothing. "Dislocated elbow (left). Crush injury to left hand. Crush injury to left ankle. Pulse low and erratic, respiration shallow. In deep shock. His right side seems okay." He pinned Tim's sleeve to his coat to secure his left arm. "Hospital ASAP."

The nurse scribbled the last of his comments on the Medical Card, and pushed it inside Tim's coat as the stretcher was lifted from the table.

His place was immediately taken by Trevor, his face and clothes covered in dried, bright red blood.

A quick check.

"No respiration, no pulse. Cause of death must be punctured lungs, possibly heart, by broken ribs. Mortuary."

As he was taken and laid out on the stage with other small bodies, their presence being concealed by the curtains, his place at the table was taken by a sobbing six year old girl, clutching an arm from which a smashed hand dangled.

As soon as Tim arrived at the hospital, his clothing was cut away and rammed into a bag, quickly tagged with his name. Five minutes later he was wheeled into an operating theatre.

The time was 20.00 hrs.

Chapter 18
Shattered dreams

As Ron cycled up his street he was smiling. Tomorrow he'd be 'phoning Anne, she would tell him the final Permit had arrived, a confrontation with May and then he would be away to Anne taking Kitty with him (he was sure), at last able to explain to her why he had not been able to get her back to Wales.

He had a new sense of freedom, of being able to be his own man again, without a carping, critical wife always putting him down, but instead a 'wife' who drew him out of himself, gave him confidence in himself. And it would be a marvellous surprise for Kitty. He was absolutely certain of that.

Not that he hated May now. Not really. His feeling against her was nothing like as strong as that. And he would always do right by her and the boys, as he was expecting they would choose to stay with her.

It was 18.30 as he put his key in the door.

He walked into the front room and stopped short, seeing Jennie with May. And May looking tearful.

So May must have found out about Jennie. Or somehow both had found out about Anne.

He shrugged mentally. What did it matter? It had just come a day sooner rather than a day later. And the children weren't in the room to hear the row, which was a good thing.

"So what gives?" he asked calmly.

"Ron, the school's been bombed. And the children were in it." May clapped her handkerchief to her face, sobbing bitterly. "And it's our fault for bringing them home from Wales where they were safe. We shouldn't have done it."

Stunned with shock, shattered, Ron was silent for a full minute trying to take it in. The very thing that he had been so worried, terrified, of happening – had happened.

Then what May had said, struck him.

"OUR fault?" he growled. "OUR fault! It was YOUR bloody fault for keeping Kitty here when I wanted her to go back to Wales when I was better. You said you'd Divorce me, which I don't give a damn about but you said you'd get me barred from ever seeing the kids again! You said that your Premonition was that if Kitty went back to Wales something terrible would happen to her there! Those were your exact words, weren't they! Do you remember? BUT THAT IS EXACTLY WHAT'S HAPPENED HERE IN LONDON ISN'T IT! So where were your bloody precious Premonitions this morning? Why the hell didn't they tell you not to send them to school today?" His voice had risen to a thunderous shout.

He stopped, glaring at her, breathing thickly under the stress of his emotions.

"So what's happened to them?" he demanded harshly.

"I - I don't know Ron. But ...,"

"I'm going to find out."

At the school Ron found the Chief Warden talking to a vicar.

"'Evening Chief ...," he interrupted brusquely, " ... I'm Ron Jackson. I've got a couple of kids in that lot." He nodded at the wrecked school and the lines of rescuers working under floodlights. "I'm a Warden at the Granville Road Post. Have you got a list of the children already brought out?"

"Sorry about your kids, Jackson. The First Aid Station in the Church Hall over there are keeping a list. Try there. Otherwise Lewisham Hospital. That's where they're being taken from here."

Ron nodded his thanks and, pushing his bike, strode across to the Hall.

There was a lull in children being rescued and he found the medical staff were relaxing over mugs of tea.

"Can I help you?" asked a tired-looking doctor coming over, carrying his tea.

"My name's Jackson. Have you had a Kathleen or Timothy Jackson come through yet?"

"Betty, has a Kathleen or Timothy Jackson come through yet?" the doctor called.

One of the Auxiliary Nurses checked her clipboard.

"Yes doctor. A Timothy Jackson has. About an hour ago. Sent on to hospital."

"How bad were his injuries?" Ron asked, tight-lipped.

The doctor tried to remember one boy out of the dozens that

had passed through his hands. Then he clicked his fingers.

"Wasn't he the boy with that unusual arm injury, nurse?"

"That's right! You said afterwards that it was like ...," she stopped suddenly.

"Well?" demanded Ron harshly.

"It was as though his arm had been pulled," the doctor interposed quickly. "Unusual in a bombing incident. They'll be able to tell you more at the hospital when he gets out of the theatre."

"Any other injuries?"

"A damaged ankle. But that was not too bad on first inspection."

Ron nodded. That was something anyway. "But nothing on a Kathleen, then?"

"No. Sorry."

"Thanks. And thanks for doing what you could for him."

Ron went into the cold darkness and hesitated. Should he go to the hospital to check on Tim? But Kitty was still under that lot. He could do nothing for Tim, the hospital were taking care of him, but for Kitty – maybe he could. He hurried back to the school.

"Did I say too much doctor?" the young nurse asked him anxiously.

"I'm glad you didn't say to him what I'd said to you. That that lad's arm injury was just as though he'd been stretched out on a torture rack."

Ron hesitated at the three lanes cleared of rubble that thrust into the wreckage. It was impossible to say which could be going closest to where Kitty was. Or where Tim had been taken out from. Or if Kitty had been anywhere near him. On impulse he joined one group at the leading edge, and swiftly picked out the Senior Warden nearby.

"'Evening. I'm Ron Jackson, a Warden at the Granville Road Post. I've got a daughter under there somewhere. What can I do?"

"Take three men and start widening this lane over that way. It looks as if there was a line of tables going along in that direction."

In the direction the Senior Warden was pointing there was a long girder partly covered at one end by some rubble sticking out. Ron picked three tough-looking men nearby already shifting rubble who had heard what he'd said.

"Let's have a crack at shifting that girder," Ron said. "With a fair bit of luck that'll give us access to smaller stuff underneath. But careful how you walk on the wreckage to get along its length. We don't want anyone to break a leg. Or to step on anyone under there."

He positioned the men.

"Ready?" He received 'okays', "Lift. Bring it this way, slow and steady."

In a few seconds the girder was away from the wreckage, and the men were back. Ron went along the length of where the girder had been, shining his powerful Warden's torch down into the wreckage.

"Clear the rubble along this line," he directed, indicating.

They soon reached splintered trestle tables.

"Kitty? Are you there? It's Dad. Can you hear me?" Ron called. In hope, not expectation.

He heard a whimper.

"There's kids here. Get clearing," he snapped.

Bare hands tore at jagged pieces of masonry, lifting them up, passing them along the line to the lane where others took the rubble away to a growing pile. Ron checked again.

"We can get this chunk away. Position yourselves," His gang got around the large section of trestle table. "Lift."

And there beneath them were at least half-a-dozen children. Ron flashed his torch around. Kitty was not among them.

"Stretcher-bearers," he yelled. "Multiple casualties."

Men and women came at a rush. Children were lifted out, some with injuries, some dead.

Ron was already moving on, probing. A mass of plaster and lathes. He dug his hands in to heave it away.

Underneath it was a body. Facing downwards, the head partly under a bench that was still in position. He cleared the shoulders.

"Kitty?" he queried, hardly believing it was possible.

He brushed more plaster and lathes away from the shoulders and back. At the knees his hand thudded against a solid length of wood, lying across them.

He went back to the head and tremblingly reached down to very gently turn the face sideways.

"Kitty!" he sobbed. "Kitty, my angel."

He forced himself to gently touch her neck, searching for a pulse.

And found it. Beating steadily and strongly.

"She's alive! Alive!" he whispered.

"Your girl?" queried a voice.

Ron nodded. "Yep. And alive," he choked.

"Bloody miracle that mate. See her face under that bench? That made an air pocket for her under all that plaster."

Suddenly galvanised, Ron turned back to the thick beam of wood lying across Kitty's legs. One end was three feet in one direction when he'd cleared it. But it went far under the rubble in the other.

"Stretcher-bearer!" Ron yelled. "At the double."

"Now lads ...," he said to his gang, " ... as soon as the stretcher gets here, you're going to lift this end right up which'll lift up that rubble there, so I can ease Kitty out. Got it? I've done it before and it works."

The men nodded, and positioned themselves.

"It can't be a heave and drop mind," Ron warned them. "I'm going to need a few minutes to get her out."

"Where's the casualty?" came a voice behind him.

Ron glanced up at the stretcher-bearers.

"Under there," he pointed. "These chaps are going to lift up that beam, I'm going to get underneath and pass her up to you."

"Gawd's s'trewth man!" exploded one of the bearers. "Those blokes let it slip or it breaks and you're a goner. Get a heavy rescue crane ...,"

"That casualty's my daughter and there's no time to mess about." Ron glanced at his gang. "Ready? Let's do it. Lift."

The three men heaved.

"Onto your shoulders," snapped Ron, as he slithered forward.

He quickly checked that nothing else was holding Kitty down and gently raised her up by her shoulders for the bearers to get a hold on her.

"Careful of her legs. They're probably smashed," Ron snapped, trying to take their weight as the bearers eased her onto the stretcher, still face down, head to one side.

"Get a move on Ron," gasped one of the men

"She's on the stretcher."

From his position in the rubble, Ron shone his torch round underneath the wreckage

"There's more kids under ...," he began.

"Get out Ron! The timber's breaking!"

Ron got. Just as the beam cracked, and broke, one end thudding down heavily just where he had been a moment before.

He stood up. "Get on with getting those other kids out, lads. You've seen how it's done. I'm going after my daughter."

He followed the stretcher into the Church Hall.

"Parents aren't ...," began the doctor. "Oh. Your daughter Mr. Jackson?"

"He risked his neck getting her out, doctor," said a bearer.

The doctor nodded.

"Kathleen Jackson," he read from the Identity Disc. The Auxiliary Nurse noted it on the Medical Card. "Some contusion on the back of the head. Arms okay. Legs – ah." He bent over to look.

"A heavy beam was lying across them. She was lying face downwards," Ron volunteered.

"Where exactly was the beam lying?"

Ron indicated.

"Okay. Nurse. Crush injuries across the back of left knee, severe bruising across calf muscle of right leg. Probable fractures of right leg. Hospital ASAP."

"How bad is it doctor?" Ron asked quietly as Kitty was taken to an ambulance.

The doctor hesitated. This father had already had bad news about his son, though not all of it, and now his daughter ....

"Not good I'm afraid." He hesitated again. "How big and heavy was the beam?"

Ron described it. "She'll lose at least one of those legs won't she?"

"That is possible I'm afraid Mr. Jackson. But the hospital will be able to tell you more when they've done a thorough check."

"Sure." Ron knew what that meant. He'd used the same form of words on more than enough occasions. "Thanks for your help."

He looked as his watch before going out into the darkness. Nearly 10.30. Maybe Tim would be out of the theatre. It was more important to check on him than going back to May to tell her that both were alive. Alive at the moment at any rate.

He got on his bike and set off to the hospital.

Once there he was directed to a room off the long corridor where he found a dozen people were already waiting, facing a notice board on which were pinned a series of lists. At the back of the room a Salvation Army lady was sitting by a tea trolley. She stood up. "Cup of tea sir?" she asked brightly.

"Thanks. What happens in here?" Ron took the steaming mug.

"A doctor comes in every now and then and reads out names from a list in her hand. Those are people on whom she can give a preliminary report. She'll then see any parents that are here. Before she goes off to see them she pins the lists on that notice board."

Ron nodded and went to check the lists on the notice board. Tim's name wasn't on any of them, so presumably he was still in the operating theatre. He went to take a seat.

Five minutes later the door opened, everyone twisting round to see who it was.

It was a young, tired-looking doctor in a white coat, carrying a sheet of paper in one hand and several files under her other arm. She went to stand by the notice board.

"I have some more names here. If any parents hear their child's name, raise your hand and I will have a brief word with you about your child's condition."

She read out seven, the last being Tim's. There was one other father waiting besides Ron.

After the other father was seen, Ron went into the doctor's office.

"Mr. Jackson?"

"Yes."

Ron sat down, already knowing the news was bad from what the Doctor at the First Aid Station had said.

"Timothy has a fairly complicated fractured ankle, but that has been put in plaster and though there may be some residual weakness it should be reasonably functional."

"Right." So that's the good news bit, he thought.

"He has also what is called a 'traction injury'. As far as we can work out from his injuries, his left hand was pinned down by a lump of rubble or something similar, and the rescuer tried to pull him free, presumably not realising that. That means that nerves were stretched and damaged in the brachial plexus area. That's the - well you could call it a knot of nerves under the armpit, just here."

Ron nodded. He remembered that had been mentioned in one of 'Doc's' First Aid lectures.

"We don't know just how extensive the effects of that will be until we've done a lot more tests."

"But I take it they'll be fairly extensive. On the best outlook."

The doctor hesitated. This Mr. Jackson really did grasp things in a way a lot of parents found it hard to do.

"Going by the dislocated elbow and injuries to the top of the spine that is likely to be so."

Ron took a deep breath. At least he now knew. His son was going to be crippled for the rest of his life. As was Kitty.

"Can I ask if there's any news on ...."

"There is one thing more about Timothy."

"More?" Ron was taken aback. The First Aid doctor hadn't mentioned anything else to him.

"Timothy received a very heavy blow to the head. He has severe concussion and ...,"

"And?" Ron asked as the doctor hesitated.

"I'm very sorry Mr. Jackson but Timothy may well have had real damage done to his brain."

"Brain damage?" Ron echoed. "Oh my God!"

One of the other Drivers at the Depot had a son who'd got brain damaged in an accident and was almost totally helpless as a result.

"It may not be too much and the effects may be barely noticeable, so we'll be doing further Tests. In the vast majority of these cases there is improvement over time so whatever the results of the Tests might be at first, that is certainly not the end of the story."

"Is there any more bad news?" Ron asked after a pause.

"No. That is everything."

"Right. Thanks. Erm - I have a daughter who was brought in about forty minutes ago. She had bad leg injuries, so I suppose she's still being checked. Her name's Kathleen Jackson. Can you ...?"

"I'll see." The doctor picked up a 'phone, dialled a number, said a few words, spoke her thanks and replaced the 'phone. She folded her hands on the desk and looked at Ron.

"She has just gone into theatre, Mr. Jackson. As you say, her leg injuries are severe. They will be doing their utmost to save them of course." She paused. "As it will be several hours before we know the outcome of that I suggest you go home, and contact us in the morning."

Ron cycled home slowly through the blackout. Searchlights were probing, guns firing as aero-engines droned high in the sky, but there was no crash of bombs falling nearby.

He arrived home and walked into the front room. Jennie was still with May, Frank had gone to bed and asleep long ago.

The two women looked at Ron fearfully.

"I'll give it to you, just as the doctor gave it to me. Businesslike and blunt," he said harshly. "Kitty and Tim are both alive ...,"

"Thank God!" gasped May.

"Alive when I left the hospital. Kitty is going to lose both legs. Tim has a smashed ankle, what amounts to a paralysed left arm and has a bad head injury which has resulted in bad concussion and is likely to have caused brain damage, how bad they don't know yet. But I know of a kid who has it and he's totally helpless. Like a baby. Everything has to be done for him. And I mean everything."

A moan escaped from May's lips as she covered her eyes as though she was trying to block out what she had really seen and what she was imagining had happened to the children to cause such injuries.

"So any way you look at it I've now got two crippled children," Ron ground on remorselessly. "And that's because they were here in London instead of in the safety of Wales. So I'll ask you again - what happened to your wonderful Premonitions May? Those 'feelings' of yours that you throw at me to prove I'm always wrong and you're always right. To 'prove' that Kitty must not go back to Wales because 'something terrible would happen to her there'. But it happened to her right here didn't it? In London. In that damned school. So why didn't those wonderful, bloody Premonitions of yours stop you sending the kids to school today? Have you, or they come up with an answer yet?"

"Ron! Don't. Please!"

"Don't what May? Don't make you face up to what YOU'VE done? Don't remind you of you saying you'd get me barred from ever seeing them again if I even tried to get them back to the safety of Wales? Oh damn it to hell! I'm going out."

He slammed out of the house and strode down the road, trying to escape from his grief, and his own guilt for not having stood up to May in the first place and taken his chances with the Judge. Yesterday - this morning – a few hours ago - everything had been so perfect. Everything had been working out exactly as they'd hoped and planned.

But now ....

He strode on.

A long time later he found himself outside the Warden's Post. He hesitated, then went in. He could get warm in here, suddenly realising how chilled he was, and he would be with people he knew and respected. There was no Alert on so it was crowded. As he went in through the inner blackout curtain, the buzz of conversation cut off.

Next moment Ralph was on his feet going towards him, hand outstretched.

"Come on in Ron. I 'phoned the hospital five minutes ago and they told me, and I've told the others. I can't say how sorry we all are."

Ron found himself drawn in, sat down by the stove, a mug of tea pressed into his hands, having sympathetic pats on the shoulder, surrounded by friendship. And with no blame, criticism or condemnation for having the children back home from anyone.

"The hospital only told me Kitty and Tim were seriously injured but alive. How bad is it?" Ralph asked.

Ron explained, and added his fears, that now to him were certainties. In this atmosphere he found it helped.

"Ron, I can only go on what you say the doctors said, of course, but looking at it more detached than maybe you can at the moment, it seems to me you're looking too much on the black side," 'Doc' said quietly. "With head injuries especially, you do have to give it time. And the doctor was right about kids too. Even when the physical injuries are bad, it's amazing how they can adapt and make use of what they've got. So don't write off Kitty and Tim too soon."

Ron stared at him searchingly, hardly able to believe that anything could be less than the absolute worst. But also knowing that 'Doc' never gave any false optimism.

"Are you levelling with me 'Doc'?" he queried at last.

"Sure am. Ever known me do anything different?"

Ron shook his head. So maybe there was some faint element of hope after all.

The ring of the telephone slashed into the silence.

Ralph snatched it up.

"Jerry's back," he snapped as he banged the Air Raid Warning button. "Off you go to your Sectors. Except you Ron." The Post emptied in seconds except for Ron, 'Doc' and Ralph.

Ralph caught 'Doc's' eye, a slight jerk of the head and 'Doc' stood up.

"I think I'll go and take a look round Ralph. See you Ron. I'm sure the hospital with do its best for Kitty and Tim."

"Sure 'Doc'. Thanks."

As soon as he heard the outer door close Ralph said, "A Miss Carruthers 'phoned me from Folkestone, Ron. Said she was Kitty's first foster-mother and that she'd heard on the Six o'clock News about the school."

"Oh?" Ron was guarded.

"She wanted to know if I'd got any news about Kitty - 'Kathleen', she called her. I could only give her the hospital number at the time."

Ron said nothing.

"She asked if you or May dropped in, could I ask you to give her a ring. But she didn't want me to send a message to your house asking you to. She gave me her 'phone number." He picked up the scrap of paper.

"I know what it is."

"She sounded really nice."

"She is. And she really loves Kitty - Kathleen. We ...," he stopped abruptly.

Ralph made guesses.

"So you've - they've kept in touch then? Even after Kitty went to Wales? And came home?"

"They wrote every week, regular as clockwork. They're very close."

"Ring her Ron," Ralph urged gently. "Obviously you can't use this one with an Alert on, but as soon as it's over ...,"

"Thanks. I was going to ring her. You see, Anne and I ...,"

He stopped abruptly as the outer door banged open and then shut. Next second the curtain was pushed aside. It was Jennie.

"Thank God! I hoped you'd be here Ron. May needs you ...,"

"Don't make me laugh!"

"She does Ron. So does Frank. He's woken up and is crying for Kitty and Tim. God knows what he must have seen at the school with May. And May's right at the end of her tether Ron. They both need you. You've got to come."

Ron just glared at her, his mouth a hard line. He wanted nothing to do with May. She could stew in her grief as far as he was concerned. Just as he had to stew in his.

"Ron." Jennie's voice became gentle. "Kitty and Tim will need you. Frank needs you at this very minute. And they'll all need their mother. And she needs you Ron. Now. To care for her, not to blame her for what's happened. Ron, May is your wife. She is your responsibility."

Ron glared at her, silent, as grim as before, then abruptly he stood up. Without a word he pushed past her to go through the door.

"Don't forget Miss Carruthers, Ron," Ralph called after him softly.

"I won't."

Jennie ran after Ron, catching him up by the telephone box fifty yards away. Ron pulled open the door.

"Ron. May needs you right now. You've got no time to make 'phone calls to anyone," Jennie said insistently.

"This one takes priority over May," Ron snapped harshly, and pulled the door closed against her.

In the dim moonlight she saw him pull out change and in the light of a small shielded torch, he counted out coins. Surprised she found she could hear the sound of him dialling and looking down, saw that several of the thick glass panels in the door were missing. She moved closer to be sure she could hear his end of the conversation, her curiosity piqued.

He asked the Trunk operator for a number, and seconds later "Anne? It's Ron. Kathleen's alive." Pause. "But there's bad news as well Anne. She's - she's likely to lose both legs." Pause, and he brushed his hand across his eyes. "There was a bloody big - sorry Anne - there was a big timber resting across her legs when I got to her in the wreckage. The doctors said they'd do their best but didn't seem to hold out much hope of saving them." Pause. "He's badly injured as well. Arm, leg, maybe even brain damage. And it's my fault Anne." He broke down, pulling out a handkerchief. When he'd recovered, "I should have taken May on over sending Kitty back to Wales. Then she and Tim would have been there and safe." Pause. "Yeah, I know your lawyer said May was bound to win the case but ...," Pause, then almost incredulously, "You mean you really don't blame me, at least in part then Anne?" A long pause. Ron wiped his eyes and face. "Anne, you're such a wonderful person. I really do love you more than I can ever say, you know."

Jennie jerked round to stare at his back through the glass

"Anne, there's something else. I've - I've got to stay here now because ...," Another long pause. "Of course I'll keep you up to date on how she gets on, Anne. Anne, can - can I ring you every day please? Would you mind?" Pause. "I love you Anne

- and - and thank God for you."

He gently replaced the receiver and Jennie moved quickly away from the box as he pushed open the door.

"Let's go then," he snapped harshly.

Kitty dazedly opened her eyes.

She felt awful, a terrible headache, a horrible 'sicky' feeling in her stomach and a funny kind of feeling in her legs.

She looked around and frowned as she tried to make sense of where she was.

"Hello Kathleen. You're awake then?" a quiet voice by her said.

Kitty looked over and saw a nurse standing by her.

"Where am I?" she asked.

"In bed, in hospital. How are you feeling?"

"I mean - where? I'm only 'Kathleen' in Folkestone. In Wales and London I'm 'Kitty'."

Poor kid's rambling, thought the nurse. Aloud, "Okay then, you're Kitty. Because you're in London."

Thoughts connected.

"Tim? How's Tim? A bomb hit and the school fell down on us." Kitty struggled to sit up, but was restrained by the nurse. "Where is he?"

"He's fine," the nurse said quickly, having no idea who 'Tim' was. "He's quite safe and he's okay. Now you just rest a for a bit."

Kitty relaxed re-assured. She looked down her bed.

"What's that big lump in the middle there?" she asked, nodding at it.

"It's what we call a bed-cage. It's to keep the weight of the bedclothes off your legs. Come on, Kathleen - or Kitty if you like - you have another sleep."

Kitty went to lift the bedclothes to see what a bed-cage looked like and why the bedclothes had to be kept off her legs, but the nurse tucked them in firmly to stop her, her arms outside the blankets. Kitty would have to face the facts eventually, but better for that to be later rather than sooner.

Acquiescing, Kitty closed her eyes and dropped off to sleep again, the anaesthetic still having its effects.

It was daylight when she woke again. She realised she was feeling much better, that horrible 'sicky' feeling had gone for a start. She lay still for a few moments, then her eye was caught by that mysterious bed-cage.

She raised the bedclothes to see what a 'bed-cage' was. And stared horrified at what she saw. And what she didn't see.

She dropped the bed-clothes and stared rigidly, sightlessly, at the ceiling, hardly believing that this was not some ghastly nightmare.

Slowly she raised the bedclothes to look again. It was not a nightmare. It was real. Most of her legs were missing.

"Oh no!" she cried. And burst into tears.

In seconds, a pair of arms went round her, hugging her tightly, as a young nurse tried to give whatever comfort was possible in these terrible circumstances.

Kitty's crying eventually died away, to racking sobs.

The nurse wiped her own eyes, then Kitty's eyes and face.

"What - what happened to them?" Kitty gasped between her sobs.

"They were so badly broken, the doctors just couldn't save them Kitty. They tried their best but it just couldn't be done."

Kitty nodded despairingly.

"How - how much is gone?"

"Above one knee and below the other. So though I know it won't be much comfort now, with what you've still got they will be able to give you artificial ones."

After a long pause, "But Tim's alright you said, didn't you? Or some other nurse did. I think."

"That's right. He's fine," the nurse lied. She knew who 'Tim' was now and how badly he was injured, lying in the 'Men's Surgical Ward'. But Kitty had more than enough to cope with just now, without hearing about him.

"I have a message for you, Kitty. Well, three really. One from your Mum and Dad sending you their love and saying that they'll be in to see you later today, one from a lady calling herself 'Aunt Anne', sending her love, and a third from an

'Uncle Hywel and Aunt Edith' sending their love as well."

Kitty's eyes filled with tears. If only she had been with them, either of them, as she'd so much wanted, then she wouldn't be lying here like this, crippled for life.

And it was all the fault of mother and father.

That afternoon outside the Ward doors waiting for the Start of Visiting bell, May braced herself for her first visit to Kitty.

She told herself she had to be matter-of-fact about even this ghastly thing that had happened. She had always been like that even when she had been as much, or even worse upset than the children over something. When they were Evacuated for instance. Because her own mother had said to her, when she had asked for advice on bringing up children when Kitty had just been born, 'Always be matter-of-fact about things, May. Never get upset when the children are because that only feeds their upset, rather than helping them control it'.

So that was what she had always done. And she'd have to do it now, despite the way she was feeling herself - her depression, her fear and, most of all, her terrible guilt. The fact that this was her fault. She had to do that to help them cope with - with everything.

The bell rang and she went in with other mothers and fathers.

But at the sight of Kitty's despairing face as she stared at the ceiling, and then her look of – was it really hatred - that she directed towards her as she turned her head to look at the visitors coming in? May's resolve collapsed.

She stood by Kitty's bed, tears in her eyes.

"Kitty ...," she whispered, " ... I'm so, so very sorry this has happened."

"If you'd only listened to me," Kitty said, stony-faced. "I've got no legs now. Did you know that?"

May collapsed into the chair by the bed and nodded. "Dad told me last night that was - was possible. And when I 'phoned the hospital this morning they said you'd had an operation but I was only actually told that about - about them when I got here. Kitty, I ...,"

"Where's Tim? The nurse said he was alright so I suppose they must have got him out pretty quickly."

"He's here in another Ward. He's - he's got an injured arm."

May had been told not to tell Kitty more than that at this stage.

"Then he's not alright is he? He's injured. How bad is his arm?"

"A dislocated elbow, a shoulder injury. That's all. But how are you feeling Kitty? In yourself I mean? Are you ...? Does it ...?"

How can you talk to a thirteen year old about an injury as awful as hers? For which you're blaming yourself?

"My legs? Yes, what's left of them does hurt. But it's bound to be like that, isn't it? How's Frank?"

May knew that Kitty had not forgiven her. Probably never would now. Just as she would never forgive herself. But she had got to still be a loving mother to her. Then Kitty might come round. Perhaps. Eventually.

"Not too bad. Aunt Jennie's looking after him right now so that I could come in to see you."

"And father?"

"He's - he's had to go to work. But he'll be in at this evening's Visiting time."

"The nurse said I'd had three messages. One from you and father. And from Aunt Anne and Uncle Hywell and Aunt Edith."

She looked for May's response, but May simply nodded.

"Apparently Anne 'phoned the Post as soon as she heard about the school on the wireless. Your father 'phoned her to tell her the news. And I suppose she must have 'phoned the Davies's. You said once you thought they'd talked on the 'phone."

"Yes."

"By the way ...," May reached for a shopping bag and tried to bring in a lighter note. "I've brought a card for you drawn by Frank, and a present from Dad and me and another from Jennie."

Kitty opened the big envelope with Frank's card, and then a bag with a story book and an Activity book.

"Thank you. And thank Aunt Jennie for me will you? I'll get some writing paper and envelopes and write to thank her properly. The nurses here found my purse in my coat pocket so I've got some money for them."

May took out her purse and gave her a ten shilling note.

"Have that to add to your store," she smiled. "Well I'll just pop off and see Tim, but I'll be in to see you tomorrow afternoon again. And don't forget, Dad will be in tonight."

She kissed Kitty on the forehead, getting no response at all.

May stood up and looked down at Kitty, feeling despair herself. Kitty was being so remote, so - so cold. Making it obvious that she was rejecting her more than ever.

Abruptly, May hurried away, before she broke down completely in front of her. Which she mustn't do.

Tim was sitting up, propped by mounds of pillows, half-unconscious from another pain-killing injection he had just had. But still his eyes flickered from time to time as fresh spasms of pain racked his arm and spine.

"Hello Tim," a gentle voice said.

Tim opened his eyes and a smile lit up his face.

"Hello Mum."

May sat down by him and took his good hand in both hers. Tim was showing a huge bruise across the left side of his head and eye, spreading far down to his cheek. He too had a bed-cage over his legs, but May knew that his left ankle was encased in plaster. He had suffered no amputations.

"How are you feeling Tim?"

"Alright. The doctor stuck a needle in me and that's made the pain go away. Mostly anyway. How's Kitty?"

"She's alright. She's in another Ward here, she's got something wrong with one of her legs that the doctors are sorting out."

"I'm glad she's okay then. And I'm glad you're here Mum."

Tim's eyes drooped as under the influence of the drug, he dozed off. May stayed with him to the end of Visiting Time, though he did not wake up before then.

At least, she felt, he did not seem to be blaming her for what had happened in the way Kitty was.

Ron walked into Kitty's Ward, trying to hit a medium between the grimness he felt and the cheerfulness he thought he had to show to Kitty.

He received the same look that May had received.

Ron kissed her, and sat down beside her, taking her hand.

"Feeling bad, Kitty?"

Wordlessly she nodded.

"God, Kitty ...," his voice suddenly broke and he grabbed for a handkerchief.

Kitty stared at him unbelievingly. She had never, ever, seen her father cry. Or even show when he was upset over something. It impacted on her in the way her mother's tear-filled eyes had not.

So she put her arms round his neck, and they cried together.

When they recovered, Ron mumbled, "Sorry about that Kitty. You must think me a real idiot, snivelling like that. But ...,"

"I don't think you are, Dad. It just shows how really, really sorry, you are. About – everything," she added.

He squeezed her hand. She had called him 'Dad', the first time for months.

"Aunt Anne sent a message to me Dad. And so did Uncle Hywell and Aunt Edith. Just sending me their love."

"Would you like me to arrange for them to come and see you Kitty?"

"What here? In hospital?" she asked, sudden eagerness in her eyes and voice.

"That's right. I'm sure they'd like to and I'm 100% sure that Anne would be able to. It might be a bit more difficult for the Davies's to manage, but we could see."

"Oh, that'd be so lovely Dad!" Kitty hugged him. "But where will they stay? At - at home?"

She mentally contrasted their shabby house with Aunt Anne's and Uncle Hywell's.

"No. I'll find a hotel for them. I think that would be better all round. I'm 'phoning Anne as soon as I leave here tonight to let her know how you are and I'll tell her that you'd love to see her. And she'll 'phone the Davies's and see what they can do. Okay?"

"Dad! You're wonderful!"

After spending time with an asleep Tim, outside the hospital Ron 'phoned Anne. Expecting the call, Anne answered on the second ring.

"Kathleen's not too bad ...," he went on giving Anne the details he could remember. "She told me you had sent your love. I asked her if she would like you to visit."

"Can I Ron? That would be lovely! How soon? But ...," with a sudden doubt, " ... does she really want me to? In - in the circumstances?"

Ron grinned. "She jumped at it. So - it's up to you how soon you could fix to come?"

"This weekend?"

"Fine by Kathleen and me. Saturday or Sunday? Visiting hours are 2 - 4 in the afternoon and 7.30 - 8.00 in the evenings."

"If there's a hotel not too far away for me to stay Saturday night, could I come both days? Or will that be intruding too much? Because - what will May think?"

"It doesn't matter a damn what May thinks. It's what Kathleen wants that counts," Ron's voice was grim. "So - if you can manage both days, Kathleen would love it, I'm sure. And so would I," he added softly. "The way things are though we'll need to be - shall we say – erm ...,"

"Discrete?"

"I guess so. I asked the hospital and they gave me a list of four hotels, one in Lewisham, not far from the hospital and three in Blackheath which is a bit further away but they'd probably be nicer." He gave Anne the addresses and 'phone numbers. "I also asked Kathleen if she'd like the Davies's to come."

"Does she?" Anne asked cautiously.

"She does. The thing is Anne, I'm going to find it difficult to 'phone them from work during the day. That's when May was able to get through to Hywell Davies at his office. Malcolm, the Yard Foreman, is keeping me on Yard duties to be on hand in case I get a sudden call from the hospital if the children have a relapse. So ...," Though Anne could have given him the Davies's home 'phone number so he could have 'phoned them in the evening, she felt it would be better for this first contact to be from her.

"I can get in touch with them and let you know tomorrow Ron."

"You angel Anne! That would be a tremendous help."

"One thing you need to think of Ron," Anne said quietly. "While I could understand I might be reasonably acceptable to May - at least she's got nothing against me as far as I know - it's a very different story with the Davies's isn't it?"

"Kathleen wants it Anne. So the only problem as far as I'm concerned is whether the Davies's feel they can come." That grim, totally determined, tone was back in his voice.

"Then I'll contact them and tell you what they say tomorrow night."

May looked up at the sound of Ron's key in the door, and went to the kitchen to get his dinner from the oven.

"How are they?" she asked, as she met him in the hall. There was no longer even the pretence of a kiss of greeting.

"As you left them this afternoon I should think."

"Is Kitty as bitter to you as she is to me?" asked May, pouring the boiling kettle into the teapot.

"I guess." Ron did not mention that she was back to calling him 'Dad' now.

When they were sitting down, "She wants to see Anne Carruthers."

May nodded. "Fair enough. When?"

"I 'phoned her tonight after seeing Kitty and she'd like to come this weekend."

"You 'phoned her before asking me about it?" May's tone was hostile.

"I was 'phoning her to let her know how Kitty was getting on, and I knew you wouldn't object to Anne Carruthers coming. Because that's what Kitty wants." He stared at her challengingly.

"No. Of course not," May muttered after a moment, looking down. "Is she coming Saturday or Sunday?"

"Both. Staying overnight in a hotel in Lewisham or Blackheath. I got addresses from the hospital."

"Oh?" May suspicions were aroused by these pat arrangements.

"And Kitty wants to see the Davies's," Ron said quietly.

"No." snapped May forcibly. "Anne Carruthers I'll tolerate. But not the Davies's. Not after ...,"

"Kitty wants it," Ron ground through set teeth.

"She'll have to want. And if you try to insist on doing it Ron Jackson, I'll ....,"

"You'll do what?" interrupted Ron as forcibly as she had been, and slamming down his knife and fork. "You'll do what exactly? Divorce me? Try to ban me from seeing Kitty again? And the boys? Even the most thick-headed Judge wouldn't go along with that in these circumstances. And don't forget that Kitty is going to be in hospital for at least six months and by then she'll be fourteen and able to choose where she lives. And where do you think she'll choose? Here? With you? After all that's happened?"

There was a throbbing silence.

"When are you contacting them?" May asked finally in a low voice.

"I've asked Anne - Carruthers - to do that. Stuck in the Yard permanently now I don't have any access to a 'phone during the day. She'll let me know tomorrow night what their answer is."

"So you're going to be 'phoning that Carruthers woman every night then?"

"Do you begrudge her wanting to know how Kitty's getting on?"

"She could 'phone the hospital if she wants to know that much. I think ...," She stopped.

"Think what?" Ron was quite ready to face anything that May wanted to throw at him now. Including any suspicions she might have about him and Anne. And if she did, he was in the mood to confirm them outright and damn the consequences.

"Nothing," May muttered. Her world was already shattered enough.

"I'm arranging for your Aunt Anne to come to see you this weekend," May told Kitty brightly the next afternoon. She had thought to use this to warm relations with Kitty.

"You are? I thought Dad was going to do it."

"He did a little bit of the arranging, but I've done most of it." May didn't think that Ron would argue over claiming credit for a thing like that. "That'll be nice won't it?"

"Yes." A pause. "Thank you mother."

Kitty was not at all sure she believed her. Not after the way Dad had said it. So she'd ask Aunt Anne if they got some time alone together.

And May noticed that while Ron was now 'Dad', she was still 'mother'.

Chapter 19

Visits

When Anne drew up outside the house early Saturday afternoon, Ron and May were ready and waiting. They were going to the hospital in Anne's car, and after Visiting Time they would take Anne to her hotel before coming home. And, despite her mistrust, May had suggested that Ron and Anne should visit the hospital that evening together while she put Frank to bed. She felt that if she hadn't, Ron would have, so it was the sensible thing for her to suggest it - and make a point of telling Kitty she had.

Kitty was staring at the Ward door as the Start of Visits bell tinged. They were the first through the door.

"Aunt Anne! It's so lovely to see you after all this time!"

Kitty flung her arms round Anne's neck and hugged her tightly, as Anne hugged her back, tears in their eyes.

Anne hid her shock at how wan Kitty looked, but the enthusiasm and love for each other were obviously as strong as ever.

May shot a jealous look at them. Kitty hadn't responded to her like that for - months. Years. In fact, not since that first Christmas they were evacuated on the railway station in Folkestone. Even in Wales there had been some reserve. And since being kept at home it had been worse. She glanced at Ron. He was not looking jealous! He was smiling at Kitty affectionately. Or was it at both of them?

It couldn't be of course! He'd only seen Anne Carruthers that once years ago. But he was 'phoning her every evening about Kitty now, wasn't he?

"Tim will be waiting for us Ron," she snapped. "We'll leave Anne with you Kitty but we'll be back shortly," she added as she turned away.

Anne sat down by Kitty's bed, holding both her hands.

"How are you my dear?"

"Could be worse, Aunt Anne. I could have lost my arms as well, couldn't I?" Kitty had made up her mind she had got to be brave in front of Aunt Anne.

Anne nodded, understanding what Kathleen was doing. "I suppose so, my dear."

Impulsively she hugged Kitty again, as though she could never bear to let her go again.

"But how are you, Aunt Anne? And the shops? And Aunt Sonia and the twins?" Kitty asked when finally they released each other.

They chattered on, swapping news, Kitty's face becoming alive with happiness. A nurse strolled down the Ward, apparently aimlessly, but really checking how the visits were going. Back in the office she reported to Sister how bright Kitty had become with this visitor.

"Aunt Anne ...," Kitty moved closer to her to speak quietly, glancing at the Ward door to make sure her mother was not coming," ... who arranged for you to come to see me?"

"Ron, I mean your father did. Why?"

"Did mother have anything to do with it?"

"Not as far as I know. Your father 'phoned the first night he saw you to tell me how you were and said that you'd like me to visit. He'd already thought to get hotel addresses from the hospital, and I 'phoned them myself to book the room, so – I'm here. Why do you ask, Kathleen?"

To Kitty, that was another strike against her mother, lying to her to take credit away from Dad, even over a thing like this.

"It doesn't matter. What's your hotel like?"

They were chatting about places Anne had stayed in around the world when May and Ron returned. Ron had pure delight at seeing how Kitty had blossomed. So had May, but this was underlain by jealousy that it was Anne, not herself, who was having this effect on her daughter.

After the visit Anne drove them home where Jennie was playing with Frank.

When introduced she looked at Anne appraisingly. So this was the woman that Ron had told how much he loved her the other night. Her rival for Ron. While she could see why Ron would fall for this well-dressed sophisticated woman, why would she have fallen for him? Unless it was all one-sided of course.

But as she watched them while May was in the kitchen making them all a cup of tea, she became sure it wasn't like that.

Because Anne kept looking at him in that certain way.

Anne and Ron were meeting at the hospital that evening, Ron going on his bike because, May insisted, she was sure that Anne did not have enough petrol from the ration to keep coming backwards and forwards for them.

Driving alone, Anne took a route to her hotel in Blackheath that went by the school. She stopped and got out of the car to look. In spite of the dark night she could see mounds of rubble still in the playground and floorboards still hanging in space from the edge of the wrecked wing.

She wondered where exactly it was that Ron had found Kitty, and risked his life to get her out. She knew what had happened from the doctor, now in charge of Kathleen, who had been on duty at the First Aid Station who had been told by the stretcher-bearers.

She had also had a long chat on the telephone with the Chief Warden at Ron's Post on a quiet day last week. He had told her of Ron's rescues near the Docks in the first big raid of the Blitz, then of his handling the incident in his own Sector later that same night and the three other incidents since then. All of which made her love him still more.

And there was the way Kathleen responded to him. In such contrast to the way she spoke to May. Such a contrast as to make Anne wonder if she already knew of May's threat to Ron those months ago.

Ron spent fifteen minutes with Tim, then joined her at Kitty's bedside for the last ten.

"What was May's reaction to the idea of Hywell and Edith coming, Ron?" Anne asked him on the way out.

"A flat 'No'. I think she was going to try the Divorce threat again, but I scuppered that."

He told her what had happened. "So - if they want to come, I'll make the arrangements as I did for you and - well May can do what she likes."

"They said they do want to come. They can come for part of the third week of February, but Hywell's not sure which days of that week yet. He's got a very important meeting that he can't miss on either the Tuesday or the Thursday that week and he won't know which it is till the week before."

"Tell them that's fine by me. I'll tell May."

"What I could do Ron ...," went on Anne thoughtfully, " ... is to come up for the whole of that week myself. I'd like to meet them and I can run them around as I'm getting to know the area. I can manage the petrol alright."

"I won't ask how," Ron grinned. They stopped by Anne's car. "That'll be really nice Anne." He took her in his arms. "Goodnight Anne. God! How I love you." He kissed her long and hard.

"You just make sure you keep on doing so, my man," Anne smiled up at him, tugging at his coat lapel. She slipped into her car. Ron watched her drive off before going for his bike.

"I expected you to be later than this," May said, looking at the clock as he walked in.

"Why?"

"You've been out with Anne Carruthers."

"And I'm on Warden Duty in fifteen minutes." Ron glanced at the clock himself. "She told me she's been in touch with the Davies's. They can come for a few days at the beginning or end of the third week of February. They won't know which end till the week before. Something about a meeting he's got to attend."

"I've been thinking about that," May said abruptly. "The best thing I think, as you're so set on them coming, is for me to spend that week at my mother's. The whole week so it doesn't matter which end they come. I'll take Frank and - and you lot can do what you like. And use any excuses you like to Tim and Kitty because I won't be going to the hospital while the Davies's are likely to be going. I've no wish to see them even if you have."

"If that's what you want," Ron shrugged indifferently. "For me, the only thing that matters, is that Kitty wants to see them. If she hadn't, then they wouldn't have been invited. But she does." He paused. "Will you be coming back here? After you've stayed at your mother's for the week?"

May hesitated a long moment "Yes. Probably," she said finally.

"Good," Ron replied unhesitatingly, and with apparently genuine feeling. He stood up. "I should be back about two if everything's quiet."

Two weeks later, May went into Kitty's Ward soon after the Start of Visiting Bell rang. Kitty looked up from the book she was reading as May reached her bedside, but there was still no smile of welcome from her.

"I've been to see Tim," Kitty said abruptly as May went to kiss her. A practice she kept up as much for appearance as in the fading hope that Kitty might respond some time.

"How on earth did you manage that?" May asked, sitting down.

"I started using a wheelchair for myself a few days ago. I found out which Ward he's in and went. He's really bad isn't he?"

"He's getting on ...," May said cautiously not sure how much Kitty knew, " ... but it'll take a bit of time."

"He says he thinks his arm is never going to get better. Never. Not really better. And you told me that his arm was hurt just a bit. Just as you told him I'd got one of my legs hurt just a bit. He got a terrible shock when he realised I haven't got any legs at all now." Kitty's tone was accusing. "So how much more is wrong with me that you haven't told me about?"

"Nothing more is wrong with you. Ask the nurses if you like. And the reason I didn't tell you exactly what was wrong with Tim at that time was because the doctors said I mustn't. At that stage you were too ill yourself to be worried by that news. And the same applied to Tim with what I told him about you. I didn't lie to you because I wanted to, you know."

May was not only hurt by Kitty's unremitting hostility which had gone on for so many weeks, months in fact, she was now resenting it. Hadn't she always acted with the best of intentions? And no one would ever have thought that the Germans would deliberately bomb a school.

"Did the nurses know you were going to see Tim?" she asked sharply.

"I didn't ask them."

"I'd better go and see if Tim's got over the shock of finding out about you then. You should have checked with the nurses before giving him that kind of news. In fact you should have done before you went to see him at all. It was very silly of you." May stood up abruptly and walked out.

Kitty shrugged and picked up her book again. Mother didn't

know anything about anything! Of course it had been a shock to both of them to find out how bad the other really was, but by the time Kitty had left him to come back to the Ward for lunch, they'd both been laughing about things.

When May returned to her nearly an hour later, she was feeling decidedly happier. Tim, having seen Kitty and now knowing exactly what was wrong with her, had stopped worrying about her so much. Kitty had even made him laugh by calling herself 'Little Miss Tin-legs' having told him she had been measured for artificial legs that morning.

"Tim tells me you've been measured for some legs, Kitty. And that you had made him laugh by calling yourself 'Little Miss Tin-legs'. That's really brave of you," May said warmly,

"It seemed the best thing to do," Kitty shrugged unsmilingly. "We've both got to learn to - to handle what's happened to us. Through no fault of ours." She didn't tell her mother that that was what Aunt Anne had written in a letter to her.

May bit her lip. That could be taken as either she was blaming the German bombers - or as blaming her for having brought them home from Wales.

When Ron called in that evening Tim repeated the story of 'Little Miss Tin-legs'. When he saw Kitty he mentioned it, patting her shoulder.

"Dad, would you answer a question really honestly? Really telling me the truth?" she asked.

"Sure," he said at once. But inwardly deciding that would depend on the question. And if necessary he would lie as convincingly as he could.

"On the basis that you're a man - could a boy ever be interested in girl who's got tin legs? Not ordinary ones, I mean?"

"Yes," replied Ron promptly. "Provided ...," he paused.

"Provided - what?" asked Kitty, thinking that because he'd answered that way he must be saying what he really did think.

"Provided she's got it there and there." Ron pointed at her chest and her head. "I don't mean your - your shape there ...," he nodded at her chest this time, flushing with embarrassment at what his daughter may have thought he meant. " I meant in your heart, and in your mind. Whether you are a kind and loving person, thoughtful and brave. With those qualities, legs become less important."

"One of the nurses said Douglas Bader, that Spitfire pilot, has got tin legs like mine. But he's a man isn't he, not a girl?"

"True enough, but what are you getting at, Kitty?" Ron was puzzled.

Kitty pulled at the bedclothes, looking down at them.

"He's a man so he wears trousers, doesn't he Dad? I'm a girl so I wear a skirt. Which means it'll be obvious I've got tin legs. And I'm sure a boy must think of the way a girl looks, at least at the beginning." She looked up at Ron. "Which could mean there'll be no beginning for me."

"I can see what you're getting at, Kitty. But what I said is more important than just appearance. But perhaps you should talk to Anne about the way a girl feels about that. One thing though on the trousers line, a lot of women have started wearing slacks now. So as you want to be a dress designer, why not design some feminine looking slacks? If stockings won't do the trick about hiding the - the legs."

Kitty's eyes lit up.

"Dad, you're a genius! Why didn't I think of that? I'll do it!"

The Saturday morning before the Davies's came, Ron carried May's suitcase to the station for them to catch the train to London. From there he would put her on a bus to her mother's home in Manor Park, as she had adamantly refused to let him go with her right to the house.

That afternoon he biked to the hospital where Anne was to meet him with the Davies's in time for the Visiting Hours.

"Good afternoon, Mr. Jackson." Hywell shook his hand with some reserve. He was glad that Ron had arranged this visit, because Kitty had written saying it was he who had suggested it and had made all the arrangements. But on the other hand it was because of him and Mrs. Jackson, that Kitty was so terribly injured and in the hospital at all.

"Good afternoon, Mr. Davies, Mrs. Davies. Shall we go in? Through the door there."

He indicated for them to go ahead, so that he could give Anne a real smile and at least squeeze her hand.

Kitty was sitting up in bed, looking eagerly towards the door as they came in on the bell.

Edith caught sight of her and rushed over to her while Hywell walked over quickly. When their first emotional greeting was ended, and Kitty had hugged Aunt Anne, Ron said that he and Anne would go to see Tim, leaving the three together. As they had already arranged.

At Tim's bedside he greeted Anne as a grown-up friend of his sister's who had come to see him in hospital too.

"Would you like Auntie Flo and Uncle Wilf to come to see you sometime?" Ron asked.

"Who are they?" Tim asked, being more interested in the toy car Aunt Anne had just given him.

Ron and Anne looked at each other, Ron suddenly grim-faced.

"The people you stayed with in Folkestone. Before you went to Wales," Ron explained gently.

"You slept with Tommy and Jack in a room like a big tent," Anne added.

Tim looked up from his car and frowned. "Did I?" He thought. "Is Folkestone seaside?"

"Yes. It's where I come from. I looked after Kathleen - Kitty - while you were at Auntie Flo's."

"Oh yes." Memories began to percolate through slowly. "Yes, that's right. Auntie Flo was a little lady who talked all the time and Uncle Wilf was big. Almost like a giant. And he was someone important on a big ship. He wasn't the Captain, though Auntie Flo used to say he used to work a lot harder. That's right. And there was Uncle Toby there too! He was a hero because he'd only got one arm. Dad, does that make Kitty a double hero because she's got no legs now?"

"I rather think she is," Ron replied, his grim look gone now that Tim was remembering. It had only taken a kick-start.

"It would be nice to see them. Is it far for them to come?"

"Just a bit. When I go back to Folkestone, would you like me to go and ask them?"

"Yes please Aunt Anne. That'll be t'r'ific!"

After an hour with him, Anne and Ron went to see Kitty. Only two Visitors were allowed to a bed but they and the Ward Sister ignored it for this special visit and so the four of them stayed with her.

Afterwards they went back to Anne's car, Ron expecting to say as formal a 'goodbye' to Anne as to the Davies's and then go home on his bike to return that evening.

"Ron, I don't want to cause you any upset but could we impose on you to show us the school? Where - where it happened?" Hywell asked. They were now on first name terms. Because of the way Kitty was treating her father, with loving respect, their attitude to him had begun to change.

"Sure. That's no problem," Ron replied promptly.

"And then we could have tea before the evening Visits," Anne put in quickly. "I found a Tea Rooms in Lewisham and booked a table for four straight away. And then afterwards we can go to the hotel where I've already booked dinner again for the four of us. I hope that was alright, Ron." she added, with a sidelong look at him.

"It sounds as though the rest of our day's been organised for us Hywell." Ron observed, smiling. And it couldn't have been better! he thought.

At the school, now more tidied up, Ron pointed out where the three lanes had been driven into the wreckage of the Dining Area had been, and exactly where he had found Kitty. Anne's hand stole into his and squeezed it.

"So it was you who rescued her then?" Edith said, taken aback, not having known that.

"Yes. I am a Warden you see so I've had some training in Rescue."

"And he risked his life to get her out quickly," interposed Anne quietly. And described what Ron had done.

Hywell and Edith looked at him with new respect.

That evening they finished dinner with coffee in the Residents' Lounge of the hotel.

"Well, I had better leave you good people, until we meet at the hospital tomorrow," Ron said at last, reluctant to go.

"I'll run you back to the hospital, Ron, as your bike is there," Anne said standing up. "Oh, I've got a present for Frank in my room. If we get it now you'll be able to take it for him."

Nonplussed for a moment Ron stared up at her, then stood up himself.

"Of course," he said. "Goodnight then Edith, Hywell."

He followed Anne into the lobby, up a flight of stairs and along a corridor, waited till she unlocked the door of her room and they were inside.

"You clever little darling!" he said admiringly, and swept her up into his arms.

Some moments later, "The bed isn't as wide as mine at home Ron, but ...," Anne smiled at him, tossing her jacket onto the bedside chair, and unbuttoning her blouse.

"Anne! What about the Davies's? What will they think when we don't go downstairs!" Ron squawked. A quick kiss and cuddle, great! But a longer, much longer, love-making ....

"Tomorrow, if they comment, I shall simply be surprised they didn't see us pass in the lobby." She smiled at him, by now almost undressed. "Unless you really think we should go and say goodbye to them again of course." She reached for her skirt on the chair

For answer, he firmly took it out of her hands, put it back on the chair and began stripping as quickly as Anne had.

Later, he roused, leaned on one elbow and smiled down at her.

"You did say once about us meeting in a hotel. Now we have."

"What I said, Ron Jackson, was to spend a night - a whole night - in a hotel, not just a couple of hours." She stroked his face. "The Davies's are going back to Wales Wednesday morning, and I've got the room booked till Friday. As May is going to be away for the week, I could see about changing it to a Double room from Tuesday night."

"And what would the Management make of that?"

Anne shrugged. "What they like. But I'm willing to bet you anything you like they won't say anything to anyone. So - shall I?"

"Roll on Wednesday!" grinned Ron.

At breakfast the next morning Edith suddenly looked up from her plate to Anne.

"Anne, you seem to know Ron pretty well, so may I ask you a question?"

"By all means."

"Do you know if he and May ever got a letter from us about Adopting Kitty if anything happened to them? While Kitty was still with us I mean."

"Yes, they did."

"Do you know how they felt about it?" asked Hywell.

"Ron was very much in favour, May totally against."

"Do - do you know if that influenced their decision to keep her here once she was back in London?" Edith asked apprehensively. It had been preying on her mind for months.

"And was Ron really ill? Or was that just a - a pretext?" added Hywell to quickly get away from that question.

"Ron was very ill. How ill I didn't discover for two weeks when Kathleen wrote and told me." Anne looked at them steadily. "Ron used to 'phone me about twice a week from before Kathleen left to go to Wales. And at the end of the two weeks I was frantic with worry and not knowing who on earth to contact because - well, I didn't know whether he had - simply lost interest in me or - or if something awful had happened to him.

"Later he told me that apparently when in delirium he was asking for Kitty, so May brought her back to London. Then when he was considerably better he expected that she would return to you in Wales. However, May adamantly refused and said that if he tried to force it then she would immediately leave, take Kathleen and Frank to her mother's, Divorce him and persuade the Divorce Court to bar him from all Access to all of them. He asked whether I knew if she could do that." Anne drew a deep breath, guessing the conclusions the Davies's would be drawing.. "I immediately consulted my solicitor. He said that in view of the arguments May had said she would put forward to the Court, he was 80 to 90% sure she would get the Divorce and Custody of the children. Which meant she would be able to totally block Kitty's return to you. And he was reasonably sure that she would succeed in even barring Access to Ron altogether, probably citing fears of kidnap. Even if the Court didn't actually bar his Access, she would have been able to make it impossible in practice. And so Ron felt he had no alternative to dropping his insistence."

"How does he feel now?" Hywell asked quietly.

"He's carrying a tremendous burden of guilt and self-recrimination." She paused. "And May's burden must be even greater."

Jennie heard the sound of a car drawing up outside Ron's house and she quickly slipped upstairs to look out of the bedroom window. In the dim starlight she saw Anne sliding out of the driver's seat as Ron got out of the front passenger side. He untied his bike lashed to the back of the car and pushed it up his garden path to the front door as Anne followed him in.

Jennie waited, timing them. Ten minutes later, Anne came down the path with him, they shook hands at the gate in the manner of acquaintances and she drove off. Ron waved once as she turned the corner, and went back indoors. An hour later he was in the Warden Duty on time. When Jennie arrived a few minutes later, neither mentioned Anne.

Chapter 20

Achievable dreams

The next day, Saturday, she watched Ron go off and later return with May and Frank.

That evening, once Ron had gone to the hospital, Jennie knocked on the door.

"Hello Jennie. Come on in. Tea?"

"Thanks. How did your week go?"

"Okay. Missed seeing the kids of course." May paused, then with a rush, "It - it might sound all wrong and terrible Jennie, but at the same time I much more able to relax." She paused again. "I suppose it was not having to see them and be reminded every day. Especially by Kitty." Bitterness and resentment was more than a tinge in her tone.

"Yes, I can understand that." Jennie paused a moment. "Ron wasn't with you was he? At night I mean."

"No." May looked at her puzzled. "He was working and then here at night. Except when he was doing Warden Duty of course." With sudden suspicion. "You mean he wasn't here?"

Jennie put on an air of puzzlement herself. "Well I didn't see him. And he didn't do any Warden Duty the whole week till last night. Still, I suppose he must have been away on overnights." Knowing he hadn't had any since the school was bombed.

"Malcolm's been keeping him in the Yard in case he was called by the hospital suddenly." May said thoughtfully. "So he certainly wouldn't have sent him away for the whole week. And Ron's never been away that long before anyway." She paused. "Now I wonder if that Anne Carruthers has been staying in that hotel at Blackheath for the whole week instead of just last weekend."

"You don't think ...? May! Surely not! Not Ron." Knowing that having sown the seed in May's mind she could now safely query it.

"Yes. I do mean Ron, Jennie. When I first laid eyes on that Carruthers woman years ago I wondered. But I thought I'd scotched anything that might have started, but maybe not."

"But that trip down to Folkestone with Kitty's clothes was a one-off wasn't it?" Jennie interrupted. "On the other hand, if it wasn't ...," she added, as if the thought just occurred to her.

"I'll ring Malcolm on Monday and find out," May snapped with determination. "And I know the hotel where Carruthers was staying in Blackheath too. I've got a photo of her with Kitty and I've got one of Ron, though that one is from before the war. So I can check on that too."

"And then you'll tackle Ron about it?"

May smiled grimly. "Not just tackle him Jennie, I'm going to Divorce him. With maximum publicity in Folkestone about it, too. I'll smash that Carruthers woman's reputation down there for good."

Jennie stared at her in consternation. That had not been her plan at all! She'd been expecting there would be a flaming row between May and Ron with a resulting swift termination of anything that might be going on between Ron and Anne - and then a re-kindling of the affair between Ron and herself that had largely died. But a Divorce would only drive Ron away from here and from her and straight into Anne's arms.

A Divorce was a rarity between their type of people. It was so expensive for a start.

"But can you afford it, May? Won't it cost a fortune?"

"Oh I won't pay for it Jennie. And Ron hasn't got a penny to his name. No, I'll force Carruthers to pay for it in return for a promise of no publicity. Then once the Divorce is through and paid for, I'll hit the Sunday papers with the story. And the Folkestone locals."

"Malcolm? Mrs. Jackson here. No ...," May added quickly into the 'phone, " ... I don't need to talk to Ron. It's you I want to speak to." It was mid-Monday morning and she'd been hoping Ron would have been sent out on a short trip if nothing more, but he was still in the Yard. "It's a simple question. You remember Ron had to do a trip down to Folkestone very soon after the children had been evacuated in 1939 and you okay'd him dropping off some clothes for the children? Has he had to do many more trips down there over the years?"

Long ago Malcolm had adopted the policy that when wives asked about their husband's activities, he would profess not to know anything at all whenever possible. He couldn't do that with this question though, because being the Yard Foreman he obviously knew all about Ron's trips - he was the one who organised them. And he knew that May would know that. In such circumstances his next policy was to always tell the truth and any consequences would not be his fault.

"A few. It's worked out roughly every couple of months I should think. But I'd have to check the records to be more exact."

"And did he always take Tony with him as Loader?" If so, May wondered why it hadn't got back to her, given the arrangement she'd made with Tony's wife long ago.

"No. They were always big lorry trips, but without the trailer, so he didn't need a Loader. Didn't you know Tony retired over a year ago? He'd had a really bad heart attack and had to finish."

"No. Ron hasn't said. Thanks Malcolm. Oh, there's no need to mention to Ron I've 'phoned."

"Fair enough. How are the children doing?"

"Making progress." May was now anxious to get off the line in case Ron walked into Malcolm's office about something while they were still talking.

Malcolm put his 'phone down slowly. Now what had Ron, of all people, been up to in Folkestone?

As soon as the afternoon Visiting Time was over, May caught a bus to Blackheath. At the hotel Reception Desk she asked the very young man on duty if she could see the Manager.

"Good afternoon," May said in a friendly tone when he arrived. "Can you tell me if my friend, Miss Anne Carruthers from Folkestone was staying at this hotel last week? I know it was one of the hotels in Blackheath."

The experienced Manager recognised a familiar opening gambit.

"I really could not say, Mrs. ...?"

"Oh I'm sure you could," May maintained her friendly tone. "There is your hotel Register open on the counter, only half of it has been used so it would obviously cover last week and Miss Carruthers would have had to produce her Identity Card when she Registered, wouldn't she?"

The Manager looked at her steadily, then turned pages back.

"A Miss Carruthers did stay here for a few nights last week. In a single room."

The young man May had first spoken to came over, eager to be helpful.

"But she changed to a Double on the Wednesday morning for that night and the rest of the week, Mr. Wilberforce," he butted in. "She said she found the single bed wasn't comfortable and she was used to a double. When she asked, as we had a Double vacant I let her have it. I was sure I'd made the entry." He peered at the Register. "Yes. There it is sir." He pointed.

"Thank ..." the Manager began frostily.

May whipped out the photograph of Anne and Kitty.

"Was that the lady?" she asked the young man.

"That's right."

"And was this man with her?" May produced the photograph of Ron from behind it.

"Yes. And there was ...," said the lad, just as the Manager growled "THANK you Mr. Higgins."

"Thank you indeed Mr. Higgins. You've been most helpful," May said triumphantly.

"I've got him! And her!" May announced to Jennie as soon as she got back.

Jennie set her lips. So not only had Ron been cheating on May, at the same time he had been cheating on her as well, as obviously that affair had been going on from the beginning of the war!

"May, why not just have a terrific row with Ron and lay down the law in no uncertain terms that he pack Carruthers in and leave it at that? After all, you've got a lot to lose by Divorcing him haven't you? At the very basics he's not going to be able to pay much in the way of Maintenance is he? Not on a lorry-driver's wages."

"Don't you worry about that! I'm going to make her pay too, Jennie. And she's got plenty of money."

"And - and - won't you be lonely without him? At least he's a man isn't he?"

"Aaah!" May said with a slight, mysterious smile. "You know Des, don't you?"

"Des?" Jennie was bewildered at May's sudden switch. "The only Des I know is Des Ackroyd, the Warden."

"That's him. You know this road is part of his Sector, don't you? You see, while you and Ron have been covering yours, streets away, Des has been popping in here every night for a cup of tea. Or cocoa. He's been doing that ever since that bomb on the flats behind us."

"You - you old dark horse, May!" Jennie made no attempt to hide her surprise. And felt that excused (if she'd wanted any) her own long-standing affair with Ron.

"Nothing's happened between us though - not in that way," May said hastily. "The thing is Jennie ...," she went on, " ... Des hasn't blamed me or criticised me even once for having the children home. Not once. Not even after the school. And Ron has done nothing but. And that's meant an awful lot to me."

The two women were silent for a moment.

"Des's wife died six months ago," Jennie said thoughtfully, looking straight at her.

"That's right. And when I've Divorced Ron ...,"

"What about Custody of the children? Of Kitty?"

"I'll get it of course. Because I'll say that those two are morally unfit to bring up children. Especially Kitty, as she's a growing girl. And I'll get their Access barred for the same reason."

Jennie wasn't at all sure that that would succeed, not if the Judge got to know how Kitty felt. And Ron would make sure that the Judge did.

"May. If Kitty should want to go with them wouldn't that be the best thing for you? And best for the boys too? She was bad enough before the school wasn't she? And the way she's acted since, going by what you've said, she's now far worse. So why inflict all that on yourself? As well as having to cope with her injury."

"And let Carruthers and Ron win? Not on your life!" May snapped.

But the thought did not go away. It would certainly make life a lot easier without her. For the boys too. Tim wasn't blaming her for what had happened, but then, he had been so delighted she'd brought him home from Wales. And Frank was no trouble. So if Kitty wasn't there to disrupt them as bad or worse than she had been before, life would be a lot better all round.

"When is Anne expecting to come to see Kitty again?" May asked Ron pleasantly that evening as he was having his dinner after seeing Kitty and Tim.

"She didn't say. Were you expecting her to come again soon then?"

"Well I'd have thought she'd have wanted to come fairly soon, seeing how well this last visit went. Didn't she stay the whole week in the end?"

"Till the Friday night. Well, Saturday morning really. She went back then."

"So you'd have seen her every day then?"

"At the evening Visits. But it was obvious she had gone in every afternoon as well from the way she and Kitty talked."

"Oh."

When they were sitting down with mugs of tea on either side of the fireplace. "And what did you both do after those evening visits?"

"Sometimes we separated at the hospital. A couple of times we had a coffee at one of the cafe's in Lewisham." Ron was wondering what May was getting at.

"Oh." May hesitated. What she was going to say now would start the count-down to her Divorce. Then she realised her questions and Ron's lying answers had really already begun it for her. "Why not ask her if she would like to come next weekend when you ring her tomorrow night? Assuming you still are ringing her after every hospital visit."

"Anne said she'll come Saturday morning, pick us up to go to the hospital and go back Sunday after the afternoon Visiting time. She'll pick us up both days as she did the first time." Ron told her the next evening.

"That's nice," May smiled. "So she could have something to eat here before she heads back to Folkestone." That fitted her plans nicely.

At the hospital Saturday afternoon May suggested that Ron go to see Tim while she stayed with Anne and Kitty. Last time she and Ron had gone together to see Tim leaving Anne alone with

Kitty, but May wanted to check Kitty's reaction to Anne and herself just one more time. Because the more she thought about it, the more Jennie's suggestion made a lot of sense. And not just from her own point of comfort either. It could be what Kitty would want herself.

Kitty being just as frosty to her and as warm and responsive to everything Anne said as before, confirmed her ideas.

Afterwards, May suggested that after they had gone to the hospital Sunday afternoon, Anne should come back to the house for something to eat before heading off for Folkestone..

"Something funny is going on Anne," Ron said to her worriedly in a brief moment he could speak to her quietly.

Anne glanced at him amused. "Funny? With who? And what makes you think that?"

"I mean funny peculiar Anne. With May. I can't put my finger on what it is but I'm sure she's up to something."

At her hotel Saturday evening, it struck Anne that the behaviour of the young Reception Clerk towards her seemed 'funny peculiar' to use Ron's phrase. As though he was embarrassed about something, and this time his eyes seemed to look anywhere other than straight at her. Not at all as he had been before.

On Sunday afternoon when Anne came for them, May suddenly announced that she was not able to leave Frank with Jennie as she'd expected after all, so she would have to miss this afternoon Visit. But they, of course, should go, and as arranged come back for tea.

When they came back they found May had prepared a sparse meal of just a few jam sandwiches. Ron was embarrassed and silently furious. He had given May extra money to get in something more special for Anne, and he was sure May could have done a lot better despite the rationing.

But May and Anne chattered brightly together, both sensing Ron's embarrassment - Anne to show it didn't matter and May was finding that she was actually enjoying it. She had already crossed her mental Rubicon. She poured out the last drops from the teapot. The moment she had planned for had come.

"I had an interesting conversation with the Manager of your hotel last week Anne," she said, beaming at her.

Anne carefully did not look at Ron. "Really? He's a pleasant man isn't he?"

"He is. And very informative. And that young Reception Clerk, a Mr. Higgins, was even more helpful."

"Really?" Anne repeated, still smiling.

Ron looked at the two women worriedly. Whatever May had been leading up to, the moment had plainly arrived. And he had not wanted Anne to be present at any confrontation between May and himself.

"They told me you had booked a single room on arrival but changed to a Double after the weekend. After the Davies's had left."

Ron and Anne immediately knew what the 'funny peculiar' thing was.

"That's right. I did," Anne replied promptly.

"And they identified Ron's photo as staying there with you, every night for the rest of that week." May paused. "Funnily enough, Ron had told me only a few days ago, that you'd had a coffee in a cafe a couple of times after the evening visits and that he came straight home the other nights. And Jennie told me you didn't do any Warden Duties that week at all Ron." She looked at him steadily. "Quite remiss of you wasn't it? Neglecting your duty like that." She paused. "But we know exactly what you two were really doing, don't we?" She looked from one to the other now in open triumph.

"So what are you going to do about it May?" Ron asked quietly.

"I'm going to Divorce you of course." She looked at Anne. "And do you remember the first Christmas of the war I told you that if I ever caught Ron up to anything I'd Divorce him and get it the maximum publicity wherever the other woman lived? To ruin her reputation?"

"I remember it very well. And I agreed with you, didn't I?"

"Do you still agree with me?" May was puzzled. She had expected a very different reaction from Anne. Wariness, even panic. Then her trying to suggest some kind of deal. Something in return for no-publicity, from which May would extract promises.

"You must do whatever you think fit, mustn't you May? After all, the ball is in your court isn't it?" Anne smiled sweetly at her.

Totally unexpectedly the plans that she and Ron had abandoned immediately after the school, looked as though they could happen after all!

But Ron was worried about May's threat of publicity. And he couldn't understand how Anne could be so off-handed about the damage that kind of publicity could do to her. But, he then decided, Anne must somehow have some kind of answer to it.

"I will. And I shall get Access to the children barred to you both on the grounds that you have shown by your behaviour that you are not fit people to bring them up. Especially a developing girl like Kitty."

As a threat May felt that had to be more powerful than publicity had turned out to be. And then, with a show of magnanimity, she would not only withdraw that but say she would not oppose them having Custody of Kitty. Provided that in return they made more promises.

"Not a good idea, May, not a good idea at all. Because if you do try that I shall cross-petition on your relationship and behaviour with Des Ackroyd," Ron looked at her steadily.

May dropped her cup with a clatter.

"What do you mean by that?"

"Well - he comes here on the nights when I'm away in my Sector on Warden Duty, AND when I'm away on overnights too, doesn't he?"

"But nothing ever happened between us! Not in that way!"

"Really? Now who in a Divorce Court is going to believe that? Especially as you took it for granted that 'something had happened' - to use your words - between Anne and me in the hotel. With no real evidence at all, of course. So I would say exactly the same about you and Des." Ron paused. "On the other hand, if you agree that we leave Kitty to make her own decision where she wants to live when she leaves hospital, and abandon the idea of dragging Anne's name through the mud anywhere, then I shall not cross-petition and Des's name will not even be mentioned in Court or anywhere else by me."

May thought furiously. If Des were cited, totally unfairly though that was, then he'd drop her immediately, even though May was sure he, at the very least, liked her. He daren't risk his reputation being affected by that kind of scandal.

He was a 'respectable' and respected member of the Parish

Church, a Member of several professional association - and he often visited wealthy clients, ladies, alone in their homes to discuss ideas and plans as their architect.

"Very well," she snapped finally. "I'll agree to no publicity and leave it up to Kitty and Tim to decide where they want to live. But Frank stays with me."

"Fair enough," Ron agreed at once. Frank was much closer to his mother than to him.

"And don't you ever dare mention Des's name in this."

"Provided you keep your side of the bargain it won't be. You break it in any way and Des gets cited." He was fleetingly surprised at himself, at how coolly he was treating the break-up of his marriage of years. "Now then, to other matters, I shall continue to send you the same housekeeping though I won't be here to eat any of it. And I'll need my Ration Book right now. And I presume you will be passing the costs of the Divorce on to me?"

"Or to your fancy woman because you've got no money, have you? Or a job if it comes to that if you do go down to Folkestone with her." May grabbed his Ration Book from a drawer and threw it at him. "And as you won't be in a Reserved Occupation any more, you will get Called Up as soon as I tell the Authorities."

"As a matter of fact I have. Got a job and it's a Reserved Occupation," Ron said coolly, picking up the Ration Book as he stood up. "Anne and I had already planned to go into partnership setting up a Transport firm down there. But we abandoned that after the school because you seemed to need me very badly then. Now you don't, it's back on. So - thanks a bundle May. Anne do you want to wait in the car while I pack?"

"I packed all your clothes this afternoon. Now get out. Both of you."

May was bitterly disappointed. The confrontation had not gone at all as she had planned.

"Thanks for doing that for me. Anne, do you want to wait in the car while I get my stuff?"

"I'll just have a word with May, Ron. You carry on."

After a moment's hesitation, Ron went to the door, leaving it open, and went upstairs, listening for the outbreak of a furious row.

He checked the cupboards and drawers but everything of his had already gone into the two suitcases and three large cardboard boxes on the floor.

Each time he passed the now closed front room door carrying boxes or cases to the car, he listened, but there was only a quiet murmur of voices from the room. When finished, he went in. Both women stood up, and Anne came to join him in the doorway.

"May," Ron said quietly. "I'm sure you'll be a whole lot happier with Des than with me."

"What the hell do you mean by that?" she snapped.

"Des comes from your type of background and he likes you, as I'm sure you know. Jill made a point of telling me that he'd told her so several months ago. She was wanting to stir up trouble of course, but as far as I'm concerned, that's fine."

Ron turned and followed Anne out, leaving May staring after him.

They went to Blackheath, but booked into a different hotel for Sunday night, because they had decided they would both go to see the children that evening and they did not know how soon they would be able to visit again.

"Can I be the one to tell Kathleen about us, Ron?" Anne asked as they approached the Wards. "As woman to woman?"

"Sure. And I'll tell Tim. As man to man."

When Anne walked up to Kitty's bed, she looked up from her slacks design in surprise.

"Hello Aunt Anne, I thought you were going back home this afternoon."

"I was, but something important has come up that I need to talk to you about. As woman to woman."

"That sounds interesting." Intrigued, Kitty put her pad away.

"It is." Anne sat down on the chair by Kitty's bed. "Do you remember your Dad bringing you some clothes very soon after you were evacuated to me?"

"Yes. And you went dashing home from your shop to be able to see him."

"That's right. On my first sight of him I got a terrible shock."

"He's not THAT ugly-looking surely, Aunt Anne!"

"I didn't mean it like that," Anne smiled. "The point is when I went into the lounge he was standing looking at that picture over the fireplace, so his back was to the door. And from the back he looked just like Gregory."

"Your sweetheart that died?" gasped Kitty.

"That's right. That's what I meant by 'getting a terrible shock'. We talked for well over an hour, at first about you, then about the war, and then about each other. And - well maybe it sounds silly Kathleen, but I began falling in love with him. Then of course, he had to go back to London and I had to go to an important meeting for which I was already terribly late. I gave him a card with my 'phone numbers on, hoping he'd ring me. A couple of months later he finally did to tell me that your mother was going to come down to see you and Timothy that first Christmas of the war. To cut a long story short we kept in touch from then on and we fell deeply in love with each other. He would 'phone me at least once a week and send me the most wonderful love letters, and every so often he'd get sent down with a special load for one of the Camps not too far away from Folkestone and we'd be able to actually meet for an hour or two."

"Golly! How romantic!" Kitty breathed. "And I'd never have thought Dad had it in him! To write love letters!"

"Well I can tell you he certainly has, Kathleen! I've treasured them all just as I've treasured all yours over the years. Anyway what happened tonight is that your mother found out and ...,"

A thought that had not occurred to either of them before, flooded into her mind, bringing mixed feelings of horror and dread.

Now that this moment had come, would Kathleen turn against them in support of her mother, feeling that Ron – and she - had betrayed her in the worst possible way? She might feel SHE had been betrayed too by them! In not telling her.

And in spite of all that had happened between May and her, she might return her loyalties to her mother and against them. Or, she might turn against them all! Though to Anne, her romance with Ron was wonderful and precious, to May's daughter it might seem very different.

"You're not going to stop seeing Dad are you Aunt Anne?"

Kitty asked at once, wide-eyed with disbelief at the prospect.

So obviously Kathleen didn't think any of those things she (Anne) had so suddenly thought of!

"No Kathleen, I'm certainly not. But the thing is my dear, your mother is going to Divorce your father and - and he'll be coming to live with me in Folkestone. Coming straight away I mean, not after the Divorce goes through. And - well if you want to, you can come and live with us too as soon as you're discharged from here. Or of course, you can live with your mother and Frank, if you prefer. Timothy will be able to make up his own mind where he wants to live."

"Can I come and live with you and Dad, Aunt Anne?" Kitty said eagerly clutching her hand. "Please! You know I wrote and asked if I could when I leave school - and if Dad's going to be there too, that would be just perfect!"

"That is exactly what we hoped you'd say Kathleen. We had already planned to set up a Transport firm down there together and to ask you if you'd like to come to live with us, but when the school happened, and your mother needed your father, and we didn't know how things would turn out with you and Timothy, well - we abandoned them. But now, with what has happened, we can go ahead with them after all! And straight away."

It was nearing 11 o'clock that night when there came a soft tap on the front door.

"Come on in Des," May whispered. "I've got something important to tell you tonight."

Enemies and Allies

The Jackson story – Part 2

The saga continues from where 'When the bombs begin to fall' ends with Ron Jackson moving in with Anne Carruthers.

He develops the Transport Section.

Suddenly worried about Kathleen still being in London he finds Anne's contacts most helpful to bring her quickly to a Folkestone Hospital.

Conflict between May and Ron continues as May moves in with Des, officially at first as 'Housekeeper'.

As World War 2 ends Ron sees an opportunity to buy surplus bombers to use as cargo aircraft. This gets a boost as the Berlin Crisis of 1948 begins, culminating in the Berlin Airlift – which could begin war with Ruissia.

Unexpectedly Tim decides that a job on the airfield is much more interesting than either of the jobs suggested by Des, now his Step-father. Des confronts Ron as Tim is packing to move to Folkestone – and then talking to others as well learns things about May and Ron that he had not known before.

You call this 'Peace'?
The Jackson story – Part 3

The saga continues from where 'Enemies and Allies' finishes, as Anne Carruthers expands her Candlers firm into the Hire and Sale of Cruisers.

The Manager she appoints (Tom Henderson) sees this as an ideal cover for a smuggling operation. His scheme jumps from a small time drinks smuggling racket into a much bigger drugs and guns smuggling operation when he is taken under the control of a London Gang led by an ex-SOE commander.

Ron and Anne are arrested with Tom Henderson but the Gang Leader, impressed by newspaper reports of Ron's wartime activities as a Warden, orders Henderson to change his false evidence against Ron where he is the main witness against Ron, and so he is Acquitted.

Animosity between the families reduces after Tim's wedding.

Frank is Called Up for National Service going to Cyprus and then Kenya where he is severely injured in a Mau Mau attack on his Air Base.

Then in 1962 is the Cuban Nuclear Missile Crisis. Though the Jackson Family are not directly involved, the threat of imminent nuclear war causes Ron to take precautions in which Des and Frank involve themselves as architects. May panics at the threat of war and the two families shelter together.

Shortly afterwards May has a severe stroke, which paralyses her legs.

Kathleen had begun to understand May's feelings about 'losing her to the Davie's's' when her own child, 'Little' Anne, is born.

Now that May has a similar disability to hers, can she find it in her to forgive her mother after all these years?